This Book Belo

_____ DATE:_____

FAIR WARNING   BOOK 2 CONTAINS

- Self-Shattering Wisdom
- Cursing Language
- Hallucinogenic Drugs
- Casinos, Guns & Thugs
- Iguanas, Dragons & Owls

Rated

P♠E
publishing

- Irreverent Humor
- Fast Cars & Motorcycles
- Life-Changing Insights
- Emotional Button Pushing
- Death & Hot Air Balloons

Welcome Back Badass

Let the Adventure Continue!

Please Leave a Book 2 Review!

Make your world a more spiritual badass place: After reading Book 2, please leave a review with your thoughts, opinions, and stars. You can do so on Amazon, Kobo, Goodreads, Bookbub, or Smashwords. Spread the love, baby. Thanks and enjoy the ride... - *J. Stewart Dixon*

Book One Fan & Reader Reviews

The ultimate spirituality book for beginners. Truly changed my outlook on life. Thanks J. It was a great ride!! Can't wait to receive the next book! -**Kelly**

This book is amazing! Get the workbook as well. Also, the Audible version of the book makes it so much better! I've bought them for friends and family; they still thank me months later. And no, I am not a bot nor paid to say this. 😄 -**Michael**

I NEED BOOK 2! Where can I get it? I've looked everywhere. Thank you...I've learned a lot from this book. -**Paula**

Loved this book!! Great life advice presented in an often hilarious way!! -**Linda**

Amazing book. ...read it in rehab after a suicide attempt; changed my outlook entirely. 💯 -**John**

This book is absolutely awesome. Buy it! Read it! Then read it again! You will not be disappointed. ⭐⭐⭐⭐⭐ -**Samantha**

Loved it; waiting for Book 2. -**Greg**

I have this book, and what I've read so far really speaks to my personal spirituality, which is through love, humor, and acceptance. -**Jane**

It's my current read. Different—but quite good, actually. -**Gina**

I've just finished this book on Audible, and it's fucking brilliant!
 -**Andy**

Loved this book! Can't wait for 2023 for the second one! -**Takara**

I bought it maybe 5 months ago and went through it in 3 days. Reflects exactly how I feel. Great! Highly recommended! -**Gerard**

I wholeheartedly recommend this book! Being aware and aware of the awareness is, well, I don't know how to put it into words, but it's brought my life into focus...XX -**Jinea**

Loved this book! ♥ -**Misti**

I'm listening to this on Audible; it's brilliant! 🦋 -**Annamaria**

Reading it now!! Great book!! -**Diana**

I'm a first-time reader of a self-help book. I'm half way thru this, and I think this book IS Badass. I look forward to Book #2. -**Billy-Jo**

Reading as we speak, and it's awesome. -**Melissa**

BOOK ONE PROFESSIONAL REVIEWS

"*Spirituality for Badasses* should be part of any self-help, spirituality, or mindfulness collection. It goes where no other books in these genres dare travel, doing so ... in a way no other book matches."
–**Midwest Book Review**

"Dixon has much to offer, repackaging mysticism, intentionality, and self-care into something proudly lowbrow and accessible. ... A jokey yet earnest and useful guide to enlightenment for badass readers."
– **Kirkus Reviews**

"Dixon has clearly done his spiritual homework, and he succeeds at distilling the effective and life-changing ingredients of contemplation and initiation. His relationship to his student/reader is like a shaman

drill sergeant cajoling and nudging and ultimately getting his team over the hurdle."
–**Pacific Book Review**

"It's this shedding of typical, formalist intonations and the possession of a good sense of fun that make *Spirituality for Badasses*, along with J. Stewart Dixon, entertaining—but never at the expense of holistically sharing material. That's to be commended."
–**The Magic Pen**

"In his new book, *Spirituality for Badasses*, J. Stewart Dixon has written an irreverent, exuberant, free-wheeling, stream-of-consciousness saga that chronicles the spiritual journey in ways that are unique, humorous, challenging, and a hell of a lot of fun. Buckle up and be prepared for a wild ride that's readable, accessible, and eminently relatable. Two enthusiastic thumbs up! Highly recommended!"
–**Chuck Hillig, Licensed Psychotherapist, Spiritual Teacher & Author**

J. Stewart Dixon is a true original…He's your irreverent, potty-mouthed best friend and big brother, but don't let the humor fool you: the teachings offered here are profoundly liberating, important pointers to awakened awareness. Dixon teaches us all to en-LIGHTEN-UP with his special blend of hilarious, profound, crazy-ass wisdom."
–**Erin Reese, M.S., Spiritual Counselor, Teacher & Author of** *Truth Seeker: A Spiritual Journey of Love, Loss, and Liberation* **and** *The Adventures of Bindi Girl: Diving Deep Into the Heart of India*

"Accessible. Compulsive. Irreverent. Fun. Practical. All the while, lacking *nothing* in richness or depth. Take an adventure with J.—a spiritual guide who comes off more Han Solo than Obi Wan Kenobi on the surface—as you journey along with the R-rated spiritual everyman with a lizard draped over his shoulders on a path that winds inside and out, through valleys and up mountains, volcanoes, and earthquakes, as you make your way toward becoming more your badass true aware self. This book is rich!"
–**Zac Cannon, Pastor**

SPIRITUALITY for Badasses Book 2

HOW TO FIND YOUR HEART & SOUL WITHOUT LOSING YOUR COOL

J. Stewart Dixon

publishing

BOOK 2 / V-1.1 / ©2023

Copyright © 2023 J. Stewart Dixon.

All rights reserved. No part of this publication may be reproduced, distributed, or transmitted in any form or by any means, including photocopying, recording, or other electronic or mechanical methods, without the prior written permission of the publisher, except in the case of brief quotations embodied in critical reviews and certain other noncommercial uses permitted by copyright law. For permission requests, contact the publisher at the web address below.

Any references to historical events, real people, or real places are used fictitiously. Names, characters, and places are products of the author's imagination. But Lenny is absolutely 100% real.

Disclaimer: The brief excerpt from *Twelve Steps and Twelve Traditions* is reprinted with permission of Alcoholics Anonymous World Services, Inc. ("A.A.W.S."). Permission to reprint this excerpt does not mean that A.A.W.S. has reviewed or approved the contents of this publication, or that A.A. necessarily agrees with the views expressed herein. A.A. is a program of recovery from alcoholism only - use of this excerpt in connection with programs and activities which are patterned after A.A., but which address other problems, or in any other non-A.A. context, does not imply otherwise.

ISBN: 978-0-9858579-7-4 (Paperback)

Cover design by
J. Stewart Dixon & Darren Wheeling
www.blackegg.com

Edited by
Mary Lib Morgan
www.perfectlypenned4you.com

Blood, sweat, teared, laughed and cried by
PIE Publishing
Charlottesville, VA
www.spiritualityforbadasses.com

Contents

Part 1: Talladega Angst

Chapter 1: Jumper Nine, Go! — 16
How to unlock your heart and soul

Chapter 2: Spiritual Awakening — 28
How to realize you're sleeping

Chapter 3: Existential Racecars — 33
How to recognize your inner angst

Chapter 4: Goat Yoga — 46
How to be completely present in your body

Chapter 5: Two Monkeys — 58
How to take small leaps of faith

Chapter 6: The Coosa Monster — 63
How to get unstuck when you feel spiritually flat

Chapter 7: Alcoholics Anonymous — 71
How to meet your black shadow

Chapter 8: Baby Goats — 78
How to avoid arrested development

Part 2: Kansas City Presence

Chapter 9: Don't Fear the Reaper — 95
How to meet vulnerability, grief, and sorrow

Chapter 10: The Gift of Presence — 112
How to exit the Wheel of Samsara

Chapter 11: Non-Abiding Awakening — 125
How to reconnect with the heart of existence

Chapter 12: Brahman's Castle — 146
How to wake up and meet your dreamer

Chapter 13: Spiritual Hangover — 167
How to deal with radical shifts of identity and reality

PART 3: Vegas Washing Machine

Chapter 14: Mescaline Medicine — 182
How to vomit up the cosmos

Chapter 15: Mirage Magic — 201
How to screw up royally

Chapter 16: Street Smarts — 224
How to travel to the city underworld

Chapter 17: Great Spirit — 243
How to travel to the spirit underworld

Chapter 18: Honda Rebel — 258
How to find your true inner voice

Chapter 19; Lenny Knows — 268
How to navigate a hot air balloon down the Grand Canyon

PART 4: Lake County Cave

Chapter 20: Plato's Cave — 291
How to escape the cave of shadows

Chapter 21: Political Debate — 298
How to be unenlightened

Chapter 22: E=MC^2 — 312
How to say goodbye to good friends

Chapter 23: Adrenaline Junkies — 318
How to jump out of a perfectly bad airplane

Chapter 24: Spiritual Disneyland — 325
How to soak your aura in a hot tub

Chapter 25: Namaste', Bitches — 332
How to get kicked out of spiritual clubs

Chapter 26: Church — 341
How to rock like a Baptist

Chapter 27: You, You, and You — 351
How to find your heart and soul

Chapter 28: Epilogue — 375
How to find your life's purpose

Author — 380
Reviews & Sharing — 381

Preface

Do I need to eat giant larva?

Okay, you can relax. Here're some ground rules I'm pretty sure you'll appreciate.

You will *not* (okay—mostly) be asked to do any of the following in this book:

- Nope—Meditate, chant, commune, frolic, dance, water-ski, or *swim* with dolphins.

- Nope—No *yoga* with dolphins either. Yep—you will be asked to do yoga with *goats*. (Yoga with goats is much better than yoga with dolphins.)

- Nope—Enhance your aura with chunks of mostly translucent pieces of the mineral kingdom.

- Nope—Walk on hot coals, hot rocks, hot timbers, hot volcanic ash, or freshly baked hot chocolate chip cookies.

- Nope—Have tantric sex for eight hours straight. (I know you *think* this sounds awesome, but it is most definitely not. You will need weeks of expensive, follow-up chiropractic adjustments.)

- Nope—Beg, bargain, hope, wish, visualize, pray, or attract, through various strange-ass laws of the universe, anything other than a good parking spot. Trust me—all you need is the good parking spot.

- Nope—Set aside fourteen minutes in the morning, seven minutes at lunch, and twenty-three minutes in the evening for precise chakra tuning, energetic alignment, and trans-dimensional communication with Norse gods.

- Nope—Place sticky notes on your refrigerator, bathroom mirror, or gym locker with declarations of how beautiful, abundant, glorious, special, amazing, awesome, or super-spiritual you are. (Finger way down throat on this one.) You *can keep* the oil change reminder sticky. Totally cool. Don't blow your engine.

- Nope—Eat giant larva. (Yes, Bear Grylls *is* kinda badass, but eating giant larva does not make him so.)

- Yep—Make me a grilled ham and swiss sandwich for lunch. (Oh, wait—shit! Sorry, my son just asked me to do that for him. I gotta go. Enough of this metaphysical hot air.)

Okay, one more:

- Nope— I hijacked my Dad's computer. He doesn't know it. Dad!? Where's my sandwich? I'm a growing boy. I read a few chapters. People actually read this shit?

- Yep—Dad here. Yes, they actually do. Go figure. FYI- I put soap in your sandwich. Foul-mouthed little runt!

- Yep—Son here. #$@!$%$!! ☺

INTRODUCTION

Something must still be nagging you

Really?

So, you think you're gonna double your spiritual badass just by reading *Book Two*?

Think again.

There is no doubling your badass. There is only *one* amount of spiritual badass and you already (sorta-kinda-you'll see) have it. You've always had it. You never lost it. You can't lose it.

But I presume, since you're back for more, something is still nagging you.

That's okay.

Actually, that's more than okay. It's fucking great.

I *want* you to be nagged.

In fact, this book really won't work for you unless there *is something* nagging you...

Something missing—Something not right.

Something wrong —Something not whole.

Something that is really pissing you off, depressing you, making you angry, making you feel unhappy, lost, irritated, frustrated, or confounded.

However it shows up for you, this nagging something is a *good* thing.

Truth be told, I also have a nagging feeling—because you and I have some unfinished business to attend to, or karma—as the

Hindus call it, or an unresolved gestalt—as some therapists might say.

You and me—we ain't done dancin'.

And believe it or not, *Book One* was just a slow dance at a rural county fair.

This book—well, it's a stage dive into a slam-dancing mosh pit at a punk concert. Don't say I didn't warn you.

But that's why you're here, I guess: You like the unfiltered punk rock truth.

Well, so do I, and I promise to serve up as much of it as I possibly can, while also serving your heart and soul.

Yes, I just said those words "heart and soul" in the introduction.

Oh, crap! They're also in the subtitle of the book. Forgot about that. My bad.

My first spiritual teacher had numerous names for his work. One of them was "The Way of the Heart." I don't care what path, way, road, teaching, or method you chose to follow or practice as a means of growing spiritually. Just make sure it has heart and soul. There is no rule that says you can't be a spiritual badass who also has a big heart. And soul size? Hmmm? Well, in my experience, ONE size fits all.

(Okay, I'm almost done blabbering here, and then we can begin our adventure.)

When I got into spirituality, my heart was pretty small, blackened, and achy—and my soul was…well…forgotten, lost, and pretty much nonexistent.

Spirituality served my heart well: My heart healed, grew, became whole again, shone, and now—despite my best efforts, sings.

Spirituality also served my soul: Before I got involved with badass spirituality, I thought I was a *somebody* with a soul. After evolving into a spiritual badass, I realized that I was—in fact—a *soul* with a somebody.

As you're about to find out, that's a big damn difference.

It's also a difference *you have to work for.*

In *Book Two*, I'm presuming you're a little more grown up, a little less naïve, less green, and a bit more prepared—*to do the real-life work* it takes to become an authentic spiritual badass. As a result, the "Badass Lessons" from *Book One* have been replaced with "Badass Suggestions" here in *Book Two*.

You'll notice that these "suggestions" are larger in scope and nature. These aren't quick fixes, tricks, or techniques; these are classes, courses, deep experiences, groups, encounters, and relationships.

Following any one of these suggestions may have a profound impact on your spiritual badass journey. Take me up on just one? Awesome! I've done my job. Take me up on *a bunch* of them? Super awesome! You'll soon *have* my job.

In short, reading about this shit is a great place to start and an excellent road map, but to really experience the fullest essence of your authentic spiritual badass heart and soul—you need to get your feet wet, hands dirty, and sweat pouring. You need to attend the concert—*front and center.*

Okay, I think I can hear the aforementioned punk rock band warming up. I'm excited about the show! It's gonna be loud and it's gonna *rock.*

Fist bump, friend—
J. Stewart
Charlottesville, VA

Part 1

Talladega Angst

Chapter 1
Jumper Nine, Go!

How to unlock your heart and soul

Yes to awareness! —Yes to the fear!
Yes to awareness! —Yes to the fear!

You got this.

Two yeses.

You got...

The 52 ft. 400 Series DHC-6 Twin Otter aircraft has reached jumping altitude—13,500 feet to be exact. You're strapped to your tandem skydive guide, Josh, and seated on a customized, ten-foot long aluminum bench that extends to the carpeted sliding hatch bay door jump area. Another jumper grabs the bay door and lifts, and like the snarling maw of a leviathan about to devour you—it opens. The rushing sound of wind, fury, fierceness, and nail-biting fear engulfs the cabin. Your palms sweat profusely. Your heart rate ticks up to maximum. Your nerve ganglia fire off a last-minute barrage of warning signals begging you to stop this insanity—

Oh, fuck. Oh, fuck.

Two yeses.

Can't believe I...agreed...to this.

There's no going back now. You and the ten other jumpers are committed. And *yes*: *You agreed to this shit.* But it's *not* the skydiving you can't believe you agreed to.

Jumper one—go!

Jumper two—go!

You watch as they jump and tumble into an abyss of sky.

Okay—scootch closer.

Oooooh...fuck!

It's the microdose of Psylocibin mushrooms that J. offered you a few days ago. He said to take it when the moment called for it. "You'll know" were his exact words. Out of sheer stupidity, brashness, or perhaps some hidden penchant for reckless abandon, you decided that *this* would be a fine and dandy *day* to take the mushrooms...and...eh, a bit more than a microdose.

Jumper three—go!

Jumper four—go!

You watch two more fools tumble into infinity.

The problem, you see, isn't the jumping; it's that the Psylocibin peaked...just as the Twin Otter jump plane peaked. So, not only are you about to jump out of an aircraft for the first time in your life. You're about to jump out of your—

Jumping out of my head?

What does that even mean?

Out of my head??...

Jumper five—go!

Jumper six—go!

Out of my head!?

Out of my head!?

Scootch more—

Jumper seven—go!

Jumper eight—go!

Oh, fuck. I'm jumper ni-

You slide along the final inches of the bench and somehow remember to crouch and scoot bent-knee into position with your jump guide.

"You ready!?" Josh yells. "Out the door we—"

Jumper nine!

Huh? What?!

Out of my head!?—

Ohhhhhhh crap!—

Out of my head!?—

Go!

Oh, wait—

Shit, sorry.

J. Stewart here.

Getting ahead of myself. All of this doesn't happen until Chapter Twenty-three. And—oops, this is Chapter One.

My bad.

Let's back up a bit, shall we? Let me see…where were we?

Oh…right!

I think *we were here* last time we hung out:

"You hear the sound of an engine, and you know a chartreuse Jeep is pulling into your driveway. A few moments later, you hear a knock at the door.

Excited, you rush downstairs and open the door.

"*Good morning, Sunshine!*" you both shout simultaneously, with laughter on your lips and joy in your hearts.

"You ready to finish this thing?" asks J.

"*Abso-fucking-lutely,*" you reply.

"Wait 'til you see what I have in store for you!" J. says with glee.

You respond seriously, but with a twinkle in your eye:

"*You know—six months ago that statement would have scared the shit out of me, but today...well, you're gonna have to try a lot harder than that to get a rise outta me, friend. A lot harder than that...*"

"I'll try my best!" J. exclaims with a smile. "I'll try my best."

Inside, you are as excited as a basket of six-week-old puppies.

"*Let the adventure continue...*"

"*Let the adventure continue!!*"

Well—okay then. Welcome to *Book Two*—and to the *next* adventure!

"Let's catch up in the Jeep." J. says.

"*Cool,*" you reply.

"Grab your things. I'll wait for you outside—with you-know-who."

19

"Lenny! Sounds good. I'll be out in a minute."

You rush upstairs and grab the medium-sized duffle you've been obsessively-compulsively packing and repacking for the last few days.

Arrangements for a part-time house sitter. Check.

Arrangements for a good chunk of time off work. The rest in digital nomad mode. (Gotta love the internet.) Check.

Wad of cash. Check.

Hiking boots. Bathing suit. Rain jacket. First aid kit. Various pieces of camping gear. Check. Check. Check.

What else? What else?

Right!—, per J.: Blank journal. Check.

That's it.

Like a mad end-of-the-world prepper about to escape an impending apocalypse, you surrender your life to the bare essentials, lock the door to your home, and courageously, fiercely…step outside into the great beyond…

Oh, Jiminy Cricket!

You go back inside. A few moments after folderol-ing around with your bladder, you're outside again approaching the Jeep.

What the…the Jeep!?

"*What the hell did you do to the Jeep!?*" You blurt out to J., who is leaning against the left passenger door, fiddling with his phone.

"You like!?" asks J.

"*It's yellow!*" you exclaim.

"Actually, *hellayella* is the technical name." says J.

"*But—*"

"Awesome isn't it!?! It was time for a change and it's every bit as ostentatious as the chartreuse!"

"*I do kinda like it.*"

"It grows on you."

You walk over to the attached trailer, note the open back hatch, and throw in your duffle. Then, excitedly, you tiptoe skip to the Jeep back panel door.

"*Is he in there!?*"

"Yes—along with…"

You grab the handle and swing open the door.

"*Lenny!!!!!!!!!!!*" you exclaim with glee.

Lenny is seated on his kingly, royal throne—the flat, sturdy section of his favorite branch—enjoying a 360-degree outside view.

You finger scratch his back. He arches it slightly in response to your affectations. He then casts a nonchalant but approving glance your way. High acknowledgement from the lizard god.

And then you see it…camouflaged among the other branches of Lenny's perch…

"*Ohhhh my! What—who is that!?*"

"Who!? would definitely be the appropriate question. That's Ollie! He's an Eastern Screech Owl."

"*Oh! Should I close the door? He could fly…*"

"He can't fly. He's wounded. Or *was* wounded. He's disabled."

"*Ohhhh—poor thing.*"

"Ha! Don't worry about Ollie. He's perfectly content. We're taking him with us. There's a wounded wildlife center near where we're headed; they specialize in owls. A friend asked me to transport him—long story. I'll fill you in later. You ready!!?? "

You look J. directly in the eyes.

"*I am.*"

J. closes the back hatch door of the Jeep and then ambles over to the front passenger side door and opens it. He throws the keys up and over the Jeep. You barely have time to react before catching them.

"Good. You're driving," he says.

"*Well—that hasn't changed,*" you mutter.

You hop in, start the engine, and put the Jeep in drive. J. gives you a few meager directions. Something about Interstate 81 South and Alabama. You use your phone to plug in the directions, and you're off!

An hour or so goes by, and J. says nary a word.

"*So, what's the plan?*" you squeak out, deciding to break the silence.

J. looks at you. He takes a *long* pregnant pause. Then he takes a deep breath. You then notice—or *feel* actually—J.'s tranquillité d'esprit. It's been a while, but you remember his poise well...

"I have no idea. It's all a mystery to me," he retorts.

"*Mystery!?*" you belch out.

J. remains calm, unbothered.

"Yep. No idea what's next. It's a mystery. *That's* the plan."

You take a minute to let his answer sink in, and then, not knowing how to truly respond…

"Oooooo-kay," you say.

Devious and charming, you think. *Devious and charming, as ever.*

I have a confession to make.

Yep. Brakes on and pull over.

Yes—*you,* reader-person holding book.

Here it is: I'm *not* psychic, contrary to what you're about to think…

For instance…

You just peeled back the next few pages or scanned the Kindle pages forward (or, at the very least, have been itching to do so)—to see when the chapter ends—because, as first chapters go, this one is getting lengthy.

Yep—I do this all the time myself.

You're slightly antsy and have got the *Is this author gonna deliver the goods or waste my time?* jitters.

Yep—I usually don't trust an author until three or four chapters in.

You're concerned that the gritty, potty-mouthed tone of the last book will be gone or watered down in this second book. *What more can he say or write that will surprise, shock, and awe? And with the same amount of detail, care, honesty, and heart?*

Yep—This is just ordinary movie/book, story/narrative, part-two, anxiety. Millions of fans suffered from this at the beginning of The Empire Strikes Back, Harry Potter and the

Chamber of Secrets, and *Debbie Does Dallas,* (um, yeah I saw it!) —*Part 2.*

You see. All predictable shit. So, no—I'm not psychic. I'm simply aware. I'm awake. (Not *woke*—big difference.) My eyes are wide open. I am here. I am now. My sensory perception and situational awareness are dialed to *max*. I am present.

What the fuck are you even talking about!?

Exactly.

Here's what I'm talking about: If you think *Spirituality for Badasses Book Two* is going to be just like *Spirituality for Badasses Book One*, you're wrong.

Book One was logical, orderly, *relatively* safe, and straightforward. *Book Two* will *not* be any of these things. There will be paradox, conundrum, enigma, and quandary. There will be *mystery*.

Fair Warning for *Book Two*: Boys and girls, leave your thinking caps at home. Throw logic out the door. If you can't handle profanity, dancing on the edge of danger, microdosing psychedelics, high-octane adventure sports, or feeling deeply uncomfortable in the face of brain-breaking, heart-expanding, and soul-realizing truth, *Do Not Enter*. Here, there be *many* inexplicable fire-breathing dragons. You have been warned.

Okay—cool. That was my confession.

The miles pile up as you cruise south on I 81. J. is preoccupied with his phone, making arrangements for places to stay and people to meet, apparently. He's terse on the phone, revealing minimal information in each conversation, so it's hard for you to glean anything other than vague plans. After a while, you stop eavesdropping and settle into the drive.

"There are two locks to pick on the road to becoming a spiritual badass." J. announces out of nowhere.

You glance at him wide-eyed, letting him know you're listening.

"One lock is on the brain—the head—and the other lock is on the heart. Each lock is unique, and to pick each requires a different set of tools. The tools are fairly straightforward: The head lock tools are mostly logical and orderly. The heart lock tools are mysterious and messy."

He pauses and thinks.

"The results of picking each lock are also different. Each lock picked results in a certain amount and quality of energy, attention, and awareness being released."

Another pause.

"During our last adventure, from what I can gather, I do believe you picked the lock on your head. What do you think?"

"So, becoming a spiritual badass is like doing one of those escape room thingys..." you reply.

J. chuckles. "Yes, the ultimate paradoxical escape room."

J. continues. "Actually, escape rooms—plural. Jumping out of the first room landed you beautifully, smack dab in the middle of awareness, which—correct me if I'm wrong—healed a good bit of your relationship with body, emotion, and mind. But—"

"True that."

"But—there's a part of you that still remains in your head. And now we enter the second escape room. In this escape room, you'll be jumping *completely* out of your head into—

J. pauses, takes a big breath, and lingers in silence.

After a minute of this you're bursting at the seams. *"Come on, man! You're killin' me. Into what?"* you implore.

"Into your heart and soul," says J. "Into your heart and soul.

Spiritual Badass Suggestion:

Well, damn. It is way cool that you're still here. You just passed a gauntlet of *Stay Out! - Do Not Enter! - Private Property! - Here There Be Dragons!* signs—and you entered anyway. I want to congratulate you, high-five you, fist-bump you, and bear-hug you all at the same time. Is that okay? Because you—my friend—seem to have moxie, which I really admire and respect. And by moxie, of course, I mean—*badass*; and it goes without saying that if you've got some badass, well, that's something I *really* admire and respect.

Why all the continued hoopla about this badass thing? I'll tell you: I've met hundreds, maybe thousands, of spiritual seekers. The word "seekers" says it all—still seeking, waiting, hoping, looking, searching, spinning wheels—lost, confused, and asleep. Still seeking and *not* finding.

Question: What's the one main difference between a spiritual seeker and a spiritual finder?

Answer: *Courage*—Courage is the secret ingredient which transforms a seeker into a finder. *Badass courage.*

Spirituality for Badasses just means spirituality for courageous people. And I'm guessing, because you're still here, that this is *you*. You've got moxie, balls, courage, and badass. So again: High five, fist bump, and bear hug. You're in my tribe, and I love my badass tribe.

Your first spiritual badass suggestion for *Book Two* is this: *Remember* where you came from. You're no snowflake, pansy-minded, or rubbery-spined fool. You've seen some life shit—some of it good and some of it bad. You're not naïve. You're not gullible.

Remember this when things start to get tough in this book. I'm going to challenge you here. I'll be inviting you to break personal boundaries and social taboos. Why? Because I want to see you climb higher, run farther, and reach deeper. I want to see you transform into your own unique, beautiful, and awesome spiritual badass. I wouldn't do this if I didn't think you were ready.

So—remember who you are, badass.

Remember who you are...

Chapter 2
Spiritual Awakening

How to realize you're sleeping

After an overnight stay at a nondescript roadside motel in Knoxville, Tennessee, you, J., Lenny, and Ollie continue on a southward vector toward Alabama. J., still playing the petulant, mysterious spiritual guide tarot card, still hasn't revealed the destination. You're strangely okay with this and decide it's probably best just to play along.

You glance at the rearview mirror often, just to catch a glimpse of Lenny and Ollie. Lenny is perched on his usual branch, and Ollie (asleep with his eyes closed most of the time) sits nearby, tucked up into a tight little feathery ball. You find it strangely amusing and ironic that a small, silent, *cold-blooded* reptile has such a large, warm sway over your heart and mind. *I'm here because of J.*, you think, *but I stay because of Lenny! Enlightened little saurian beast...*

You drive for another hour. Your previous accepting, patience-filled thoughts are blown to smithereens as you cross the Alabama state line. You summon your best whiney kid's voice and blurt out:

"Mooom!...Daaad!??? Are we there yet!?"

J. chuckles. "Sorry, kids. Another few hours."

"*Might you proffer at least a clue?*" you chime.

J. pauses, thinks, and then finally relents. "Well—okay. Let's continue the child-adult role-metaphor thingy. Quite apropos. We're headed for adulthood—awakened adulthood to be specific. But that's not until Kansas and Nevada. In Alabama, we're going to visit my good friend Ray, who lives in asleep adulthood, much like you do, but is moving in fast on awakened adulthood—also much like you. After these three states, if I haven't scared you off, we're headed to California where we'll visit a...," J. pauses. "Well, I'm working on that one." That's sorta-kinda in a round-about way—the plan." J. looks at you and smiles cannily.

You acknowledge J.'s smile and widen your eyes in response as you begin chewing on the mountain-sized revelation he just dumped nonchalantly in your lap. You slowly swallow it and then begin digesting. Finally, you reply.

"I got plenty of sleep last night and feel quite awake. Not sleepy at all."

J. smiles. "Yeah, that's the problem with being asleep and dreaming. You don't realize it. But from my vantage point, you very clearly are."

"Sleeping, dreaming? Of what exactly?"

"That you're a *somebody* inside the amusement park."

"As opposed to?"

"That you're a *nobody,* and the amusement park is *inside* you."

"Totally confused, but I'll ask anyway because I think you're goading me to: 'I'm asleep.' Got it. How the hell do I wake up?"

"Bingo! I'm an excellent goader, don't you think?"

"I don't think goader is a valid Scrabble word."

"I accept that." J. pauses and then, looking directly in your eyes, speaks again. "Existential angst."

You wait for him to keep going, but realize the ball is in your court.

You pause, then ask:

"Oooooh–kay. What about it?"

He replies. "That's how you wake up—angst."

You let that sink in. "*I don't know if I have...existential angst. Is that a problem?*"

"Not a problem at all...but trust me, you have angst. It's just buried. That's the point of this trip. We're going to dig it up."

You take a deep breath and sigh.

"*Oh, boy.*"

"Yep. Oh, boy. Keep driving. Ray's place is just outside of Talladega."

Alrighty then. I suggest pulling over for this one. Yep, *you* out there with the book in your hand. I just threw a shit-ton of stuff your way.

Let's have a quick talk. Specifically, let's talk about this term "awake" or "awakening" or—as it's more popularly known—"spiritual awakening." (Don't worry; we'll get to *existential angst* in the next chapter.)

First of all—my apologies. I hate confusing vernacular, coded spiritual talk, or nonsensical religious verbiage. *Absolutely hate it.* But at some point in this process, as a spiritual author/guide, I have to cry *Uncle* and relent to using popular cultural words or terms.

So, okay...*Uncle! Spiritual Awakening*:

The term "spiritual awakening" is a modern, hackneyed platitude stolen, recycled, and altered from that Buddha dude of long ago. "Spiritual awakening" is bandied around by everybody and their brother, and their brother's wife, and her uncle, and his second cousin, and so on. Everyone from Oprah—who long ago had a live online thingy with Eckhart

Tolle, marketed by the ridiculous slogan *"Prepare to Awaken!"*—to Jim Carey and Russell Brand, have all had "spiritual awakenings." It's gone Hollywood. Ugh. BUT—

But, BUT; BUT!—Damnit, it's accurate. The spiritual badass process, the spiritual growth process—any good spiritual teaching which instigates a transformation or change in your life—when it works, *feels* very much like *waking up* from a bad dream. It *feels* like you've just snapped out of something. It *feels* like you've just altered your life course for the better. But, saying you've had a spiritual snapping or a spiritual course correction is a bit clunky. So—"spiritual awakening" it is.

I've had two major "spiritual awakening" events in my life. Both of them were hallmarked by embracing and dissipating large chunks of internal fear. These two "spiritual awakenings" are quite common in the grand playbook of most spiritual seekers.

Spirituality for Badasses Book One (no surprise here) was based on my first awakening experience, which occurred after a long student phase where I learned about awareness, mindfulness, and came to grips with the mechanics of ego and mind. This period culminated in a pivotal moment where a huge "chunk" of this internal emotional fear and shadow was seen, encountered, and embraced completely. Afterwards, I felt much lighter, freer, and —as indicated by the term—yes indeed, more "spiritually awake." Imagine unshackling a bowling ball from your ankle, after a lifetime of dragging it around. It felt very much like I had just picked a lock and set myself emotionally and mentally free—hence the whole "lock" metaphor.

Spirituality for Badasses Book Two, which you're now holding in your hands (again, no surprise here) is all about my experiences leading up to and including my second "spiritual awakening." Again, the generalities of this awakening are common to most spiritual seekers who encounter it. I'm not going to describe that awakening to you right now. Instead, through the magic of prose and a smidgeon of fanciful, authorly, story-telling BS, I'm going to drag you wholesale, right through it...with extensive, emotionally charged, heart-tugging and excruciating detail.

That's the end of my "spiritual awakening" rant. It's a crappy and overused word, but a necessary bit of modern spiritual lingo.

Prepare to awaken! (Really? That is some cheeseball shit.)

Spiritual Badass Suggestion:

Let's back up, shall we? I mean waaaaay back—all the way to *Book One*. There's something I'd like you to do, which is very much in alignment with the principles and techniques of this book: Take a mindfulness course. Yep, you read that correctly. Your first big spiritual badass suggestion is to sign up for a local eight-week mindfulness course.

Why?—Because any good mindfulness course will help you minimize stress, anxiety, unhappiness and/or depression.

Book Two is all about this—engaging with the world, meeting new people, and trying new things on the spiritual menu, even if they don't appeal to you at first. This is how boundaries are broken, goals are met, and positive change is achieved: trying new shit.

So—*if you are feeling stressed, anxious, unhappy or depressed*—I suggest taking an eight-week, in-person, mindfulness course at your nearest college or yoga studio. (Google it.) It may cost you a couple hundred bucks, but it's money well spent.

Remember, my books are just spiritual roadmaps.

Your life is the road...travel it.

Chapter 3
Existential Racecars

How to recognize your inner angst

Before we continue, I want to begin this chapter with a gentle preemptive warning about an erroneous expectation you might have: We won't be speeding through a bunch of quick fixes, exercises, or techniques—if that's what you're expecting. The lock-picking process for spiritual awakening—spiritual *badass* awakening, that is—takes time and patience. The pacing is slower, and the buildup is longer. But the payoff, as you'll soon find out, is *huge*. So—take a deep breath, find your inner space of awareness, slow down, and enjoy...

Now that's a combo you don't see often, you think, nearly out loud, as you pull onto a long, flat, gravel driveway, where a small quirky entrance sign reads *Ray Halloway's High Performance Engine Repair and Goat Ranch.*

As you slowly make your way down the driveway, your attention is hijacked by exactly that which was advertised: fenced in on both sides of the driveway are dozens of goats in all shapes, sizes, and colors.

"This should be interesting," you remark to J.

"Oh, it will be. I promise," J. replies.

"So, how in the world do you know Ray?"

"Seven Dragons. A few years ago, I taught a course there. Ray was a participant. He's been inviting me down here for rides ever since."

"Rides?—on what? Goats?"

"There he is."

You arrive at what looks like a highly functional and practical, but not so pretty, circular compound of buildings. There's a small, red brick and white trimmed single-story ranch home; a barn-like structure built from a hodgepodge of wooden and metal materials—you ascertain it's a barn from the high concentration of goats milling around it; and a large, concrete block, triple-bay garage, which is, very clearly, Ray's place of business. Each bay has a sign overhead, charmingly labeled *Billy, Nanny,* and *Kid.*

Ray, a buzz-cut, grey haired, sinewy, sixty-something, Steve McQueen-Clint Eastwood look-alike, stands at the opening of the center Nanny bay, wiping his hands on an old, blue oil rag hanging from his brown, worn leather belt. He's wearing blue jeans and a white t-shirt with the ubiquitous blue and yellow NAPA auto parts logo on it.

You pull into an obvious parking space, then flip the ignition key to the off position. J. hops out and greets Ray with a handshake, hug, and laugh. You step out of the Jeep and join the reunion.

"Ray, this is my latest victim—er, uh, I mean protégé," J. cracks.

Ray extends his hand. "Don't listen to him. Howdy, friend. Welcome. And pardon my greasy hands."

You shake Ray's hand, unbothered. *"Very nice to meet you. Interesting place you have here."*

"J. told me you were on a jaunt with him. J. and I drove around on a similar adventure." Ray directs his attention to J. "What was that…three, four years ago?"

"Something like that," J. responds.

Your eyes widen. *"You also did this? Did he make you drive?"*

"Hell yeah, he made me drive. Most of the way, but *not* during the rattling parts, thank God."

"Rattling parts?"

"You know—dark night of the soul stuff: anxiety, fear, emotional lows; all that fun stuff that rattles you to the core."

"Oh, that rattling. Thought you were talking about the Jeep."

"Speakin' of which...you changed the Jeep color. It's awesome!"

"Indeed, I did," responds J. with a big smile. "Thought you might like it."

Ray redirects the conversation and deadpans: "So J. tells me you're interested in doin' some goat yoga."

You pause and look incredulously at both Ray and J. *"Goat yoga?"*

"Yeah, yoga with baby goats." Ray deadpans again.

You take a few seconds to respond. *"Well, um, okay if that's..."*

You then notice the gleam in both Ray's and J.'s eyes.

"I'm just kidding." Ray places his hand on your shoulder. "We *are* going to a yoga class tonight, but sorry—no goats." Ray looks at J. "Have you told your friend about the yoga class?"

"Nope," J. says, "and I don't plan to."

You interject, *"He does that."*

"Yeah, he's been doing that for a while. Mr. Mystery is what I used to call him."

"Mr. Mystery!" You chuckle.

"Well, you're in for a treat," Ray continues. "And you're going to *love* this yoga class, if you don't puke in the first part."

"*Puke?*"

"You'll be fine, I'm sure. Listen up, guys; J., you remember where the room is, right? Get unpacked. Make yourself at home. I have a leaking head gasket that needs to be repaired. Should take another hour or two." Ray begins to turn away, but then hesitates. "Actually—just one more thing, J.—Lenny?"

"Of course!" J. responds.

Wise to the Lenny reunion drill, you allow J. and Ray to commune with the great green lizard god on their own. You grab your things out of the trailer and wait it out near the entrance of the Billy bay. You poke around inside and notice what appears to be some sort of covered sports car. On the interior garage wall, you also notice a framed, autographed photo of Ray holding a large silver NASCAR trophy, standing next to a skinny, funny-looking old guy with a feathery, black cowboy hat and black sunglasses. A handwritten cursive note below the photo reads: *To the GOAT! You earned this one!— Richard Petty.*

Damn, you think. *Richard fucking Petty. Who the hell is this Ray guy?*

After the Lenny fawning, you follow J. around to the back of the small ranch house where you encounter a wide-open, beautifully decorated patio.

"*Wow, this was unexpected,*" you utter.

Before you, spanned majestically, is a well-maintained and thoughtfully designed Alabama-Zen garden. Large, potted Camellias ostentatiously flaunt large, green leaves with fluorescent pink flowers; purple Grandpa Ott Morning Glory vines creep up vermillion wood trellises; a handful of moss-imbued, mostly eastern-themed statuary poise stately and elegantly here and there; and a koi pond with an intricate rock waterfall gurgles and splashes away.

"Ray has got his Zen shit on," you comment again.

"Yeah, he does," J. responds. "He wasn't always this way. That man tore through a mountain of existential angst to find the peace that this garden represents."

You reflect, then reply. *"Existential angst. Is that the Mr. Rogers word of the day?"*

"Yes, it is, boys and girls."

J. hops on a small, stone walkway which quickly leads to a small, detached guesthouse on the edge of the garden. "Here we are." J. opens the double sliding glass door, revealing a small, tiled kitchenette and a nearby living space. "There are two rooms in the back. Pick one," J. says.

"Cool. Sure thing."

You pick a room, unpack your things, and take a much-needed hot shower to wipe away the road grime from the last two days of travel.

It's late afternoon when Ray knocks on the sliding glass door. You answer his knock and open the door.

"You guys all settled?" Ray asks.

"All four of us," you say, pointing to the nearby pop-up cages which house Lenny and Ollie.

"Excellent. So, J. tells me you're ready for the Black Shadow," he announces.

Slightly taken aback, you reply, *"Eh, the Black Shadow? Not quite sure what that is."*

"That," says J. from behind you, "is exactly why we're here—the word of the day."

"*Oh, the word of the day,*" you reply. "*Angst.*"

J. looks at you with approval. "The Black Shadow and existential angst go hand-in-hand. You'll see."

"We're going to do some yoga in order to coax it out," Ray adds.

"*Cool. I'm game,*" you reply.

"You say that now," J. chides.

"Meet you around front in my car!" Ray exclaims.

"Cool. I'll fire up the Jeep," replies J.

Ray vanishes around the corner. J. tells you, oddly enough, to bring a bathing suit, a towel, water bottle, and change of clothing.

So—let's talk about *existential angst* because, very clearly, I'm about to place you in its lethal crosshairs. I think a little background might be in order. Shall we?

For starters, I should probably address the elephant in the room. I've been hearing it thump across your brain since Chapter 1: "But, but, but—we already dealt with fear and anxiety in the first book. I already met fear!"

My answer to this?—No sir/madam, you fucking have not. The fear you were introduced to in *Book One* was your garden-variety psychological and emotional baggage fear, which gets released when healthy amounts of mindful awareness are applied to the slightly-below-the-surface machinations of mind, emotion, and body. You see that fear, accept it, meet it, and then, bingo-bongo—Fear *Lock One* opened.

The fear, talked about here in *Book Two*, is accessed through existential angst and its gatekeeper, the Black Shadow. (And just in case you try to cross-reference these terms in the annals of some highfalutin', college-level, psychological reference book—don't bother. I'm using total storytelling / poetic license here to make this easier for you to understand and digest.) This fear is buried *deep*. *Meet it* and bingo-bongo—Fear *Lock Two* is opened.

Here's the spiritual adult stuff:

I can tell you that meeting the fear accessed through the existential angst/Black Shadow lock is a little like having your own personal lightsaber dual with Darth Vader.

I can tell you that meeting this level of fear is similar to the scene in *The Matrix* after Neo swallows the red pill and wakes up in a cyber-genetic soup pod to discover that he's nothing more than battery acid.

And I can tell you that you're Bruce Willis's character in *The Sixth Sense* listening to your young patient tell you, "I see dead people," and then realizing that you are, in fact, *the dead person*.

But all that would be child's play compared to meeting this fear *for real*. There are no words, no feel-good spiritual pep talks, no possible earthly descriptors I can provide or use to convey the sheer, raw, horrifying existential terror of what I am speaking about. You will run. You will cower. You will shit your spiritual pants. Okay? Anyone left in the room? Hello? Anybody?

Really? Cool. Alrighty—you asked for it.

Existential angst:

Truthfully, existential angst is not something I can teach or give you. We can dance around its perimeter. We can poke at it from a distance. We can ruminate about it over two fingers of whiskey. But existential angst is *your bag. You* have to feel it. You have to realize that it's always been there, and it's been so damn numbed, drugged, ignored, or drowned in life drama that you barely noticed it.

What is it? Existential angst is the deep, nagging feeling that something fundamental is sorely missing from your life; and—for most of us—*fuck if we know* what that fundamental missing something actually is.

Existential angst is a very strange place that—for no *one* particular reason—but rather and usually, for *multiple* reasons over time, you just wake up one day and find, for better or worse, that you're in. No sane person signs up for existential angst, but no sane person remains so *without it.*

Bottom line is that, for most people, shit has to get super bad before they come to the very grown-up, adult conclusion that existential angst is a good thing. You have to be *very* done with the connect-the-dot, "normal" life bullshit, so much so that the moody, ill-tempered, black clad emo-club looks really appealing—*because you have no other alternatives.* Some part of you has to *feel* like an old-soul.

I know this is supposed to be a spiritual and *not* a religious book, but I'd feel remiss if, at this time, I didn't point out the old-school corollary to the term "existential angst." Here it is. The Buddha dude said it very well long ago: "Life is suffering." Discovering your own existential angst is in 100% alignment with my friend Siddhartha—the Buddha.

So, I imagine if you're still here reading this—well then, indeed, *some* part of you identifies or feels *old-soul* and you're ready to bring existential angst into laser focus. So how does one do this? Simple: You turn off as much mental distraction as you can and *return* to your body. Goat yoga is *exactly* what you need…

It takes you a few minutes to gather the required things, and then you and J. depart the guest house and meander back through the Alabama-Zen garden. As you round the side of the house, you hear the deafening growl of a high-powered car engine come to life.

"*Holy shit!*" you say to J. "*Is that what I think it is?*"

"Oh, yes—it's going to be glorious," J. comments.

You round the corner of the house just in time to see a bright yellow Chevrolet Corvette Challenge roll out of the Billy garage bay. It's printed with an obscene amount of race car manufacturer and product logos and a large numeric black 4. You see *Ray Halloway* printed at the top of the driver's side door and, sitting relaxed in the driver's seat, with his left elbow draped over the top of windowless door, is Ray. He pulls the beast alongside you and J. and, for effect, revs the car's mighty engine before speaking.

"Only got room for one. Which one of you wants to ride with me?"

You look at J. He waves and gestures his right arm while slightly bowing. "All yours…"

"*Oh, hell yes!*" you reply. "*You'll follow in the Jeep?*"

"That's the plan," J. replies.

You hop in and notice immediately that this is no street car. You have to duck under roll bars as you enter. There's no seat belt—it's a harness, which Ray helps you get into. There's no radio or air conditioner or USB port for your phone. There's a gas gauge, odometer, speedometer, and that's it. It's built like a tank, paradoxically made to take a high velocity beating.

"*Why no windows?*" you ask.

"Makes it easier for extrication," Ray replies.

"Oh shit, that is intimidating," you squeak out.

"Don't worry. Haven't crashed since '89 and that was no fireball, just a roll and spin. They didn't have windowless regs back then, so it took a good twenty minutes with the jaws."

"Jaws?"

"Jaws of life—heavy-duty hydraulic cutters."

"Yikes. Bet that was no fun."

"It wasn't—but I survived, and the next day I won the damn championship. Go figure. I love telling that story."

"Is that the same championship...?"

Ray interrupts you. "One second." He looks in the rearview mirror. You do, too, and see J. pull up behind the Corvette in the Jeep. Ray sticks his arm out the window and gives J. the thumbs up. Ray shifts into gear, and both cars slowly roll down Ray's long gravel driveway.

"Sorry 'bout that. Yeah, that was 1989. I was thirty-two. Bested Dale Earnhardt and won the NASCAR Die Hard 500. My one and only claim to fame."

"That's the same championship picture in your garage with Richard Petty?"

"Ah, you saw that. Yeah, Richard started the whole 'goat' thing. Everyone saw that picture. Ironic that Richard Petty—who was in fact the real Greatest of All Time—referred to me as the goat that year. I ate that shit up."

"Awesome."

You reach the end of the driveway, and Ray pulls out onto a small country road, followed by J.

"So, what did you do after that?"

"After that?" Ray chuckles, "I became a professional alcoholic."

"Oh."

"Yeah. Quite the conversation stopper. I never won another championship, lost my sponsor two years later, and then replaced both with a twelve-pack of beer and whiskey chasers every night for a solid decade. I was a bad NASCAR country song. But fast-forward a bunch of years—or decades—and that's how I met J. ...at a week-long addiction retreat offered by my local AA."

"At Seven Dragons Sanctuary, right?"

"Yes. J. told you, I presume. That's my story. What's yours?"

"*I don't know. Typical screwed up childhood, I guess. Ran into J. and here I am.*"

"That's it, huh? And now you're on the hunt for the Black Shadow?" Ray says with a smile.

"*I don't know about that. I'll just settle for some yoga.*"

"That we can do."

Ray pulls out onto interstate I 20. A few minutes go by, and you spot the Talladega Superspeedway off to the right. Ray takes the Superspeedway exit and works his way toward the massive track."

"Where exactly is this yoga class?" you ask.

"Why—it's right there, of course." Ray points to the massive complex now looming over you.

"*At Talladega? Really?*"

Ray pulls up to an electronically gated entrance labeled "Mechanics and Drivers." He flashes a key card at the kiosk,

43

and the gate arm swings up. He pulls forward, stops the car, gets out, and does the same for J.

You, Ray, and J. pull into an underground garage a few minutes later. J. parks the Jeep and gets out. Ray flashes another thumbs up to J. and points to a nearby door. You and Ray continue forward and finally work your way to a large open garage area. It looks like a staging ground for race vehicles. Ray turns off the Corvette and gets out. He helps you unstrap the harness and has you get out.

"Here we are," announces Ray. "Pick a helmet." Ray points to a wall of helmets in all shapes and sizes.

"*I thought we were going to a yoga class?*" you say, surprise in your voice.

Ray looks directly at you and smiles. "Oh, we are, but the first part of *this* yoga class is a track run at 175 miles per hour."

"*Oh, Lordy me*," you whimper.

"What!? Haven't you ever driven at 175?" You turn and see J. entering the room...

He's grinning devilishly...from ear to ear.

Spiritual Badass Suggestion:

I suggest purchasing a blank journal or notebook and get to writing...

Specifically, you should address your own internal existential angst. What really bothers you? How are you unsatisfied? What's missing? Why are you an unhappy fuck? Write that shit down! Be honest. Be brutal. Don't hold back. No one else is going to read it.

The point of this simple but powerful journaling exercise is to burrow deep into the inner workings of your psyche and find the existential shit. Draw it out; see it; accept it; and—finally—love it.

Spiritual maturity *does not* happen for any old reason: It happens only when your angst—your suffering, your deepest sense of separation—is brought to the light of day. In doing so, all of your fears—just like dragons—are seen, met, and slain.

So don't just sit there...Get a journal and start slaying.

Chapter 4
Goat Yoga

How to be completely present in your body

Yoga is *not* what you think it is.

Every small town in America has half a dozen yoga studios these days. Most of them offer weight loss, physical fitness, or rehabilitation—all worthy causes, but not what the original 3,000-year-old Hindu Vedic creators of yoga intended. Yep...yoga is some old-school shit.

The word "yoga" is derived from the Sanskrit root 'Yuj,' meaning 'to join' or 'to yoke' or 'to unite.' As per the hoary Hindu Vedic scriptures, the practice of yoga was meant to lead to the union of individual consciousness with universal consciousness—a fancy way of saying "Know Thyself," which is, as you know, right up the spiritual badass alley.

Yoga is cool. I give most of it (not all of it) two wholehearted thumbs up. As a matter of fact, I'm taking a hot yoga class right now—entirely for rehabilitative purposes. I was diagnosed with prostate cancer recently and had my prostate surgically removed. I'm cancer-free and good now, but post-surgery recovery has been tough. So hot, sweaty yoga in this nearby studio has been beautifully brutal, challenging, and healing.

But I digress. You, my friend, might just benefit from some yoga in order to "Know Thyself." Here's how that shit works...

I can't believe I let them talk me into this. You stress think over and over. You feel like you're sitting on a tarmac, waiting for takeoff— in an F-14 Tomcat. *Oh shit, shit, shit...*

"You ready to do this?!" Ray says loudly through the mic system built into the helmets. His words are barely audible over the loud revving noise he applies to the Corvette's engine.

"*As I'll ever be...*" you shout. "*I guess.*" You're now strapped in crazy tight to the harness system built into the passenger seat.

"Relax as much as you can. Sink into the moment. Sink into your body. Don't push the fear away—whoop and holler as much as you like! Okay?" Ray exclaims and asks.

You look around you and can't believe you're actually about to be propelled high-speed around this behemoth NASCAR track. The Corvette is poised at the black and red checkered start/finish line. The red, white, and blue seated grandstand stretches to infinity both in front of and behind you. The grey asphalt track surface looms into the distance where it meets a menacing looking 33-degree banked turn.

An official looking man, dressed in a white collared shirt and black pants, walks out onto the track holding a matching checkered flag. He raises it up.

"Hang on, baby. Here we go!" Ray yells.

The flags come down, and Ray drops the engine into gear.

"*Oh shiiiiiiiiiit!*" you reply.

The G-forces mount immediately, and you feel your helmet press into the back of the seat. The engine, which you *thought* was loud before, now roars to a whole new level of cacophonous life. Head immobilized, you glance down with eyeballs only and see Ray deftly maneuvering the gear shift and gas pedal. He is a master driver; seeing his skill relaxes you— *but only a little*— because all that gear shifting amounts to one thing:

"*Holy crap!*" You manage to squeak out as you watch the speedometer climb: 60-70-80-90-100-120-140 miles per hour down the first straight stretch of track. Ray notches the gear shift back one, and the car maintains a steady speed as it approaches the first turn.

"Hang on! You might feel this one." Ray laughs.

"*Ohhhhh, man!*" is all you can manage as you peel into the turn. Something unholy and unnatural about the laws of Bugs Bunny physics allows you to travel *vertically sideways* as you round the mighty corner. You glance beyond Ray, out his window, and see the road blurring by with unnerving ferocity. The G-forces continue to mount as you swing out of the massive turn. Ray upshifts again and you…black out.

Ahh, there we are. Finally…I am here. Can you hear me? I'm speaking to you…

Allow me to introduce myself: I am…ahem, YOU. We have not spoken before, but we have much to talk about. I know this is confusing, but just give me a sec of your time…

How can I possibly be—you? Simple. I am—in part—your body. I know. I know. You just blacked out—but that actually did the trick and allowed for this communique…

Everything in your life has led up to this moment. I am—the clear open presence of your internal awareness, your truest essence, which your whole badass life has pointed to.

Yes, I am you. Your body—your awareness—speaking to you, paradoxically, right now. I am that. I am you. I am the black…

"Wake up friend! Wake up!"

You open your eyes. Ray is jostling your left shoulder and speaking to you through the helmet headset mic. "You okay? Probably too many Gs for you on that turn. You passed out!"

"*I did?*" you ask.

"Sure as hell—," Ray laughs. "Keep going?"

"Yeah, *I'm fine. Keep going. I'll never hear the end of it from J. That was just strange…*"

"You sure you want me to…?"

"*Really. All good. I'm fine. Give me all you got.*" You point forward.

"Ooooo-kay." Ray smiles. "Hang on tight!"

The rest of the ride is a literal blur and blast. Ray launches the Corvette down the main 4,000-foot stretch of Talladega and achieves, for a split second, 175 miles per hour. You both whoop and holler. He reduces speed so you don't black out on the second turn and then crosses the finish line.

"Again?" Ray asks.

"*Abso-fucking-lutely!*" you reply with a big grin.

Ray loops the track one more time. You cross the finish line, delirious with joy and completely ragged out. Ray maneuvers the car back toward the garage, passing J., who just witnessed your whole experience. You arrive at the garage. J. meanders in and helps both you and Ray out of the Corvette. You're a wobbly-kneed mess upon exiting the vehicle.

"Well? Whaddya think!?" implores J. with excitement.

You take a moment to gather your thoughts and find your balance. "That was…absolutely amazing—and a little strange."

"Your friend passed out," Ray interjects.

"Really!?" comments J. "And...?"

"*I think I may have seen, or—eh—experienced, the Black Shadow thing,*" you reply.

"No shit," says J.

"*No shit.*"

J. approaches you and pats you on the back. "Well done, amigo. Well done. We'll talk about it later."

"Let's get some chow," Ray gestures to the exit, "and then go to yoga class."

After a light meal at Big Bill's, the open-air restaurant food court at Talladega, you, J., and Ray jump into your prospective cars again and exit the raceway compound. You head south on Route 77.

A minute or two passes by, and you speak up. "*Ray, if you don't mind me saying so—you don't seem like the yoga type.*"

Ray smiles and glances at you. "It's a Zen thing. Think about it. How did you feel after the track experience? How do you feel now?"

"*Well, truthfully—a little wobbly and queasy.*" You think some more. "*And present, very present—now that you ask.*"

"Exactly. All the best drivers are *present*. You have to be—in order to survive, excel, and win—if that's your thing. Yoga helps you do that; something, unfortunately, I learned a little too late in my racing career."

"*Present—,*" you calmly repeat to yourself.

"Yep. No past. No future. Just now, now, now. Body and awareness only."

You pause in silence and allow the seconds to tick by. Then, like a tortoise peeking out of its shell, you risk another question. *"Have you ever met this Black Shadow thing J. talks about?"*

"Yes, I think so. It's different for everyone, of course. I still have my limitations. Scared the shit out of me. Still working on that one."

Another long pause of silence.

"Me too, I guess."

Ray arrives at the outskirts of Talladega city and weaves his way to a small, nondescript strip mall. You park in front of a shop with a large, exterior glass window painted in letters that read *Talladega Yoga Center*. J. pulls up. All three of you get out of your cars and enter.

It's a humble little place, but neat, clean, and—typical of most yoga studio lobbies—contains a gift shop. T-shirts, yoga mats, incense, and various trinkets are strewn about sparsely on shelves.

What stands out is the wall of photographs behind the counter: It's a who's who of NASCAR racecar drivers—some photos of drivers next to their cars; some of drivers with trophies; some just headshots. What they all have in common is the word *Thank You!* written in a variety of fonts in black sharpie pen. You ascertain that this isn't just any old yoga center—it's *the yoga center* for NASCAR stars.

"Pretty impressive, huh?" says Ray when he sees you gawking at the photos. "I get credit for quite a few of them."

"Credit?"

"I introduced them to yoga," Ray proudly says.

"Really?"

Just then a woman in her late forties swings around the hallway corner.

"Ray!" she exclaims.

"Mariam!!" Ray smiles. He walks over to her and gives her a hug. "How ya been? Got room for three more tonight?"

"For the hot-class, right?" Mariam replies.

"Yes, ma'am. Do you remember J.? This is his friend."

"*Nice to meet you*," you chime in.

"Likewise," she replies. Mariam looks at Ray and them fumbles with the white iPad on the counter. "You're all signed in. Go get ready, and I'll meet you in the studio."

"Awesome," Ray says. "Just one more thing. Listen, would it be okay if…"

J. taps you on the shoulder and gestures *follow me* while Ray continues his conversation with Mariam. You and J. head to the showers and bathrooms at the end of the hall.

"Put your bathing suit on," J. announces. "You're about to sweat your ass off."

You and J. enter the studio with yoga mats, towels, and water bottles in hand. You're immediately accosted with an oppressive blast of heavy, hot air. *Oh, crap*, you think. *This ain't gonna be easy.* Ray and Mariam are already seated on their mats along with about a half-dozen other students who meandered in while you were changing. It's a fairly large room, probably forty some feet front to back.

Mariam sits at the front of the class. Behind her is a large wall-to-wall, floor to ceiling mirror. The room is dimly lit with multiple LED colored lights. There's a large, generic-looking mandala on the back wall. There's also a NASCAR sticker, humorously posted at a deliberate angle below the mandala. Some light, New Age-ish music plays on the ceiling speakers. You like the peaceful feel of the place, but suspect it's about to deliver you an ass-whoopin' ... and you're not wrong.

Mariam turns down the music slightly and then chimes a small glass bowl sitting behind her adjacent to the mirror. The hot-yoga class begins. You do poses like downward-facing dog, mountain, eagle, standing bow, triangle, and more. It's a pretty defined set of movements all flowing together and clearly coordinated to accomplish one thing: to make you sweat your ass off, just as J. promised. You also grok that doing this kind of thing repeatedly would probably make you a rock-steady, powerful, and flexible *physical* badass.

It's tough—*really* tough.

You struggle through the set and see that J. and Ray are no yoga masters themselves. They, too, struggle with many of the poses—modifying and short stepping them as needed. You're relieved when Mariam invites you into vipassana, the final pose where you lie flat on your back and allow all the hard work to sink in. And sink in it does...

"*Holy fuck, I am present...,*" you think while lying on your back. There's a taut singular feeling of razor-sharp clarity that manifests itself with an odd pressure on your temples. Thoughts are mostly burned up. Emotions are clear and empty. You feel empowered, straight as an arrow, and clear as a bell. *Wow, this is some powerful shit.* You close your eyes and hear Mariam speak...

"Well done, everybody. So, tonight we have a special guest who is going to lead us through a unique meditation. This is last minute, so if there's anyone who can't stay—it's all good. Thank you so much for joining us, and we'll see you in the next class. Namaste."

Everyone replies. Just one person gets up to leave.

"So J., the stage is all yours."

J. rolls over and out of vipassana, gets up, and then seats himself next to Mariam. She takes J.'s spot. J. invites everyone to get in a comfortable cross-legged position.

"This is called The Shut-Off Valve Exercise," he announces. "It's meant to power down your mind: thoughts, emotions, dreams, delusions, wishes, and what-ifs…all of it…so that the only thing left is the body. I hope you enjoy. Mariam, thanks for letting me hijack your class."

Mariam laughs and so do a few other people.

The Shut-Off Valve Exercise

J. continues:

"We'll begin with three deep breaths. Inhale one…two…three.

Imagine a garden spigot with a red rotary on/off valve and a brass body."

J. pauses.

"Now—imagine about a dozen of them surrounding your body. Water is leaking out of all of them. In this case, *water* is your vital time, energy, and life resources. You're leaking like an iceberg-struck Titanic…

Each valve has a particular name and function. We're going to turn each valve all the way off, and the only thing left will be your body—in its purest, wisest, and most natural state. No leaks. Just the body. Got it? Cool. Here we go…"

You follow J's lead and settle into the exercise…

"*Thoughts*—In order to understand, accept, see, and feel the complete wisdom of the body, let's shut off all thought. Turn the valve which *shuts off* thought. No thought—high or low, good or bad—is going to save you, help you, enhance you, or improve you. You are *only* the body and the body has all the wisdom you need...Take a deep breath."

You do so and recall your previous conversation with Ray. *Body. Present. Here. Now. Perfect sense...*

J. continues...

"*The Future and the Past*—In order to understand, accept, see, and feel the complete wisdom of the body, let's shut off the future and the past. Turn the valve which *shuts off both* the future and the past. No future—good or bad—is going to save you, help you, enhance you, or improve you. No past—good or bad—is going to save you, help you, enhance you, or improve you. You are *only* the body and the body has all the wisdom you need...Take a deep breath."

Just here and now...

"*Hopes and Dreams*—In order to understand, accept, see, and feel the complete wisdom of the body, let's shut off our hopes and dreams. Turn the valve which *shuts off all* hopes and dreams. No hope or dream—good or bad—is going to save you, help you, enhance you, or improve you. You are *only* the body and the body has all the wisdom you need...Take a deep breath."

No fantasies or delusions either...

"*The Separate Soul*—In order to understand, accept, see, and feel the complete wisdom of the body, let's shut off our ideas about having a separate soul. Turn the valve which *shuts off* the separate soul. No soul—high or low, good or bad—is going to save you, help you, enhance you, or improve you. You are *only* the body and the body has all the wisdom you need...Take a deep breath."

"*Guides, Angels, Gurus and Teachers*—In order to understand, accept, see, and feel the complete wisdom of the body, let's shut off our ideas about guides, angels, gurus and teachers. Turn the valve which *shuts off all* guides, angels, gurus and teachers. None of these—high or low, good or bad—is going to save you, help you, enhance you, or improve you. You are *only* the body and the body has all the wisdom you need...Take a deep breath."

You notice some resistance to this one, but allow those thoughts to come and go...

"*Higher Self & God*—In order to understand, accept, see, and feel the complete wisdom of the body, let's shut off our ideas about a higher self or god. Turn the valve which *shuts off* all ideas about a higher self or god. No higher self or god—high or low, good or bad—is going to save you, help you, enhance you, or improve you. You are *only* the body and the body has all the wisdom you need...Take a deep breath."

You feel yourself sinking, shifting, dropping and sweating. Deeper and deeper, you fall into the very still, present moment state of the body...

"*Spiritual Awakening or Enlightenment*—In order to understand, accept, see, and feel the complete wisdom of the body, let's shut off our ideas about spiritual awakening or enlightenment. Turn the valve which *shuts off* spiritual awakening and enlightenment. No awakening or enlightenment—high or low, good or bad—is going to save you, help you, enhance you, or improve you. You are *only* the body and the body has all the wisdom you need...Take a deep breath."

J. pauses and stretches out his legs. "Thanks everyone. That's the end of the exercise. I hope it helped you find the deep, still presence of your flawed, amazing, wise body."

J. pauses for another quick beat. "And now, if you'd like, you can join my friends and me—sorry, Ray; I know you don't drink—at the bar across the street where we'll be turning the cold beer valve—all the way on."

Everyone in the room laughs. You can barely move; you are so still and present. You don't *want* to move. Somehow, though, you muster the energy, gather your things, and exit the room—still drenched with sweat from the heat and yoga.

As you leave the room, you are silent, solid, grounded, and fucking amazingly…beautifully…*present*.

Spiritual Badass Suggestion:

No surprise here: Take a yoga class! Just about any yoga will do. You know your strengths and weaknesses, likes and dislikes. Try a few *different* yoga classes, even—until you discover one that speaks to you and helps you uncover the innate wisdom of your body.

Why do this? Well, it's not going to turn you into an overnight spiritual badass; and it's not going to turn you into a NASCAR superstar; it's not even going to give you the power to levitate or see auras. But, if you take a good class, it will get you in touch with the wisdom and *presence* of your beautiful and flawed body. Combine this with the spiritual badass work you've already learned and the spiritual badass work you are *about* to learn—and you'll shave years off your efforts.

Yoga is a good thing—even yoga with goats.

Chapter 5
Two Monkeys

How to take small leaps of faith

What if you ain't feelin' it? What if you're just not ready? What if...none of this is resonating? All good. All acceptable. All *okay*. Here's what I suggest: Take *one small step*...

Here's an allegory that just might help you:

Once upon a time, there were two white-faced monkeys who lived on opposite banks of a large river in the jungles of Coast Rica. One monkey, whose name was Jinga, lived on the east bank of the river. The other monkey, whose name was Mongo, lived on the west bank.

Jinga and Mongo lived two very different lives because, for whatever reason, the river's west bank was much more fertile than the east bank. The west bank was flush with coconut palms, mango trees, banana groves, and a wide assortment of berry and nut bushes. The east bank was dry and barren and proffered only the occasional banana, fig, or pecan.

Mongo lived in a cornucopia of plenty and rarely worried about his next meal. Jinga, on the other hand, spent most his days scraping and scrounging for very little.

Rarely did the two monkeys venture to the shoreline simultaneously, but having both gone down to the river's edge to quench their thirst one day, it happened.

Mongo noticed Jinga first and waved to him. Jinga, a bit slow to respond, finally noticed and waved back.

When Jinga raised his hand to wave, Mongo immediately saw how gaunt and malnourished he was. Mongo didn't know why he spoke up, but he did, and this is when the essence of our little story began...

"Hey, you over there. I'm Mongo! Come join me! Swim across the river. There's plenty of food over here for both of us. What's your name?"

Jinga looked up, hesitated, but finally replied: "I'm Jinga. I can't swim. There are crocodiles!"

"It's safe. The water is actually shallow. The crocodiles won't hurt you." replied Mongo.

"That's okay. No thanks."

And with that, Jinga disappeared into the forest. Mongo shrugged his shoulders and meandered back into the forest.

As Mongo headed home, he noticed the amber rays of the setting sun and thought to himself: "Hmmm. I wonder...? I'll return tomorrow night."

And so he did, and there again at the water's edge at the same exact time was Jinga.

"Hi again!" yelled Mongo. "Really! It's safe. Swim across!"

"No thanks," said Jinga. "Snapping turtles!"

Mongo, not surprised, was now determined to help his new friend (at least that's what he considered Jinga) and so, for several more nights, he showed up to the river's edge and tried to convince Jinga to cross. Nothing worked. Jinga was equally determined *not* to cross for various reasons, but mostly because of all the scary crocodiles, snapping turtles, boa constrictors, poisonous frogs, and other creepy, crawly things that Mongo found laughable and absurd.

And that's when Mongo thought of it. "Ha!" he laughed to himself. "Perfect."

The next night, after having made a few arrangements with friends, Mongo sauntered down to the water's edge and, sure enough—there was Jinga, gaunt and thin as ever, out for his nightly drink.

"I brought you something. Just step out onto the rock!" Mongo yelled across.

"Rock?" questioned Jinga.

"That one." Mongo pointed to a rock near the water's edge of the east bank. "It's a banana!"

Sure enough. Jinga saw the rock Mongo pointed to and on it was a big, ripe banana. Jinga, hadn't eaten a banana in *weeks*. It didn't take long for him to make the leap. Jinga pounced on the banana and ate it whole in a matter of minutes.

"I also got you a fig!! On that log!"

Jinga looked around and, sure enough, also within leaping distance was a log with a fig branch and several figs on it. Jinga leapt and quickly gobbled down the figs.

"Mangos—my favorite! There's one on that stick!!" yelled Mongo.

Jinga saw the mango on the small, winding stick and jumped. Jinga had not eaten a mango in over a year. His mouth exploded with delight as he gulped down the juicy mango.

"Pecans and almonds!!" shouted Mongo. "On the small grey stone."

Jinga saw the stone and the nuts. It looked tiny, but he didn't care. He hadn't eaten like this in years. He leapt again and, within a few minutes, his belly was filled with nuts.

"Now take my hand," said Mongo.

"What!?" said Jinga. "How did you get to *my side* of the river!?"

"My friend," said Mongo, "I'm not on *your* side of the river. *You* are on *mine*."

Jinga looked up and, sure enough, he recognized the dry barren path he frequently used—on the opposite side of the river.

"But, but, how?" uttered Jinga.

"Quite simple—," said Mongo. "Got some help from my friends. Okay boys, show yourselves."

Then—from out of the water emerged his friends: one big snapping turtle whose back looked like a rock; one six-foot crocodile whose back looked like a log; one boa constrictor whose back looked like a branch; and one frog whose back looked like a small grey stone.

Jinga stood with his mouth open. When he finally spoke, all he could say was...

"Thank you. Thank you! Thank you, friends! You have done for me a great service ...Thank you."

Jinga never stepped foot on the east bank of the river again. He became best friends with Mongo and *good* friends with the turtle, crocodile, snake, and frog.

What's the point of this story?

Life is about small leaps of faith; *not giant, impossible bounds—* and our fears are quite often...good friends in disguise.

Now leap, friend, take one small step...and eat that banana.

CHAPTER 6
THE COOSA MONSTER

How to get unstuck when you feel spiritually flat

It's the next morning, and the effects of the racing and hot yoga are still with you. You're seated outside at a small iron table in Ray's beautiful Alabama-Zen garden patio. The koi pond is gurgling away in the background. You've helped yourself to a large cup of coffee and are enjoying its earthy taste and aroma.

"Good morning, Little Sunshines," you hear through the screen door of the guest house. Inside, you see that J. isn't speaking to you but to Lenny and Ollie. You smile at the familiar phrase. After a few minutes, J. joins you outside with Lenny and Ollie in tow. Lenny is drooped around J.'s shoulder, munching on the remnants of what looks like a grape, and Ollie is in the pop-up cage. J. sets the cage down next to the table.

"You mind?"

"*Oh, sure,*" you reply.

J. hands Lenny over to you. "Be right back." You place Lenny around your shoulders, and he settles in. J. leaves for a moment and returns with a small plastic container.

"Chicken gizzards. Breakfast of champions," J. comments.

"*Yuck...,*" you reply as J. opens the container and you see what's inside.

"Ahhh—but it's good!" J. replies.

Ollie, still in the pop-up cage, immediately perks up—his eyes excited and wide when he sees breakfast. J. begins cutting and preparing the gizzards and, for the first time, you hear Ollie speak. It is the cutest damn thing you've ever heard—a warbling, sad little sound similar to the cries of nested fledgling baby birds with Mama nearby. It melts your heart, despite the somewhat gruesome follow-up behavior.

J. forks a piece of the chicken gizzard into Ollie's beak. With reckless abandon, Ollie rips it apart and swallows it whole down his gullet. It's both cute *and* brutal. After his breakfast, Ollie is wide awake and chirpy. J. reaches into the cage and coaxes Ollie to jump onto his gloved hand.

"Here. Take one. His talons are sharp." J. hands you a glove from his pocket. "Put it on."

"Now, hold it out." You do so, and J. shifts Ollie from his hand to yours. And then—*oh my!* You get a close-up, intimate look at Ollie for the first time. You immediately drown in his big, beautiful, innocent yellow and brown eyes.

"*You are so cute!*" you mutter. Ollie squeaks again.

"You're a goner now!" J. proclaims.

With your other hand, you scratch the top of Ollie's head. His eyes squint and close slightly as you pet and rub the soft down between his small ears. You do this for a few moments and lose yourself in the presence of this darling little creature.

"*Kinda puts Lenny to shame in the charm department*," you say as you transfer Ollie back to J.

"Lenny heard that!" J. laughs.

"*I don't think he cares*," you reply, noticing that Lenny is in his happy spot on your shoulders.

"I imagine not," says J. "Ollie's a wise one, just like this little dude." J. gives Lenny a scratch.

"*I believe that,*" you reply, wondering what this little, feathery animal teacher has in store for you.

Just then, Ray rounds the corner of the house and walks over to the table.

"Ahhh, feeding time at the zoo, I see," says Ray.

"Chicken gizzards and grapes. Want some?" counters J.

Ray smiles and offers Lenny a head scratch. "What's on the agenda today, friends?"

J. looks at you. "I thought we'd walk down to the river, maybe take a swim; and…you know what else I was thinking, Ray? Could we go to a meeting?"

Ray doesn't hesitate. "Sure thing; they're public. There's one every night in town."

"*Meeting?*" you ask.

"AA," replies J.

"You guys make yourselves at home. I've got some work to do in the garage." Ray looks around at his garden and takes a deep breath. "Enjoy! We'll meet at five tonight."

He walks off and, as he does so, chimes in again, "Maybe you guys will spot the Coosa monster! Never know." Ray rounds the corner and is out of sight in a second.

You look at J. "*Coosa monster?*"

"The Loch Ness of Alabama," J. replies.

Great. More shadowy monster weird shit, you think. You take a deep breath and then, for whatever reason, start feeling annoyed.

An hour or so passes, and you meet J. again out on the patio. Lenny is wrapped around J.'s shoulder. Your mood is less than chipper; you summon minimal enthusiasm for this little jaunt.

The Coosa River marks the western boundary of Ray's property. There's a trail, and apparently a pier and a decent swimming spot. You stand. Your body language divulges the inner turmoil. J. assesses it immediately.

"Not feeling it, huh?" J. asks.

"*No, I'm not.*"

"We can wait and go later."

"*That's not it. I'm not feeling ... any of this. Why am I here? What am I doing?*"

"Like it's all flat?"

"*Today—very.*"

"Come on…let's walk...and talk."

You reluctantly follow J.; Lenny bobs his head up and down and seems excited for the walk. *At least someone's into it*, you think.

You follow J. around the house, past the garage bays, and over to the barn. J. opens a small gate, and you both step through. You pass by a small group of goats and then, with J. leading the way, catch a single file trail through a field of light green brush and grass dotted with small yellow wildflowers. Crickets chirp. Insects buzz. Birds flit up and away as your feet swipe and crunch the grass below. It's peaceful and pretty.

"It's called spiritual flatlining," J. speaks and then continues. "It's very common. No highs or lows; peaks or valleys; challenges or disappointments; profundities or banalities; good guys or bad guys; heroes or fools. It's all just the same…and it's flat as a board. Many, many spiritual seekers have encountered this, and it's absolutely no different than the Coosa monster."

"*The Coosa monster?*" you query.

"That's right...the Coosa monster. It's a bunch of horseshit—a made up story you tell yourself and others for drama, effect, and fun. There's no such thing as the flatlined boogey monster—not really. You haven't been abandoned. The spiritual process is still alive and kicking inside of you. You're completely worthy and you, my friend, totally got this. The spark, the pizazz, the juice—it's just dormant, that's all."

"*That's great to hear, but I still don't feel it today.*"

J. stops walking and turns to face you. "Bullshit. It's there. This is the part where I pull out my bamboo Zen stick and slap you on the back of your hand. There's something under that flatness. I'm not denying that you feel flat. But I'm adamant that you don't abandon hope, interest, courage, or intention. It's *very* easy to get sucked into the flat, erroneous, self-pitying belief that nothing will change *for you*, nothing will work *for you*, and nothing can save your sorry ass. That's the Coosa monster—a big stinking pile of nonsense."

J. turns and continues walking…

"You with me?"

"*I am. Thanks for the slap.*"

"Listen, you know you have my utmost admiration and respect. This shit is difficult, and it's actually the *most* difficult when everything seems utterly flat and pointless. But—and this is a very big ol' but—you wouldn't be here putting up with Lenny and me if there wasn't something deep down inside you that, however fucking faint, you couldn't hear calling out your badass name. Right?"

You pause in silence and think before responding. "*You're talking about that existential angst thing again, aren't you?*"

"Yes. Sometimes you have to poke and prod at that shit to get it to come out of hiding."

You take a deep breath. *"Understood."*

"Good. Not done yet. There's one more thing." J. pauses. "Gratitude."

"Okay...gratitude?"

"I know what you're thinking. Most of the time when I hear or read about gratitude, especially in the spiritual context, it makes me want to vomit big spiritual chunks. It's hyped, over-done and about as effective as a three-day old wet noodle."

"I'm guessing there's another big ol' but comin' "

"Yep. But, but, but—use it in the *right* way, and gratitude can extricate you from flatness and other shitty feelings. Here's how: Be *grateful* for the shitty feelings, and be *aware* of the shitty feelings— that's what you do. When something shitty-crappy-awful *like feeling flat* comes down the pike, instead of wallowing in it, dramatizing it, or getting stuck in it—*be aware of it and be grateful for it*—because that shit is trying to tell you something."

"So—I should thank the flatness?"

"Yes. Witness it. Notice it. Be aware of it—you know exactly how to do this now...and express a big internal thank you to it, because it's the next doorway. That's how this spiritual stuff usually works. Every shitty obstacle is usually *the next* awesome doorway. It's the phoenix archetype."

"I know that one all too well."

"Yes—you do. Out of the destruction, death, fire, and ashes—rebirth."

"Damn, you're good."

J. takes some time before responding. "I get all my spiritual-teacher power direct from source."

"*Source?*"

"Yeah—," J. points to Lenny. "Source."

You crack a big smile. "*You'd be nothing without the supreme power of Lenny.*"

"Oh, I'm *nothing* alright. And someday you will be, too."

You continue through the field. It eventually takes you through a small, sparse forest of willow and poplar trees. You begin seeing the river through the trees. The water flow is hardly noticeable, and the river's half-mile width makes it look more like a lake. A small, sandy, sloped embankment appears, and the path continues down to a small, white, paint-chipped, wooden pier which jetties out about ten feet over the water. It's not much, but it serves its purpose.

You watch J. strip down to his bathing suit and then place Lenny on the end of the pier. J. jumps in. You watch in amazement as Lenny, like a damned, water-loving, black Labrador Retriever, leaps off the end of the pier and swims right up to J.

"*He never ceases to amaze me!*" you shout.

"He's the real Coosa monster!" J. shouts back.

"*Yes, he is.*"

You, J., and Lenny spend the next few hours splashing, swimming, and cavorting in the warm waters of the Coosa River. It's a delightful afternoon. The water absorbs and smooths out most of your previous feelings of flatness. The day slips by, and soon you don't remember what all the fuss was about.

J. brought a power bar which he graciously shared with you, but it wasn't near enough food for the two of you. So, when the grumbling in your stomach starts up again in earnest, you know it's time to head back. You pack up your things and take one last look at the Coosa River.

"See—no river monster there," says J.

"*Just a silly story...*" you reply.

You walk back in silence through the buzzing green fields bathed in the languid, late day Alabama sun.

Spiritual Badass Suggestion:

If you're feeling flat, lost, unworthy, or bereft of spiritual umph, do exactly as prescribed: write about this shit in your journal. *Be aware of it. Be grateful for it.* See what happens. It may take some time before the doorway *out of* flatness appears, but it will appear.

As spoken, most teachings about gratitude make me want to hurl big spiritual chunks, but I think there's a place for gratitude in Badass Land, especially if done in a non-woo-woo way...

With humor and awareness, just say "Thanks a fucking lot for *that* shitty experience, universe. I get it. I'm grateful. Can we move on now?" You get the idea...

CHAPTER 7
ALCOHOLICS ANONYMOUS

How to meet your black shadow

Okay—you still hanging in there with me? Like I said earlier in the book, the pacing at this level of teaching is *slower*. You might be feeling a bit of resistance, right now. Good!— No whining or complaining!

You know why this shit is difficult?

Because—no ego in his or her right mind *wants* it. *Because*—it means *death* to that very same ego and on the flip side *life* to your truest badass self. Sorry friend—you can't have it both ways.

In this chapter you're going to have a major breakthrough, but as you're about to find out, all the spiritually flat, existential, Black Shadow, angst shit was literally and figuratively *the fertilizer* that nourished and birthed it.

So? You ready? Cool. Let's continue...

In 1935, a stock broker from New York City and a surgeon from Akron, Ohio got together to discuss a particular shitty condition that had afflicted them both: alcoholism. Both Bill Wilson and Dr. Bob Smith had reached the literal and metaphorical bottoms of their individual whiskey barrels when they surmised that a higher power (literally *any* higher power) might just be the ticket to sobriety and sanity. They were correct. Fast forward three years later with over a hundred alcoholics transformed into sober citizens, and *Alcoholics Anonymous*—along with its famous *Twelve Step* program— was born.

Today, *Alcoholics Anonymous*, or AA as it's commonly called, "can be found in approximately 180 nations worldwide, with membership estimated at over two million. There are more than 123,000 AA groups around the world and AA's literature has been translated into over 100 languages." (Thanks, Wikipedia.)

AA must be doing something right; that's a lot of hurting people being helped.

With the name in the title of this chapter and previous references in *Book One*, you may have noticed that I'm slightly gung-ho for *Alcoholics Anonymous*. No denying it. Here's why: I think AA utilizes a very solid set of practical, open-minded spiritual principles to achieve its goals. *The Twelve Steps and Twelve Traditions* book, written by Bill Wilson and published in 1953, miraculously hit the spiritual phoenix nail directly on its fiery head. The steps work. No bullshit. No drama. No sex scandals. No tax evasion. No Rolls-Royces. (And no fucking fun say all the dead gurus from the '70s and '80s.) The powerful spiritual fire of the *transformational phoenix* is alive and well in *Alcoholics Anonymous*. Shitty situations transform into awesome doorways.

So, why am I gettin' all preachy and in your face about AA? Because—*Step Five*, as you're about to find out, is of particular interest to our badass adventure. *Step Five* is fucking genius...

You, J., and Ray enter the lobby of Peace Wesleyan Church, located just north of Talladega. It's typical of any drywalled, tile, drop-ceiling entrance area found in buildings everywhere. You walk down a short hallway and enter a large, open community hall filled with dozens of beige plastic chairs.

About a dozen people have helped themselves to the chairs. Also seated, at a white plastic table front and center, is a gentle looking man in his mid-fifties wearing blue jeans, a black t-shirt, and sporting a five o'clock shadow and wire-rimmed glasses. Draped over the back of his chair is a black leather jacket, which you surmise compliments the black Suzuki motorcycle you saw parked out front.

Ray introduces you and J. to the man seated at the table.

"Thom, this is J. and his friend."

"Welcome, guys. Happy to have you. Please, take one for the class and grab a seat. We'll start soon." Thom points to a pile of books, all of them titled *Twelve Steps and Twelve Traditions*. All three of you sit down with books in hand.

A few silent moments pass. You note the rather bland and nondescript décor of the room. You also note—and it's not bland *at all*—the very surprising, but much appreciated, return of the deep, grounded, peaceful presence of what J. had called "The Sobering Truth." It catches you completely off guard. You had been feeling a bit self-conscious, awkward, an imposter for not identifying as an alcoholic—but this awkwardness quickly dissipates into a deep pool of grounded awareness.

The meeting commences.

"Let's begin with the Serenity Prayer," announces Thom.

You listen as the others recite the prayer:

> God, grant me the serenity
> To accept the things I cannot change;
> Courage to change the things I can;
> And wisdom to know the difference.

After the prayer, Thom continues speaking. "Welcome everyone. We'll continue where we left off last Friday. Judy, we read Step Four last week, correct?"

Judy, who is seated several chairs away, replies, "Yes, I can start reading Step Five if you'd like."

"Please do," replies Thom.

Judy begins reading Step Five from *Twelve Steps and Twelve Traditions*. You follow along in the same book. After about a page, she passes the baton to another member who also reads a page. This cycle continues over the course of about twenty minutes. By the end, about a half-dozen members have read Step Five.

It takes you a minute to catch on, especially since the step is out of context for you, but you soon relax and begin to get the gist of it. Step Five is pretty damned profound, not because you *think* it's clever or even psychologically accurate, but because you can feel the raw, sobering truth and power of the words: Step Five is about *confession*.

Confession is the key to this whole thing!, you think.

It stirs up a whole litany of insights: *This isn't some hokey, stiff, institutionalized, religious confession. This is the authentic, ego- deflating, humility-inducing transformation of the body, mind, and spirit—through the spoken word and hearing heart.*

After the final page of Step Five is read, Thom gently assumes front and center again and speaks.

"My name is Thom and I'm an alcoholic. I'd like to reread a section that, years ago—and still today, I might add—had a powerful impact on my sobriety." Thom picks up the book and begins reading the following passage:

> "Until we actually sit down and talk aloud about what we have so long hidden, our willingness to clean house is still largely theoretical. When we are honest with another person, it confirms that we have been honest with ourselves and with God."

"I remember just *not* getting this step." Thom continues, "I had stopped drinking. I had reached rock bottom. I had even reached out to spirit or God or whoever and—no answer. I was *this* close to hittin' the juice again. But then my very cool, superstar sponsor…," Thom points to Ray, "…clued me in. I was trying to do it *by myself*. Step Five was hard for me. It took time before I was willing to confess and lay it all bare, in front of others and with others. But I'm very glad I did. Because of Step Five…I found myself and got my life back."

Everyone in the room speaks simultaneously: "Thank you, Thom."

Judy speaks again. "Hi, I'm Judy and I'm an alcoholic. I remember struggling to connect with this concept of a higher power. It was just flat—just as flat as when I was in Catholic high school. It wasn't until I started speaking my truth—my ugly, angry, mad-at-the-world truth—that I began to connect. I began to understand that I didn't need God to talk to me—you know, like in some crazy, bat-shit, in-my-head way. I just needed you guys to talk and to listen."

Judy pauses and places her hands over her heart.

"I remember very clearly realizing that a higher power *does* speak to me. It speaks to me every time one of you confesses and is honest and true. I am so grateful for this group. My anger and my drinking really didn't go away until I let it all out—as you all know, through my big, fat, beautiful mouth, here in this room."

Everyone in the room laughs and chimes in with "Thanks, Judy."

As you listen to the brutally raw and honest confessions, you find yourself sinking deeper and deeper into the sobering truth awareness.

Everyone's listening, you think. *They're not just blowing hot air. Everyone is actually listening, hearing, and seeing one another here. It's really beautiful.* Then, and it's no surprise, you recall the deep sadness over your uncle's death and the anger over your father's unabated alcoholism and abandonment. Anger at your dad; Sadness over your uncle's death. Anger and sadness; anger and sadness; anger and sadness. Over and over and over you see it spin in an endless cycle of life-drama-bullshit.

And then—for the first time ever—you perceive it, obscured all these years by the constant repetition of these two demon forces. Below the anger and below the sadness—a huge black hole. You then realize *exactly* what it is you're perceiving...

There—screaming at you your whole life, but hidden by your own emotional baggage—is the very core of your existential angst. *Something is missing. Something is missing. Something is missing.*

Holy shit, you think.

Judy stops speaking and you instinctively raise your hand to speak next. Thom acknowledges you. You look toward J., who gives you a big thumbs up. You blaze through the nerves which protest in fear over what you're about to do...

"Hi, I'm J. and Ray's friend. I'm fairly confident I'm not an alcoholic, but I'm definitely an addict. I just had, I think, a pretty major epiphany. I'm addicted...to...sadness and anger."

You then proceed to tell the story about your father and uncle to the whole group:

"So, as I said, I'm not an alcoholic...but I'm definitely addicted to being sad and angry. I avoid the real hurt, the real pain by dramatizing and repeating my grief and anger over and over with myself and others. I've sabotaged personal relationships with this pattern. I've ruined goals and dreams. It sucks. I see now that what I'm really doing is avoiding this giant black hole in the center of my heart."

You look toward J. and Ray.

"I think these two have been shouting this to me for the last couple of days. It's my existential angst."

You then, with very clear eyes, look around the room and, in a steady voice, confess:

"*Something deep, deep in my core is missing. It's been shouting to me for years, and I think meeting it scares me to death.*"

"*Thank you,*" you end.

Everyone in the room thanks you in return. J. leans over and offers you a fist bump. Ray pats you on the back. You slump in your chair, exhausted and relieved. Over and over you recount the epiphany in your mind: *Something is fucking missing. Scares me to death. Something is fucking missing...*

...What you didn't confess is that you saw the faint outline of a black shadowy form, standing over that deep, black, existential hole...

I think part two of this adventure with J. actually just began, you finally surmise.

Spiritual Badass Suggestion:

Perhaps you're still in the beginning phases of your spiritual search, where your willingness to clean house is still largely theoretical. Might I suggest you apply some real-world, hands-on practicality and hang out with a group of awesome folks like the ones you'd meet at an *Alcoholics Anonymous* meeting? (It doesn't need to be an AA meeting, but that's a good place to start.)

Why do this?: Because—It's emotionally healing. It's socially nourishing. It's spiritually challenging. It's existentially cathartic and fulfilling. And — if you're willing to confess your inner most truth, fear, pain and sorrow in front of a group of your peers—you'll be absolutely stunned by the amount of spiritual badass progress you'll make.

CHAPTER 8
BABY GOATS

How to avoid arrested development

It's 4:35 a.m. the next day.

You maneuver the craft's left aft thruster engine and engage the ion throttle by thirteen percent. The craft slowly swings around, just enough to maintain the delicate balancing act needed on the event horizon's gravitational pull edge. You scan the overhead display panel in front of you for any plasma jet or magnetic irregularities. All is clear. *I got this one in the bag,* you think. *Easiest black-hole power conversion I've had all year.* But then—

In a nanosecond, dozens of deep black, ghost-like, tendril arms reach out of the hole and grab your ship. The ship shakes, rattles, and rumbles violently. It cantilevers sideways, and the tendril arms begin dragging the whole craft into the center of the black hole.

Then somehow, one of the black arms penetrates the front hull of the ship, grabs you, and extricates you from the craft. *How am I still alive?* is all you can think. The tendril arms pull you and the ship deeper into the black hole. And then you see it—

A giant mechanical owl swoops in and, using its razor-sharp talons, cuts through the tendril arms and grabs you. In an instant, you fly out of the black hole's maw. You watch as your ship is swallowed whole by the deep blackness. The owl swoops its wings and, in another instant, you're transported to a nearby planet. Another swoop—you're descending through the atmosphere. A final swoop—the owl gently releases you into the middle of a large, bucolic, verdant field set on the side of a snow-capped mountain. The owl lands. As it does so, it transforms into a giant flesh and blood owl.

You look up at the owl and ask: *Who are you? What are you?*

The owl looks down at you and speaks: *I'm you, of course*—and then, to your horror, out of its beak you can see the black tendril arms again reaching out to grab you.

Hey you! Wake up! Wake up!

No—not from the owl dream—I mean YOU who is dreaming the dream! Wake up!!

Can you hear me? It's me again.

I know all this is confusing, but listen up. I seem to have limited time here...

This is what I need to say to you right now: You're it. Do you understand? Subtract the ego personality and what's left? Just awareness. But what you don't understand yet—and I know this because you and I are the same—is that there's just one awareness. I'm it. You're it! You're the black...

You wake up in a sweat, discombobulated from the strangest dream within a dream you've ever had. *Fucking bizarre.* Even more bizarre was the dream character you seemed to inhabit. You can barely wrap your head around it.

A few minutes later, you're sitting at the iron table in Ray's Alabama-Zen garden with a fresh cup of coffee, a pen, and your blank journal. The morning bird symphony is in full swing, and you rest deep in the moment, contemplating the fading memories of the strange dream and the more vivid memories of last night's *Alcoholics Anonymous* meeting.

You decide to give this journaling thing J. talked about a try. You open your notebook to an expanse of fresh, white, empty pages. Pen in hand, you write...

> Where to begin? Well, there's no doubting that these adventures with J. deliver. Sometimes in a good way, often in ways that are disconcerting and maddening.
>
> Major epiphany from the AA meeting last night: I'm an anger-sadness addict. I've been avoiding this dirty deep-down feeling that I'm missing something, that - life- is really missing something. Can't say what that thing is. I'm scared of it. Why? Why am I so scared? Where is all this headed, exactly? I have NO clue. My existential angst?
>
> Dreams of a weird persona who speaks as me to me somehow. Can't wrap my brain around it. Black holes and owl robots? WTF? I think that's Ollie in my dreams. Am I doing this right?

You set the pen down, satisfied with your very first attempt at journaling. J. called it "spontaneous stream of consciousness." James Joyce, William S. Burroughs, Virginia Woolf, Hunter S. Thompson, Jack Kerouac, and even Kurt Cobain were famous for it.

Okay, maybe not James Joyce level prose, you muse internally, *but perhaps Kurt would be proud.*

Just then, Ray pops out of nowhere and strides up to you.

"Morning friend. Seen J. anywhere?"

"*I think he's still in bed,*" you reply.

"Spare a minute to help me? Need help feeding the goats. There're a couple of new kids—very cute."

"Yeah, of course, no problem."

You follow Ray around the side of the house and over to the barn. In route, you strike up a conversation.

"I'm impressed."

"About my goat ranch?"

"Well, that too—but about how many people you've helped. Thom at AA last night said that you were his sponsor; all the drivers at the yoga place—not to mention you're an awesome racecar superstar, and you even won a trophy."

"Well, I wouldn't say superstar. *Thank God* I wasn't that."

"No, I mean it. I'm really impressed. You seemed to have really turned your life around. I'm sorry your racecar dream didn't pan out."

"I'm not. Geesh, that would have doomed me to a life of arrested development hell."

"Arrested development? How so?"

You and Ray arrive at the barnyard gate entrance.

"Let's go in and get these guys fed, and I'll explain—best I can anyhow."

You follow him through the gate and into the barnyard. You enter the barn through a large, maroon, wooden door. Inside are several large stables and a big area with piles of old, yellow, musty-smelling hay bales. Ray grabs a bale and hands it to you. He grabs another.

"Follow me."

Ray steps outside through another large half-door into an area where a bunch of goats are milling around.

"Watch this," he says to you. Ray drops the hay bale, cuts it with a knife, and then kicks it several times to spread it out. He then turns around and clangs a large, old, brass bell located on the exterior of the barn. All mayhem breaks loose. Goats from everywhere come running and bleating.

"Oh my god. How many goats do you have exactly?"

"Fifty-two, including the new kids; they were born several weeks ago."

"Hilarious."

"Drop your bale, and we'll spread out the hay. Then we'll go get some more."

You do so, and over the course of about fifteen minutes, you repeat the operation multiple times. You can't believe how fast the goats tear through the hay bales.

"Would you like to see the baby goats?"

"Yes, please," you reply.

You follow Ray back into the barn and over to one of the smaller stables. In the stable are three goats, one very clearly Mama and the other two, the kids. Mama bleats when she sees Ray, and he offers her a handful of hay. The kids are beyond cute—they romp around on unsteady legs and bounce and jitter under and around Mama while she eats. You can tell she's slightly annoyed with them while she consumes her breakfast.

"Imagine if these goats, the kids that is, stayed that age their whole lives?"

"That would be so cute. Can you breed them that way?"

"You *cannot* and it would be *disastrous*. Goats, in general, aren't genius creatures, and the kids are particularly naïve and clueless. They'd get into all sorts of trouble without their mamas: They'd eat stuff that would endanger them; they'd get lost, even on my small ranch; they'd get stuck in trees; they'd get eaten by predators. Arrested development would do them no good. And that's why, to quote Garth Brooks, "Sometimes I thank God for unanswered prayers."

"*Your racing career?*"

"Yes. Winning a few more championships would have been nice, but then I wouldn't have failed and hit rock bottom."

"*How can that be good?*"

"Had I succeeded in establishing some sort of successful racing career, I would never have become an alcoholic, and I would never have grown up and gotten on the *Know Thyself* path. So, I thank God for *unanswered* prayers every single day. I wouldn't trade *knowing thyself* for all the championships in the world."

"*Makes perfect, but painful sense.*"

"Easy, it was not. But am I glad I went through it. I think last night you also just sidestepped a whole lotta arrested development, don't you think?"

You pause before answering. "*You may be right. I've been arrested at the anger-sadness phase for so long I can't even remember not being in it. I think I saw that for the first time last night.*"

"I think you did, too. *You*, my friend, impress me."

"*Thanks, Ray. Appreciate that....*" You pause and reach down to pet one of the baby goats that prances near you. "*But I still think it's a shame these cute little fuzzballs have to grow up.*"

"I know what you mean, but the adults also have their charm."

"*Like J., you mean?*" you respond with a twinkle in your eye.

"Yes, exactly like J. ...charming *as the devil*."

You both laugh and, after a few more minutes of fawning over the goats, you and Ray head back to the house.

Let's talk about *arrested development* for just a minute. It's important. You'd be surprised at the number of people in the world (including, more than likely—*you*) who are caught in arrested development hell. It saddens me. It frightens me. It makes me want to write faster, teach better, and shout louder from all the mountain tops in the world: Grow up! Grow up! Grow up! You are so much more! And you've settled for so little!

So, what exactly is *arrested development*? Most definitions dance around halted emotional growth springing from early childhood abuse or trauma...

This type of arrested development is everywhere: the husband who physically or verbally abuses his wife because he has the arrested emotional development of a ten-year-old; the unlovable or unworthy woman who has arrested social development due to childhood abuse; the meek and timid office worker who is taken advantage of by his superiors due to arrested inner confidence development; the overtly positive New Age spiritual seeker whose arrested development prevents him or her from tackling shadow issues.

But arrested *emotional* development is *not* what I'm referring to here. I'm talking about arrested *evolutionary* development; arrested *Know Thyself* development. Unless you're a spiritually awakened adult, you just can't see it. Why can't you see it? Because *everyone's* afflicted with it. You don't recognize the crazies in the looney bin because *you're in the looney bin with them!*

What modern society refers to today as "adulthood" is a farcical two-dimensional cardboard cutout of the real thing. Ever see one of those giant life-sized cardboard posters of Marvel or Star Wars action heroes? Greeting one of those cardboard cutouts and then expecting a high five, bear hug, and an autograph from it is about the same as expecting adult behavior from "adults" who just happen to have the bone structure, weight, and age of a forty-five-year-old, but inside, spiritually speaking, are wearing diapers and sucking their thumbs.

Arrested *spiritual* development is tragically epidemic and there is absolutely no excuse for it. I ain't talking about supreme pizza enlightenment here, I'm talking about a basic handle on mindful awareness and the workings of our poor, flawed ego-minds. This is *secular, scientific* shit—not esoteric Buddhist shit. This stuff should be taught in grade school, or at the very latest in early high school.

Arrested development is a tragedy and, all by itself, if addressed and healed, could help to prevent *so many other* tragedies: domestic violence, drug abuse, alcoholism, suicide, gun violence, and more. (Did I mention politicians and presidents with arrested development? Oh yeah, we got those too.)

I know I'm having a what-if, could-have, pie-in-the-sky moment here, but dare I say that one of us loonies has gotta speak up at some point? Well, I'm as looney as they come, so I got no problem hoppin' on my soapbox and shouting:

Don't just grow up! Wake up! Wake up! Wake up! You are so much more! And you've settled for so little!

After hanging out with Ray, you head back to the guest house and find J. and the gang enjoying breakfast. You join, have a bite to eat, and watch again as Ollie devours some slimy chicken gizzards.

"*Ollie, please don't grow up to be a giant, soul-sucking, robot owl!*" you say playfully in front of J.

J. looks at you with his best *WTF?* face.

"*Strange dream I had last night.*"

"Owls have that effect on people." J. pauses and changes the subject. "Well, Kemosabe, time to pack. We should be off by noon or so."

"*I gathered that. I think we've done our job here.*"

"Me, too," replies J.

You and J. spend the next hour packing and cleaning up the guest house. With everything ready to go in the Jeep, you prepare to say your final goodbyes to Ray.

Ray greets you from the garage when he sees that you and J. are packed and ready to go. The same iconic blue mechanic's towel hangs from his leather belt.

"Sorry, greasy hands haven't changed much," he says as he moves in for a shake.

"*You're not getting off that easy!*" you reply as you move in for a bear hug. Ray obliges and hugs back.

"Anytime you're in need of a track ride or some…" He gestures all around. "…goat yoga, you know where to find me."

"*Yes, I do. I certainly do. Thank you so much for having us, Ray.*"

J. moves in. "Ray, I will see you, sir, at Seven Dragons next summer, right?"

"Absolutely. I look forward to it. You guys drive safe. Sure you don't want to take a goat along for the ride?"

"Eh, pass on that one," replies J. with a smile. "Maybe next time."

You put the Jeep in drive and pull forward down the long, gravel driveway.

"That was some good goat yoga," J. comments.

"*Yes, it was. Where're we headed, Mr. Mystery?*"

"We're goin' to Graceland! Memphis, Tennessee! Just an overnight stay. Tomorrow, we have a long drive to Kansas City."

"*Roger that.*"

It takes four hours to get to Memphis. No *Graceland* tour this time; just a quick overnight at a Motel 6. You and J. check into your separate rooms and then meet out front. There's a Denny's within walking distance—not exactly five-star cuisine, but it suffices.

The parking lot is *packed*. You can't tell exactly how packed or with whom, but you decide to chance it anyway as your options are limited.

J. swings open the glass double doors, and you're swarmed by a very large group of black clad goth kids sporting make-up and hairdos better suited for a Halloween night. Your first thought: *What in the fuck is this?*

Your heart skips a beat or two, because this group doesn't come off as exactly the friendly, sociable type. You squeeze into the lobby area. It's super crammed. Everyone is waiting to be seated. Tension is getting high, and the energy turns rambunctious as you try to get through.

J. nods his head and points to the black rock band t-shirts that many of them are wearing: *Marilyn Manson.*

You try to squeeze through and accidently bump into one tall, particularly rough looking fellow with quite an impressive mohawk.

"Where the fuck you think you're going?" he says loudly and in your face.

You turn pale and start to mumble apologetically. "*Um, yeah, sorry man. My bad. I was just...*"

J. interrupts you and says very loudly, "*Antichrist Superstar.*"

The mohawk guy immediately turns to J. and says, "What about it?"

"That's his best album. Produced by Trent Reznor. Hands down—one of the best albums of the nineties."

"Album, huh? Old man. I don't know about no album—but that sure as fuck is one of his best. But *The Golden Age of Grotesque* rocks and has..."

"*This is The New Shit* and *Mobscene*. Agreed; another stellar um, album, but I still like *Superstar*."

The mohawk guy scans both you and J. up and down and asks, rather incredulously "You guys going to the show?"

"There's a show!?" J. exclaims.

While J. is talking, and very effectively hijacking the mohawk guy's attention, you take the opportunity to slip out of the packed fray and over to the hostess stand where you get your name on the waiting list. Miraculously, you see a vacant chair in the waiting area and sit down. Through the packed mayhem you see, but can't hear, J. continuing a very animated conversation with the mohawk guy. Fifteen minutes go by, and the hostess calls your name. You see J. fist bump the mohawk guy and walk away.

"*Well, you seem to fit right in,*" you say to J.

"Big fan," he says.

The hostess takes you to a table, and you both sit down. She hands you menus. You look around and see that ninety percent of the restaurant clientele is clad in black. The hostess leaves.

"Holy shit!" says J. "Talk about synchronicity and coincidence. What are the fucking odds?"

"*Don't understand*," you say.

"This!" J. emphasizes. "It's the Mack-Daddy grand prize, ground-zero for arrested development angst!"

You smile and then chuckle. "*Holy shit. You're right. I hadn't thought of that. So funny. Or sad. However you want to look at it.*"

"These guys are cool. Just a little misplaced, misfit anger. Actually, healthy for their age." J. looks at the menu. "But, yeah, sadly, most of them probably won't escape it. They'll get caught in it, and due to the lack of *actual adults*, will stay caught in it their whole lives. But—that doesn't mean we can't enjoy the shit out of their company tonight." J. looks at you with a devilish grin. "I totally scored."

"*Scored what?*" you ask with trepidation.

"Be right back."

You watch as J. gets up and heads over to where the mohawk guy and a bunch of his friends were just seated. You see J. pull out a wad of cash and slap it down on the table. The mohawk guy counts the money and then hands J. a white piece of paper. You see J. scan it with his phone. He fist-bumps the mohawk guy again, returns to the table, and sits down.

"*What in the world did you just do?*"

"I told you. I scored!"

"*Yes, I know. Scored what!?*"

"Two tickets to *Marilyn Manson* live in fucking concert! Boooyah! Arrested development heaven. It is going *to rock!*"

You cringe at the thought of being packed into an auditorium with two thousand black-clad, goth, emo kids, but like most other moments during your badass adventures with J., you're sure there's a damned good reason for it—albeit a slightly fucked-up and borderline insane one—but none the less, a *spiritually badass* ...damned good reason.

You take a deep breath, let go of all control, and prepare yourself for a wild night of all things black, shadowy, arrested, and angst-ridden.

Strangely enough, peacefully, deep down in your heart, perhaps near that existential black hole you came in contact with just the night before, you hear or feel—you don't know which, exactly—a low, murmuring voice recite over and over again:

Yes, yes, yes, yes, yes, yes, yes...

Spiritual Badass Suggestion:

So no, I won't suggest that you need to score some tickets to see *Marylin Manson* or *Metallica* or *Nine Inch Nails* or *Tool*— or *Heilung,* for that matter. (Although *any and all* of these guys rock live.) What I will suggest, now that our little adventure in existential angst has come to a conclusion, is that you pick at least one of the *Part One* suggested things to do and run with it. All of them, in one way or another, will help you get in touch with your own existential angst *Black Shadow*:

1. Sign up for an 8-Week Mindfulness-Based Stress Reduction course at your local college, hospital, or yoga studio.
2. Purchase a journal and start free-form stream of consciousness writing about what you suspect your existential angst might be trying to tell you.
3. Sign up for a yoga class, and get in touch with the innate wisdom and presence of your body.
4. Keep a gratitude journal about all the shitty things that have happened to you, and see if you can sense or find the phoenix transformational doorways that come with them.
5. Attend an *Alcoholics Anonymous* group and experience the raw, brutal, and beautiful honesty available there.
6. Okay, I lied. Experiencing and immersing yourself in the shadow of exterior life (like a hard rock concert) can help you get in touch with the shadow of your interior life. Buy some tickets, go to a show, and slam dance your sweaty badass off.

END PART 1

DON'T JUST READ ABOUT IT.

EXPERIENCE IT.

This is your invitation to a whole new world badass.
There's a life-changing *experience* waiting for you online. Something you've been longing and waiting for *your whole life*. You ready? Of course you are…

Go here:
www.spiritualityforbadasses.com

Part 2

Kansas City Presence

CHAPTER 9
DON'T FEAR THE REAPER

*How to meet vulnerability,
grief, and sorrow*

You'd think a guy who writes books with the word "spirituality" in them wouldn't have waited until page 95 of his fourth book to address a pretty damn fundamental—ahem— *spiritual* topic: Death.

I guess I shy away from the topic of death like I shy away from the topics of politics, sex, enlightenment, love, and God. All of these subjects have just been so done—ahem again—*to death* in the arena of spirituality. Therefore, another random bowl of alphabet soup disguised and sold as a book *about any one of them* hardly seems necessary. Yawn—I'm just not that interested in speculation, philosophy, or faux quasi-spiritual intellectualism about tired old themes that humanity has been chewing on—with limited, dubious insight—for millennia.

Yes, I do have my *own* asshole opinions about this, that, and the other spiritual thing—but most of these tend to be backed up by leading edge science (mindfulness), social proof (meditation), psychology (shadow-wound-trauma work), my own hard-earned personal experience (spiritual awakening), or channeled wisdom from the Romulans in the alpha-binary quadrant of the Tirian-5 Galaxy (awareness / fist bump, all ye Trek nerds). You get my drift.

I don't know jack shit about God, gods, classically hawked enlightenment, tantric sex, world economy, or politics—at least not in any way that makes me an authority. And, to get to my point here, I also don't know jack shit about *death*. How could I *or anybody*, for that matter?

I've had a few out-of-body experiences, some pretty crazy hallucinogenic-induced insights, and a bunch of meditation-induced epiphanies about the topic, but—at the end of the day—my opinion, the Bible's opinion, the Bhagavad Gita's opinion, opinions from the Tibetan Book of the Dead, or Shirley-fucking-MacLaine's opinion (No offense, Shirley—that was just fun literary hyperbole.) about *death* all amount to the same damn thing: mostly delusion, a lot of speculation, and a bunch of hopeful, wishful thinking.

Fuck, even *I* fall prey to this cartoonish shit—hoping I'll see all my beloved long-dead pets (R.I.P. Lilly, Rocky, Kit, Gypsy, etc.) across the "Rainbow Bridge" in the afterlife. Fuck me, what a highly probable load of horseshit that is. (Lilly—if I'm wrong, I'll treat you to a T-bone steak and play ball with you for hours.)

Okay, pause, slow down—deep breath: Aside from a bunch of foul-mouthed, fun blathering, here's what I *do* have to offer on the subject of *death:*

Life.

I have a hunch; I have a very big hunch that the following is probably, most likely true:

Death is the ultimate roller coaster ride. You are either going to meet this roller coaster ride with fear in your heart and being or with peace in your heart and being. Your unique response is most likely—probably—I'd wager—going to determine your experience of death and your experience after it. You feel me? I have no idea how this roller coaster ride unfolds, but I do know, from decades of spiritual badassery that how you meet an experience determines your relationship, feelings about, quality, and results of that experience.

So, the quick and dirty is this: Obsessing about death or what happens after death is *mostly* a waste of time. Obsess about *life* instead. Be present to life. Meet your fears in this life. Handle your karma, dawg. Meet the boogeyman before death. Leave this world with zero regrets. And probably, most likely, odds are—your experience of death and the afterlife will be spiritual badass okay, awesome, and just fine. Don't fear the reaper.

With that said, let us continue our strange, badass adventure which takes us deep into the spooky underbelly-netherworld of a twisted and paradoxical state called...*Kansas*.

"Toto, I have a feeling we're not in Kansas anymore," you declare loudly, waking J. up right as you cross the border. *"But, but...wait for it... wait for it...."* You pass a big blue and yellow *Welcome to Kansas* sign. *"Now we are!!"*

"How long have you been waiting to say that?" yawns J.

"454 miles, give or take."

J. points to the road. "Keep going. We're off to see the wizard, and we've got another fifty-some miles."

"I'll get you, my pretty, and your little iguana, too."

"Right. Are you done yet?"

"Maybe. Never been to Kansas. Just getting it out of my system."

"Good for you."

J. rolls back to sleep while you check the GPS on your phone. *Samsara Farm* actually has its own Google business address and website. It's situated about twenty miles southwest of Kansas City proper. You're curious, but in the spirit of *Mr. Mystery* and, mostly due to the king-sized *Marylin Manson* concert hangover you've had all day, you haven't bothered to take a peek at the *Samsara Farm* website. But you are *very* curious...

A few minutes pass by when J.'s phone rings. Out of character, he wakes up and takes the call. You quickly surmise that something is wrong.

"Right. That's a shame. I'd thought we'd have more time. We're okay with that." He pauses. "In an hour or so…yeah. Got it." Another pause. "No worries at all. See ya soon."

J. hangs up the phone and takes a deep breath. He's visibly shaken.

"What's going on?" you ask.

"I knew she was going downhill, but I didn't think she was this close." J. takes another deep breath and gazes out the window. "Rosie is dying—maybe a day or two at the most."

You silently let the news sink in and then reply.

"You know Rosie, I presume?"

"Yes…Rosie is—well, for all practical purposes—Lenny's mom."

You give J. your best quizzical expression. He responds.

"*Samsara Farm* is a women's shelter. That was Cam on the phone. She founded it two decades ago. One of the ways the farm makes money is through their small herpetology, …eh, reptile program. Lenny was born there. Rosie ran the program. She's been living and working on the farm for the past fifteen years. She's seventy-nine and…has pancreatic cancer."

You pause again, allowing J. to have space.

"That sucks. Rosie sounds awesome. Should we cancel or reschedule or something?"

"No, no—it's all good. Cam invited us, and she's still happy to have us." J. pauses and stares out the window again. "Rosie was actually…," J. chuckles to himself, "…a real pain-in-the ass."

"*Oh*," you respond and check the GPS. Fifteen more miles...

Despite her being a total stranger, the news of Rosie's impending death drops you into a somber melancholy. You realize this feeling might define the next couple of days. This was not the next experience you were expecting—at all.

The small, modest wooden sign reads *Samsara Farm Women's Shelter*. Circling the name are three more words printed in elegant font: *Empowerment - Freedom - Safety*.

Nice, you think.

What's not modest is the vast expanse of farmland sprinkled with numerous patches of forest and several old homes you see from atop the small hill where the Jeep is paused. A curvy, black asphalt road stretches out and down through what looks like acres and acres of corn and soybeans. The sunlight is beginning its evening transformation from whites and golds to ambers and reds, the light splintering and glittering in a thousand shards through the undulating corn and soybean fields. You put the Jeep in drive and meander down the road.

You arrive at the business center and main hub, which is surprisingly busy with lots of people milling around, talking, and working. Numerous old, paint-flaked, white wooden buildings make up most of the architecture. You pull into a parking space adjacent to a small building labeled *Office*. You get out, stretch, and follow J. inside.

There's an empty reception desk and a couch nearby.

"J.—is that you?" you hear from a distant back room.

"Yeah, just arrived," J. responds.

"On the phone. Be out in a sec." The voice reaches you from a distance again.

J. sits on the couch. You follow suit. On the table in front of you is an assortment of magazines: *Journal of Hospice & Palliative Nursing*, *Reptiles*, and a Buddhist-looking one entitled *Lion's Roar*.

Strange collection of magazines for a farm in the middle of Kansas, you think. Just then, the voice you heard earlier takes human form.

"Hi, J."

J. stands. "Hi, Cam." J. offers Cam a long, gentle hug and she reciprocates. You stand.

Cam is a big woman in her late sixties. You're both shocked and pleased by her appearance: Her long grey hair is wound tightly in a thin, braided ponytail. Her classic farmer's garb includes blue jean overalls, a white t-shirt, and a pair of old, black rubber boots. Finally, for good measure, and by no means out of place, a black leather biker vest adorned with numerous patches and symbols hangs loosely from her broad, strong shoulders. Cam is a sight to behold. *Fierce, strong, and not a woman you want to fuck with*, you think.

"Cam, this is my friend." J. gestures toward you.

You reach out a hand. She grips it firmly, shakes, and says with a smile on her face, "Don't worry, I'm all bite and no bark—," She pauses for a quick beat, then laughs deep from her core and it instantly relaxes you. "Sorry for my appearance. I was just in town …on my bike. Not my usual office getup. Very nice to meet you. Any friend of J.'s…"

"*Same here*," you reply.

"Well, you guys picked a helluva time to join us. Rosie's got this whole place in a tiff. What else is new, right?" Cam looks at J.

"There's no stopping her; not even in death," J. replies.

"God love her. She's a wild one!" Cam says while belly laughing again. "When I told her you guys were coming, would you believe the first thing out of her mouth was 'Lenny'? She's got a steel-trap memory, that one."

"Lenny's actually in the car right now," proffers J.

"Perfect. Rosie will be pleased. Well, you guys should get settled and unpacked. After that, if we can catch her lucid, we'll surprise Rosie with a Lenny visit. Sound good?"

"Sounds excellent," J. says.

"I'll have Janine show you to your room; then after dinner we'll meet up. ...that okay?" Cam turns and faces the hallway and yells. "Janine. Our guests are here."

"Perfect," replies J. "Thanks again for having us, Cam. I know the timing isn't great...."

"Nonsense. You know as well as I do that the timing is *perfect*," Cam interjects.

"I know. Just a social courtesy." J. smiles.

"You don't need to social courtesy me, honey."

"Yes, ma'am. I mean yes, Cam. Roger that," J. says, slightly stammering.

Cam laughs deeply again and, just then, a younger woman in her late twenties enters from the same hallway.

"Janine, take these two vagabonds to their room. We had 3-B cleaned out today, yes?"

"Absolutely," replies Janine. "You guys want to follow me? The guest suite is just down the road."

"J., I'll catch up with you guys after dinner—alright?" Cam says as she exits, making her way down the hallway.

"You got it," J. replies.

Janine waves her hand forward, toward the door. "Shall we?"

Janine hops into a small golf cart out front while you and J. enter the Jeep.

"*You stammered! I have never heard you stammer,*" you immediately say to J. with a grin on your face. You put the Jeep in drive and follow Janine on her golf cart.

J. gives his best *mea culpa* look accompanied with a shrug. "She's my peer. I told you. Cam is a rarity, a real awakened adult..." J. pauses to think. "...and besides that, she could kick my ass in a heartbeat if she wanted to. So yes, I defer to my spiritual badass-ness and stammer happily. Cam is brilliant."

"*Slightly confused. What exactly is Cam's role here again?*"

"Cam inherited this farm from her parents. Before converting it to a women's shelter, she worked in the hospice industry. Now she runs the show here and, from what I understand, has the occasional death doula gig on the side.

"*Death... Doula?*"

"Hospice nurse without the western medical degree. Cam hires nurses for the medical stuff, if I recall correctly."

"*So, then what does Cam do?*"

"Of course." J. pauses. "Cam provides the spiritual presence of an awakened adult. She's the island."

"*The island...*" you ponder. "*I like that.*"

"Me, too. That's why we're here. I want *you* to experience that island."

Janine stops at a newer structure that has the look of a small motel or apartment building. Within a few minutes, you and J. wrangle your bags up to the third floor and into room 3-B. It's a simple little apartment, similar to an extended stay suite of a large hotel. There's a small living/dining area, two bedrooms, a full bathroom, and a small kitchenette.

"If you guys need anything else, just call the front office," announces Janine. "And you know where the dining hall is, right?"

J. makes dinner arrangements with Janine while you fetch the two little creaturely beings from the Jeep. You set up two pop-up cages and get Lenny and Ollie settled. You're pooped from a long day of travel, but feel welcome in your new environs. *Samsara Farm* is way cool.

You plop yourself down on the living room couch. J. finishes talking with Janine. He enters the living room looking at his phone.

"*What's samsara mean?*" you ask.

J. snaps out of his phone reverie. "Oh—It comes from Buddhism. Means the cycle of birth, death, and suffering."

"*That's an odd name for a women's shelter, don't you think?*"

"No—not if the goal is to *escape* the suffering. Most of the women who come here have suffered plenty. This place is a reset button."

"*I guess that does make sense.*"

"Escaping the Wheel of Samsara is an ancient Buddhist concept."

You pause and reflect before speaking. "*Is that what we're doing here?*"

"Yes." J. pauses. "That's *exactly* what we're doing here."

It's after dinner and dark outside.

You, J., Lenny, Cam, Janine, and another woman, Rosie's slightly younger sister, Mariam, to whom you've just been introduced, all enter a small farm home slightly outside the hustle and bustle of the main operations center. Several more women and an older gentleman are in the living room. Introductions are made.

Some of the women are shelter participants. Some are employees. The kind looking older gentleman, Carl, is the groundskeeper and maintenance supervisor. The lighting is dim. Candles are lit. Eyes are wet. Everyone speaks in hushed tones. You've arrived in the middle of a vigil. Rosie is upstairs with the hospice nurse...

"How's she doing?" Cam asks Carl.

"She's in and out. Very weak. We just visited. Asking for Beatrice a lot. Helen is with her now," Carl replies.

"Of course," Cam whispers and then turns to you, J., and Mariam. "I'll be right back." She heads upstairs.

You take a seat along with everyone else.

"She was fiery today, I'll tell you," Carl comments. Everyone laughs. "...berated me for my tears. I tried to hold back. Goin' out the same way she was here." Carl laughs and shakes his head.

You sink deeper into the moment and begin to feel the sacred weight of the occasion. Cam comes down from upstairs.

"Okay. We'll visit probably for just a few minutes. She's awake and mostly lucid. Don't be surprised if she rambles or has an outburst. She's all over the place. Before we go, I want to make sure we're all on the same page. So, take my hand."

Cam holds out her hand to you. You stand, not knowing what this is about, and take her hand. Mariam, J., and Janine seem to be more in the know and follow suit by forming a small circle with everyone holding hands.

"Eyes open. Deep breath," Cam coaches in a low voice. "Pick a partner and keep eye contact. You do so hesitantly, then give in and go with it. You look J. directly in the eyes. He reciprocates. It's awkward.

Cam continues. "Breathe. Hold eye contact and notice your own aware presence. Notice that same aware presence in the person you're holding eye contact with. Breathe. Notice the vulnerability of this moment. This isn't just a vulnerable occasion for Rosie. We're all vulnerable here. We're all dying here. Great mother—thank you for the reverence and sacredness of this occasion."

You hold eye contact for another silent minute, then everyone releases their gaze and their hands. You feel like you've just been shoved off a cliff and are still free-falling. Your arms and legs are feather light. You feel slightly dizzy. *How did that just happen?* you think. *What was that?* You cast a quizzical look in J.'s direction.

He leans toward you and says one word: "Presence."

You silently acknowledge this new information. Cam slowly and very mindfully leads the way upstairs. Mariam goes next, followed by J. with Lenny wrapped around his shoulders; then Janine; then you…

Cam opens the door to Rosie's bedroom. It's dimly lit. A woman in her late forties, dressed in a white professional nurse's gown—Helen, you presume—sits next to the bed. There's a silent, still energy in the room, no doubt heightened by the short hand-holding eye contact thing you just experienced.

Rosie, very thin and frail, lies on her back with her head propped up on a pillow. Her thin, silvery grey hair is disheveled. Her face is gaunt; skin, pale and blotchy. Her eyes are open. She stares blankly ahead, not acknowledging the five people who just entered her bedroom. Everyone takes seats on either side of the bed. J. sits next to Helen, the hospice nurse.

"Rosie, you have some visitors," Helen says gently.

Rosie looks up at Helen. She then shifts her gaze to J. and Lenny.

"Is that Lenny! Goddamn. Goddamn. Look at that old rascal. Give him here. Give him here."

J. looks to Cam for approval. Cam nods. J. very gently places Lenny on the bedsheets covering Rosie's lap. Helen helps Rosie adjust so she can maneuver an arm.

J.'s eyes visibly tear up, and you can feel your lips start to quiver.

Rosie strokes the back of Lenny's neck.

"Oh, Lenny, look at you. It's been years, darlin'. You're so goddamn handsome." Rosie's sunken eyes beam. Her gaunt frame seems to have new life briefly.

Rosie looks around at everyone. "I named him, you know!"

J. takes another deep breath. A few tears run down his cheeks. He smiles and wipes them from his face.

"Yes, you did. You sure did," J. whispers.

Lenny bobs up and down. Rosie continues petting him and then looks at Cam and asks, "Where are Wilbur and Wilma?"

"They're not here today, Darlin'," Cam says.

J. leans into you and whispers, "Lenny's parents."

"Rosie, you remember J.? And this is his friend," Cam says.

Rosie looks at J. "I remember you. I didn't much care for you. Iguanas shouldn't live in cars. Lenny looks good. Is my boy happy?"

"I think Lenny is very happy, Rosie," J. responds.

"Runt of the litter. Now look at him. I raised a bunch of his brothers and sisters also, you know?"

"Yes," replies J., but he's interrupted when Rosie tilts her head back and lets out a loud moan.

"Oh God, I'm achy…so tired of this." Rosie coughs and adds, "Just take these old bones, goddamnit. Why are they here?" Rosie looks around at no one in particular.

J. leans over and carefully extracts Lenny from Rosie's lap.

"Sissy, is there anything we can get you?" Mariam asks.

"I told ya before. No, Mariam. No! I'm oldest! Where's Beatrice? Oh…my little Beat…" Rosie coughs again.

"Here Darlin'," Cam offers Rosie some water from a strawed water bottle. Rosie slowly takes a small sip. Cam puts the bottle down and takes Rosie's hand.

"Oh dear. Oh dear." Rosie's moaning conveys anguish as her head rolls back and forth on the pillow.

"We're here for you, Darlin' Rosie. We're here for you," Cam whispers.

"Just need some goddamned sleep. Didn't know death would be so goddamned exhausting." Rosie smiles. "I'm good. I'm good."

"We'll visit tomorrow if you'd like," Cam interjects.

"Oh yes, that handsome gentleman can visit anytime," Rosie says, glancing toward Lenny. "Okay, okay."

"Goodnight, Darlin'," Cam says, signaling the end of the visit. Everyone except Helen gets up, slowly exits the room, and walks downstairs.

You breathe out a big sigh of relief and collapse on a chair in the living room. J., Cam, Mariam, and Janine all take seats. The only one left from the previous group is Carl.

"Let's finish the evening properly," Cam states calmly. "Carl, you're welcome to join if you'd like."

"Yes, Ma'am," says Carl.

"Hands again, everyone. Choose a partner and keep eye contact."

Before you know it, you've locked eyes with Cam. Slowly you feel an intimate, vulnerable, and powerful presence. You notice that this presence comes from both you *and* Cam. It's the combination.

Cam continues to speak while holding eye contact with you.

The Vulnerability Bubble Exercise

"Great Mother, who gives all and takes all—thank you again for this sacred occasion…

"Notice your own awareness and presence of being. Notice the same presence in the eyes of the other…"

You do so, fighting the awkwardness of the experience and resisting the urge to look away.

"Breathe …"

"By being vulnerable, open, honest, and present with *each other*, we can transform the deepest grief and sorrow into a sacred and reverent occasion…"

"Breathe…"

"Notice any lightness in your limbs or body. Notice any anxiety, nervousness, awkwardness, or feelings of exposure…"

Still resisting the urge to peal your eyes away, you breathe deeply and consciously. You continue steady eye contact with Cam.

"Imagine this vulnerability as one big, raw nerve..."

"Imagine this raw nerve forms into a clear bubble. Now, the bubble begins to grow in size, from your heart..."

"Breathe..."

"Allow yourself to feel the bubble completely...vulnerable, on the edge of tears, on the edge of a breakdown, on the edge of sorrow, grief, and pain..."

Oddly enough, the experience gets easier. You feel yourself dropping deep into an ocean of calm. Your eye contact with Cam remains steady.

"Be present with it..."

"Imagine the bubble expanding...beyond your heart and chest, beyond your body...and into the room."

"Now imagine that your bubble begins to touch the bubbles of the others in the room..."

You can almost feel the experience she's describing. Some indescribable, ethereal part of you intermingles with everyone else in the room. The intimacy and vulnerability are overwhelmingly powerful.

"Breathe..."

"The bubbles intermingle, touch one another, and meld. Imagine that the bubbles combine into one large bubble and take the shape of the room.

"Breathe...

"This sacred, reverent space we are all now in—vulnerable, raw, heartfelt, sad, lonely, painful, lost, afraid, angry, melancholy, inadequate, confused, unhappy—and simultaneously conscious, aware, and present—is acknowledged, seen, held, experienced, accepted, and loved."

"Breathe…"

"Death, loss, sorrow, and grief *transformed* into a sacred, vulnerable space…"

"Everything here is welcome…"

"Everything here is *just* as it should be…

"Thank you, Rosie, for gifting us with this… Thank you, all."

Cam pauses in silence for a minute.

"Is everyone good?"

Everyone nods yes.

Cam pauses before breaking eye contact with you.

"Goodnight everyone. Shall we leave in silence?"

You close your eyes, grateful for the strange and amazing island of presence Cam and everyone else just shared with you.

No idea such an experience existed, you think.

No idea such a thing was possible….

No idea at all.

Spiritual Badass Suggestion:

I'm a pretty creative sort and have no problem coming up with my own spiritual badass exercises, techniques, or devices, but I stand on the shoulders of giants for this one: Shared eye contact with other spiritual badass awakened adults was a crucial part of my own badass adventure. It's an odd one for sure and not everybody's cup of joe, but, as chronicled in this chapter, if you allow yourself to get over the initial awkwardness, it's a profoundly powerful practice.

A few things about it I'd like to convey: We're a society (especially Western culture) *bereft* of true heart and soul intimacy. Take stock in the amount of time you've spent gazing into another human being's eyes. Most of us can point to two occasions: 1. When we were babies and received the loving gaze from our mother or father. 2. When we were young and dating someone and gazed into our lover's eyes. And then…nothing. The only time we receive the steady gaze of another human being is usually from an actor or talking head…on a screen. (And, in that case, most of the time—it's anything but loving.)

So, here's my suggestion: Practice shared eye contact with an open-minded, willing friend, relative, or partner. Yes—initially it will be extremely awkward; but persist beyond the brain's amygdala defense mechanism, and you'll gradually experience a profound state of open, vulnerable, aware presence which has the power to transform your life. No shit—the eyes are very much the windows to the soul.

Chapter 10
The Gift of Presence

How to exit the Wheel of Samsara

Before we continue with our *Samsara Farm* adventure, let's take a moment to blow holes in that argument currently boiling in your brain:

So you think you can solo climb Mt. Everest, huh? You think you don't need sherpas, guides, maps, training, guidance, or help? You think you got this one—all by your lonesome?

Yeah, right you do. Call me when you get to the top. Please don't forget to take a selfie; I'll require proof.

And now, you think I'm exaggerating. *Mt. Everest? Really? There's no way that's a legit comparison.* You're right; it's not. Mt. Everest is easier.

I hear this argument all the time. It's common. We all suffer from it: hyper-masculine, Western, do-it-yourself, John-fucking-Wayne *independence*. We're sold this bill-of-bullshit goods every day in the West. (It's actually sold worldwide, but Western civilization seems to wallow in it the most.) It's sold in politics, government, education, business, religion, and of course... spirituality.

Let's focus on the *spiritual* bill-of-bullshit goods. I get it. *Totally. 100%.* I, too, abandoned groupthink religion, culture, and society. I utterly abandoned *the herd*. I grew a badass pair and became an independently thinking and autonomous human being. And of course I applied this independence to my spiritual path and pursuits. *And* it worked...*until it didn't*.

Allow me to jump right to the point here: Your independent ideas, thoughts, attitudes, and biases, relative to spirituality, will only get you *so far*. Don't get me wrong; you absolutely need that independent character card. But, sooner or later, you and your card will hit a very hard and impenetrable wall. There's no way through, around, over or under that wall—without a helping hand or heart. You need to swallow that hyper-masculine, Western, do-it-yourself, John-fucking-Wayne *independence*—and acquire help.

Indulge me in a quick metaphor, and then I'll shut the hell up about this. Have you ever water-skied? Water-skiing is a balancing act. When you're being dragged full-bore behind a 300hp Mastercraft powerboat, there are two things you need: *inertness and flexibility*. If you don't have the *inert* badass independent power and strength to hold the fuck on—you'll fail. Simultaneously, if you don't have the *flexible* humility (to ask for help) suppleness to ride the wake and waves— you'll also fail. You need both.

I *love* your independence. Fist bump to that, my friend: It's what attracted you to the *Spirituality for Badasses Book One* basecamp. But now, we've arrived at the mountain peak. You're going to need help—nothing to be ashamed of. We all do.

Shall we climb?

It's the next day. Much to your surprise, at breakfast Cam invited you for a private tour of the farm—without J. Cam was ebullient and professional as ever, walking around the main building complex, but her tone changed considerably after inviting you to experience something she referred to as "the wheel."

"I think you're ready to dispense with the pleasantries, yes?"

Slightly taken aback, you realize now that maybe J. had something to do with this whole event. *"Did J. arrange this?"* you ask.

"No, dear. You did. All of it. Hop in."

You and Cam hop onto one of the many golf carts and head out of the hustle and bustle of the main center. You meander down a gravel road for some time; then Cam steers the golf cart onto a grass path. The path zigzags in and out of some tall wheat grass, passes a chest-high field of corn, and comes to a dead end at a beautiful, pastoral, forested corner of the farm.

You're on a slight hilly rise overlooking a very odd sight: A walking maze a hundred feet in diameter in the rough shape of a wheel is landscaped into the earth before you. You're impressed. It's composed of smooth, glinting, yellow, white, and light brown pea gravel. The edges are precise. The grass is immaculately mowed. The whole thing is blanketed in a silence only slightly disturbed by the rustling leaves from trees in the nearby forest.

"Welcome to the wheel—of Samsara Farm," Cam announces. "J. tells me you're ready to leave it."

You pause, reflecting on the conversation you just had with J. about this subject. *"Yes, well, um—I guess so. I don't know."*

"You don't know? That sounds like some bullshit talkin' to me, dear. I think *in fact* you do know." Cam glances at you with a funny look of suspicion. "No one drives around in J.'s Jeep, on the adventures he arranges, *without knowing*. Now, I'll ask you again. ...you ready to get off the wheel?"

You take a deep breath and continue to think it over. On the one hand, you feel a little cornered and overwhelmed. On the other hand, you're grateful for this big, wise woman's *no bullshit* approach and attitude.

"If what you mean by off is an end to my angst—my constant sadness and anger—then yes, hell yes, I want off."

"There ya go...much better." Cam pats you on the back. "Look, sweetie, all the poor lady folk that come here are in the exact same place. They're abused. They're frightened. They're lost. They've been treated like dirt most of their lives. I know this isn't *exactly* why you're here, but it's similar."

Cam takes your hand and very deliberately leads you to where the Wheel of Samsara walking maze begins. She gestures to your shoes as she removes her own. You do the same. Your bare feet crunch the small crystalline pebbles on the path.

"The first thing we have to establish—and it's the price of admittance here—is whether or not you want to take charge or responsibility. This is the first question you need to ask yourself." Cam looks you directly in the eyes as she speaks. "So—do you want off the wheel?"

"*Yes.*" You reply with some trepidation.

Cam continues to lead you through the maze holding your hand. "Now, take a deep breath." She walks slowly and quietly before speaking again.

"Good. You have to *want* to get off the Wheel of Samsara: make something of your life; be who you were meant to be; find out what you're really made of, and—most importantly—find out *who you really* are."

Cam continues slowly leading you through the maze. A slow, creeping sense of weight and seriousness begins to overtake you. You begin to recognize your old friend...the sobering truth. You drop further and further into your body. Your feet crunch the pebbles as you walk, but you are unaware of the sound.

Cam speaks again. "Now dear, the second question you must ask yourself is whether or not you *feel worthy enough* to be the best version of yourself. This is a big one, because just like many of the women who come here, especially after a lifetime of suffering and beatings, most of us *don't feel worthy* of being our best selves."

Cam pauses the walking and looks you directly in the eyes again. "Notice your own internal awareness. Notice mine. See that we are exactly the same. Breathe... So...do you feel worthy?"

With this question, you flush with nervous, tear-inducing emotion, because you realize that, in fact, you *do not feel worthy*. "I...I...don't know. It hurts so much." Tears stream down your face. "*I am sooo angry—sooo sad*." Your gut is now wrenching tight with the realization of this deep sense of unworthiness.

Cam keeps your hand, placing her free hand on your shoulder. She gives it a soft, comforting squeeze. "That's all right, dear. Let all that hurt out. You *are* worthy. You are most worthy. Take a deep breath. Look at me."

You look directly into Cam's eyes through a blurry waterfall of tears.

"I am with you. We are the same. I also once felt unworthy. But now—my strength is your strength. My awareness is your awareness. These tears, this release, your vulnerability, your courage—all of this is *worthiness itself*. You are so worthy."

You continue to shed tears through big chest heaves of inhalations and exhalations. Your legs feel light and unsteady. The unworthiness works itself loose, and like some lifeless ghostly apparition, slowly evaporates from your body. You *feel* heavy. You are silent, clear-eyed.

Cam continues to guide you through the maze. You both work your way toward the center. After a few moments of silence, you reach the center of the wheel.

"Such beautiful work you're doing here today," Cam says gently. And now, the final question you must ask yourself while walking the Wheel of Samsara..." Cam pauses. "...Close your eyes and keep them closed—no matter what." Cam waits again.

Not sure if she really means for you to do it, you close your eyes. And then...

"Do you trust the universe?" Cam asks loudly.

Cam begins leading you out of the maze by the hand. Your eyes are closed. It's very difficult *not* to open them. Your balance becomes unsteady; you're unsure of your next steps.

"Do you trust the universe!?" Cam repeats even louder as she guides you.

Every ounce of your being screams to open your eyes.

"Do *you trust* the universe!?" Cam repeats forcefully.

Inside, behind closed eyes, you are screaming for control; screaming for security; screaming for identity; and screaming and screaming and screaming until...

"Do *you trust* the universe!!?" Cam yells with absolute fierceness.

It breaks. You collapse on the ground with all control gone, and all anxiety broken, in a heap of deep relaxation. You slowly get back up, eyes still closed.

"*Yes,*" you reply and then pause before saying, "*I trust the universe.*"

"Well done, dear." Cam then resumes her lead in guiding you out of the maze. Again, she reminds you, "Continue to keep your eyes closed." You do so and slowly find that your steps become steady and sure again, even with closed eyes. "Yes, well done," Cam repeats.

After a few final moments of walking in blind silence, you reach the end of the maze, right next to where it began.

"Open your eyes," Cam says.

You do so, and the world is anew. Exhausted, you look around and experience everything in a deep glow of clarity and softness: the glistening Wheel of Samsara maze before you; the crisp chatter of leaves falling, then settling on the forest floor; the birdsong meandering aloft in the air. The world is right, okay, and present.

"Now you're ready to get off the Wheel of Samsara," Cam says while patting you on the back. "Now you're ready."

"*Thank you*," you reply.

"Of course, dear. Shall we go get some lunch?" Then Cam belly laughs, puts on her shoes and hops onto the golf cart. You jump on and enjoy a mostly silent trip back to the farm center.

En route, you break the silence. "*Thank you for your presence, Cam. J. told me that was your thing, and he was right.*"

Cam looks at you while driving. "My absolute pleasure. J. knows how to pick 'em, and he picked a good one in you."

Cam parks the golf cart in its designated location outside the main office. You agree to meet up for lunch in the dining hall in about thirty minutes and then part ways. In the interim, you meander around a bit until finding an ornamental, white iron bench couched beneath an old, decrepit chestnut tree. You park yourself there for a while, contemplating the Wheel of Samsara maze and glowing in its after-effects...

There's no end to the surprises on this spiritual badass journey, you think... *no end.*

J. and Lenny make appearances at lunch. J. takes note of your glossy-eyed, relaxed look and laughs. "I see the wheel has made its mark upon you," he comments. "Cam knows her shit, don't she?"

"Well yeah, that's one way to put it." You smile back. "*Pretty powerful. Unexpected, as usual. Thanks for arranging it.*"

"I didn't arrange that. He did," J. says as he smiles and points to Lenny drooped across his shoulder.

"*Of course he did.*" You laugh.

Cam shows up to lunch with Janine and Miriam in tow. Your group enjoys lunch together at one large table.

"I think Rosie is having her rally day," Cam shares joyfully, yet somberly, while eating.

Everyone except you seems to acknowledge what this means. You give J. a questioning look.

"Cam, tell my friend here what a rally day is." J. speaks to the group.

"Oh, sorry." Cam says, then looks at you and continues. "It's pretty common during the dying process. Most individuals "rally" out of the low-energy dying stupor for a day or so, regain some strength, and become lucid—talking, laughing, even eating—one final time before death. It's the last hurrah for the dying, both beautiful and sad at the same time."

"*Got it,*" you reply. "*Are we going to visit her again today then?*"

Miriam interjects. "Everyone's invited. She's awake right now. I think we should go right after lunch."

"Me too," Cam adds.

"Awesome," J. states. "Can I bring this guy?"

"Lenny is always welcome," Cam replies with a smile. "Always welcome."

Everyone makes plans to meet up after lunch. You finish eating and then head back to your guest quarters. You shower and get on some fresh clothing. You meet up with everyone near the golf carts. The group piles into two of them and heads toward Rosie's farmhouse.

You, Cam, Mariam, Janine, J., and Lenny enter Rosie's room quietly and reverently, but quickly ascertain that such solemn gentleness is unwarranted. *Rosie is on fire compared to yesterday,* you think.

You see Rosie sitting mostly upright; her hair is combed, and she's eating ice cream spoon-fed from Helen, the hospice nurse in attendance the previous night.

"Goddamned butter pecan. Isn't there any chocolate fudge? I want the fudge!" Rosie spouts.

You can't help but laugh along with everyone else who hears her ice cream diatribe.

"Beatrice and I always liked the fudge. But we gotta eat the goddamned butter pecan 'cause it's Miriam's favorite. Not even on the death bed am I allowed a proper indulgence."

Miriam laughs. "Rosie, I'm sure you can have all the fudge you want when you see Beatrice."

"Oh, my Beat. How I want to see my little Beat." And then, on a dime, Rosie starts crying in high pitched wails.

The mood turns somber and sad as you realize that while Rosie is definitely more awake than before, she's still a little loopy and confused.

"Oh Rosie, Beat loves you so much," Miriam replies.

Janine reaches out a hand to Rosie. "It's all right, dear. We'll get you some fudge."

"I don't want the goddamn fudge. I want my Beat," Rosie replies.

"Beat is waiting for you, Rose. She is..." Miriam interjects.

"So long I've lived with this torment. So long," Rosie moans.

J. leans over and, out of Rosie's earshot, whispers to you. "She died while Rosie was babysitting her. Accident."

You silently acknowledge the information, and your heart goes out to Rosie, who is wailing again.

Cam takes over. "Rosie dear, look at me. Find your beautiful center, dear. Find your beautiful center."

Rosie stops wailing and looks at Cam.

"That's it. Breathe and find your center. We've talked about this before. Not your fault. Beat loves you. No blame. Just an accident. Find your center."

"Not my fault. I know. I'm good. Am I good?"

"Rosie, you are most definitely good," Cam replies. "Look who we brought again today." Cam steers Rosie away from the Beatrice topic and points to Lenny, wrapped around J.'s shoulder.

"Oh, there he is!" Rosie beams with a smile. "Maybe Leonard would like my goddamned butter pecan ice cream!?"

Everyone laughs, biting their tongues, not knowing how this wild, unpredictable interaction will unfold.

J. interjects, "Lenny would love some." J. then deftly pulls out a small baggie of dried blueberries and hands one to Helen.

"Are you done with the ice cream, Rosie?" Helen asks.

"Hell yes, I'm done with that shit ice cream."

Everyone laughs again. Helen places the blueberry in the bowl of ice cream and then dips it out again with the spoon. Helen looks at J.; J. acknowledges this and gently places Lenny on Rosie's lap. Helen holds out the spoon with the blueberry on it and then…Lenny skillfully licks the blueberry into his mouth with a single tongue tine.

"I had a boyfriend with a tongue like that once," Rosie says with a devilish grin.

Everyone groans and laughs at the same time.

"Okay," Cam says. "You are a pill today, aren't you, dear?"

"What are you goddamned talkin' about? I'm a pill every day."

"That's my Rose," quips Miriam.

"I am so happy to see you like this. Did you find your beautiful center, dear?" Cam looks directly into Rosie's eyes. Rosie gets very serious and quiet.

Rosie begins to pet Lenny. "Such a beautiful boy."

Again, Cam states gently, "Your beautiful center."

Rosie breaths a big sigh of relief. Lenny seems to know what's happening and plays his part. Very slowly, he makes his way up to Rosie's small shoulder and curls himself up between Rosie's neck and the pillow. Rosie's eyes shine as Lenny snuggles against her. Rosie tilts her head in affection toward him.

"Find your beautiful center," Cam whispers very gently.

Rosie continues to pet Lenny with care. She looks out at everyone with clear and gentle eyes. "Thank you, Cam; I have. Me and Beat are gonna be just fine." She then looks at Miriam. "And you too, Miriam. We'll all be together again someday. And we'll all be just fine."

"Yes, we will," Miriam replies through tears.

Rosie continues to pet Lenny for some time and then abruptly breaks the silence. "Now get me that goddamned fudge ice cream." Rosie laughs and moans nearly simultaneously.

Everyone laughs again.

"I think if Lenny were a cat, he'd be purring right now," says J.

"Oh, he's purring," Rosie replies. "Deep down inside. He's purring. ...such a good boy."

After some time, Rosie starts to get heavy-eyed, and Helen concludes the visit. You stand, gently pick up Lenny, and say your goodbyes. There's a heaviness in the air as all of you leave the room, not knowing if you'll ever interact with Rosie quite like this again.

As you walk out, you can't help but feel how much richer you are to have had this brief encounter with this crazy old soul, who also seemed to be ready and waiting to exit...the Wheel of Samsara.

Spiritual Badass Suggestion:

Well, we're in a pickle this go-round, aren't we? I can't exactly suggest Wheel-of-Samsara Maze Therapy or a visit with your crazy dying Aunt Rosie, can I? And *you* can't exactly go out and do those things.

Or wait a minute...can I? Actually, yes—yes, I can!

Here's how: It's not the context, it's the *content*. Your progress on the road to spiritual badass peace and happiness isn't dependent upon particular people, places, or things. It's not dependent upon those; it's dependent upon the field of *depth, honesty, and truth* you interact with, in whatever form or fashion you can find or receive.

Is there someone you can speak with or *be* with who is willing to be real, honest, and true with you? Seek that person out. Seek that group out. Seek that friend or family member out. Seek that therapist, priest, minister, or lord of the fairy kingdom out. Who it is on the outside doesn't matter. What matters is who they are *on the inside*.

Will they listen? Will they really hear you? Will they be true with you? As a general life rule, these are the people you want to meet and hang out with!

And yes, you are right. This is not necessarily easy, but it's most definitely worth the time and effort to look...

Again, if you find the content, the *context* won't matter. But, if you do happen to find a Wheel-of-Samsara Maze therapist, well then, damn: High-score fist bump to that!

CHAPTER 11
NON-ABIDING AWAKENING

How to reconnect with the heart of existence

The rest of the day passes without much in the way of activity, which you're grateful for. You've been at *Samsara Farm* less than a day and it feels like time was drugged and hypnotized by some external, mystical boogeyman who slipped it a mickey and filled it with a year's worth of experience. Or, maybe, like your mama always said, "You ain't been eatin' your veggies." No matter—you're super content to do zip, nada, nothing, with *nobody*.

Time passes and dinner rolls around. You stroll over to the dining hall and find yourself seated alone across from a young woman named Hana. She's in her late twenties, has short brown hair, and speaks with some Eastern European accent you can't quite pinpoint. She also has a bruise the size and color of a plum around her left eye. You presume she's a visitor and struggle to strike up a polite conversation without mentioning the elephant in the room.

She beats you to it, pointing to her face and asking, "Is the eye still purple? I haven't looked at a mirror in three days."

"*Yes, with shades of brown and black,*" you reply.

"Cool. That's new development. Eye liner is free!" She chuckles and adds, "Look on the brighter side, yes?"

"*Um, yeah, I suppose you're right...*"

She interrupts you and holds out her hand. "I'm Hana. I live here four months now. You just arrived? Not seen you before."

"Yes," you reply. *"I, or eh, we just got in last night."*

"You are here with family, yes?"

"No. Not exactly. Just a friend. It's complicated."

"Yes, complicated. *Always* complicated. You see my eye? Very complicated." Hana laughs and so do you.

You like Hana and decide to lay your cards on the table. *"I'm not here because I was abused. I'm here with my friend, J. We're visiting with Cam. I'm here because, well, because I'm unhappy or eh, sad and angry and I want to get off the Wheel of Samsa...Samsara... and um, maybe wake up or something..."* (You catch yourself rambling and nervous, but notice how good it feels to admit all this to a total stranger.) *"...like that."*

"Oh, you are here for Auntie Cam meditation stuff, yes? I know she is very good with it. She teaches me to be very present and still. Up here." She points to her head.

"Yes, meditation. I'm not very good at it. But yeah, I suppose so ...and yes, her presence is very good."

"She teaches me to be okay and stand up for myself. Find my woman's inner power and feel better also here." She points to her heart.

With that gesture, you *really* begin to like Hana and go all in with your next question as you point to her eye. *"Boyfriend do that?"*

"No. Complicated, as I say. Living with aunt and uncle in, you know, Kansas City. Uncle, how do you say...? ...mean sons of a bitch, with too much alcohol. Thinks I am his servant and treats me as you can see. I had enough. No more family here in U.S.A. so I leave—and lucky I find this place. This place, *Samsara Farm,* saved me. My new Auntie...Cam makes available to me a big reset."

You smile and point to your own head and heart and reply, *"Yes, big reset."*

You continue to chat with Hana and realize just how deep the work that Cam is providing here goes. Despite Hana's outward appearance, there is a shine and happiness to her inner world that you guess hasn't seen the light of day for quite some time.

Hana tells you about her background and her dreams of becoming a veterinarian's assistant or even a veterinarian. She's unapologetically honest and forthright. You think, *...so refreshing to meet honest people. Honest even about their pains and struggles.* You continue your conversation with Hana until the dining hall empties and it's time to go.

You leave with yet another small amount of renewed hope added to your own personal armory on your badass adventure to escape the wheel. *If Hana can do it, I can, too...*

It's 2:30 a.m. back at your guest suite. You're sound asleep. There's a light tapping on the door. It takes you a few seconds to come to your senses and fumble with the light function on your phone. In your heart, you know exactly what this is about…

"One sec," you reply.

"Sorry. I know it's late." J. speaks with a hushed tone.

You walk across the room, your heart sinking and blood draining from your limbs. You open the door. J. is standing there with a look of open sympathy and caring. He doesn't need to say it, but of course does.

"She passed…about a half hour ago."

Chills rush up your spine. The somber seriousness of the moment grips you. You become a thousand pounds heavier. Your eyes slightly water. You struggle to form words.

"I figured."

"Cam just sent me a text."

"Is there anything we can do to help?"

"No. No. They're going to remain with her body overnight and in the morning sometime, call the coroner. I just wanted you to know tonight, so you aren't surprised by everything in the morning."

"Thanks. Appreciate it."

"Don't know what funeral arrangements they've made. We'll find out tomorrow, I'm sure." J. pauses a few seconds and looks directly into your eyes. "She was a crazy old hoot."

You smile. *"Yes, she was."* You extend your arm and pat J. on the shoulder. He continues looking directly at you, nodding his head in gratitude.

"I think I'm going to read a little and then try to get some sleep. Probably a long day tomorrow."

"Sure. Sounds good."

"Well, okay," J. responds, then pauses another long beat. "Goodnight." Tears slowly drip from J.'s glassy eyes. He smiles, nods his head affirmatively, then turns and walks away.

You shut the door and walk back to your bed…Phone light off... Place it on nightstand...Lie down…Pull covers up…Shut eyes…Breathe a few deep breaths…Slowly...fade...to a fitful… dreamy…black…sleep.

In your dream, you're standing before a full-length mirror. You can see yourself from head to toe. The problem is—you're seeing the backside of yourself, not your front reflection, which is what you're supposed to be seeing.

You push on the mirror. You spin around several times. You jump up and down. Nothing works. Every time you face the mirror directly, all that is reflected back to you is—your back.

Then it dawns on you…and you get nervous with the realization: You're being watched from behind. You slowly, nervously turn around and, weirdly enough, with no shock at all, there's *you*—the *you*—you were looking for, standing right in the middle of the room—and *not* a mirror image.

The other you speaks:

That took you long enough!

No, dumbass—not the dream character of the YOU in the book. I'm talking to the YOU out there—the you holding the book.

Yeah, it's me again, or eh, the real you—to be more precise.

Really? Still confused? How many times do I have to communicate this to you?

There's only ONE character…

You're it.

There's only ONE player in this holographic video game…

And you're it.

There's only ONE of us here…

And…you…are…it.

I know, I know. You think you're Thom or Melinda or Jesse or Bill or Susan…but all that identity-personality stuff is just *the black illusory shadow of the real you. The Black Shadow dies. The Black Shadow always...dies.*

Do you see me now?

Can you see me now?

Do you see—

The dream ends abruptly.

You hear J. gently tapping and speaking at the door. "We overslept. It's 9:30."

"*Oh, crap,*" you moan, rolling out of your dreamy stupor. "*Should we go to the dining hall?*"

"Yeah, I think that would be smart," J. replies.

"*Okay. Give me a few. Was totally out of it.*"

"No worries. I'll meet you down there in five. Sound good?"

"*Okay. Sounds good.*"

J.'s morning revelry does a pretty good job of squashing the brain cell department in charge of dreams, but the memory vapor is still there, and you can't shake it. *Fucking weird...Fucking weird...*is your mind's passive aggressive response to it. *Mirrors? Characters? Book? Video game? What the fuck?* After you hop in the shower and get dressed, it evaporates—*mostly.*

The tone in the dining hall is not at all what you expected. There is laughter, conversation, and the hustle and bustle of activity. You see Cam, Janine, and J. all seated together at one of the numerous small round tables. Their mood is happy and bright— far from the somber, grey expectations your mind held. Hell, now that you think about it, not even the weather is cooperating with today's events: It's a bright, clear, bluebird day with nary a cloud in sight. You grab one of the last bits of breakfast from the buffet and join the group, which is mid-conversation.

"I don't think there's enough firewood down there yet," Janine says to Cam.

"Well, we need to get on that. I thought we prepared the sight," Cam replies.

"Just the circle of rocks and a few chairs. I'll take my group down there after breakfast and get on it."

"I expect there to be fifty or sixty people tonight. So make sure there're enough seats for everyone and enough wood to burn past midnight, at the very least."

"Got it," Janine affirms her next steps.

J. interjects, "When did you say the coroner was coming?"

"Should be here around noon. That's what we requested. They'll bring her back tomorrow after the paperwork and legal pronouncement," Cam replies.

"And she'll be buried on the farm here?" J. questions.

"Yes, in the old grave site down near the wheel."

J. nods, then acknowledges your presence. "Morning, Sunshine," he says with care and heart.

"Oh, crap. Sorry. Good morning," Cam says directly to you. "Busy one today."

"*Oh, no worries. Sorry to interrupt. Don't mind me.*" You pause and then add, "*My condolences.*"

Cam looks appreciatively at you. "Thank you, dear," she says softly.

"Does Helen have the filing papers ready for the funeral home lawyer?" Janine asks.

Cam and Janine continue their conversation while J. scoots next to you and talks low enough not to disturb them. "Sleep okay last night?" he asks.

"Oh, you know, okay...considering."

"Yeah, me too." He pauses for a sip of coffee. "There's an outdoor bonfire ceremony tonight in celebration of Rosie. That's what we've been talking about. We're invited, of course."

"Cool. Sounds, um...perfect. Is there anything I can do to help out today?"

"I don't know. I'd ask Janine. After breakfast, I'm going to go sit with Rosie and Mariam until the coroner comes. You're welcome to join me if you'd like."

"I think I'll pass, but thanks. I'm probably better at a distance today."

"Understood."

Just then, you have an idea. "Will you have Lenny with you today?"

"Probably. Why?"

"Oh, nothing big. I was thinking about taking a hike and thought his company would be good."

"Hmmm? I have a better idea. Take Ollie! He'll be fine. He can't exactly escape. Keep him next to you, and he'll be perfectly content. Oh, and pack something for him to nibble on."

You pause to think about it, then ask, *"Well, why not? Are the gloves near the pop-up?"*

"Yep. Trust me. He'll be great."

"Can do. Settled."

You go back to eating your breakfast. The other three continue to talk about all the necessary preparations for the funeral home, celebration, and burial. After some time, their talk winds down and you take advantage of the lull.

"Janine, would you like help at the fire circle pit thing?" you ask.

"Sure. I'm headed down there now. Happy to have you."

"Great. Some physical labor would do me some good."

After breakfast, you join Janine for several hours cutting, carrying, and stacking firewood for the bonfire celebration. You also drive the golf cart, transporting a variety of chairs down to the firepit. It's sweaty work, perfect for keeping your mind off all the death and dying highlighted today by both your reality and dreams.

Once the firepit preparations are complete, you break for lunch. Afterward, you grab a shower and put on fresh clothes. J. isn't around, but Ollie is. You walk up to his pop-up cage...

"Okay, little dude. You wanna go for a walk?" Ollie doesn't speak much, but when he does—like in this instance—his warbly, little, innocent squeak tears into your being and plucks every last heartstring available. You can't resist. You grab a small backpack and throw in the small, sealed container of chicken livers, a water bottle, your phone, and your writing journal. With the handling gloves on, you carefully extract Ollie from his pop-up cage. He's perfectly content and calm perched on your right hand.

Janine graciously gave you permission to use a golf cart, which you adroitly maneuver with your left hand. Ollie doesn't seem to mind the bumpy golf cart ride that takes you down to the wheel walking maze where, you've been told, the entrance to a long hiking trail in the forest is also.

You park the golf cart and spot the trail. You pause to take a deep breath and then take a moment to try something.

"*Okay dude. We're gonna give this a go.*"

You lift Ollie up to your right shoulder and gently place him there. He flutters slightly, but soon grabs a perch. His talons slightly dig into you, but the hoodie you're wearing is thick enough to prevent them from digging into skin.

"*Perfect!*" you say with laughter. "*Oh—Lenny is going to be soooo jealous! Ha!!*"

You grab your backpack and get out your phone. *This will probably tick J. off, but it'll be so worth it*, you think. You snap a selfie of you and Ollie and text it to J. with the tag "competition" on it. You snicker with delight.

You step onto the trail and into the canopied forest. The trail is a generously wide, worn dirt path that winds its way through red cedars and white oaks. Like many forests you've hiked in, this one contains a soft, mysterious, and quiet beauty you immediately recognize. There's no breeze. It's perfectly still. You can even hear Ollie breathing. You also notice the muffled pad and plop and slight crunch of your shoes on the hard, bare earth. You drop deep into your body, and deep into thought...

Death. Death. Death.

Okay, let's wrap our brain around this Black Shadow thing.

First things first... just a dream.

Second thing. Our brain? Are there two of us here? More than that, maybe?

What the fuck?? Too much. Too fast. Back up.

Black Shadow...keeps saying there's just one of us. What does that even mean? One of us?

But I'm me. And J. is J. and Lenny is Lenny. And Cam is Cam. That's a lot of us, we, whatever—not to mention the seven billion other people on the planet that make up us, we, whatever...

There's just one?

Okay. Hypothetically strip away personality. Strip away dreams and hopes. Strip away...my life. What's left?

Rosie's dead. What's left for her? Is there a Rosie still left? Somehow, I doubt that.

What's left?

The question is not what. The question is who...

Who am I?

You stop dead in your tracks because *that thought* got you, and *not* in a good way.

Oh fuck. Oh fuck. Oh fuck.

Your heart starts racing because you've exposed something: Something that didn't want to be exposed—and it's now revolting. You haven't had an anxiety attack in some time, but you sure as fuck are having one now. A primal rush of fear courses across your brain and sends fight or flight signals to your whole body. Your system flushes with cortisol. Your breathing turns shallow and rapid. You collapse to the ground in a heap. Ollie flutters off your shoulder and onto the ground in front of you. He doesn't go far—thank God. You continue to panic. It comes on in deep waves echoing monstrosities from your deepest existential parts.

Death! Run! Distract!

Death! Run! Distract!

What the fuck?!

Who am I? I am…. I am…

You're doubled over. Both your hands are flat on the forest floor, and your forehead is low. You almost feel like vomiting, it's so bad.

I am the fucking Black Shadow!

I am the fucking Black Shadow!

And then you look up—and to your utter surprise and amazement, you are met by two huge, beautiful, brown and yellow eyes…

Ollie! Holy fuck! Those eyes. Those deep, gentle, aware eyes.

You are aware!

Ollie is aware! I am aware! J. is aware! Cam is aware!

And then, just before it feels like your whole being is going to burst, the anxiety attack dissipates …and is gone.

Oh crap, that was powerful.

"Thank you, Ollie. Thank you, little dude."

Ollie sits and stares like he always does, and then he lets out a tiny warble.

You let out a slight laugh and whisper, "*Was that 'You're welcome' in owl talk? I think it was.*"

After a few moments, you're able to stand again. You pick Ollie up and gently place him back on your shoulder and, God knows why, continue your walk through the forest—minus the deep thoughts this time.

An hour or so passes by with no further anxiety attacks. You stop at one point and take a few minutes to feed Ollie, who, as always, is very appreciative of raw chicken parts. You resume your hike, and the trail eventually dumps you out on the opposite side of the walking wheel maze. Within a few minutes, you're traveling back on the golf cart.

That was zero fun, you think. You gaze at Ollie, still perched on your shoulder...

"*What about you? Did you have fun?*"

Ollie responds with a quiet warble as you scratch his downy soft, feathery head.

"*I'll take that as a yes.*"

Author J. Stewart Dixon here, reporting for duty. ...don't mean to disturb you because I know you're knee deep in the narrative now, but I'd like to share something with you, briefly, if you don't mind...

There's an old Buddhist story that goes something like this: Imagine every year a bird migrates over the Himalayan Mountain range and its wings slightly brush the top of the mountains. Now imagine the amount of time it takes for that great range to be completely worn down *to nothing* by that single bird; that's the same amount of time it takes for a soul to become enlightened.

Well, fuck that shit.

I'm no Buddhist. I'm a distant fan, but I certainly don't identify as such. Here's why:

For the most part, I think the Buddhist religion business is no different from all the other religion businesses available here on our fine little planet. On some days, yeah sure, it seems like Buddhism is slightly closer to the truth. It certainly kicks ass over Mormonism or Scientology, that's for sure. But like most belief systems, it's still filled with traps and dead ends that can get you thinking that your salvation, Heaven, enlightenment or whatever can be attained—after about eight billion years and three thousand lifetimes—*if you get your shit together.* So yeah, um— hard pass, thank you very much.

I think what Buddhism does get right (in a general sense) is its famed three legs: Buddha (enlightenment), Dharma (teaching), and Sangha (community). These are the three things that, according to most Buddhist practices, one needs in order to exit the Wheel of Samsara.

I agree. (Generally speaking…I know—lots of caveats here.)

I'm calling your attention to all this because, if you haven't figured it out, that's exactly what we're doing on our little spiritual badass adventure here—and it's how *most* spiritual adventures actually and authentically unfold: through the use of the *three legs…*

Leg One – The Buddha: We hang out with enlightened characters and beings like Lenny, Tenzin, and Brent in Book One and, in this book, Ollie, Ray, and Cam (and more to come).

Leg Two – The Dharma: We learn, formally or informally, from the teachings and living examples of these "enlightened," wise, or awake beings.

Leg Three – The Sangha: We hang out in a community of others who are also interested in enlightenment, spiritual wisdom, or waking up.

One, two, three. Pretty simple stuff. Again, I'm no Buddhist but I like the *three legs*.

One final note:

Personally, I'd probably have built this thing out of four legs: Buddha, Dharma, Sanga, and Foul-Moutha. In my esteemed, irreverent, low-brow, potty-mouthed experience … you reach a shitload more people with Foul-Moutha.

Author, J. Stewart Dixon here, checkin' out—

Fuckin' A.

I should have known better...

You knew in the back of your brain that the Black Shadow-anxiety-attack-thing wasn't finished with you today, but you just didn't imagine, *couldn't even comprehend*, how in God's name it could return...on the same *damn* day.

It's after dinner and dark out. You're sitting in front of a roaring, crackling, white-hot bonfire. There are about fifty people gathered around and more streaming in as the evening stretches to its midnight zenith. The stars are out in crystalline, pinpoint clarity—the perfect celestial slideshow for Rosie's ceremony of life send-off.

You're seated near Janine and your new friend Hana. Cam, J., and Mariam sit nearby. They look exhausted, but manage to talk and laugh and express good spirits despite the day's challenges.

A gaggle of musicians, each holding various acoustic instruments, shows up accompanied by what you presume is a group of belly dancers. *Well, that's different for a funeral,* you think. There's a small stage adjacent to, but safely distanced from, the firepit where the musicians set up their instruments.

After they set up, everyone quiets and settles a little, waiting for something to happen. One of the musicians walks over to Cam and whispers in her ear. She stands and nods her head and follows him back to the stage. And then, *something indeed happens...*

Cam steps onto the stage. She's wearing blue jeans and a polished, pearl colored, loosely fitted blouse adorned with tasteful, ornamental stitching; the blouse hangs below her waistline. Around her neck is a big, bold necklace crafted from silver, opals, and turquoise. What's most striking about her, however, is that her silver hair is *loose and down*. Gone is the tightly controlled, braided ponytail. With her hair down, Cam is an unleashed, mighty, and powerful woman. The fire throws shadows and orange-red bits of flickering light across her face, transforming her into an ancient, face-painted Norse goddess—ready to go to war.

But she does not go to war. She goes to heart. She goes to the heart of every person seated around that fire. She goes and she does *not* let go. It is powerful, intimidating, profound, and so very, very...*real*. Before your eyes Cam becomes Shakti, Kali, Freyja, Mary Magdalene, and every other divine goddess combined from all of history. And yet...*and yet*...she remains humble, flawed, vulnerable, exposed, and so very painfully human...

"Welcome, everyone. So, I am not here to blow snow up your asses about our friend who passed away very early in the morning of this day. Rosie told me, very specifically, that I was not to do that. So, I'll honor her wishes by *damn well doing it anyway!* which, as we all know, our beloved, obstinate, rule-breaking Rosie would completely approve of."

The gathering unleashes a torrent of laughter, whoops, and hollers. The musicians clamor their various drums and instruments. Everyone claps. It continues for several minutes until the Norse gods are sated.

"Rosie certainly wasn't one for conventions, rules, or rituals! So in honor of you, my beautiful Rosie—*our* beautiful Rosie—we blow a raging snowstorm of gratitude, love, respect, laughter, strength, and wisdom straight from our collective asses right up yours, dear. You were, and are, one of a kind, Rosie!"

The gathering goes wild again, unleashing the same boisterous clamor of approval. Eventually, the collective energy of the group dissipates. A calm, serious tone returns to the crowd. Cam then assumes the mantle:

"Rosie lived on *Samsara Farm* for fifteen years, but she escaped samsara long ago. Rosie escaped her abusive past. Rosie escaped her painful childhood. Rosie escaped a world where she was told 'no,' repeatedly and forcefully, over and over again."

Cam pauses briefly.

"What did Rosie do instead? Rosie did not accept this 'no' in any way, shape, or circumstance. She did not accept the pain, the suffering, or the limitations of this little box that so many of us are told we must live out our lives in. She shouted indefatigably to that box—'Fuck You!'"

Everyone at the gathering whoops and hollers again and then quickly quiets down...

"Allow me to repeat that in gentler, more Buddhist terms: Rosie said to the Wheel of Samsara and to suffering, 'I will *not* comply. I will *not* fall in line. I will *not* be imprisoned... I *will* instead find out *who I am*. I *will* empower myself. I *will* be the best version of myself. Or I *will die* trying.'"

Cam pauses, allowing the fire to flicker, crackle, and burn.

"Does this mean that Rosie was a saint? Hell, no—it doesn't mean she was a saint. It means she embraced life completely, with all its ups and downs and all her numerous..." Cam smiles and pauses. "...flaws."

"Rosie lived on her own terms in a world of her own making. The word 'no' which echoes from the countless small boxes of small-minded and small-hearted men *did not* penetrate her world."

Cam looks deep into the bonfire flames as they dance into the infinite starry heavens....

"We should all aspire to be like Rosie. We should all aspire to *get off* the Wheel of Samsara. Have we not suffered enough? Have we not endured generations of folly and ignorance? Have we not *all had enough* of this dream—now soured into a nightmare?"

Cam's words penetrate into the darkest recesses of your being. You feel something primal stirring and awakening. *Oh shit, not now, not here...*

"Tomorrow, when we lay Rosie to rest in the old graveyard down by the walking wheel, we will be one less than our whole. We will be missing one spoke. We will be bereft of one human part. But..."

Cam masterfully pauses again for the starry universe to seep in and work its magic in the hearts of all in attendance ...

"But—do not allow this missing piece, this sadness for the loss of our dear friend Rosie to define you for long. Yes, embrace the sadness. Yes, embrace that hole in your heart. Yes, embrace the very pain it means to be human. Embrace death... And then, embrace this life and live as Rosie did—free, unencumbered, liberated, wild, flawed, messy, and in absolute defiance of the Wheel of Samsara and all the many 'nos' which spiral out of it."

Cam takes a deep breath and takes a moment to look at everyone, *including you*, directly in the eyes and finishes...

"Instead, like Rosie... say yes! Say yes! Say yes!"

Cam repeats "Say yes!" and this time everyone around the bonfire joins in. *Say yes!* echoes into infinity chanted by the sixty-some human beings gathered around the bonfire in communal primal urging to the universe to know itself, better itself, and be, at last...free from the great Wheel of Samsara.

The chanting ends and, just as smoothly, the musicians transition into a haunting, drumming incantation which goes on for a good thirty minutes. You lose yourself in the moment and allow the drumming, chanting, dancing, and mesmerizing body movement of the sacred gathering to utterly sweep you away.

Lost in the reverie, you forget the apprehension you felt during Cam's speech. But—destiny has a date with you tonight and, at long last, it arrives...

You are sweaty with dance and heat from the bonfire. Your eyes dart in and out of contact with your friends old and new who are also lost in the boisterous dancing revelry. You see J., Hana, Janine, Mariam, Helen, and, of course, Cam.

When your eyes meet Cam's, she works her way over to you, looking at you directly and deeply. She places both her hands on your shoulders and says fiercely, "There is only one of us here!"

That *thing* which was disturbed and stirred earlier during Cam's speech now fully awakens. *There is only one of us here* ricochets across your brain—from the dream of the Black Shadow you had earlier this morning and the anxiety attack you had with Ollie in the forest to the deepest essence and singularity of this very moment around the bonfire.

There is only ONE of us here!

There is only ONE of us here!

Yes, there is only one of us here.

Holy shit! I am that ONE! I am the Black Shadow! I am Cam. I am J. I am Hana. I am Rosie. I am YOU, dear reader.

Oh, FUCK! Holy Christ, God Almighty—I am NOT real. I am a character in a book. I am fiction. I do NOT exist. I am a character—in a book!

You look deep into the bonfire; out of its infernal depths, a monstrous, black, shadowy dragon appears....

With a sickeningly slow, dragging, crawling sound, the dragon moves and gathers itself directly in front of you and rears up on its hind taloned haunches. Its eyes penetrate yours and sear away your being with white-hot fear.

"*You are mine now!*," it bellows in a low, terrifying, guttural voice.

It inhales deeply…and finally exhales a shower of nuclear-sun-mantel-core-hot fire, which rains down upon you and incinerates every last ounce of your fictional being. You stand in place, utterly aware, present, and alone.

*I am…I am…I am…*is the *only thing* you have to stand on.

In an instant, the dragon disappears.

Cam is no longer next to you. The bonfire is still burning. The musicians are still playing. The belly dancers are still dancing. J. is still smiling. Everything is *everything*, just as it was.

But *you*, YOU are forever changed. Because *you* have just realized the truth: *you* do not exist.

You…are a character in a book…

…a character in the dream book of Brahman.

You pause, take a deep breath, and allow your nerves to settle.

Finally, after several moments of reconstituting, you manage to birth a single, powerful, solitary thought:

Who in the fuck…

…is this Brahman dude?

Spiritual Badass Suggestion:

We're in the wilds now, and in the wilds it's best to travel light...

At this point, making spiritual *to do* suggestions will just weigh you down, because what's mostly needed from here on out is actually—*undoing*. So, for now, we'll pause these suggestions and I'll let you hike solo for a while...

This doesn't mean I won't be back to join you on the trail; it just means I think you're ready to go it alone for a bit.

Trust me...you have all the badass tools you need for your continued adventure.

Fist-bump, my badass friend.

You got this...

Chapter 12
Brahman's Castle

How to wake up and meet your dreamer

Wish number one:

About five thousand years ago, on the Indian subcontinent, about eighty miles south of the city now known as Lucknow (the capital of the state of Uttar Pradesh), there was a small, rural Indian village named Kanpur, washed and blessed by the holy waters of the Ganges River.

In this village lived a diminutive nine-year-old boy named Atman. Atman grew up with four brothers and sisters, all of whom labored with their mother and father as subsistence farmers, toiling away on a small plot of scrubby, mostly dirt, wind-swept land granted to them by the local raja.

Atman's life was filled with routine. Early each day, Atman would haul his two buckets and carrying yoke on a long downhill trek to the Ganges River. When his buckets were filled, he would commence with the laborious business of lugging the water back to the farm for cooking, cleaning, and refreshment for the cow, goat, and half a dozen chickens his family kept. On some days, because the crops needed extra water, Atman would have to labor through this trip several times.

On one such day, halfway back from his third bucket filling, Atman tripped and fell, and his water buckets emptied themselves onto the arid, hard earth. Atman collapsed in tears at his misfortune. After a few moments, he stood up.

Unfocused, feeling sorry for himself, and no longer on task, he began following the stream of water created from his emptied buckets.

The spilled water meandered and trickled through the underbrush in a slow, serpentine fashion—around boulders, through crevices, and, finally, down a deep gully on the side of the hill. Atman had never seen this gully.

Enticed by *something—anything*—new, little Atman eagerly followed the trickle of water down the gully. After setting his buckets and yoke down, Atman scrambled on all fours down its craggy, rock-filled walls. With his eyes still on the ground, he continued to follow the slowly dissipating stream of spilled water. Atman was paying little attention when, after a short time, he looked up—and there, in front of him, was the entrance to a cave.

He had certainly never seen this cave before; nor had any of his brothers or sisters ever mentioned it. Now that he thought about it, no one from his village had ever mentioned it before either. He was mesmerized...enticed. After all, what nine-year-old boy could resist the magical beck and call of a hidden, unknown cave?

Atman looked around and hesitated. He knew his parents would not have approved. He knew that somehow what he was about to do was *deeply* forbidden, but by what or whom— he couldn't imagine. All he knew is that even though the outward appearance of the cave conveyed *Do Not Enter!* every inward urge said *Yes, Please—Do Enter!* He was torn, but soon gave in to the building blocks that make up all little, mischievous nine-year-old boys. He simply couldn't resist...and entered.

The cave entrance was small, but the interior opened up into a giant, cavernous hall filled with light streaking in from various crags and openings in the ceiling, and numerous foreboding dark corners and tunnels. Atman looked around. The rocks glistened with moisture from an unknown water source, giving everything a magically colored sheen washed in varying shades of ochre, burnt umber, and dark marigold. The cave was magnificent and utterly enchanting.

Atman spun slowly around, taking the whole wondrous thing in, when he spied one dark tunnel which beckoned him even further. There was just enough light for him to risk venturing in. His small feet crunched the scattered cave floor pebbles as he tentatively moved down the crawlway.

The tunnel grew smaller and smaller—darker and darker, tinier and tinier—until, at last, there was just enough room to squeeze his thin body through the entranceway into what appeared to be another well-lit room. He could detect the light in this room but, from where he stood, he could only see its floor. Atman got on his stomach and squeezed his body through the slender entrance…

He kept his eyes closed while he was slowly slithering along, so when at last he squeezed through, stood up, and opened them, what Atman's eyes fell upon was the thing of dreams.

The room was diminutive, maybe twelve feet in diameter and height. A small hole in the ceiling allowed a single shaft of light to pour in. The beam shone down on a very plain, brown rock altar. That was what he called it in his mind anyway. Atman wasn't *sure* it was an altar, but because of *the object* perched there, he knew it was, at the very least, some place very special or sacred. On the stone altar was a brass oil lantern strewn with a blazing assortment of jewels, the likes of which were reserved for only the wealthiest rajas in all of India. It was breathtaking in its beauty.

Atman looked around, worried that he might be caught in the act of theft or trespassing. Not a single soul, or any sentient creature for that matter, made its presence known. Atman was all alone with his find.

He took a deep breath and, in one brave move, grabbed the oil lantern off its perch. Nothing. He looked around again, feeling all the more guilty. Nobody...just the crunch of pebbles beneath his feet echoing in the small chamber. Silence. He was feeling bolder. He held the lantern in the shaft of direct sunlight. No markings, names, or indications that it belonged to anyone. *Not that I could read it anyway,* he thought. No owner. He shook it. Nothing.

Only one last thing to check—the lid. Very carefully, Atman set the oil lantern on the ground while he sat down cross-legged. Atman opened the lid—squeak, clang, plop—and nothing—*again.*

"Hmmm? This can't be." Atman finally risked speaking aloud. "Is there nothing more to this silly lantern? Just a mere empty, useless bauble? Some old forgotten bangle?"

Atman looked around the room, and his eyes fell upon something he had missed—a small, indistinct brown feather, also on the rock altar.

"Hmmm. Maybe?" Atman grabbed the feather and lightly brushed it against the lantern. Once again—nothing.

"Oh, for the love of Shiva! This thing is worthless!" And with that, Atman knocked the oil lantern with the back of his hand.

With that whack, the handle of the lantern bent just the right way on its hidden hinge, unlocking a secret internal compartment in its lower half. With its unlocking complete, the lantern immediately began to buzz and vibrate. A trickle of smoke began undulating from the lantern's mouth.

"Oh Shiva! Shiva!" Atman cried in fright and turned, looking for the exit. But before he could extend himself in the prone position to crawl out of the small room—it happened. The genie who lived in that great oil lantern appeared. And this genie did not disappoint. Atman was lying on his back looking straight up at the djinn (as they call them in India) when the djinn spoke:

"Greetings, Atman. I am the Djinn Brahman, and I grant you three wishes from my castle."

Atman could hardly believe his eyes or ears. The djinn towered above him. His skin...his appearance was that of the starry night sky. Atman had only ever seen such a thing while looking up at the evening firmament. Here it was embodied in the undulating, wispy form of this djinn.

Clearly the djinn was also taking on human form, but the truth was evident and plain to see—this was the djinn of the infinite universe.

"I...I...How do you know my name?" Atman was surprised at himself for uttering these as his first words.

"All men are Atman to me," the djinn replied.

"And—?" Atman paused to see if the djinn was going to follow that statement up with a clarifier, but after a brief moment, "...that's all you got?"

"Ahem—," the djinn cleared his throat, as if caught off guard. "I mean, I am *all* men, and all men contain Brahman, and *I am* Brahman, therefore...I contain all men. All men are Atman to me."

Atman began to relax, realizing that this djinn was perhaps not the almighty God he had initially presumed, regardless of outward appearances. Atman, still on the ground, rolled to his side and sat upright, wrapping his arms around his bent knees.

"You're not very good at this, are you?" Atman couldn't believe he said such a thing.

"I am Brahman. Umm..." The djinn paused and scowled slightly. "Yes—it *has been* some time. Two thousand, four hundred and seventy-six years, four months, three days, nine hours, and twenty-one minutes...to be exact...and—." Djinn Brahman looked down at the watch on his ghostly arm. "—thirteen seconds." The djinn looked slightly flustered. "...long time in the bottle."

"Yes—that was very exact. It's not a bottle," Atman replied.

"What's not a bottle?"

"The thing you were trapped in. It's not a bottle. It's an oil lantern."

"We are *waaaaay* off topic!" the djinn boomed, causing Atman to slightly cringe. "I am the Djinn Brahman, and I grant you three wishes from my castle. But be warned! The only *true wish* is to *return*...to Brahman. What is your first wish?"

Atman stood up. "How does this work? Is there a special way I need to ask? And what do you mean—*return* to Brahman? Very confusing."

The djinn scowled again at Atman's many questions. "Not confusing. Simple. All of this—," the djinn gesturing to the cosmos, composing his body, "—is a dream I am having. All wishes within the dream are just that—d*ream wishes.* I am Brahman. To return to Brahman is the only true wish. But you are Atman. The choice is yours. Just ask."

The djinn paused to think. "And yes, to formally file a wish, you must begin with the following: *Oh Great Djinn Brahman, grant me the wish of...*" Then the djinn bowed and waved his hands in a ridiculous circular fashion as if he was handing over command of a circus sideshow to Atman.

"Are you shitting me?!" Atman immediately put his hand to his mouth because cursing was strictly forbidden in his family. But he couldn't help himself in this instance because what the djinn had just spoken was so preposterous. "I have no clue what you mean by returning to Brahman or any of that." Atman then points to the starry makeup of the djinn. "But I do know that I am sick and tired of being poor, and I am most definitely sick and tired of carrying water. I want to be rich!"

"You are Atman and may wish for anything you desire."

Atman waited, expecting something to happen. A minute or so ticked by with awkward silence. "Okay. Um? Aren't you going to—you know—do it?"

The djinn gestured quickly with his right hand. "You must file the wish formally."

"...oh, right." Atman interrupted the djinn and sighed. "Okay." Then Atman spoke again, using a slightly obligatory tone of ridicule: *"Oh Great Djinn Brahman, please grant me the wish of being absolutely, stupendously, fantastically...rich!"*

The djinn, in classic djinn fashion, hovered above Atman with his arms crossed and a menacing scowl on his face. After the wish had been filed, the djinn's scowl transformed into an obsequious, vapid look. Then, another awkward pregnant pause unfurled...

"Okay. Wish granted," Djinn Brahman spoke.

Atman looked around the small cave. Nothing had changed. He felt no different...looked no different...thought no different. "That's it?"

"Yes. Go home. You will see."

"Really?" spoke Atman.

"Really," replied the djinn.

"What about my other wishes?"

"Come back anytime. They'll be here waiting for you. Just place me back on the altar."

"Oh Shiva! Shiva! I mean...Great Brahman! Thank you!"

"You are most welcome. Don't say I didn't warn you. The only *true wish* is..."

Atman interrupted the djinn. "Yes, yes I know—to *return*...to Brahman."

"I am Brahman. You are Atman. That is correct." And with that, the djinn returned to his bottle, or rather...his oil lantern.

Atman could hardly believe his good fortune. He got down on the floor, shimmied through the small entrance, and made his way into the big, open cavern. He looked around. Nothing different here. Within a few minutes, Atman had scrambled into daylight and was hoisting himself up the steep side of the gully where he had left his buckets and yoke and—*Oh my! something was very different here!*

The first thing that caught his eye was the glint of sunlight off his yoke, which had been transformed into pure gold and steel—no longer was it the old, wooden, dilapidated thing used to tote water. It was lavished with jewels and carved with writing. The second thing he noticed was that he could actually *read* the writing! And finally, he noticed his buckets had been transformed into silver and steel, both containing countless jewels and golden treasures. Atman was so excited he knelt down and cried tears of relief and joy. His life had changed.

Very quickly, he took off his shirt and tore it into two pieces, then covered each bucket of treasure. He was no fool. After some time, he made the voyage up the hill and back to his home, or *at least* he thought *where his home had been*. In its stead was a palace of epic proportions, surrounded by lush gardens and adorned with exotic flowers, statues, walking paths, and animals of every kind and breed. Cautiously, he walked up to the front entrance gate. His mother ran out to greet him.

"Atman! Great Shiva! Where have you been? We've been worried sick."

Atman looked at his mother, who was dressed in a manner he had never seen before: opulent and beautiful. "I…I…was down at the river gathering water," Atman spoke.

"What!? Why in the world would you be doing such a thing? We have servants for that!"

Atman set his buckets and yoke down, then collapsed to the ground. He pinched himself in the neck, making sure that what had happened wasn't all a dream conjured by that great Djinn Brahman.

But of course a dream is *exactly* what it was.

Wish number two:

Atman grew up immersed in wealth and cushioned in opulence. He never wanted for anything again. His life extended into those years when he remembered nothing but wispy tendrils of his former youth. He grew to be a man. He married and had children.

He gained access to the political courts and stages of nearby royalty through his wealth, and eventually he became raja of his own town, which his small village had transformed into. His life was perfect.

Until it wasn't.

It was the spring of his forty-fifth year. His eldest daughter, Sita, was to be married to a prince hailing from Jhansi, a much larger town in the adjacent province to the south, Madhya Pradesh. It was an arranged marriage. Atman was very proud and extremely happy. His daughter was the joy of his life, and his heart sang at the thought of the upcoming union.

It was, however, not meant to be...

When one thinks of snakes in India, what comes to one's mind, of course, is the great king cobra. But there is another lesser known, but much faster and deadlier serpent known as the saw-scaled viper. This smallish, golden brown and cream-colored beast with black double diamond etchings down its entire back can camouflage itself perfectly in the rocky, scrub underbrush which permeates most of India. Over the centuries, it's been called the *population killer* due to the prodigious number of people its strike and quick-acting venom has taken to the grave.

Sita was bitten one week before her wedding date. She lived for one hour after the bite...and Atman was destroyed.

The seven stages of grief mean nothing to the man who is embroiled in them. The first six stages—shock, denial, guilt, bargaining/anger, depression, and reconstruction—become only his tormentors. The final stage—acceptance—becomes only a foe he barely tolerates. Atman had *zero tolerance*. He refused to accept this dreadful event because Atman realized ...he had a bargaining tool, *unlike any other*...

After weeks of lamentation, outrage, and complete shock, Atman *remembered*...he remembered a small boy who had stumbled upon a gully long ago...and he remembered a cave which contained a stone altar and an oil lamp...and he remembered a djinn who lived in that oil lamp. But more than anything else, of course, Atman *remembered* that the djinn owed him something: Djinn Brahman owed him *two more wishes...*

Upon remembering, Atman immediately set out to find the gully again. It took some time. It was well hidden—perfectly camouflaged amidst numerous ruts, crags, and gullies which eons of monsoon rains had carved out of the hillside's downward descent to the Ganges River. But he found it—and this time, Atman was prepared. He descended into the gully with numerous digging tools in case the years, for whatever reason, had obstructed the passageway. The entrance to the cave had indeed been obstructed, and it took some time to clear it, but once he entered, he saw that the cave was precisely how he remembered it from decades past. Within several minutes, he found himself at the small, earthen entranceway to the inner sanctum of the djinn's resting place. He dropped to the floor and used his tools to widen the passage, and within an hour, Atman entered...

There on the altar was the answer—the solution to his deep grief. The oil lantern was resting, along with the useless brown feather, in the exact location he had left them. Without hesitation he grabbed the oil lantern, twisted its handle, and— immediately it sprang to life.

Djinn Brahman appeared and Atman, even in his distraught state, couldn't help but gasp at the djinn's other-worldly appearance. The infinite expanse of celestial bodies, which made up the djinn's *body*, shone with such living, breathing, three-dimensional precision that it seemed if Atman were to choose such a thing—he could fall into that celestial depth and slip away, lost forever, in another realm of time and space. It frightened him. The djinn spoke...

"Greetings, Atman. I am the Djinn Brahman and I grant you two wishes from my castle."

Atman had no time for folly this time around...

"My daughter—she was bitten and killed by a pit-viper a month ago. I had forgotten about...about this place—and *you!* Please...I beg you. *Oh, Great Djinn! Bring her back now!*"

The djinn, after listening to Atman's desperate lamentation, once again, in classic djinn fashion, crossed his arms and scowled deeply. "*Oh, Great Djinn!*...really? ...haven't seen you in...what!? Thirty-six years, four months, three days, eight hours, seventeen minutes, and..."

Djinn Brahman looked at his watch.

"...thirty-seven seconds!?...and this...*this*?...is how you greet me? Oh Atman, have you learned nothing? Have some respect for yourself, good man. It is *you* who wanted all this."

Atman looked aghast, irritated, and insulted. "I did not *want* any of this! I demand that you bring back my daughter—now! *You owe me a wish!*"

"Actually, I owe you *two* wishes. Clearly, you've forgotten protocol."

"Protocol? *Protocol!?* What idiocy is this!? Bring back my daughter this instant!"

"Oh, my, dear Atman, my very own self—you have grown into a cranky old man, have you not? All that wealth—all that opportunity, luxury, and security—*all of it*...and you don't seem any happier."

Atman collected himself, finally realizing the futility of arguing with the djinn. He was clearly outsized, outclassed, and coming very close to being *outwitted*—something Atman had no tolerance for in his old age. He collapsed to the ground.

157

"Great Djinn Brahman, please bring my daughter back." Atman spoke with sadness and defeat in his voice.

"I've told you before, my beloved Atman: the only *true wish* is to *return*...to Brahman."

"Yes, yes. Still I do not know what you mean, and I do not care. I simply want my daughter Sita back. Please! I beg you."

The djinn paused briefly before speaking.

"Is this what you truly desire, Atman?"

"Yes, it is—*with all my heart.*"

Djinn Brahman looked down upon Atman, taking in his sad, shell-of-a-human state, and had sympathy.

"Atman, you are my very self, and I cannot deny your wish. Repeat these words..." And the djinn spoke the magic words required for wishing. Afterward, the djinn rolled his arms fancifully and bowed his head and torso to Atman. Atman recalled the very same ridiculous gesture Djinn Brahman had made all those years ago and his heart sang with hope...

"Thank you, djinn!! Thank you!"

Atman then stood and returned a bowing, arm-waving curtsey and spoke, with tears in his eyes.

"*Oh, Great Djinn Brahman, grant me the wish that my daughter Sita comes back—alive—never bitten by that dreadful serpent. All of it—and Sita just as she was before!!*"

"Done," the djinn replied.

"Really!?" Atman had forgotten how simple the wish-granting process was. "That's it?"

"All is now as it was. Wish granted. But I must speak it again, because it is my heartfelt duty: the only *true wish is to return...to Brahman*." And with that, the djinn shape-shifted and vanished into his oil lantern.

Atman made his way out of the cave and back to the gully. He scrambled up the rocky embankment and then walked up the long hill back to his palace. The wish had indeed been granted. Greeting him at the gate was his daughter Sita.

"Father, where have you been? We have much to prepare. The wedding is a mere week away! And Lord Shiva! You decide, today of all days, to go off adventuring!"

Atman smiled and dropped to his knees. "Oh, Great Djinn! Thank you! Thank you! Thank you!" Atman got up, ran to his daughter, and hugged her like he was embracing the divine goddess herself...

Wish number three:

Another decade slipped by, and Atman was now fifty-five. His daughter Sita and her husband, the prince, bore him three grandchildren. Sita and her family lived in the palace, as was the usual custom. Atman's other children and their husbands and wives and all their grandchildren also lived in the palace.

Atman's life had become a constant stream of activity and busyness, all oriented around his familial tribe. There was an unending litany of celebrations, weddings, births, and rites-of-passage. All was happy and well in Atman's life. All was *very* happy, indeed...

Until of course, once again, it wasn't...

The pursuit of happiness is a mercurial beast that one can never quite completely tame, no matter how skilled one thinks they are at doing so. During the summer of Atman's fifty-fifth year, that beast grew weary of its sedate captivity and rebelled mightily, creating one final act of tragedy and turmoil in Atman's life.

The monsoon winds and subsequent rains arrived in June that year just as they had predictably done throughout Atman's entire life. Nothing about this season's rains portended anything particularly dramatic or unusual—but then most people aren't looking underground for portentous signs.

Rock fissures are hidden even if those fissures are right beneath one's feet. This was exactly the case with the fissure than ran the ground and stretched to its zenith at the top of the small mountain—the location of Atman's palace, town, and *his entire life*.

Over the years, with the monsoon's predictable rainfall, that underground fissure had grown and widened. This would be its final growing season. Like a hidden tumor finally ready to slay its host with a cancer that had set in years ago, it didn't take much. The monsoon rains arrived. The rains filled that fissure one final time, and, like the final breath of a dying, suffering beast, the fissure exhaled...and the life force within it completely collapsed.

It was 2:30 in the morning. Everyone was asleep. It happened so quickly—most were killed before waking. The side of the mountain gave way. The ensuing cacophonous, boulder-filled avalanche engulfed and collapsed the entire palace, most of the town, and a good portion of its roadways. Kanpur was no more. It lasted only a few minutes. By the end of the tragedy, those who hadn't died during the avalanche's downward descent drowned when they reached the river Ganges. It was mercifully quick, but brutally ruthless in its scope. Only a handful were spared, and Atman—much to his utter dismay—was one of them.

The ensuing days and weeks of Atman's life could not really be called *life*. It was just death...and death...and more death. He now lived behind a solid impenetrable wall of insurmountable grief. There really was no more Atman, as far as he was concerned, just as there was no more family, and no more palace, and no more town of Kanpur. It was all over, *he was over*...

Until he remembered...

He had one wish left!

If...he could get to it...

Could he?

Could...he...get...to...*that* wish?

He had to try.

So he did...

It took him three long, grueling months, but he did it. He got to that wish—and it *changed everything*.

Atman was thin, malnourished, unshaven, cloaked in rags, caked with mud, and bloody with the scrapes and wounds from the non-stop digging by the time he got near what he thought *might be* the vicinity of the cave.

He knew he had found it when, after having fallen through a hole and down twelve feet to the ground, he woke up from unconsciousness staring at an old, familiar brown feather. The oil lantern was still perched on its altar.

With what little energy he had left, Atman grabbed the oil lantern and turned the handle mechanism... The lantern sprang to life!

Atman collapsed to the ground again when the great Djinn Brahman appeared.

"Greetings, Atman. I am the Djinn Brahman, and I grant you one wish from my…"

The djinn paused and looked at Atman—a barely recognizable shell of his former self, bunched up in the fetal position on the ground.

"…castle. You look like cow dung, Atman! What in the name of Lord Shiva happened to you?"

"Wish…I want my last wish…" is all Atman could squeak out.

"My poor Atman?! Oh, dear goodness—what happened to your good soul? If only I could mend you, my poor, dear old self. Look at you! Miserable wretch. The things this dream does to my Atman… Dreadful. Delightful. Astonishing. Amazing. Have you had enough now, my Atman?"

"Wish… Last wish." Atman spoke barely audibly and then pushed himself up, leaning his frail body against the cave wall.

"Your wish is my command, Atman. What can I change? What can I give you this time around? You clearly have lost everything. Do you wish for it all back!?"

With that Atman screamed: "NO! I do *not* wish it all back! I wish none of it had ever been! I wish, I wish…to return to…"

"You wish to return to Brahman? Aha. I see," said the djinn. Then he paused. "Are you sure, Atman? This cannot be undone. There is no returning from this wish."

"Anything—*anything* is better than the torture I have suffered. I am done."

Djinn Brahman crossed his arms as he always did when serious. "Are you sure, Atman? You must be sure that you are done with the dream. Are you done with it?"

"I do not know what dream you speak of," Atman croaked out. "I only know that I am done with the pain...done with the loss...done with the triumph—and its inevitable opposite...failure. I am done. *Please! Please spare me this!*"

"Very well," said the djinn. "But you *must* say the words. My dear Atman, you must say the final words which will relieve you from this dream that has now soured into a nightmare."

Atman took a deep breath. He remembered those words—just as he remembered being a poor, small boy carrying water buckets on an old wooden yoke, toiling under their weight... just as he remembered the joy of getting married ...the joy of having children... ...of becoming raja... ...of becoming a grandfather. He remembered it all, and now it was all gone, and so was he. It was time.

"Oh—Great Djinn Brahman, grant me the wish of returning... to Brahman!"

"Done."

Atman waited. Nothing. He waited some more. Still nothing. He looked questioningly at the djinn.

"You must go outside. It will sting a little bit, but it will happen fast."

"Really?!" said Atman.

"Sorry..." said the djinn. "That's the way it works. See ya soon." And with that, Djinn Brahman shape-shifted once again and returned to the oil lantern. Then—the oil lantern vanished into thin air.

Out of the thin air, a knotted rope appeared from above. Atman stood up, and, with what little energy he had left, hauled himself up the rope and out into the light of day.

Atman stood blinking and squinting in the bright sunlight. Off in the distance, he saw what he thought was a large bird flapping its wings. But it was no bird...

Within seconds, something dreamed of only in myths and nightmares swooped down out of the sky. An unimaginably monstrous, black, shadowy dragon swooped down. Before Atman could flinch, the black wyvern breathed a volcano's worth of molten flame directly down on Atman's old, frail, thin, and worn-out body, evaporating him instantly.

The plot twist:

Atman opened his eyes. He was somewhere dark, but *exactly where*—he couldn't tell. He felt *different*. And he *looked* different, too! His appendages, what little he could see of them, were softly undulating and filled with a cosmos of stars, just as the djinn's had been! And then, he realized it: Yes*! It had all been a dream!* None of it real, at least from the point of view of his *Brahman* self. Then Atman turned and concentrated his attention and awareness on something very strange. Something *very strange* indeed...

A computer screen. A small room. Brightly lit. Fingers typing. Aware that his fingers are typing. Aware that words are being written; a book is being written...a book and a story about people, adventures, jeeps, iguanas, owls, a fable about an Indian man named Atman and a djinn who lives in an oil lamp. And then Atman refocuses. He is the reader of the book now...He sees *his* or *her* hands holding the book...aware of the words...aware of *himself*...aware of *herself*. Aware of the strange paradox that he is everyone, everything, and everywhere *all at once*. He is Brahman dreaming of Atman—dreaming of all Atmans, in all of time, in all of space. *Aware* that there never was an Atman. *Aware* that there never was a djinn. *Never was* an author. *Never was* a reader... Only the timeless ONE behind them all.

And in *that* moment, which is paradoxically also *this* moment, Atman dissolves into the singular, pure conscious nothingness of Brahman, because...

There is only ONE of us here!

There is only ONE of us here!

Yes, there is only one of us here.

Holy shit! I am that ONE! I am the Black Shadow! I am Cam. I am J. I am Hana. I am Rosie. I am YOU holding a book in hand!

Oh, FUCK! Holy Christ! God Almighty—I am NOT real. I am a character...in a book. I am fiction. I do NOT exist. I am a character...in a book! I am a character in the dream book of... of...Brahman!

Do you get it now?

It's me again—the Djinn Brahman, who lives trapped in the oil lantern of *your* heart.

I am here waiting for you...

I am here waiting for you to discover me—your true Brahman self...

I am here waiting for you to say those magic words...

"Oh, Great Djinn Brahman! Grant me the wish of returning..."

Wake up, Atman! *You are dreaming...*

Wake up, J.! *You are dreaming...*

Wake up, beloved reader! *You are dreaming...*

There is only ONE of us here!

Wake up...Wake up...Wake up...

...and Know Thyself.

And with that, Atman finally understood: To return to Brahman is the only...true wish.

The End.

CHAPTER 13
SPIRITUAL HANGOVER

How to deal with radical shifts of identity and reality

I know I just unloaded a whole lotta poetic, allegorical, and story-telling metaphor in your lap, so allow me, please, if you would, to briefly unload some *for-reals* on you...

No—dragons did not incinerate my soul or ego. And no—I've never met Brahman or Atman or any other character from the Bhagavad Gita. But yes—I did go through a spiritual awakening that revealed my true self, and, if I could describe that experience using a single phrase, it would be this: *Meeting fear with awareness.*

Briefly—because I could write a whole *other* book about this event—here's what happened in prosaic, brown paper bag, layman's terms:

I'd been chewing on the *Know Thyself* bone for quite some time... (like maybe fifteen years). I'd done *pretty much* everything taught and suggested in *Book One* and in *this* book: I paid attention. I became self-aware. I became mindful. I understood the nasty *and beneficial* bits about my ego, mind, and personality. I smoked some pot and, of course, tried a few psychedelics. I also did some yoga and meditation, read a ton of spiritual books, and probably most importantly—hung out with a bunch of *Know Thyself* teachers and authors. I did retreats and workshops with them. I met them in their homes and hometowns. I invited and hosted them to teach in my home and hometown. I went canoeing down rivers with them. I smoked cigarettes and drank beer with them. (Contrary to what most people think about spiritual teachers, once you get to know them, like me, most of them aren't prudes.)

Long story short: I did a shit-ton of spiritual things that led up to a ten day "event" that took place in late August / early September of 2004. It's difficult to put into words the exact unfolding process that happened to me, but I'm the blabbering, fool-of-a-took (Thanks J. R. R. Tolkien) spiritual author, so I should probably try...

Spiritual breakthroughs, *Aha* moments, or gestalts almost never happened to me while I was busy doing, you know, spiritual shit. So, it was no surprise that while drinkin' beer and swimming with friends at a local quarry, my brain decided to split open and allow the full and mighty power of bodily-being-awareness-presence to flood it.

That description pretty much sums up one half of what this experience felt like: I went from being a meek, demure Clark Kent to a full-on fearless Superman. It felt like an entire heretofore hidden, unused ganglia of critical, neural brain pathways had suddenly come online. They simply woke up...causing me...to *wake up* and experience absolute undifferentiated, non-dual awareness and presence. Time stopped. There was only now...and the next now...and the next now...

It was fucking, goddamned amazing and *bizarre*. I was flabbergasted and thunderstruck. Spiritual awakening was *not at all* the thing I had imagined, fantasized, or thought it to be. Spiritual awakening was not *out there*—it was *right here*, in this very flawed body and mind I had so desperately, during my whole grand spiritual adventure, tried to change or escape.

Like a drunk schizophrenic on a roller coaster ride, I also experienced a deep, raw, heart-pounding, existential *fear*, the likes of which I had never experienced. My neocortex and amygdala were furious: *You fucking dumbass. Just had to go poking your nose into Smog's Lonely Mountain layer! Now that giant fire-breathing beast has smelled your putrid, fear-ridden, human form—and you will be incinerated and eaten for breakfast!* Something like that—some fear you just can't quantify on a scale of one to ten.

This shit went on for about ten days. It was a maddening, washing machine mix of spiritual sanity and insanity. I had sleepless nights. I had moments of abject fear. I had moments of divine bliss. These events occurred in my home, in the grocery store, in my car, and on the toilet seat. Some days were quiet and peaceful; others were a cacophony of intolerable, high-decibel madness.

I tried to speak with friends, relatives, and even some of my spiritual teachers about all of this—but my brain was too far gone—and my *being*, too much on fire. No one could help me or offer an iota of useful advice. I was on my own. I asked for this shit, so I badassed up, accepted the situation as best I could, and tenuously held onto what tiny, little puffballs of sanity I could call my own.

After the ten-day period, the ride got smoother, and, believe it or not, about a month later—a true testament to the tenacious, super-glue power of ego—I was my old, miserable, unhappy self again. Of course, this wasn't the end of my spiritual journey. That swan song would arrive several years later, but this *had been* my first real encounter with spiritual awakening—and what a doozey it had been.

So, let's end the *for-reals* here. I have a lot more of them, of course, but you're paying for *the story*, not just my own personal, blathering memoir.

And *the story* just reached *its* doozey point...

It's the next day. You slept fitfully, and you have a whopper of a spiritual hangover. Still lying in bed, you're writing in your journal...

Hangover? Maybe that's not the right term for this...A fifth of tequila and an ass-whoopin'? Yeah, closer... Insanity...? Ahh, there we go...spiritual insanity.

This is weird—like looking at the world—at reality— through an entirely different lens. Never thought awareness, spaciousness, consciousness...what should I call it?...could feel like this—so close and intimate.

In my bones. In my head. In my emotions. Presence. In everything I see, touch, and experience. I'm not just in it. I don't just <u>have</u> it. IT has me. I am IT. IT is me. Fuck, fuck, fuck, fuck...why is this so maddeningly difficult?

I am struggling here. New feet. New hands. New eyes. New ears. New lungs.

Ego. Separation. Contraction. Holy shit! See it very clearly in others. Avoidance of eye contact. Lost in my head. Lost in thought. Rambling. Hurting. Crazy.

Presence kills all that. Presence is slow, vulnerable, open, here, now, open, spacious. Fuuuuuuck. What have I done?

Feel like I am living life in first gear—with access to all gears and speeds. Before, only one gear—fifth. Speeding. All the time...

There's a knock at the door. It's J. He has a vague sense that you went through something last night, but you never filled him in on the details. You know he's just checking in on you.

"You doin' okay in there?"

"*Gimme a sec... Is it time for breakfast?*" You look at your phone and see that it's past 9 a.m. "*Oh, shit—be right out.*"

"All good. Morning, Sunshine. You hungry?"

"*Yeah... Let me shower up and get my head on straight.*"

"I'll wait."

You put your journal down, get out of bed, and hop in the shower. The warm water feels good, even though it only surface splashes the oceanic abyss of your spiritual hangover.

You and J. say little as you head over to the dining hall. You find seats quickly and get down to business. Once you've eaten something and taken the edge off your hangover, you relax. Your hands palm the warm surface of the coffee cup that sits on the table in front of you.

"So—what's up, Kemosabe?" J. questions me.

"*Is it that obvious?*"

"Written in black Sharpie on your forehead. I know you went through something last night. Still stewing over it?"

"*Stewing's not the right word. I'm on fire.*"

"Oh—okay. Is that good?"

"*Good and bad. Feels like I'm in a deep, primal sobering truth hole. Everything is crawling, heavy, and present—blissful and horrible at the same time. I'm astounded, actually—that is, if what I'm experiencing is what you call spiritual awakening.*" You explain and look at J., questioning.

J. pauses and reflects. "Well, let's see. Feeling astounded is *not* atypical."

"*And, and...that Black Shadow thing or person or—in this case, dragon—also showed up.*"

"Last night?"

"*Yes, last night. And just rocked me to the core. ...was absolutely terrified and horrified.*"

"Ah, yes. Part of it."

"*So...*" You pause, take a sip of coffee, and feel yourself falling, this time refreshingly into the *calmer* depths of the sobering truth presence. "*...so, is it always this maddeningly difficult?*"

"Yes!" J. says emphatically, without skipping the slightest beat.

"*Yay for me! Progress, I suppose.*"

"It is progress! Our last serious conversation was about spiritual flatlining, and now you're confessing that you've had an awakening. That's awesome! And yeah, this shit is difficult." J. pauses and looks you directly in the eyes. "Here's why: I may not need to tell you this, but spiritual realization or spiritual awakening is the *ultimate unexpected twist* in most spiritual badass adventures. Your mind imagined one thing and what you get instead is something entirely different—and not just *next town* over different, but *next galaxy* over different. So yeah, this stuff is inevitably disconcerting...and shocking, even."

You breathe and allow what J. just said to ripen. "*Reminds me of an Agatha Christie novel or an M. Night Shyamalan movie.*"

"Yes. I see dead people, and you're dead! And—holy shit! It was the church pastor who committed those murders! I did *not* see that coming. So think about it! How cool is the twist!? Movies or books with no twists and plot turns—that are completely predictable—ya know...*suck*. Right?"

You nod. "*Agreed. This makes for an epic story, but still, it hurts—because I'm the goddamned protagonist.*"

"Yes! But...I'm here with you, and so is Cam, and so are all the other travelers, teachers, and guides you've met and will meet along the way. We keep you on track. That's our role. We can't and won't stop the Black Shadow antagonist super villain monster from getting to you, but we can warn you of its whereabouts, advise you on how to do battle with it, and—when it arrives—shout words of encouragement to you from the sidelines."

J. pauses, then continues with a twinkle in his eyes.

"I mean shit, what would *Lord of the Rings* be without Mordor or Sauron? Just a bunch of cosplay nerds hiking across the New Zealand plateaus. Kinda cool—but, um, kinda lame also."

"*Is what I'm experiencing spiritual awakening?*"

"I would guess so—yes. Based on your description, you just experienced your first glimpse of non-abiding awakening."

"*Non-abiding?*"

"It means now ya got it—and now ya don't. Most spiritual awakening unfolds this way…in caustic, starting and stopping coughing fits—like a flooded car engine that turns over but won't run smoothly or steadily. This phase can go on for years. Mine did."

"*Years?!*"

"Yep. But it's different for everybody. …can't predict how long it will take for you. Maybe years; maybe months. I doubt days—but ya never know."

"*Ya. Fucking. Hoo.*"

"Oh, and it's also quite common during this phase to experience all sorts of overly dramatic, sometimes ridiculous…shall we say…plot themes? Like, um, dragons and black shadows. If you were the religious type, Beelzebub himself would probably be getting involved."

"*Beelzebub!?*" You guffaw loudly. "*The fucking devil?*"

"The one and only. I wrestled with him on more than one occasion during my own dark-night-of-the-soul, non-abiding awakening phase. Absurd!? Right!?"

J. pauses, takes a deep breath, and slows the pacing and tone of his delivery way down…

"Eventually you'll come to realize, like a weary soldier surmising the battlefield from afar, that there isn't a single part of this whole goddamned *thing* that *isn't* absurd."

You rest in silence for a few beats and then reply, "*By thing, you mean life…*"

J. interrupts, "…and death and birth and spirituality and enlightenment and God and awakening and all of it. The whole…damn…thing."

"*I'd like to take a pill, please—to make this thing go faster and smoother.*"

J. gets animated again. "Ha! Sure—and there's a phone app that'll do the same thing. My advice: Get used to it. You signed up for this *and* the spiritual hangover you have right now…"

You chuckle. "*Hangover. That's what I called it in my journal.*"

"That spiritual hangover is the price you pay to enter the *adult* section of the human amusement park…where only fully awake, fully aware, and fully responsible spiritual badasses hang out. It's the price we all pay."

"*The ticket's expensive.*"

"Very. It will bankrupt you completely. Nothing left." J. pauses and holds his index finger up for emphasis. "…except…"

You interrupt him. "*Let me guess. Except for Brahman.*"

"Damn! How'd you know I was going to say that?!"

"*There's only one of us here. Cam told me that last night. That's what the Black Shadow keeps telling me. I looked up the name Brahman online. Brahman is also Lord Krishna from the Bhagavad Gita, apparently.*"

"Yeah. I was going to mention Brahman because I was just perusing that copy of the Bhagavad Gita in our room. Did you see it on the shelf? Not my teaching cup of tea or lingo, of course, but I won't argue the point. I have found it to be strangely true. Right now, for instance, from Brahman's point of view, I'm just talking to myself. Fuckin' bizarre, right? There's only *one* of us here."

"*I think 'fucking bizarre' sums it up nicely—yes.*"

"Well, don't worry, my friend; that realization and $3.45 will buy you a Grande Dark Roast at Starbucks. Speakin' of which, I need a refill." J. shakes his coffee cup. "...you good? I mean with the whole spiritual awakening hangover thingy?"

"*I'm good. Thanks, J.*"

"You're most welcome—Atman." J. winks at you as he says this, gets up from the table, and heads over to the breakfast bar to replenish his coffee.

You sit, contemplating Atman, Brahman, black shadows, dragons, spiritual awakening, and other frivolous, world-shattering shit. Mostly, though—you're wondering what unexpected plot twist will take place *next* in your story...

I mean, ultimately, I'm just a made-up character in a book. How could it get any twistier than that?

That afternoon, you attend Rosie's burial at the small family graveyard located near the walking maze. Rosie had requested Lenny's presence, so you and J. were happily invited to the service. It's a diminutive gathering attended by a fellowship of mostly family and close friends, many of whom you don't recognize. There's an elderly pastor, dressed in traditional black and white garb, officiating the burial.

It's evident that this event will not be on par with last night's raucous bonfire. That was Rosie's wilder-side-of-life send-off celebration—for friends. Today's burial is more traditional and suited to her conservative family. You're fine with this. You've had all the bonfire dragons you can take in the last twenty-four-hours. You're happy not to flirt with shadowy things for a spell.

But *there are* shadowy things... It's just that in your current semi-awakened, sobering truth depth, you're seeing those shadowy things *in others*. Your calm, still presence has a two-fold effect:

For those *not* in their hearts, you very clearly see the unconscious shutdown and tightly closed side effects of their egoic fear, isolation, and contraction. They avoid your steady, calm gaze and open state at all costs. They shun any sustained eye contact, real conversation, or meaningful engagement; the light is too bright for their own shadowy undealt-with emotions and issues. Their internal suffering may as well be announced on a roadside billboard. It's that evident to you.

For those *in* their hearts, your open-eyed, vulnerable, energetic disposition is welcoming and inviting, for both you and them. They accept your unconscious invitation to be present and aware, and somehow it seems an unspoken bond is formed. These are people on the path, not bereft of love or light; people, perhaps, who have done a little of their own internal exploration.

The funeral-burial unfolds in the same way that so many do: Solemn words are spoken. Prayers are invoked. Token platitudes are tossed about—and then it's over, as quickly as it began. It's a bit of a shock compared to last night's event, but you understand the need for it.

What speaks to you the most and has almost zero to do with the burial proceedings is this idea of "being your heart." You've heard this term bandied around the halls of New Age spirituality for so long that it never held any serious weight with you. But today, because of the non-abiding awakened state you find yourself in, as J. called it, you have a profound, clear, and tacit understanding of what this phrase actually means.

Being in your heart…?

Until one's heart opens, you think, as you watch the ornate, glossy, black casket being lowered into the ground, *…one can never quite know or even possibly imagine just how severely closed off it had been.*

What a genuine gift it is to realize the open heart.

What a genuine gift…

You look off into the distance. You see storm clouds gathering, boiling, and looming on the horizon. You reflect on the day that's ending. You recall your earlier conversation with J. about characters, books, and plot twists…

Portents and omens?

Ominous dark brewing clouds?

Oh, fuck.

What does that shit mean?

Me again.

Yes, yes—I might well be a made-up character in this story—but I can and will *certainly do* as I see fit—and when I see fit. For instance, dear reader, I do believe this is the first instance you've heard from me, your own Black Shadow self, *outside* of the strict narrative timeline…Yes?

Let's get one thing straight, shall we? Fuck restrictions. Fuck the timeline, and fuck your expectations. If you can't do that within the context of a book, then just how in the hell do you expect to break free from the restricted context of your own life? Ponder that one. A hard-earned lesson in my own case...

It's now been over a week since Rosie's death and the night of the mighty bonfire dragon with Cam and friends...

Oh, what a week it's been.

In many ways, it was my own fault...poor Lenny. Poor, poor Lenny! I am so, so sorry.

It was my own...damn...fault.

Poor Lenny.

END PART 2

Don't Just Read About it.

Experience It.

This is your invitation to a whole new world badass.
There's a life-changing *experience* waiting for you online. Something you've been longing and waiting for *your whole life*. You ready? Of course you are…

Go here:
www.spiritualityforbadasses.com

PART 3

Vegas Washing Machine

CHAPTER 14
MESCALINE MEDICINE

How to vomit up the cosmos

You probably picked up *Spirituality for Badasses*, in part, because of the secondary subtitle: *The ultimate spiritual but-not-religious book.*

As you've no doubt noticed, and perhaps been flummoxed by, there's been an awful lot of talk and writing recently about this idea of there being just "one." And you just might be thinking, *Shit man, that smells an awful lot like religion.* And to that I would have to say—Yep, my bad.

Honestly, I don't quite know what to do about this. It's called pantheism: The belief that there's just one "thing" happening here and it's all taking place in and as that "thing." I'm paraphrasing here to save you from a massive headache: Google pantheism -nonduality-advaita and you'll trip down a semantic rabbit hole, the likes of which you're not likely to return from any time soon.

The belief that there is only *one* god, *one* way, or *one* truth is exactly the type of supercilious religious hoopla that a book called *Spirituality for Badasses* should be railing against, and, I might add, those types of beliefs are probably something you abandoned 119 exits and 500 miles ago. *How about something a little less rigid, without so many definitions, rules, or regulations...?* is probably what you were thinking when you lost or were in the process of losing your religion. *How about something that just makes me feel a little better—and the world a little lighter?* Yeah, exactly.

And now I've gone and fucked all that up for you. What are we to do about this?

I suggest these five simple tenets as a remedy to all the recent *I'm one–You're one–We're all one with everyone–Rah, Rah, Sis-Boom-Bah.*

Tenet One: *No Apologies*

I'm just relaying the spiritual badass process as it unfolded in my own case. That unfolding led to the recognition of the one dreamer who is dreaming this dream. If that unfolding had led to the realization that I was a leprechaun who enjoyed riding unicorns bareback and chasing rainbows through fields of golden yellow daisies, buck-naked—well, then that's what I'd write about. (That scenario is not entirely off the table, btw.)

Honestly and without drama, I offer no apologies because, well—who gives a fuck? So what if I've recognized the dreamer who is pissing this whole reality out? As written in Chapter 13, that recognition and $3.45 will get you a Grande Dark Roast at Starbucks. Congrats. *Methinks you can now take out the trash.*

Tenet Two: *Something's True Here—Extrapolate*

Attention. Awareness. Mindfulness. Ego. Meeting fear. Discovering that part of you which is untouched by fear. Recognizing your true aware self. Some part of this journey must be ringing true.

Therefore, it's not heresy, gullibility, or stupidity to do some basic extrapolation here: If all that shit about the nature and power of awareness is true, then how far-fetched is to surmise that the origins of awareness are from a singular unitive pool? *Methinks it's not that far.*

Tenet Three: *Perennial Philosophy*

My friend, in case you hadn't realized it, you're dabbling in the dark arts. The underlying foundation of every mystical school in the halls of perennial philosophy is the monad: the one, singular, original substance (usually consciousness) from which all other things are born.

Primary colors are a good metaphor here: Three colors—red, blue, and yellow—give birth to over ten million other colors detectable by the human eye. Systems, groups, and hierarchies almost *always* rest upon solid, simple foundations. *Methinks reality is no different.*

Tenet Four: *I Never Said Religion Was Bereft of Truth*

I never really said much about religion at all, actually. I'm just not a fan. I think all religions carry some seeds of truth, of course, but the obligatory swamp crawling needed to get to those seeds, in my asshole opinion, *sucks*. I'm also not a fan of exclusivity, which most religions push as if life, reality, and the human experience can be summed up in one singular book or creed and there ya go—live your life by it. One book or creed? Seriously? I prefer the whole damn library, thank you very much.

So—might I suggest that you take this same approach with this book? *Spirituality for Badasses* is just one very irreverent, opinionated voice. Read, study, and experience other voices; other books!—many other books! Draw your own conclusions. *Methinks the library is vast.*

Tenet Five: *Stick to Your Guns*

Contrary to the old cliché, "when meeting the Buddha on the road," you actually need *not* kill him. In other words, you can still go to church or temple. You can still be Christian, Hindu, Buddhist, Jewish, or Atheist and be objectively spiritual. No problem. (I'm not saying this is easy, but it can be done.) *Methinks you should just be authentically you.*

There you have it.

Hopefully this shotgun blasts some holes in all the "one" spiritual talk I've been layin' down and retains the integrity of a book that claims to be *the ultimate spiritual but not religious book*.

But—this doesn't mean I'm gonna stop talkin' or writin' about this theme 'cause fact is—my personal investigative experience in these matters has *not* revealed a multitude of buck-naked dancing and prancing leprechauns at the end of a rainbow. I only found *one* leprechaun, my friend—and both you and I *are it*.

> "Swing low, sweet chariot
> Coming for to carry me home,
> Swing low, sweet chariot,
> Coming for to carry me home."

The leprechaun asked that I include that quote in this section of the book. ...no clue why. Sometimes I just don't even ask.

Now, where were we?

"Welcome to Fabulous Las Vegas, Nevada."

If there was ever a sign absolutely destined to be the poster child of all impending apocalypses, in whatever asteroid-smashing, zombie-walking, or dinosaur-stomping apocalyptic format we may desire—the iconic, 1959 *Welcome to Fabulous Las Vegas, Nevada* sign, located south of town on Las Vegas Boulevard, is unquestionably *it*.

And—after two and a half days of driving (which J. did indeed share), J. added another superfluous forty-five minutes to the trip on the Las Vegas bypass just so you could see the damn thing as you entered the city.

"When the end comes, that sign will be all that is left of civilization," J. comments with a smile.

"This place is like one giant, loud, tacky, mini-golf course," you reply.

"Yep. Welcome to Mt. Vesuvius Mini-Golf—on steroids. Love it or hate it, but you can't deny it. Viva Las Vegas, baby! Viva Las Vegas." J. chuckles as he drives the Jeep with the windows wide open along the Las Vegas strip.

It's been three days since your last morning of farewells at Samsara Farm...

Much of the experience there lingers in your heart and bones but, to your vast disappointment, much of it *does not*. The landscape en route seems to have dictated the change: The Colorado Rockies complimented the stunning grandeur and height of your first spiritual awakening experience. For days, your heart sang an open song as magnificent as the passing mountains. Free of worries, mind, and stress—you experienced an unencumbered state of deep, sublime, happy presence—something you could never have imagined possible.

And then, as the landscape transformed into something deader, flatter, and more barren—so did your heart. The Utah desert and now this loud, man-made behemoth called Las Vegas have all but killed that free, open song. You're back to your old, flat, normal, ego self. Yuck.

The sensory overload that Las Vegas now assaults you with doesn't help matters either. J. senses your deflation.

"The first time is always the hardest. Has the high totally worn off?"

"For the most part."

"I feel ya. It sucks. Nothing you can do about it. It'll return. And then you'll lose it again—and then it'll return again. Back and forth. Up and down."

"Washing machine, I think you said."

In a singsong fashion, J. bellows, "Welcome my friend...to the machine."

"*I think Pink Floyd was referring to a machine of another sort.*"

"What are the badass rules?"

"*Say yes to awareness and yes to the fear.*"

"And...?"

"*Be aware of the shitty feelings. Thank the shitty feelings.*"

"The shitty feelings are..."

"*...a doorway. I know.*"

"You got this. Now relax. It's Vegas! Trust me. My friend Emmitt has hooked us up."

J. slow crawls the entire Vegas strip so you can gawk. There's no end to the bombastic insanity of the whole thing: The Luxor, The MGM Grand, New York-New York, The Aria, The Bellagio, Caesar's Palace, The Eiffel Tower—on and on it goes, one extravagant, themed, behemoth hotel after another. There are people—tourists, businessmen, businesswomen, call girls, street performers, vendors, the homeless, and more—milling on the sidewalks and in the streets everywhere. Taxis dart in and out of traffic lanes. Buses packed with hordes of tourists lumber up and down the thoroughfare loading and unloading passengers. Horns are honking. Music is blaring. You can even hear the distant singsong, cha-ching-ching chatter of slot machines as you pass casinos with open doors. It's orchestrated mayhem and simultaneously in some odd, Faustian way—fantastically, out-of-this-world, charming, and enticing.

Even a deaf person would consider this loud, you think.

Finally, J. pauses the Jeep at a stoplight in front of a massive hotel complex located off to your left. He points out the window with his free hand and exclaims. "*That* is where *we're* stayin!"

You look out the Jeep window, past a large, blue lagoon festooned with palm trees and an island volcano. *Oh crap, not a volcano again,* you think. You peer up and into the vast Nevada skyline and read the massive billboard plastered upon the upper windows of the hotel.

"The Beatles. LOVE. By Cirque du Soleil"

Next to it is the hotel's name.

"*Wow!*" you exclaim. "*We're stayin' at The frickin' Mirage!?*"

"The frickin' Mirage indeed. …told you Emmitt hooked us up."

"*Who is this Emmitt I need to thank!?*"

"He works security there."

"Well, that makes sense. How in the world do you know this guy?"

"Emmitt's Hualapai Indian. He's a shaman-in-training, I think. I did a sweat lodge with his uncle a long time ago."

"*Wow.*"

"Yep. Emmitt's a total spiritual badass. This is going to be amazing."

"*I have no doubt.*"

Oh-hi.

Let's just skip the hotel check-in shit, shall we? And the part where we first meet this Emmitt dude. I mean—you know the drill. He's J.'s friend. He's cool. He's got some Native American spiritual street cred and all that. What say ye?

Shall we just skip right to the part where shit goes sideways...?

That's a rhetorical question. You really have no say in the matter. It's all been decided for you. So...

Sit back.

Relax.

And enjoy.

Let's go here:

You're nervous and stressed out as you make your way through the back streets of this part of town. It was J.'s idea to rent e-scooters. You'd never been on an e-scooter in your life and here you are, Day Two in Vegas, slightly hungover from tequila shots with J. at the bar last night, navigating sidewalks and alleyways in a totally foreign town on totally foreign transportation—if that's what you could call this. E-scooters are deceptively tricky bitches.

"Come on! Come on, slowpoke!" J. shouts to you looking over his shoulder as he navigates another street crosswalk. "GPS says it's just a few blocks from here."

You scramble to follow without spilling, bumping, ramming, knocking, or a myriad number of other less than desirable outcomes on the cursed thing. *What the hell was J. thinking?*

But more than him, you're cursing *yourself* for saying yes to Emmitt's invitation....and not just the invitation to visit his home Hualapai Indian reservation and participate in a sweat lodge ceremony, but to do so with the very specific requirements of having acclimated to the "medicine." The

189

"medicine" meaning Mescaline—the psychoactive hallucinogen gleaned from the peyote cactus.

Apparently, Emmitt's uncle, Kuruk, is the ceremonial gatekeeper of such things and is meeting you, J., and Emmitt this morning at his Native American antiquities shop on the west side of town. You're anxious, to say the least. This shit is *way* outside your comfort zone.

"This is just a test run. You realize this, right? A very small microdose to see if it gels with you…" J. told you this last night at the bar. "Totally legal. The Hualapai have religious sacrament usage rights. So—nothing to worry about."

But you *are* worried. The bowling ball-sized stress knot in your stomach is sloshing around as you zip from street corner to street corner on the e-scooter. You can't imagine taking a more uncomfortable mode of transportation to get to your Mescaline "medicine" date.

J. finally stops on his e-scooter and points to the sign above his head. You roll up and read it: *The Navajo Feather Antiquities and Art Shop.* You've arrived. *Thank* God, you ruminate, *that was torture.*

You dismount from the e-scooter and park it next to J.'s. J. opens the door for you and you both enter. The door activates some sort of chime heard storewide. You're pleased—and actually *relieved*—to see a beautifully well-lit and laid out retail store filled with a cornucopia of Native American art and artifacts. Everything is kept on clean, uniformly sized and colored shelves, or behind locked glass counters. Artwork of all types hangs on the walls. You see paintings, dream catchers, kachina dolls, earthenware, jewelry made from silver and turquoise, a collection of gorgeously ornamented knives, leather clothing items, and a variety of statuette knickknacks whose use is probably more form than function. You're *relieved* because the place looks *professional.* You hope this foreshadows the experience you're about to have.

Emmitt strolls in from the back, his six-foot three stature and long black hair an odd juxtaposition to the nerdy black glasses resting on the bridge of his nose. He's wearing the same black slacks and white collared shirt he wore at the hotel casino last night. Today his hair is down and loose, which makes him look even nerdier. You like him even more this way. There's a big cuddly teddy bear quality to his persona, so it's no surprise when you hear an older, gruffer voice from the back shout out "Little Bear! ...they here?"

"It's them," Emmitt replies. "Howdy, guys."

Emmitt walks up to J. and, once again, oddly out of character and appearance, fist-bumps J. He does the same to you. *How many shamans greet you with a fist bump*? you think.

"You guys like my uncle's shop? Nice, huh?"

"Indeed. Beautiful..." J. responds, and you nod in agreement.

A few seconds later an older, greyer, more dilapidated version of Emmitt, probably in his late sixties, walks into the room. He's wearing jeans, a bright blue turquoise colored t-shirt, and a white Stetson hat. His long grey hair is tied in a ponytail and rests on his strong, muscular back. This guy clearly has no problem assuming the mantle and appearance of a modern, elderly Native American. He wears it well.

"Welcome friends. I'm Kuruk. Little Bear—my nephew Emmitt here—tells me you're seeking medicine initiation for a sweat."

"Yes sir," J. replies.

"Both of you?" Kuruk asks.

Emmitt interjects. "Not my friend J. He's initiated. Remember the spring ceremony during the big flood six or seven years past?"

"Long time." Kuruk looks at J. "Right. I remember you now. That was a strong sweat. You handled it...not so well."

"Yeah, I was pretty green," J. responds.

"Yes. Big green face as I recall..." Kuruk smiles. "Lots of puking." Kuruk looks at you. "And you? Sweat lodge ever?"

"No sir," you reply.

Kuruk pauses before speaking again; then he smiles. "You both call me Kuruk, okay? Follow me to the back. Little Bear, lock the shop door, and place the Lunch Hour sign out."

Emmitt nods silently and heads to the front door. You and J. follow Kuruk to the back of the store. You head down a long hallway. Kuruk stops and opens a nondescript door, and all three of you enter. The dimly lit room you enter contrasts sharply to the main shop. It takes a moment for your eyes to adjust...

There's an abundance of plush furniture and artwork in the room, giving the space a warm, soft ambience. Two giant-sized, six-foot tall Kachina doll totem statues, however, define the room: They look like Native American gargoyles of some sort, each with fierce, toothy growls or grins. On the center rug at ground level is what appears to be the initiation space. It's surrounded by a plethora of soft, earth-toned Back Jacks, pillows, and blankets. There's a small table with an abundance of candles and sacred looking items resting on it—a rattle, a small drum, an antler, and half a dozen brown pottery mugs. Kuruk gestures to you and J. to have a seat on the floor. You do so, grabbing the nearest Back Jack and claiming a spot. Kuruk lights several candles. Emmitt enters the room.

"All set, Little Bear?" Kuruk looks at Emmitt.

"Locked up." Emmitt takes a seat next to you and J.

You're extremely nervous now and remember J.'s famous words. "Say yes to the fear and yes to awareness."

No different here, you think. *I got this. I got this...*

Kuruk announces the ceremony with little fanfare. "Let's begin."

So—yeah, you knew this was comin': Just a quick badass check-in before we proceed here. I'd like to take a moment to preface this whole experience and make sure you know where it *and* I are coming from: Relax—nothing serious or dire here; just a respectful setup that I think the use of psychedelic hallucinogens for spiritual purposes deserves.

For Native Americans the use of Peyote-Mescaline is a sacred act reserved for sacred occasions, and for *spiritual badasses,* it will also be treated as such. A few simple things to consider...

One: What you're about to read here is a fictionalized amalgamation of experiences I've had over the years with various psychedelics under a variety of circumstances. I've participated in sweat lodge ceremonies both formal and informal. I've ingested psychedelics both formally and informally. I've done this type of thing alone and in group settings. And—I've done all this stuff enough to know that no two experiences, settings, or ceremonies are *ever* the same. So—*mea culpa* if the ceremonial aspects of this account don't jive with what you may know or with what you may have experienced. There are five-hundred and seventy-four federally recognized Indian Nations in the United States—tribes, nations, bands, pueblos, communities, and native villages—and each of them has distinct ways of practicing similar ceremonies.

Two: I wholeheartedly condone the safe, *adult* use of natural plant-based psychedelics (Mescaline, Psylocibin, Ayahuasca, and Salvia Divinorum in particular) for spiritual practice and growth. I don't condone the hedonistic partying use of these psychedelics at all. I don't condone the use of psychedelics without proper guidance, right intention, and a positive setting. I'm all about using these "medicines" for healing, insight, and growth, but distinctly *not* about using them at parties or nightclubs. (Burning Man burn-outs—I'm talking to you.) Yeah, I'm an old-school fuddy-duddy when it comes to this shit. Deal.

Three: If you're squeamish, righteous, indignant, and/or repulsed by the use of ceremonial hallucinogens—well, um, then ya might wanna rethink this whole "I'm a spiritual badass" thing. …'cause if you can't handle a few mind-altering substances granted by Mother Nature herself, ain't no friggin' way you're gonna tolerate having your head, heart, ego, and entire being split open and torn to shreds by the cosmos itself. Just a thought.

Okay. Let's proceed…

Kuruk laughs as he speaks. "You *know*—this is *not* the sweat. This is just the medicine initiation for the sweat. Yes?"

"We know," J. replies.

You chime in simultaneously: "*I know.*"

"Good. Making sure. Some greenies think *this* is the sweat. This ceremony is just to see if the medicine accepts you." Kuruk looks directly at J. "Been a while. You gonna take the medicine today?"

"Yes."

"Good." Kuruk points to Emmitt. "Little Bear will be your chaperone today once the medicine enters you. Okay?"

Emmitt nods his head affirmatively; so do you and J.

Kuruk picks up the rattle. Emmitt picks up the small drum. They both begin chanting, using the instruments to accent the chant. It's in a language you don't understand, but the gist of it is haunting and beautiful. You see that J. has closed his eyes. You do the same. The rhythm of the drum and rattle create a soft, buzzing meditative state. You occasionally peek through open eyelids and see Kuruk and Emmitt swaying their bodies. You do the same and soon you're lost in the gentle incantation. It's completely foreign to you, but also somehow deeply familiar and comforting.

The chant comes to a slow, quiet conclusion. Kuruk reaches under the table and pulls out a small Tupperware container of milky liquid. He arranges three of the earthen pottery mugs for use. Emmitt begins drumming to a new rhythm, a little slower—more intentional. Kuruk matches his pacing with spoken words:

"To the four directions..."

"Great Spirit who comes out of the East, come to us with the power of the East. We are thankful for the light of the rising sun. Let there be light on the path we walk. Let us remember always to be thankful that you give the gift of a new day."

Kuruk pauses and pours the milky tea into the first mug, then speaks again. "We offer this sacrament." Kuruk takes the rattle and shakes it over his own body. He continues...

"Spirit of creation, we turn to the South. We are thankful that you send us warm and soothing winds from the South to comfort us and caress us when we are tired and cold. Unfold us as your gentle breezes unfold the leaves on the trees. May we be grateful and grow close to you."

Kuruk pauses and pours the milky tea into the second mug and speaks again. "We offer this sacrament." Kuruk takes the rattle and shakes it over J.'s body. He continues...

"Great Life-giving Spirit, we face the West, the direction of sundown. Let us remember every day that the moment will come when our own sun will go down. Give us beautiful color; give us a great sky for setting, so that when it is time to meet you, we may come with strength and courage."

Kuruk pours the milky tea into the final mug and speaks again. "We offer this sacrament." Kuruk takes the rattle and shakes it over your body. He continues...

"Great Spirit of Love, come to us with the power of the North. Make us courageous when the cold winds of life fall upon us. Give us strength and endurance for everything that is harsh, hurts, and makes us squint. Let us move through life ready to take what comes from the North."

"Everyone may drink the sacrament."

Kuruk hands both you and J. your individual mugs. Kuruk takes his and puts it to his mouth. You and J. do the same. It's bitter and sweet at the same time. *Not half bad,* you think. Then the bitterness really kicks in and you nearly gag. You look to see if J. drinks all of his. He does.

You follow suit—very slowly you ingest the warm, milky tea. Almost instantly it upsets your stomach. You can hear your bowels arguing against the foul contaminant. You start to feel like vomiting, but resist. Your body temperature begins to rise, and you flush with heat.

Fuck! This shit takes hold fast. You look at J., worried. Your brow begins dripping with sweat.

J. looks back and advises, "Just breathe. Deep breaths."

You follow his lead. It helps. Deep breathing staves off the vomiting.

Kuruk looks at you and smiles. You notice, for the first time, a deep wise presence in his eyes. You look at Emmitt and see the same presence.

"Allow the Great Spirit to travel through you with the medicine. Accept it in your heart. Open to it in your mind. And...if you need it, there's a greenie bucket for vomiting." Kuruk chuckles when he says those final words.

Emmitt stands and walks across the room. He returns with the bucket.

Kuruk picks up the rattle and begins a new haunting chant. Emmitt joins in with the drum. Kuruk reaches under the table with his free hand and pulls out another drum and rattle set. He gestures to you and J., who picks up the drum and joins in. You do the same with the rattle.

Deep breaths. Take deep breaths. Say yes to awareness. Yes to the fear.

You miraculously continue to stave off the vomiting. The breathing helps and so does the sound of the drumming and chanting. You develop a pattern of breathing, drumming, and *sinking*. *Sinking* deeper and deeper into the dizzying grip of the Mescaline medicine. It's disconcerting but also freeing and familiar. The chanting, drumming, and sinking goes on for the better part of an hour...

Parts of the experience you recognize—the deep feeling in your body of sobering truth. And other parts are completely foreign to you—like the dizzying auditory effects of the chanting. You hear other things, other voices, other sounds from behind a just-out-of-reach hidden veil. You sink deeper and deeper into the medicine...strange voices and sounds swirl all around you. You lose complete track of time...

Eventually, you stand involuntarily. You have little control as the medicine seeps into the deepest, most sacred spaces of your being. Kuruk, J., and Emmitt all join you in standing. You begin rocking back and forth, the medicine blurring your vision and sending you into a deep hallucinatory state. You sway, rattle, move, chant, breathe. and convulse...

"*The medicine has me! The medicine has me!*" you shout.

You're delirious. You continue shouting. J. takes your hand and looks you in the eyes. Kuruk takes your other hand and does the same. They steady your stance and keep you from falling over.

You're not sure how much more of this you can take; then suddenly, out of nowhere—you vomit...*hard*.

Emmitt is quick with the bucket and places it beneath you just in time. An ocean of putrid yuckness flows out of your mouth purging the bowels deep within you. This is not drunken beer vomit. This is not spoiled food vomit. This is *cosmic, existential, spiritual* vomit. It's violent and painful, and it yanks your insides all the way out.

You collapse to the ground exhausted, yet simultaneously free, present, and completely clear...

Something more than the Mescaline medicine brew has escaped your body... a wickedness...a stench...a rottenness...a vapor...a death. In your delirious state, you can't quite put your finger on it, but you know that whatever that something was, it had been in your body *for a very long time*, and it's now gone—purged by the medicine and the vomiting. You feel the difference! Lighter! Freer! Empty! Exhilarating!

You look up at Kuruk, J., and Emmitt and smile through the deep muscle ache of the vomiting. You then begin laughing and laughing and laughing...

You laugh deliriously into the void of nothingness. Time spins out of control for you. A deep resting presence overtakes your body—the same spiritually awakened presence you temporarily attained at Samsara Farm!

"I see the medicine has accepted you," Kuruk states with a twinkle in his eyes.

"Yes, I think it has," you squeak out.

J. pats you on the back. "Well done, friend. Well done."

You stand again. Emmitt gazes upon you with admiration and offers you a fist bump as he looks at his uncle. "Not bad for a greenie, hey uncle?"

"I think the Great Spirit approves," Kuruk replies.

"*I certainly hope so*," you whisper in a raspy voice. "*That was hell.*"

"Sometimes traveling to the underworld is necessary, my friend," Emmitt says softly.

"And what about you?" Kuruk asks J.

"I'm cool. That was awesome," J. replies.

"*Are you fucking kidding me?*" you rasp out in response to J.s nonchalant report.

"What!? It was!" J. adds.

Kuruk and Emmitt begin laughing.

"*Holy crap. I puked my brains out and you…?*"

"What can I say!? I'm a professional." J. smiles and laughs along with Kuruk and Emmitt. "I'm a badass professional."

Kuruk gets serious. "This medicine will last several more hours; it's not finished with you yet. Treat it with respect. Integration is important. Listen to it. Little Bear will take you back to your lodgings. Rest and respect the medicine. Understand?"

"Yes sir," J. replies.

"Call me Kuruk."

"Thank you, Kuruk. Deeply appreciate your guidance today."

"Not my guidance. Great Spirit's."

"Yes, of course. Thank you both," J. responds.

"Donadagohvi," states Kuruk.

Emmitt chimes in, "…means until we meet again."

"See you in two days at the sweat," says Kuruk.

"Donadagohvi," J. repeats.

Emmitt leads you and J. out of the room. All three of you head out to the main store area.

"My truck is around back," Emmitt states as he unlocks the front door. "Get your scooters. We'll put them in the truck bed. My shift starts in a few hours."

"Thanks, Emmitt," J. replies.

"No worries, man. How you guys feel?"

"I'm great!" J. replies.

"*I'm high as a kite and stoned off my rockers...*" you state.

"Your friend's an honest one, hey?" Emmitt laughs and J. joins him.

"All my fault," says J. "All my fault."

CHAPTER 15
MIRAGE MAGIC

How to screw up royally

What's so bad about all that, you might be asking?

Well, we haven't gotten to the bad sideways stuff yet; that's just about to happen. There's more to the story than I've let on: Last night, while you were drinking shots with J. at the hotel bar, someone put a mark on you. You know what a mark is? It's a target. Do you know why you were targeted...?

Lenny.

Let's rewind 16 hours...

9:07 pm / The Previous Day...

There's a knock at your hotel door. It's J. You can tell by his trademark dun-ta-da-dun-dun thrumming on the door. You hear his muffled voice.

"I know it's late, but…any interest in some tequila at the bar?"

"*Oh, man. No interest in getting mindfully drunk if that's what you're thinkin'.*"

"No, no. My treat. Just some people watching and a bit of a celebration."

"*Celebrating what?*"

"You, of course! And all the good badass work you've been doing. Relax a little. Take your mind off shit. Tequila's good for that."

"*Arm twisted.*"

"Awesome. Lenny and I will meet you down there—the lobby bar under the big glass dome."

"*Will do. I'm gonna take a quick shower.*"

"Cool beans. See you in a few."

Showered up and with fresh clothing on, you make the trek down to the bar. The stunning tropical foliage lobby bar of The Mirage is, by any other standards, a world class hangout, but relative to Vegas and the other bars in The Mirage, it's just a convenient, centrally located watering hole where you can see everyone—and *everyone* can see you.

You arrive, and now you get it: J. has Lenny wrapped around his neck, and the two of them are hamming it up for a gaggle of tourists all wanting photographs. Lenny is the perfect photographic complement to the sea of palm fronds and flowering hibiscus which surround the bar. You take a seat next to the circus, barely noticed. Within a few minutes, the Lenny side show calms down and J. takes notice of you.

"*I'll have two shots of Patron. Thank you very much.*"

"Ouch. Okay—I deserved that," J. states. You then watch as J. ponies up his credit card for two *very* expensive shots of tequila. The shots arrive quickly. You hold yours up for a toast.

"*Here's to Lenny—the real star of the show.*"

J. lifts his tequila shot up and toasts. "And to you—I'm serious. You deserve it. You've been through a lot…in a very short time. You deserve some street cred."

"Thanks. I'll take it." You down the shot. *"Spiritual awakening, black shadows, and dragons will drive you to drinking."* You laugh and J. joins you.

"Your friend Emmitt is a total character. Not what I expected for a shaman."

"Did I say shaman? Pretty sure I said shaman-in-training."

"Right. Forgot. That makes more sense."

"His uncle, whom you'll meet tomorrow, is more the full-fledged shaman."

"Hey. Speaking of which..." You point to Emmitt, who happens to be walking by with another younger fellow.

Emmitt and his friend catch sight of you and J. sitting at the bar. They stroll over to you. Emmitt's dressed in the same black and white coat and tie you saw him in earlier. His friend, probably in his early twenties, is dressed similarly and also seems to be a security personnel staff member. He's holding and fiddling with a big, black walkie talkie.

"Hey, guys," Emmitt cheerfully greets you both. "Getting along, I see. ...he drink tequila also?" Emmitt points to Lenny.

"Oh, God no. He'd be an angry drunk," J. laughs.

"This is my nephew, Kai. Trying to keep him out of trouble. He's new to the job."

"Cool. How new?" you ask Kai.

Kai looks at Emmitt. "Lemme see. When did I get out!?"

"That was six months ago. Can't even remember your last day of juvie."

"Yeah, so it's been four or five months," Kai answers.

"Trouble follows this one. I'm trying to help my brother and his wife. I look after him." Emmitt places his hand across Kai's shoulder. "Show him what it means to work and have responsibilities. Grown-up shit." Emmitt looks directly at Kai.

"What's your lizard's name?" Kai asks J. as he looks at Lenny lounging on J.'s shoulders.

"This is Lenny. He's a green iguana. His family originally comes from Costa Rica."

"*I didn't know that!*" you chime in.

"Cool lizard, man. How much he cost?

Emmitt interrupts Kai. "Leave the iguana be, man. I'm sure J. and his friend wanna finish their tequila. You guys need a ride tomorrow or what?"

"I have the address. We'll find it. Thanks, man. I've got a different sort of transportation in mind," J. replies with a devious smile.

"Cool. Don't be late. My Uncle Kuruk is a stickler about that kind of thing, but he's good at administering the medicine."

"We won't be late!" J. adds.

"You guys enjoy your tequila. Kai and I have to get back to work. Shift ends after midnight."

"Cool. Nice meeting you, Kai," J. says.

"*I'll be dead asleep by then,*" you quip. "*Nice meeting you, Kai.*"

Kai holds out his fist waiting for you to bump it. It takes you an uncool second to respond, but you do so finally, awkwardly. Emmitt and Kai walk away laughing and bickering.

And that's when Lenny was marked.

Let's now hop back to the next day after your medicine initiation.

1:35 p.m. / Medicine Initiation Day

You, J., and Emmitt are all piled into the front cab of Emmitt's Ford F-150. It's an older model, not exactly in great shape, but adequate for hauling and moving. Hauling equipment that is—*not ass*. Emmitt, however, seems to think differently. He's swerving in and out of traffic like a New York City cab driver on cocaine. You can't tell if he's driving like a churlish madman, or you're just stoned off Mescaline. Either scenario—not good.

"You doin' okay?" J. checks in based on your troubled-looking face.

"I'm okay. Still a little upset in the stomach. Not really high. I was joking, but definitely in a mildly altered or awakened state."

"Yeah. Microdosing will do that to you. Puts you right on the edge. Not really baked but not lucid either."

"Baked?" You laugh. *"Haven't heard that term since college."*

"Right. Probably not the best post-event description of a sacred Mescaline journey."

Emmitt chuckles at your conversation and keeps on swerving.

"You in a hurry?" J. asks Emmitt.

"Nope. Aggressive driving. Only way to survive in this crazy town."

"Well, this is certainly faster than the e-scooters."

"You want to make it on time, right?" Emmitt asks.

"On time for what?" J. replies.

"The magic show man. I comped you two tickets to see that famous internet magician!"

"No shit! Awesome!" J. replies. "Shouldn't we be taking it easy, though? Your uncle said..."

"Nahhh... You'll be fine, man. My uncle's just old-school. I mixed that stuff myself this morning. That was like just four buttons between the three of you. It won't last."

"You sure?"

"What's a button?" you ask.

"That's the plant, man. The little cactus peyote plant that looks like a green button. Grows low on the ground. Hand harvested somewhere down in Mexico." Emmitt switches the topic of conversation in the same manner he switches truck gears. "This guy is a card wizard. You're gonna love his act. I've seen it three times now myself."

"When's it start?" J. asks.

"Three p.m. So, I need to get you back by 2."

J. shrugs his shoulders and looks at you, grinning.

Emmitt continues his mad dash across the back streets of Vegas. You and J. settle into the chaos and have no choice but to trust his driving. Within a few minutes, the dash is over, and Emmitt pulls his truck into the parking area reserved for Mirage hotel employees.

Emmitt helps you unload the e-scooters. You and J. each grab one and walk them alongside Emmitt.

"Listen, man. No drinking tequila today. No heavy foods. Just stay around the hotel. You can reach the magic show without even leaving. Do all that and you'll be fine. Four buttons is…just a buzz. No worries. You have your key cards and the hotel phone app, right?"

"We do," says J.

"Look on your phones, man. I downloaded the show tickets right to your account. Way cool. All taken care of."

"That is cool. Thanks again, Emmitt. That is awesome."

You arrive at a triple set of hotel elevator doors.

"I'm goin' down. You guys head up one floor. Get off. Turn right and the main elevators to your room are right down that hall. …you guys need anything, you know how to reach me. Okay? I told Kai you'd be at the show. So, we both got your back. Enjoy!"

"We will, man. Thanks again!" J. replies.

Emmitt's elevator arrives before yours. He hops on while tucking in his shirt for work and disappears as the large steel doors close. You take a big breath and sigh.

"*I need a break.*" You look at J., exhausted.

"Me, too. Let's go to our rooms, see how we feel, and then decide. We have an hour."

"*Sounds good.*"

Your elevator door opens. You and J. push the e-scooters in, and within a few minutes…you're lying down on your hotel bed, stone-cold asleep.

The dream you have is like no other…

Because I am in your dream.

Because I am not here merely as a timekeeper or part-time narrator of your adventures...

No.

I am here purposely guiding you to a resolution.

Guiding you to a very specific and final destination...

I am not random.

I am not purposeless.

I am here to wake you—

The voice comes and goes, sometimes with clarity and other times through a haze of mist and cloud. You dream of diminutive green cactus buttons, scattered across a desert landscape. On each button sits a tiny human being. Some of the humans are silent. Some are joyful. Some are sorrowful. Some are angry. Some are in pain. Some are in agony. You walk looking down, searching for yourself...

I am over here...

You hear your own voice calling out...

No, this way. I am here...

Not there. Over here.

You hear yourself calling. You search and search, but can't find yourself. You walk, then run, then fly across the desert surface—on an e-scooter. Dust, sand, and dirt swirl up curlicue style as you shred across the landscape. Something immense looms in the distance. You head toward it. At the last minute, you realize it's a canyon stretching as far and wide as your eyes can perceive. You try, but can't stop the e-scooter! Instantly, you launch headlong out and over the canyon rim. Then, like Wiley-Coyote defying the laws of gravity, you hang in the hot dry air for a split second. You look down. Your heart sinks. Your skin crawls. You try with every fiber of your being to let out a scream, but it won't come. And then—you wake up.

You adjust your eyes, roll over, and grab your phone. *Oh shit. It's 4:15! The show started an hour ago. Bummer.* You touch a speed dial logo with a small picture of Lenny on it. *Rrrrrinngg...* J. picks up.

"Don't worry your awesome little self. I just fixed it."

"*Really? I feel like a real schmuck.*"

"I just spoke with Emmitt. There's another show at 7. He can also get us into that one."

"*Oh, good. Did you apologize?*"

"Profusely. He understood."

"*What now?*"

"Now I think we should do some washing machine integration."

"*Huh?*"

"Swing by my room."

"*Okay. Will do.*"

A few minutes later you knock on J.'s door. He lets you in. His suite is the same as yours—surprisingly modest given the bombastic and overzealous mothership it rests in. You take a seat at a small table in the corner near a window overlooking a large green area splattered with blue-green swimming pools and tropical foliage. You can see dozens of tiny human forms lounging around the pools. You recall your dream. J. takes a seat across from you.

"My apologies for the rough and tumble nature of today. Emmitt is a little rougher around the edges than I remember him."

"*On the other hand...*" You gesture toward the open window. "*We're staying in a five-star hotel in Las Vegas—at a discount price, no less, I presume.*"

J. nods in agreement. "Still, no excuses. I knew it would be a little raw, but even this is a tad beyond my comfort zone. So, let's reset, shall we? We should take a minute to digest and integrate your Mescaline trip. Sound good?"

"*All in.*" You appreciate J.'s concern and empathy. Sometimes his wild, frenetic nature gets the best of him, but not now.

"First off—how the hell are you? Where are you? What's happening?"

You take a big breath and then speak. "*I'm surprisingly good. A little wobbly from the experience. My stomach still hurts from the vomiting, but the awakened state of presence is back—a little different, but very similar.*" You pause to reflect. "*I just had another Black Shadow dream. I'll share that if you want. I do think something left me during the purging...during the vomiting.*" You pause again. "*That's it, I think. All in all—I'm fine.*" You look J. directly in his eyes. "*What about your experience? You took the Mescaline medicine as well, and I haven't heard a peep about it.*"

J. takes a moment to gather his thoughts. "Right. Well, I'm relieved. I'm glad you're okay, albeit a little discombobulated—totally normal and to be expected in this case. Good...good." He takes a deep breath. "Okay. I'll share with you my thoughts and, if you'd like, my experience."

"Yes, please!"

I'm going to try to be brief here. I'm speaking to you, reader, with book in hand...

Allow me, for just a quick minute, to do you another legit solid regarding this whole psychedelic-hallucinogen-spiritual-vision quest thing. Let's inspect and deconstruct it a bit more. It'll be worth your time.

But first—I'd like you take a deep breath—b r e a t h e—Come on. Big inhale. Big exhale. There ya go! Find your center. Find awareness. Got it? Good. Here we go...

Hallucinogens:

In a nutshell, like everything else bought and sold in the grand spiritual grocery store of this odd life (and in the grand illusory dream of *Brahman* for that matter) psychedelic drugs are *over-sold*, *over-hyped*, and of course—way *overused*.

Sure, I've done my share. I've tripped. I've had visions. I've hallucinated. I've benefitted. I have zero regrets. But, but, but...

But after a lifetime of spiritual seeking; after a lifetime of spiritual experiences; after a lifetime of spiritual highs, lows, breakthroughs, and insights, here's what I think about psychedelic hallucinogens: *They're just fucking drugs.* Let me be very clear here: *Ayahuasca, Mescaline, Psylocibin, DMT and Salvia Divinorum* (to name just a handful) *are just—fucking drugs.* Period.

I think the word *delusion* isn't used enough when users, believers, zealots, and aficionados pile on in praise of hallucinogens. Like anything else in this wicked dream-state duality, one has to be able to *discern* between the cautious, right, and proper use of such drugs and the vacuous, pseudo-scientific, *delusory* use of such drugs. Let's do some discerning, right now.

The Upside:

Three eras of hallucinogenic drug use can be examined to confirm our suspicion that *something* positive, healing, and beneficial can be gained from the ingestion of psychedelics:

The modern era of microdosing and healing – Take a look around, man. The decriminalization of Psylocibin, Ayahuasca, and Mescaline is happening more and more with each passing election, in a variety of states and countries. (This is not the same as *legalization*. Decriminalization means a person can't be threatened legally for growing, having, or using a small personal amount.)

Why is this? Microdosing hallucinogens has been proven effective in helping with anxiety, trauma, PTSD, drug addiction, alcoholism, depression, and more. There are professionally run hallucinogen healing centers popping up all over the United States and Central America. Google "ayahuasca retreats" and see for yourself.

The perennial era of indigenous use – It's no secret that indigenous peoples from all over the world, throughout time immemorial, have been doin' drugs. The use of these drugs by priests, shamans, and mystics has allowed man to feel closer to and interact with his own soul, the dead, animal spirits, God, Heaven, Hell, and any other person, place, or thing associated with *above, below, and beyond*. This shit works: Lick a frog, eat a mushroom, smoke some tree bark, and *bam!*—instant enlightenment, revelation, and/or connection with the divine or universe. It's hard to argue with this type of extensive historical use.

The ancient Greek era of kykeon – Because I'm a "Know Thyself" fan, the ancient Greeks are worth mentioning here. Socrates, Plato, Aristotle, Sophocles, Plutarch, Hadrian, Julian, and Cicero were all rumored to have been members of the highly venerated *Eleusinian Mystery School* which was oriented around the fertility goddess Demeter and her daughter Persephone. One of the ongoing initiation rites of this school was the sacramental ingestion of a barley and pennyroyal beverage called kykeon. No surprise here—the kykeon was spiked. One theory proposes that ergot, a fungus that grows on barley and emits ergometrine and d-lysergic acid amide, was found in the kykeon. D-lysergic acid amide is a chemical precursor to lysergic acid diethylamide, otherwise known as LSD. No proof; that's just a theory. Other theories propose that the psychoactive ingredient in the kykeon was psilocybe cubensis—ye old magic mushrooms. However one wishes to stack it up, it's pretty reasonable to theorize that the founders of modern civilization, were...um...stoners.

The Downside:

Three shadow characteristics of hallucinogens can be examined to confirm our suspicions that there's a ton of hogwash and perhaps even some danger surrounding the ingestion of psychedelics:

Pseudoscience – As much as I like the term "medicine" that Native Americans use when referring to hallucinogens, they're not, by any modern scientific standard, "medicine" at all. As a matter of fact, hallucinogens are actually *toxins*—poisons that make the body sick, causing one to purge and vomit, and then sending the user into a post-vomit altered state. There's a difference. Selling them as "medicine" is pseudoscience.

Delusions of grandeur – Hallucinogens are not sentient. They're not alive. They're not *aware* in some weird transdimensional way that imbues them with mystical intelligence. They're not planted or seeded "gifts" from ancient, astronaut aliens meant to assist in the cosmic evolution of our planet. They're just naturally occurring plants containing a psychoactive element which very conveniently attaches itself to the serotonin 2A receptor subtype in the neurons of our brains. No supernatural qualities need be assigned. They're just really cool plants that get you stoned.

Gullibility and highly suggestable states – Holy fucking shit! Have I been here 1000 billion times?! Ingesting hallucinogens places most users in a highly suggestable and gullible state of mind: You'll believe just about *anything and everything*. So, when someone tells you, while you're high off of magic mushrooms, that your cancer has been removed by a small army of little green gnomes, you'll probably believe it—hook, line, and sinker. Harmless enough, until the following week, when you visit the oncology cancer ward and your doctor tells you the *exact opposite*. Danger, Will Robinson...

Where do I stand on all this? Clearly, as I've stated in the previous chapter, I'm a believer in and supporter of the use of hallucinogens as part of a spiritual practice. But, but, *but*—like anything else in the spiritual marketplace, some healthy, skeptical discernment should always be in place...before, during, and after use.

Now—back to our story...

"In summary, the only real lasting value of hallucinogens is their ability to make you aware of the *one awareness* which is experiencing the hallucinogenic experience or vision," J. says with a matter-of-fact gravitas.

You get it. In that one sentence, J. summed up the value of psychedelics: It's not the vision; it's not the trip; it's not the geometric colors or alien shapes; it's not the contact with dead relatives; it's not the communication with your higher self or God; it's not even the unfinished emotional business of your soul (although that's important)—none of that. It's about noticing the *one awareness who is* experiencing the effects of the hallucinogen. It's about that *one*.

His words sink in like a football field-sized boulder into the ocean of your mind. It has *always* been only and forever about just *one* thing. Over and over and over. You're *finally* beginning to get it. ONE thing. The Black Shadow dragon has been roaring to you all this time: "There's only ONE of us here." Over and over and over it washes over you. *There's just ONE of us here.*

You respond internally, in the only intelligent manner that one *can* respond in the face of such things: *Fuuuuuuck.*

It's 5:30 p.m. and time to get ready for dinner and a show. After the talk with J., you're dizzy with insight, sobering truth, and Mescaline. You're drunk, high, and spirited away on the frenzied winds of truth *and* delusion. You're in no state to be making decisions *but you do.* And the decision you're about to make has repercussions which reverberate for days, weeks, and months...

You *decide* to take Lenny. Oops.

For dinner, you and J. wisely order room service. It's delivered at 6:15. You eat, then get dressed for the magic show. It's 6:45 now. You knock on J.'s door.

"Be right out." J. opens the door a minute later and is just about to lock it behind him.

"*Let's bring Lenny!*" you quip.

"Do we really want Lenny paparazzi? I'm pooped," J. responds.

"*Yes! I'll carry him.*"

J. hesitates and then gives in. "Okay."

A few minutes later, you're taking the elevator to the first floor with Lenny wrapped around your shoulders. *The David Leone L'Enchantement* show at The Mirage Theater is packed. You're surprised that no one, not even the security personnel or the numerous ushers, bats an eye at the large reptile wrapped around your shoulders. *It is, after all—Vegas,* you surmise.

As you're taking your seats, there's a commotion on the far side of the theater. Two disheveled younger looking guys donning baseball caps and hoodies are arguing with one of the ushers and an older couple about seating arrangements. From what you can tell, there's a dispute about the seats.

"Already taken."

"Those are our fuckin' seats; we have legit tickets."

"No sir, you do not. We've told you guys before…"

You only hear snippets from your distance. Emmitt and Kai show up and get involved in the tussle. It's evident that both Emmitt and Kai are familiar with the two guys. Eventually the two young men are escorted out. The commotion dies down, the curtain rises, and the show begins.

Much to your disappointment it's a cheesefest and a sad mockery of the mystical arts. The show's schtick—*L' Enchantement*—is a cartoonish brush with meditative states that supposedly allow *Mr. Leone* to achieve fantastical, magical, and *enchanting* feats: levitation, disappearance, and beastly transformation among other things. You're bored. At one point you lean over and whisper into J.'s ear, *"This guy could use some magical enchanting Mescaline."* J. chuckles, but seems to be enjoying the show nonetheless.

"I'm going to the bathroom," you whisper again to J.

"Lenny?" J. offers.

"Nah," you reply. *"He's fine. I'll take him with me."*

"Okay…" J. whispers.

You get up with Lenny wrapped around your shoulders and bump a few strange knees as you exit the theater. You locate the bathroom. On the way back, you notice a small gift shop containing a large assortment of *L' Enchantement* merchandise. It's packed with quite a few people. Despite this, bored with the actual show, you enter…

Oddly enough, you're pretty sure you see the two hoodie-wearing, disheveled young men who were just ceremoniously kicked out of the theater. They're loitering just outside the shop's large open entranceway. You walk by them, not giving them much thought. You don't know why (and later look back upon the whole stupid occasion with regret) but decide, more as a joke than anything else, to purchase a black *L' Enchantement* t-shirt for J.

The shop is crowded. You're shoulder to shoulder with lots of people. You're rummaging through a pile of t-shirts. And finally, most significantly—you're still slightly high off of the Mescaline, and therefore *not* paying attention to your surroundings.

It happens without you even noticing. You pick out a t-shirt. You stand in line. You purchase it. Bag in hand, you make the short trek back to the theater, bump some knees again, and sit down next to J. A few seconds later, J. taps you on the shoulder. You look at him. He leans over and in a very matter of fact way says to you out loud:

"Where's Lenny?"

You place your hand on your shoulder and your heart skips a beat. *"Oh, shit!"* you blurt out. It's loud enough for everyone within a twenty-five-foot radius to hear. You immediately stand up and once again, awkwardly, stressfully make your way out of the theater. J. follows.

You run down the short hallway and enter the gift shop. You look everywhere. No signs of Lenny. Not at the register. Not on any shelves or counters. Not on the floor. Not in the hands of anyone else. You rush out again and scan the various patrons coming and going in the hallway. Nothing. You notice J. inside the gift shop talking to the retail attendant. You also notice that the two guys in hoodies who were loitering outside the gift shop previously are now conspicuously absent. You rush up to J.

"Call Emmitt," you say to him.

"Calm down..." J. says to you. "He's gotta be around here somewhere. Why do I need to call Emmitt?"

"*Just do it. Call Emmitt now.*"

"Why?"

"*Because I know who took Lenny.*"

"You think someone *took* Lenny!?"

"*I absolutely do. And I have a feeling I know who.*"

"Who in the world would *take* Lenny?" You can tell by the tone of his voice that J. is getting worried. He pulls out his phone and fumbles with it until you hear it ringing. Emmitt answers. "Hey man. Yeah, it's me. You still here working?" J. pauses. You can't hear Emmitt's response. "Can you come to the *L' Enchantement* gift shop?" Silence again. "Because Lenny is missing or maybe someone took him or something. I can't find him anywhere." Another pause. "We're here now...okay, cool. We'll wait."

You look at J. and see a deep concern spread across his brow. You don't know what's more disconcerting—the fact that Lenny is missing, or the fact that J. is close to losing his shit.

"*I'm really, really sorry,*" you say to J. "*I wasn't paying attention. I don't know what I was thinking. My bad. I'm so, so...*"

Mid-sentence, Emmitt rounds the corner and walks up to you and J.

"Hey guys. What's goin' on? So where was the last place you saw..."

You interrupt Emmitt. "*Those two guys you escorted out of the theater...*"

"Yeah, what about them?"

"*I'm pretty sure they're responsible. When I was in the gift shop, I saw them.*"

"Ohhhhh, man. They were here?" Your heart sinks when Emmitt speaks, confirming your suspicions. "That was Derek and Little Buck, old friends of Kai's. Not smart guys. Constant trouble."

"Would they take Lenny?"

"They're mostly just petty scammers. Maybe. Kai knows them better. Let me…"

J. interrupts Emmitt. "Why would they take an iguana?"

"Gimme a sec. I'm gonna get Kai down here." Emmitt dials Kai on his phone. While he waits for the phone to connect, Emmitt looks at you and J. and very somberly says "Black market, most likely."

"Fuck!" J. replies.

"Oh, man…" you sigh.

"Kai. It's me. Get your ass down here…the theater gift shop…it's Derek and Little Buck again…Yeah, we're right outside in the hallway... Hurry up." Emmitt hangs up and places the phone in his pocket.

"Yeah man. There's a big black market here in town. Anything. Everything. Exotics included."

"Exotics?" J. asks.

"Exotic pets, animals, illegal pets. Everything. Monkeys, parrots, snakes, frogs. Shit—I even heard there was a black panther for sale a few years back. Totally illegal stuff, man. Not good."

"I'm going to snoop and ask around a bit. Be right back," J. states.

"Okay. We'll be right here," Emmitt assures him.

You're at a loss to do anything and remain with Emmitt. The situation has sobered you right up. Gone are any of the once-lingering good feelings of the Mescaline. Emmitt reads your mind and inquires: "Shit! Man, I totally forgot. You guys are still on the medicine. How are you doing?"

"Fine," you reply. *"It mostly faded. I feel like an idiot."*

"Not your fault, man. It can happen to anyone. Vegas is full of thieves and con men. They don't tell you that on the billboards or YouTube ads."

"No, they do not." You nervously check your phone and scan all the passersby in the hallway for the hundredth time. *"If those two guys took Lenny...where do you think they took him?"*

Just then, Kai shows up. He overhears your question and responds. "I *know* those two boneheads took your lizard, man. They're probably in Naked City by now."

Emmitt looks at Kai with consternation. "What did you do!?"

Kai looks at the ground in defeat and embarrassment. "Nothin', man. I told them not to mark the lizard. But those boneheads..."

"You tell them about the lizard?" Emmitt says angrily.

"I just thought it was funny. I told you..." Kai's voice cracks with sorrow and fear. "...told them the lizard was out of bounds, man."

"Why did you even mention it!?" Emmitt says, exasperated. Emmitt then fumbles with his phone and calls J. He answers and Emmitt fills him in. A minute later, J. returns.

"So, what can we do?" J. asks.

"File a police report first and then see if we can figure out where they may have taken him," Emmitt replies.

"Needle in a haystack. There's a dozen warehouses and garages in Naked City that are holding houses," Kai adds.

"Holding houses?" asks J.

"Places where illegal contraband, drugs, electronics…" Emmitt pauses and takes a big breath. "…and the animals…are held before transport or sale."

"*Transport?*" you ask.

"Los Angeles or Phoenix, usually. Sometimes Albuquerque."

"*Shit. We need to act fast.*" You look at Kai. "*You have their phone numbers?*"

"Who? Derek and Little Buck's?" Kai asks.

You nod affirmatively.

"No, man. My parents took that phone, before juvie. I still got it, but not on me. It's at home, but it's just a brick now."

"*But the numbers are still on it!?*"

"I would think so. Yeah, man."

"You can't call them. Not tonight. They'll know…" Emmitt interrupts.

"*Where's home?*"

"Tule Springs. Half hour from here," Kai replies.

"Hold up. Hold up, everyone," J. interjects. "Okay. Let's take a breather here and think this through. First things first." J. addresses Emmitt. "Should we file a police report?"

"Yes!" Emmitt replies.

J. addresses Kai. "You sure you have this phone at home, and their numbers are on it?"

"Yes."

"How long do we have?" J. addresses both Kai and Emmitt.

"How long for what?" asks Kai.

"Until they transport Lenny out of town?"

"Twenty-four, maybe forty-eight hours *if* we can find the transport van."

"The transport van?" J. asks.

"Yeah, man. They use transport vans that look like service vehicles. Plumbers, electricians, contractors, and shit."

"And where are those vans kept?" J. digs.

"I told you, Naked City; sometimes Whitney."

"Not great parts of town, I presume?"

"Nope..." Kai responds dryly.

J. takes a deep breath and then he smiles. He looks at you, Emmitt, and Kai, nodding his head slowly up and down as if just figuring something out. It's an unreasonably big smile, especially given the current dire circumstances. You're puzzled and relieved by his smile, but mostly worried...

J. speaks again. "Sometimes traveling to the underworld is necessary my friend."

"*Huh?*" you ask.

"Those were the last words Emmitt said to you this morning after the medicine initiation."

You're jolted by the memory. The Mescaline medicine initiation seems like it was *days* ago, not *today*—not *this morning*. J. imparts these words to you with a clear sparkle in his eyes. You see Emmitt nod his head in agreement. Then you watch as Emmitt also slowly smiles...

"Looks like we're going into the real underworld then, heh?" Emmitt says.

"Looks that way…looks *exactly* that way."

"*What have I done?*" are your last words before Emmitt calls the police and several hours of questioning, interviewing, and reporting unfold. It's exhausting.

You go to bed in your hotel room that night with a jumble of thoughts bouncing around your head. *The underworld. The underworld. What the fuck have I done?* But the most painful thought that grips your brain and *will not* let go is the one of your abducted… little… green… reptilian… friend.

Poor Lenny. Poor, poor Lenny.

Chapter 16
Street Smarts

How to travel to the city underworld

Strides on the spiritual path that result in breakthroughs, insights, or radical positive changes, as much as we'd like them to, seldom happen on that new $100 meditation pillow we purchased on Amazon or during the cushy Costa Rican retreat with the latest, popular nondual teacher or during the weekend workshop at the Zen center in the Pocono mountains. If only...

The hard truths, the real lessons, the unshakeable experiences that define our lives *usually* happen right in the hard, gritty, middle of our sweaty, stressful lives: during the commute to work; at the breakfast table in the early morning; in the shower; while we're arguing with our spouse; when we're stressed at work; after a big defeat or loss; when someone shares the bad news; on the phone at midnight dealing with a tragedy on another continent; on the treadmill at the gym. You get the idea...

The real long-term spiritual changes we're after, like peace, happiness, love, security, confidence, or the hard-won sense that everything is okay, need to be validated over and over again throughout the tough, daily minutia of our lives. Why is this? Because, my friend, if this peace, happiness, or tranquility you've laid claim to *doesn't* hold up during these hard, tough times, then it's probably not quite the attainment you imagined it to be. It was just wishful thinking.

I'm telling you all this because I want you to know there's a *reason* for the harrowing, gritty chapter you're about to read, beyond the fun, adventure, and danger. *When shit gets real in your own life,* those spiritual attainments you think you've made will get tested on these *very same* rough and tumble streets. Take heed.

It's 10 a.m. the next day. You, J., Emmitt, and Kai all meet at *The Navajo Feather*. Twenty-four hours ago, you were here sipping Mescaline in the back room. Today you're here trying to amend the giant fuck-up that occurred partly due to that Mescaline and partly due to your own naïveté about the Las Vegas black market. Apparently, that market likes iguanas.

The shop doesn't open until noon today, so Kuruk isn't around and the store is empty. Kai is last to show up. He's the linchpin—or at least his phone is—for the whole plan. He enters with the same look of guileless shame he had the previous night. You feel sorry for him. He's not a bad kid, just young and typically naïve. Without saying a word, Kai walks over to the sales counter where you, J., and Emmitt have gathered and rests his old phone on the counter. It's charged and displays the time and date against a screenshot of a *Rage Against the Machine* album cover. Everyone is palpably nervous.

"Per the plan," says Emmitt.

"Per the plan," J. replies as he picks up Kai's phone and hands it back to Kai. "Read me one of the numbers. I'm going to call."

"This is Little Buck's—or at least it *was*." Kai reads off the ten digits. J. repeats them, dialing them on his own phone. J. places the phone in speaker mode.

Immediately, everyone hears the distinct three-toned beep followed by an automated female voice: "We're sorry. You have reached a number that has been disconnected or is no longer…"

"Nope. Next number," J. says.

"This is Derek's," Kai offers and then reads off ten more digits. J. confirms the number and dials it on his phone. He hits the speaker button again. Everyone is on pins and needles...The phone rings...followed by a collective sigh of relief... It continues to ring....no answer...more ringing... then, finally:

"What? Who is this?"

"Yeah, man; I got some dope bumps I wanna unload. I was told you could hook a brotha up." J. speaks and you're astonished by his acting acumen and street talk fluency. You're also glad you rehearsed the whole 'stolen audio gear' thing with him earlier this morning, or you'd be clueless right now.

"Who the fuck is this? I ain't giving you no hookup."

"Come on, man. I got four bumps—all of them Vegas quality. Fifteens. ...snatched from of an out-of-town whip yesterday. At least tell me who's holding right now. I need the cash."

"Fuck that. Look, I don't know who's holdin' electronical this week. Not my scene. Ask one of the newbie recruits at the trap house."

"Which trap house?"

"Fuck you, man. Pebble Beach smoke."

Derek hangs up the phone. "Well, that went as expected. Anybody know where or what Pebble Beach smoke is?" J. asks.

"It's in Meadows Village. Neighborhood east of downtown off 95," Kai answers. "Pebble Beach is just a bunch of potheads."

"Nice 'n seedy," adds Emmitt.

"I can deal with potheads if they can steer us in the right direction!" J. proclaims. "It's our only lead. Let's get out of here."

Everyone leaves the shop. Emmitt locks up. Emmitt and Kai pile into Emmitt's Ford 150. You and J. take the Jeep. It takes about twenty-five minutes to wind your way westward to the part of town where Pebble Beach Boulevard is located. Kai knows the area. You park the Jeep next to the Ford 150 in the parking lot of a cigarette and vape shop called *The Smokehouse*, the landmark Derek crudely alluded to before hanging up.

"This is as good as it gets for parking," Kai says, "but I should stay here with the cars."

"*Understood*," you reply. "*Is this place safe?*"

"Should be," Kai responds. "It's a party house. Mostly pot, MDMA, and Ketamine." Kai looks at you after spewing off the list of club drugs. "You know—ecstasy?"

"*I know what MDMA is, and I'm sure it's peddled like candy on Halloween in this town.*"

"Trick or treat!" Kai responds, smiling for the first time in a while. "Good luck and remember—you're looking for the *active* holding house this week. They rotate," he adds.

"Got it!" J. says.

You, J., and Emmitt head around the corner and then turn left onto Pebble Beach Boulevard. "Pebble Beach smoke" is what they call on the street a "trap house" or drug den. It takes just a minute to arrive. The house looks like every other dilapidated, white, single-story rancher on the block…

There's an ugly chain link fence surrounding the property. A double-wide concrete driveway passes from the street over a sidewalk and butts up against the house beneath an aluminum car portico. Old dirty pea gravel is everywhere, substituting for grass. An ugly, monstrously sized air conditioning unit rests directly on the rooftop. Finally—an old, dying palm tree valiantly tries to give the place some life, but accomplishes exactly the opposite, given its withering presence. There might as well be a sign out front that reads: *Welcome potheads, users, and druggies. Your life has now reached a dead end.*

Emmitt walks up to the main door and knocks. You notice for the first time that Emmitt is carrying—not a gun, but a large, ostentatious, mean-looking buck knife, strapped to his hip with a dark brown leather carrying case. You also notice that he's wearing black cowboy boots and has his long black hair hanging loosely. He's donning a very intentional "Don't fuck with me" look. You like it.

There is, of course, no answer to the knock. Emmitt knocks again. Everyone waits another minute. There's no noise or evidence of inhabitants inside....

"Fuck it," Emmitt says as he opens the door. You and J. follow him in.

The stench is overwhelming—mostly an old, rancid marijuana smell that could easily be removed—if the home were bulldozed. It's dark. Graffiti everywhere. In the dim lighting, you make out pizza boxes, beer cans, dirty old blankets and pillows, a chewed-up sofa, and several white plastic chairs. There's a flatscreen TV. You're surprised to see that it's in working condition. It's on. The screen reads "Grand Theft Auto Online." *Well that's cliché,* you think.

Peering through the dank gloom you're not surprised when your eyes make out a human form on the sofa. *He...she??* Passed out.

J. puts his finger to his mouth upon noticing the person.

"Wait here. Gonna check the rest of the rooms," Emmitt whispers.

Like nervous school kids who just broke into the local graveyard late at night, you and J. wait until Emmitt returns.

"No one else here," he whispers. "Let's wake this guy up and see what we can glean from him. Cool?"

J. gives a thumbs up. You grab the two plastic bucket seats and place them near the sofa. You and J. each take a seat. Sitting closer, you see that the passed-out person is a guy, probably in his early thirties. He's thin and bearded. Emmitt rifles through the sofa and surrounding area.

"It's safe. No weapons that I can see. Let's do this." Emmitt then leans over the guy and gently nudges his shoulder. It takes a few attempts, but eventually he comes around.

"Hey, Buddy, don't be alarmed. We're not here to hurt you," Emmitt says plainly.

The man rolls over and places his feet on the ground. He leans over and rubs his face with both hands. "What is this? Rick send you? You got Dottie? Bring back my fuckin' dog, man. I told him I don't got the money right now." He looks up and sees that none of you have any idea what he's talking about.

"We don't have your dog, Buddy. We just got a few questions for you. You answer them—you get this." Emmitt gestures toward J., who sticks his hand in his pocket and pulls out a $100 bill.

The man looks at all of you and laughs. "You got ten of those? That's how much I owe. Fuck."

"What's your name, man?" asks J.

The man looks at J.; inexplicably, he answers readily. "Evan. My name's Evan. Who the fuck are you guys?"

J. looks at Evan directly in the eyes. "What's your dog's name, Evan?"

"My dog's name? How did you guys get in here? You guys know Rick or what?"

"Does Rick work any of the holding houses?" Emmitt asks.

"Fuck man, my dog's name is Dottie. She's got dots. She's a Dalmatian. Yeah, Rick works the holds, man! Why? What the fuck do you guys want?"

"We got some audio gear we want to unload. Tell us which holding houses are active this week, and we'll give you two of these." Emmitt points to the bill in J.'s hand.

"Three," Evan counters.

"My dog is also missing," J. adds.

"Three then," Emmitt replies.

Evan takes a big breath and then rubs his eyes. "Shit. What kinda dog you have, man?"

"He's a Pitbull named Lenny," J. replies.

"Alright. I'll tell you—for three. Show 'em," Evan says.

Emmitt nods to J., and again J. reaches into his pocket and pulls out several more $100 bills.

"Alright, Evan—which holding houses are active this week? Super simple. Then we're out of your hair," Emmitt says.

"Sal's Garage on Pinecrest and The Billiard Palace warehouse on upper Birdwood."

"You're not lying to us just to get the cash, are you?" Emmitt asks sternly.

"No, man. Not lying. I'm in enough shit," Evan replies.

"You take these," J. hands Evan three $100 bills. "Thanks and I hope you get your dog back."

"Yeah, me too. I hope you get yours back."

"Me, too," J. replies and then he adds, "Evan, aren't you sick and tired of being sick and tired?"

Evan looks up from rubbing his eyes again. "Who the fuck are you guys? Of course, I'm sick and tired of being sick and tired. I just want some peace man, like everyone else. I just want some peace…"

"Evan, look at me." J. speaks with authority now, perhaps to that part of Evan which is far away, asleep, and lost to the world. "You have to *want it*, my friend. You have to *really* want it. Understand?"

"Yeah man, whatever. Don't tell Rick I sent you. That fucker's got a mean temper."

"Okay, Evan—We'll let you get back to doing whatever it is you were, um, doing before. Thanks, Buddy," Emmitt says. You and J. stand and then follow Emmitt out the door.

"I thought that went very well," Emmitt says while walking out into the street again.

"Me too," J. replies. "Poor guy."

"*Am I the only one with a giant knot in their stomach?*" you ask.

"Nope. I got one; I just hide it well. That was a little intense at first."

"Greenies," Emmitt says, patting the knife at his side and grinning from ear to ear.

An hour later you park the Jeep several blocks away from The Billiard Palace warehouse. It's in another seedy part of town called Naked City, named after the showgirls who commonly resided there in the 1950s and sunbathed naked in the back lots. Now Naked City is just tons of ugly concrete, warehouse space, empty lots, garages, and ubiquitous "Available for Rent" signs. No naked showgirls here anymore.

In order to save time, Emmitt and Kai split off to investigate Sal's Garage by themselves. You don't like the idea of prowling around warehouses in dubious parts of Vegas without Emmitt and his knife, but you understand the logic.

It takes you and J. a few minutes to walk to the warehouse. While walking, you're lost in thought, anxiety, and stress. You notice that J. is as calm as a bluebird on a sunny day.

"*Aren't you the least bit worried? I'm pretty wigged out here.*"

"Of course I am." J. stops and looks at you. "Take a deep breath. Come on…deep breath." You follow his instruction. "Don't fight the stress. Allow it. Welcome it. Be it. To awareness, this is no different than any other roller coaster you've ever been on. Capisce?"

"*I have zero superpowers today.*"

"I understand. You're in the awakening washing machine."

"*Yes, I am.*"

"One minute in your heart—grounded, present, and aware. The next minute a paranoid schizophrenic—back in your head again. Only solution is to…jump out of your head."

"*Jump out of my head? What does that…?*"

J. places his finger to his mouth indicating silence. You pass by the gated and locked front entrance of *The Billiard Palace* warehouse. It carries the appearance of a retail store, but now it looks abandoned, gutted, or lost to the whims of time. You can't tell. It's bleak. You keep your head down as you walk by and then turn right down an alleyway.

"This conversation to be continued later, okay?" J. speaks softly. You nod your head in agreement. "Breathe and find your center."

The back lot of *The Billiard Palace* is immense. There are a dozen street level access bays, with large roll down doors. Two of the bays are open and look to be in use. The chain link fence which surrounds the property contains an access gate which is wide open. You and J. risk it and walk in through the gate, then immediately hook a right and crouch behind a long row of tall grass and shrub which hugs the inside fence. You make your way along the fence line until you arrive at a steel fire escape staircase built into the back corner of the warehouse.

"Worth a try, I'd say," J. whispers. He points to the large grey steel door at the top of the staircase. You both creep to the top of the stairs as quietly as possible. J. risks the door. It's unlocked! He slowly and carefully opens it and peers in. You see a dark, six-foot wide steel balcony which overlooks the whole warehouse. You both enter and quickly close the door. The balcony appears to span the entire warehouse, providing access to several small upper-level offices and storage areas. On the concrete floor, twenty-feet below, you see endless rows of large furniture-sized boxes stacked three, sometimes four high. You see multiple forklifts, dollies, conveyor belts, and packing tables. There are numerous brightly lit red EXIT signs hovering like menacing demons over doorways everywhere—*and you see two white cargo vans.*

"*Bingo!*" you whisper to J. while pointing to the vans. He nods in agreement.

"No one around. We need to see what's inside those vans. You take that one." J. points to the closest van directly below your vantage point. "I'll take that one." He then points to the van on the far side of the warehouse. "Let me go first. Shit! You got your phone? Silence it." You do so quickly; J. does the same.

"I'll call you when I'm done. Just wait here. Call me—my phone will buzz—if you see *anyone* around. Got it?"

Your heart pounds like a kick drum at a *Van Halen* concert. Your palms are sweaty. Your insides are in knots. Your cortisol stress levels are at Defcon-5. You try to breath and struggle to find your aware center. No go. "*Got it.*" You squeak out through dry throat and mouth.

"Wait here!" J. repeats. "You got this."

J. then shuffle-crouches along the steel balcony gangway for several minutes. You lose sight of him. The dark recesses of the warehouse swallow him whole. You alternate between staring at your phone and the very distant van. You think you can see someone now in front of the van, but aren't positive it's J. You're so nervous you could vomit, and then—your phone buzzes. It's J. You answer...

"I looked inside. No Lenny, but definitely animals. I don't think this one is it. You need to check out yours. I'm gonna creep back up to the..." And just then, *holy fuck*—you can't believe it—your phone battery dies. *Really? Oh, shit! Breathe. Breathe. Breathe...*

You steel your nerves as much as you can and then move toward the closest inside staircase. You slowly make your way down to ground floor. You creep along a warehouse table filled with packing odds and ends and then boldly cross an open space to the back of the van. You peer inside but can't see a damn thing, so slowly...excruciatingly...you open the rear door. No animals. Just electronics, TVs, computers. It's a *Best Buy* yard sale.

"Who the fuck are you and what are you doing in my fucking van!"

And that's the last thing you remember hearing before the butt-end of an AR-15 slams into your right temple.

Ouch.

Yeah, that hurt.

Just thought I'd check in with you to see how you're doing.

Well, clearly the book-you ain't doin' so hot, but I'm talking about the you-you, who's *reading* the book.

Yeah—YOU.

So what's the point of all this? you might be asking yourself... You'll never get a rifle-butt slammed into your head for breaking into a van—right? Wrong.

Oh, it may not be a rifle-butt. But. shit. will. go. wrong. You'll lose your job. Your car will break down. You'll lose fifty grand in an investment. There'll be a death in the family. ...Another pandemic. ...Another hurricane. ...Another terrorist attack. Shit. will. go. wrong.

And that's perfect. Perfect!

Shit is meant to go wrong here.

Shall I repeat that? Shit. is. meant. to. go. wrong. here.

So, I suggest you do what J. spoke about earlier: Jump the fuck out of your head and find yourself.

One more time: Shit is meant to go wrong here.

And YOU were meant to jump out of your head, wake up... and find yourself.

Arrivederci- See ya soon...

A sickening, crunching, violent sound of metal against metal wakes you from your stupor. *Oh, shit! Days? Hours? Minutes?* You can't tell. You only know that your hands are bound behind your back, and you're lying on the floor in the back of a van with a bunch of boxes toppled all over you. *Right. Remember. I must be in that Best Buy van or something. Yes?* You attempt to look around but can't. Too many boxes. You then hear someone pulling hard at the rear door. It opens—and the interior floods with broad daylight. You squint.

"You okay, man!?" It's Emmitt and *boy*, are you relieved to hear his voice.

"We'll get you out." You hear J. speak as well.

After a minute of digging through boxes and throwing them onto the ground, J. and Emmitt reach you. They pull you out and sit you down on the van's rear bumper. Emmitt uses his buck knife to cut the ropes that had bound your wrists and arms.

"*What happened?*" you say softly. Looking around, you see that the front end of the van is smashed up against a wooden telephone pole. You're in the street not far from the back exit of *The Billiard Palace* warehouse. Nearby, steaming slightly, rests Emmitt's Ford 150, the front bumper and hood bent to hell, evidently from careening into the van. Sitting on the ground, tied to the telephone pole with legs stretched out in front of them are two rough looking, disheveled guys. You barely recognize one of them as the rifle-butt owner. It takes you a minute to gather your senses.

'*What the fuck happened?*" you ask again.

"Those two idiots happened," Emmitt replies, pointing to the men tied to the telephone pole. "And then us two idiots happened." Emmitt then points to Kai, seated in the front cab of the Ford 150. "I slammed into them. Not pretty, but it worked."

"I think we need to do this quick," J. interjects.

"You're right," Emmitt responds.

You watch as Emmitt walks over to the two idiots on the ground and kicks them both.

"Wake up, assholes."

Both slowly respond to Emmitt's repeated, not-so-gentle foot taps.

"Fuck off, asshole," is all one of them manages to say.

"Is one of you idiots named Rick?" Emmitt asks loudly. The larger of the two looks up. Emmitt takes notice. Emmitt then reaches into his back pocket and pulls out his Mirage Hotel security badge. He flashes it in front of Rick just long enough for a glance, but not long enough for a solid look.

"I'm gonna give you one chance here Rick. I don't give a damn about your electronics. My unit has been chasing the other van, with the animal contraband, for weeks now. Here's the deal. Tell me where the drop-off locale is, and I'll cut you lose. Don't tell me where the drop-off is, and my unit—the Las Vegas Metropolitan Police Department, in case the badge wasn't clear—is gonna be here in five minutes. And five minutes after that, you'll be in handcuffs. And five minutes after that...you get the idea?"

"Fuck you. How do I know you ain't lyin'? You already called it in."

"You don't, asshole, but that's a chance you take," Emmitt replies.

"What do you want with the animals? Just a bunch of fuckin' birds "

"Yeah, well, one of those birds is owned by someone you *do not* want to piss off. He's Las Vegas royalty and not the good kind."

"So, we snatched a mob bird. Big fuckin' deal."

"It'll be a big deal when I tell him Ricky Waites stole it." Emmitt nods to J., who holds out a wallet clearly belonging to Rick.

"Fuck me." Rick moans and then spits blood on the ground.

"Yeah, you got two minutes now and then you will be fucked— by the Vegas Metro Police and the mob. What are the locales?"

"Alright, alright. Devil's Gulch off 95 and fuck—Bobby, wake up! I can't remember if it's Earl's or the Exxon on 15." Rick kicks Bobby.

"Bobby! The animal drop-off. Is it Earl's or the Exxon?"

Bobby is bobbing his head around, largely incoherent. He clearly needs medical attention, but manages to mumble something.

"Girls…" Bobby moans.

"Earl's Gas on 15 in the desert past those stupid, colored fuckin' magic mountain rock things."

"So Devil's Gulch on 95 and Earl's on 15. You sure about that!?" Emmitt asks sternly.

"Yeah, I'm sure about that, motherfucker! Now cut me and my buddy loose."

Emmitt takes a big breath and then crosses his arms. "I don't think so pal. Bobby here is looking pretty banged up. He needs medical attention, and someone's gotta explain all this shit."

"Fuck you, I knew you was lying."

"Just about the mob. At least you don't have to worry about them. My police buddies, on the other hand, are going to love pickin' you idiots up." Emmitt looks over to Kai. "Kai, start it up. We gotta go." Emmitt looks at you and J. "Get in the truck bed. I'll take you to the Jeep."

Emmitt walks over to the Ford 150 and gets in on the passenger side. You can hear him dial 911. He reports the whole scene briefly and anonymously to the police. J. helps you into the back of the truck bed. You both sit with legs dangling over the tailgate. The Ford hobbles off slowly down the back alley. You and J. watch as the white van and the two fools tied to the telephone pole gradually get smaller and smaller. You turn off the alleyway, happy you'll never see *The Billiard Palace* or its inhabitants again.

A few minutes later you're in the passenger seat of the Jeep. J. is driving. He slowly follows the Ford through the back streets of Las Vegas toward *The Navajo Feather*.

"One important question I think we need to ask..." you begin while J. is driving.

"Sure. What?"

"Was the van marked?"

"Yep. Vinnie's Plumbing"

"Thank God."

"No shit. Can't be many of those around. Right?"

"Vinnie's fucking Plumbing. Hilarious." You laugh, even though it exacerbates the pounding pain in your head.

You, J., Emmitt, and Kai arrive at *The Navajo Feather* late in the afternoon. Kuruk is there. He's brought up to date about the whole Lenny disaster-adventure. He's very understanding and absorbs it all with compassion and understanding.

"Great Spirit giving you folks a Vegas adventure. Come with me to the back. You need medicine for that."

"No-no! No medicine today. I'm exhausted," you reply.

"No, greenie. Not that type of medicine. You need an icepack, Tylenol, and a place to lie down."

"Ahh...that I can do," you reply.

Kuruk takes you to the medicine initiation room and has you lie down on a sofa. He brings an icepack, some water, and several Tylenol. You gratefully swallow the pills and place the icepack on your head. Within a few minutes you're out cold.

Several hours pass by. You wake up. J., Emmitt, and Kuruk are sitting on the floor Back Jacks eating Chinese carryout. J. notices you waking up.

"Ah—back from the dead. *Ming Dynasty Chinese*. Want some?"

"Yes, actually. I'm starving."

J. fixes you a plate, and you dig in.

After a few bites you speak again. *"Where are we with stuff?"*

"Stuff?" Emmitt asks.

"Yeah—you know. Lenny stuff?"

"While you were out..." J. begins, "I went to Earl's. Gave the attendant there—Gus is his name—a $100 bill and a description of the van. If the van shows up, Gus will call me."

"Hope that works."

"Yeah, me too." J. says.

"And what about Devil's Gulch? Is that what it's called?"

"Kai is there now. On lookout," Emmitt replies.

"He's just going to wait there?"

"Partly his mess. So yes, he waits."

"Oh man, I feel so bad. I feel really guilty."

"Not your fault." Kuruk replies. "Great Spirit intended it so."

"Maybe. Still, I feel bad for everyone involved."

"Great Spirit has you. No need for worries."

You try to find solace in Kuruk's words but struggle to do so. Famished, you continue to burn through a box of Lo-Mein and General Chow's chicken. After dinner you collapse into the soft, plush depths of the sofa again. Your lean your head far back on a pillow and gaze up…

There, painted on the ceiling is a beautiful mural you hadn't noticed before. Depicted is a rocky ochre landscape containing a vast canyon with impossibly high walls, a river, and a moonlit horizon splattered with a galaxy of stars. It's stunning.

"That is amazing. Is that an actual place?" you ask, the angle of your head indicating the mural on the ceiling.

"Sure is," answers Kuruk. "Hualapai Grand Canyon, where our sweat is tomorrow night."

It takes a moment for that to register. Given recent disastrous events, you had completely forgotten, if not *entirely blocked out* any possibility of a sweat lodge or *holy fucking shit*—more Mescaline medicine.

"Really? We're still doing the sweat? While Lenny's missing?"

"Great Spirit doesn't wait for anyone, friend," Kuruk replies.

"I think we need the sweat now more than ever," Emmitt adds.

You look at J. with a profound, fearful dread in your eyes. *"And you, what do you think!?"*

J. takes a minute to reply. You know he smells fear on you, and you don't care. You're exhausted.

"You wanna jump out of your head or don't you?" J. asks.

"*Yes, but...*"

"Then it's settled. We visit the Grand Canyon *and* the Great Spirit tomorrow night. I agree with Kuruk. The Great Spirit doesn't wait for anyone."

But, but, but—is all your inner screaming mind can come up with.

But, but, but...

Chapter 17
Great Spirit

How to travel to the spirit underworld

The Great Spirit doesn't wait for anyone...

No truer words have ever been spoken. Before we continue with our adventure, let us examine these profound words and bow our heads in respect for that small chunk of ego which is about to die a gruesome death because of them...

Let us examine that old, stale *"Then I Can"* mantra:

I'm waiting for my life to improve; *then I can* work on my inner self... I need to get fit and healthy; *then I can* work on my higher self... When the stars are aligned, and Mercury is no longer in retrograde, *then I can* work on my badass self... When I get that fat amount of money in my bank account, *then I can*... When the kids are off to college, *then I can*... When I'm older and wiser, *then I can*...

Then I can never arrives.

Never.

There is no grand, delicate, *perfect* time to unravel the mysteries of life and find out who the fuck you really are. Life has other plans for you while you're making plans, and those plans fuck up other future plans... and those plans morph... and those plans change...

Maya, the great queen of illusion, has you and *your plans* in her infinitely greedy, sticky little fingers. You know that famous John Lennon quote, right? "Life is what happens when you're busy making other plans." I wonder what plans John had when he was brutally shot down in the streets of New York City during the prime of his life? I bet he had plenty—and Maya? That bitch just shrugged.

So—take heed, my spiritual friend...

"Out there beyond that fence every living thing that crawls, flies, or squats in the mud wants to kill you and eat your eyes for Jujubes." – Colonel Miles Quaritch

That's a quote from the movie *Avatar* about planet Pandora, and, regarding your plans, it's true of planet Earth as well. Fuck your plans. The only time to work on your inner, higher, badass self is *right now*. Your badass self doesn't have a clue what you *even mean* by making plans for the future. Why? Because your badass self exists only in the present moment.

So, what did Kuruk mean by "The Great Spirit doesn't wait for anyone"...?

He meant...you can do it *right now*, dawg.

Right now.

There's no better exhibit in contrast than the one experienced when leaving Las Vegas. *There's a reason for that movie name*, you surmise. You watch as the garish, eyeball-exhausting *Mirage Hotel* and all its ugly brethren get quickly swallowed by the harsh, barren, relentlessly brown desert landscape. *The Mirage couldn't be a more fitting name—for Las Vegas, for life, maybe even for existence.* Your thoughts empty themselves as you drive.

With the Jeep fully packed, including Ollie and excluding Lenny, you reluctantly step into the next part of your adventure with a heavy, but hopeful heart. You have to stop yourself from neurotically watching, waiting, and listening for J.'s phone to ring. It's agony.

You pass by the Hoover Dam, unfazed. The miles pile up as you and J. make your way to a small village in Arizona called Peach Springs. It's a three-hour trek. J. shares the driving with you.

You arrive at the desert meeting spot: a small gate and cattle grid stretched across a rocky dirt road, serving as the entranceway to the great Hualapai Indian Reservation, the Grand Canyon, and the Colorado River. Kuruk is there waiting in his Jeep—an old, red, two-door Wrangler. You pull up and shamelessly park the fancy, four-door, Stella-yellow Rubicon and trailer next to his.

"Trade Jeeps?" Kuruk says, smiling as he gets out of his.

"I like my pimped ride, thank you very much," J. responds.

"We should wait for Emmitt. He's on a motorbike today. Should be just a minute…"

"Okay, cool."

"Any news?" Kuruk asks.

"Nothing yet," J. replies.

"Spirit animal, right?" Kuruk asks.

"Yes."

"Then nothing to worry about. Spirit animal has to come home."

"I hope so."

"*This place is spectacular!*" you interject, breaking the seriousness.

"It is. My people's home since 1883. Official United States government nonsense at any rate. Before that, our home for thousands of years."

"No one really owns the land, do they?"

"Everything here...belongs to the Great Spirit. You'll see tonight." Kuruk pauses and looks south toward the town of Peach Springs. "Here he comes."

You look in the same direction and see a cloud of dust and dirt stirred up in the distance. You hear the telltale cough and roar of a motorcycle. Within seconds, Emmitt pulls up on an older, but mint, black Honda Rebel. He cuts the engine.

"I just spoke with Kai," Emmitt proclaims. "So far, no activity at the gulch."

"None at Earl's, either. I just called the attendant an hour ago," J. adds.

"Nothing we can do, then. We got the sat-phone unit in the Jeep, so we should have cell service where we're going. You guys ready for a Grand Canyon Hualapai medicine sweat?"

"Can one really truly prepare?" you respond.

"Nope. Rhetorical question, I guess," Emmitt says with a grin. "Let's go. Follow me. We'll be on *that* for forty-five minutes." Emmitt gestures to the dirt road stretched out beyond the gate and cattle grid. "Hope your Jeep's got good shocks." With a quick full body movement and leg jerk, Emmitt fires up his Honda. Kuruk jumps in his Jeep.

"I'll drive. This is going to be one of the most spectacular roads you've ever been on. Enjoy!" J. says as he jumps into the driver's seat.

"No argument here," you reply, putting on your seatbelt. You look in the back seat and are happy to see Ollie sitting contently on his branch. *"Something new for you too, huh, Buddy?"* Ollie responds with a languid blinking of his large yellow eyes. You're happy he's happy.

You cross over the cattle grid. A small sign reads *Diamond Creek Road – Beach area 19 Miles – Property of Hualapai Nation – No access without permission.* Your desert trek begins...

No words can describe the views and the *emotions* they elicit as you drive along Diamond Creek Road. "Road" really isn't the right term. It's an old, dried-out, hard-packed creek bed, suitable for four-wheel drives and motorcycles only.

So this is what driving on Mars is like, you think. The flat, barren desert soon erupts with massive, skyscraper-sized canyon walls. The brilliant abstract color variations of the protruding rock wall abutments put to shame the man-made, pseudo-blitzkrieg of Las Vegas.

But the *size* of it all is what *really* gets you. Something about the size echoes deep in your heart and being. The *infinite* resonates here. *Mystery* resides here. Something *other-worldly* lives here. About thirty minutes into the trip, you finally get it—the *Great Spirit* lives here. *Nothing* compares to the inner-sanctum depths of the Grand Canyon; it's all overwhelming—and you haven't even stepped foot into this thing called a sweat lodge yet. You're getting nervous.

You arrive at a small Arroyo enclave nestled between two massive cliffs. Several roof-only shelters, two porta-johns, and a small storage shack are the only visible structures. Everyone parks and exits their vehicles. Kuruk gives you the lay of the land: the areas best suited for camping tents, the path to the river, the path to the sweat lodge, the bathroom facilities, and even a hand pump for fresh water. He reminds you that several more guests are due to arrive. *All good.*

Several hours of tent, food, fire, and sweat lodge preparation take place. There's some lingering amber and red-shift light left over from the sun, which settled behind massive canyon walls an hour ago. *Twilight in the Grand Canyon. Travel to Mars. Check,* you muse.

A young couple arrives at dinnertime. You're introduced to Will and Emily, both in their mid-twenties and full of energy and enthusiasm. It's good to have the extra company. You learn that they, too, are sweat lodge "greenies," as Emmitt and Kuruk like to say. Now wise to the whole Mescaline puking-purging thing, you're conservative with food intake—a handful of rice, beans, and a few vegetables only. You don't want to vomit up a complete meal.

The sun sheds the last vestiges of its light. It's dark out now and...it's time.

A brief musing about sweat lodges:

Listen—I know that a "sweat lodge" may not sound like a particularly badass thing to do. More than likely, you're thinking "New Age, hippy-dippy"—but hear me out: I've done multiple sweat lodges...and trust me when I say there are fewer things more badass than subjecting yourself to the heat, steam, fire, smoke, incense, and/or herbal-hallucinogenic features of an authentic Native American sweat lodge. They are the *very definition* of badass.

Sweat lodges have been used as a means of purification, spiritual initiation, emotional catharsis, and inner soul work by Native Americans (and Vikings!) for thousands of years. Sweat lodges are older than Freud, Jung, Dr. Phil, and the entire history of the pharmaceutical industry—combined. I know that longevity doesn't necessarily correlate to scientifically proven efficacy, but there's something to the sweat lodge experience that can't be denied.

I'm not blind to the dark side of sweat lodges either: Combining high heat, steam, fire, smoke, hallucinogens, and human bodies is inevitably inviting a tightrope walk of safety concerns. You can *die*, and people *have died*, from participating in sweat lodges.

My badass opinion: As long as you have a trained, trusted, and old-school guide who knows what the fuck he or she is doing, you'll be just fine. But—build one of these things in your backyard and hire a New Age, rent-a-shaman from Craig's List—well, *that* might be sketchy. Operate at your own peril.

You've been seated on the bare earth inside the ten-foot diameter, plastic-tarped, domed sweat lodge for maybe ten minutes—and already what Kuruk told you *would* happen *is* happening: *You want the fuck out.* Not because of the medicine—you haven't even had that yet; not the herbal concoction he placed on the hot stones either—you're okay with the smell of pine and sage; And not the nearly pitch dark, claustrophobic confines of the actual hut—enclosed spaces don't bother you. It's the damn hot steam, which causes every pore in your body to sweat profusely. In other words, you want to get the fuck out of the sweat lodge because the sweat lodge is making you *sweat*.

Kuruk said the *Prayer of The Four Directions* and now is adding ladles of water and herbs to the hot stones in the center pit. Earlier, you learned that the hot stones create the engine that make a sweat lodge tick. You're now experiencing that firsthand. Each stone—you see about a dozen—is glowing red hot. They had been smoldering in a nearby fire outside the lodge for the last several hours. Now, when Kuruk adds the herbal water mixture, the stones provide needle hot steam and sage infused smoke. It's a potent combination.

"Breathe, deeply and slowly," Kuruk reminds everyone. "This is the first doorway. Allow the heat in and the sweat out."

"Oh, my god, it's hot!" your new friend Emily squeaks out.

"That's the idea, babe," her boyfriend Will replies.

"You doin' okay?" J. asks.

You nod your head. *Deep breaths. Deep breaths...*you keep telling yourself.

After some time, you adjust to the hot steam and find a good breathing rhythm. You're drenched with sweat and getting used to it. Soon you sense that the first doorway is complete.

Briefly, Kuruk opens the side deerskin flap, and what feels like a hurricane of cool night air wafts in and gives everyone a reprieve from the heat.

"Time for doorway number two." Kuruk closes the flap and adds more sage water to the stones. Once again, the sweat lodge fills with an oppressive steam heat which causes you to squirm and fidget.

Kuruk declares his needs: "Little Bear—medicine and the bucket."

Emmitt nods his head and pulls out a large thermos and six mugs. He fills each cup with the same milky liquid used the other day at *The Navajo Feather*. You're pretty sure Emmitt didn't hold out on the peyote button quantity this time. He hands everyone a filled mug.

"Great Spirit, we offer this peyote sacrament to you—so that all gathered here tonight in your name may know you, see you, and be held, supported, and healed by you. A'ho."

"Okay, folks. Down the hatch." Kuruk laughs.

Emmitt smiles. You and J. slowly sip your Mescaline medicine like a rare tequila. Emmitt and Kuruk swallow theirs with an easy laissez-faire you envy. Will and Emily drink theirs like it was chocolate milk. *Ooooh, they're going to regret that,* you think.

Within seconds, you can feel your stomach objecting to the medicinal peyote poison. *Let's call it what it is*, you think. *J. called it a wise, self-regulated poisoning. Better than the thousands of other ways people poison themselves. At least this poisoning gets you a date with the Great Spirit…*

Your thoughts come to a dead halt as you watch Will and Emily vomit whatever they ate today, yesterday, and maybe even last week. Their naïveté got the best of them. Not surprisingly, they trooper through it. Emmitt is skilled with the bucket as he helps them purge.

"Oh, god that's strong shit," Will grumbles through fits of vomiting.

Kuruk speaks: "Good, good. Allow the medicine to purge. Gateway number two is powerful. Don't resist, push, or fight. The more you can allow and welcome it, the better off you'll be— and the sooner the purge will end."

You look at J. He looks a little nauseous, but no worse for the wear. He smiles at you, and even looks a little…dare you think it…inebriated! If this medicine can make J. loopy, you're in trouble.

But oddly enough, you don't feel much of anything yet. Kuruk adds more sage water to the stones. Steam heat rises. You practice your breathing technique. It's difficult, but doable. Kuruk and Emmitt begin a slow haunting chant, using a small drum and a rattle. The chant, steam, heat, and now finally the Mescaline medicine invite you…on a deep journey into the underworld. You begin to lose orientation. Before accepting the invitation, you point past J. to a water bottle. He hands it to you and you drink. *One last drink for the road*, you think. You set it down—and realize that it *wasn't* a water bottle. It was your Mescaline medicine mug, and you just polished it off. *Oh, fuckity duck*…are your last coherent thoughts.

Okay, let's go…

Where shall we go?

Isn't there something you wanted to show me?

Oh, right—yes, that. It's over here. Come on...

You're heavy as a stone and light as a feather. You crawl over to the sweat lodge deerskin door flap, open it, and step out into the night air. You breathe the most exhilarating breath of your entire life. Cool, fresh oxygen enters every part of your body, covering it like a blanket of newly fallen virgin snow. You are clear, empty, and alive!!

Hey—look up.

You look up and see the Milky Way Galaxy span horizontally across canyon walls.

Oh, my god. That has to be one of the most beautiful things I have ever seen.

I know. Right!?

Is that what you wanted to show me?

No. That's over here.

Are you the Black Shadow?

Not anymore. I've changed.

You arrive at a small, stone campfire ring you hadn't seen before. There's a small fire burning and several logs to sit on surrounding the fire.

Sit here.

You sit on a log and look into the fire.

What now?

Now this.

Another person appears out of nowhere, now sitting on one of the logs. You can't quite make out who it is. You lean in to get a closer look. Immediately upon recognition, you have tears in your eyes; you collapse to the ground. You knee-crawl over to the person…

"Oh, Pappa. Oh, my god, Pappa!" You're so overcome emotionally; you can barely speak. You wrap your arms around your father and grab him tightly. You wail out an eon of tears, heaves, and cries. It goes on for several minutes.

"*How, how, how is this…*"

"Shh…Little Bird. I don't know, but I am here."

"*I have missed you so, so much!*" The tears continue to roll.

"I have missed you too, little one. I have missed you, too."

Then you remember all the shadowy, bad stuff about your father. His alcoholism, the separation, the divorce, the abandonment, and…his eventual death. All of the memories *and feelings* flood back in. You look at your arms and your body. You're eight years old again…

You look deep into your father's eyes, remembering how the anger began—how it boiled inside of you; how it consumed you; and how you carried it with you throughout the rest of your life…

"I forgive you, Papa."

Tears form in your father's eyes. "I am so sorry, Little Bird. I am so sorry. I was miserable. So miserable. Your forgiveness means more to me than you'll ever know."

"I know Papa... I love you, Papa."

"I love you too, Little Bird."

And then—as quickly as he appeared, your father vanishes. You collapse again to the ground, wailing. You eventually stop, the catharsis released. You sit staring into the fire for several moments. The utter stillness of the canyon Arroyo and the astounding firmament above your shoulders soothes your wounded, and now partly healed, spirit.

You good?

Mostly, I think. Was that real?

Does it matter?

I guess not.

There's more.

I figured.

You glance at your hands, arms, and body again. You're a teenager now. Another person instantly appears sitting on a log across from you.

You get up and walk over to him. You know it's a *him*, because there's no one else it could be. Uncle Sam was also your father. He stepped in when your biological father abandoned you and your mother.

"*Hi, Uncle Sam.*"

Uncle Sam stands. You embrace. It's a familiar love that has never left you—a love that you have so desperately missed since his tragic death in a car accident when you were fourteen. You begin crying again, wondering how much more of this you can take. He says nothing, but gently pats the back of your head.

"Let me look at you."

You release the hug and step back. Your hands, arms, and body now match your older self.

"My, how you've grown. I knew you'd be fine. Look at you!"

"I was so sad for so long when you died."

"I know. I am so very sorry that happened. I don't know why, but it did. Look at you now! You're just fine."

"I love you so, so much, Uncle Sam."

"I love you, too. I love you, too. You will do great things, won't you? Promise me that."

You begin crying again, knowing that your beloved Uncle Sam is also probably going to vanish.

"Yes, I will. I will do great things."

"I love you."

"I love you, too, Uncle Sam."

He vanishes. You sit down again on a log and sob into your hands. You're exhausted. Sadness—so much sadness—continues to bubble to the surface of your consciousness. You look up and see wafts of something floating off into the starry sky above. And you realize that those wafts are the last vestiges of sadness finally leaving you, floating off into the cosmos…

Almost done.

There's more?

One last thing.

Who now?

Me.

You?

Yes, look.

You look up and see an older, gentler version of yourself sitting on a log across the fire from you. A version of yourself who has *arrived*—aware, present, content, awake, and happy.

You're me?

Of course not.

Then who are you?

I'm the Great Spirit, silly. I'm the Great Spirit.

You open your eyes. You're back in the sweat lodge. You look around, confused, but mostly astounded by what you just experienced. *That was so real! Holy fuck! That was real. But it wasn't. Or was it? Does it matter? Holy fucking shit—that was real.* Your thoughts are back and they're reeling in the face of a mystery they can't comprehend. You notice Kuruk glancing your way.

"I see you stepped through doorway three. Good job, greenie." Kuruk speaks to you gently, then smiles.

"*What's doorway three?*"

"The underworld—where the Great Spirit shows its face. I can tell."

"*You can tell what?*"

"...that the Great Spirit showed you its face."

It takes a moment for you to respond. "*Yes... I suppose it did.*"

A few minutes pass, and you watch as, one by one, J., Emmitt, Will, and Emily come back to waking consciousness. You presume that they, too, visited the underworld and met with the Great Spirit. Kuruk begins chanting something clearly meant to facilitate the group's return. He no longer continues to ladle sage water onto the rocks. The temperature inside the sweat lodge drops to a more tolerable level. He invites you and everyone else to chant along with him. You do so, haphazardly and out of tune.

Within a few minutes, all of you are standing outside the sweat lodge, the ceremony complete. The stars are out in their resplendent multitudes. You breathe deeply and completely.

The last thing you realize before heading off to your tent is that the awakened state of presence has returned with a fierce, strong, and palpable quality. It feels good—*really* good.

Chapter 18
Honda Rebel

How to find your true inner voice

It's 5 a.m. You're cozy deep in REM sleep when you hear J.'s phone ring in the tent next to yours. He answers on the second ring...

"Yeah?...all good...okay...you sure?...okay...hold on, let me get a pen..." You hear J. rummage through his backpack. "Okay, go ahead...got it. Thanks, man. Really appreciate it. I owe ya."

J. hangs up the phone. You scramble to get dressed, unzip your tent, and then...

What's the hurry?

I dunno. You're right. There's no hurry, not even now.

Breathe. Be in your body. Notice awareness...

That's it?

That's it.

Instead of reacting, you respond. You catch yourself and notice the deep aftereffects of the medicine sweat lodge. You're present, still, aware, and grounded. You step out of the tent. The sun is rising. You can see its dawning glow over the eastern edge of the Arroyo Canyon wall. It's going to be an immaculate, clear day.

J. steps out of his tent. Your eyes meet. He knows, you know. And what *you know* is that he's feeling what you're feeling—the same awakened presence. *No need to even mention it...*

"What's up?"

"That was my guy at Earl's. He sighted the van. It pulled in for gas and then went around back to the exchange spot. We got lucky. No one showed."

You nod in approval.

"They're coming our way...headed to Phoenix. Devil's Gulch."

"He's sure?"

"Said they came in to use the bathroom. One of them was on the phone and pissed off. The gist was some sort of fuck-up, wrong drop-off, wrong city. He heard one of them say 'Devil's Gulch—two hours.' That's all I know."

"Fingers crossed. We should call Kai."

"Yeah. I'll get Emmitt to do it. We gotta pack and get the hell out of here immediately."

The early morning conversation wakes Emmitt and Kuruk from their tents. They exit, stretching, awake.

"Good news, then?" Kuruk asks.

"We gotta get to Devil's Gulch ASAP," J. responds.

"Did Kai call?" Emmitt asks.

J. brings both Kuruk and Emmitt up to speed, and a plan is devised. Emmitt's motorcycle is the fastest method out of the canyon and desert. You and Emmitt will travel on it. J. will stay, pack the Jeep, and join everyone as soon as he can. If estimates are correct, Devil's Gulch is about an hour and a half away *by motorcycle*. With any luck you and Emmitt will arrive before the van does. What happens after that is anyone's guess.

You agree to the plan with zero hesitation. Normally, this kind of rapid-fire planning and daredevil execution would have you shitting your pants, but you're calm as a napping kitty as it all unfolds. Even the thought of bouncing through the rocky desert landscape for forty-five minutes on the back of a Honda Rebel doesn't faze you.

"You feeling okay today, greenie?" Kuruk asks as he helps you adjust the spare motorcycle helmet.

You smile, look deeply into his kind, wise, old eyes, and reply, "*Great Spirit—no problem.*"

"A'ho," Kuruk responds with a smile. He completes the adjustment then taps your helmet, affirming the fit.

"You good?" asks J.

"*I'm fine. Let's get Lenny back.*"

"I'll meet out there as soon as I can," J. says.

"*Roger that.*" You reach up and pull the helmet's visor down.

You hop on the Honda. Emmitt shows you several different methods of holding on, using feet, arms, or hands. It's not difficult, but the bouncing hasn't started yet. It'll be rough, but you're ready. Emmitt kick-starts the bike. It roars to life with a loud pop.

As you're leaving, you look toward Will and Emily's tent and see them exit, groggy and barely clothed. They look run-over-by-a-Mack-truck hungover. You smile and, for good measure, flash them the peace sign. They're too hungover to respond. Inside you laugh. *They'll learn*, you think. E*veryone eventually learns…*

The ride is excruciating. It's a lot harder than you imagined to hold on in any comfortable way, but you manage. Humorously *and* seriously, your thoughts gravitate to the months of chiropractic, rolfing, and physical therapy sessions you'll need in order to put your muscles, organs, and bones back in their proper places.

Despite the jarring ride, the *Great Spirit* is indeed with you. The magnificent desert canyon walls and spiraling abutments, married with your post-sweat lodge awakened state, make *everything* A-OK. Your heart sings, and the *Great Spirit* of the Grand Canyon joins you in the singing.

You're keeping close track of time. In forty-two minutes, you arrive at the entrance gate.

"You need a bathroom break?" Emmitt asks. He's said all of three words the entire trip, so you're surprised when he asks.

"*Um, yeah—sure,*" you reply, lifting your helmet's visor shield.

Emmitt stops the bike and points to a scrubby island of cactus and junipers. "Bathroom's over there."

You hop off, absolutely ecstatic to piss in a grove of cacti in exchange for a minute or two's reprieve from the back of the Honda. You return with a giant smile on your face.

"Well, you're feelin' good today. Medicine worked its magic, hey?" Emmitt smiles.

"*No complaints here.*" You hop on the bike—your muscles very much complaining.

Before taking off, Emmitt twists slightly and speaks through his open helmet. He points to the side of his helmet. "Touch this spot on yours." You do so, and you can hear an internal mic and speaker system come alive.

"Can you hear me?"

"*Holy shit. I didn't know these could do that.*"

"Yep. Pretty cool, huh? I needed to concentrate in the desert. But on asphalt, I'm fine using the speaker system."

"*Awesome,*" you reply, finding it a hell of a lot easier to communicate this way.

Emmitt continues: "The rough part's over. Now's the *fast* part. It's normally an hour to Devil's Gulch from here. We're gonna try for forty-five minutes. You cool with that?"

"*Cool.*"

"Great. Hang on. We'll be on a smooth road shortly."

You fasten down the visor shield of your helmet. Emmitt guns the motorcycle and, within a minute, you're on smooth, buttery asphalt. It's glorious.

"*Holy shit. This is Heaven!*" you exclaim, joyful to be on a smooth surface and loving the ease of the internal mic system.

"Yeah, the canyon road is rough on the ass," Emmitt laughs. He maneuvers the bike through the township of Peach Springs and then, once past it, switches to a higher gear and throttles the engine. Immediately, Emmitt's humble, black Honda Rebel motorcycle transforms into an unstoppable, two-wheeled, crotch rocket. You're grinning from ear to ear when, during this maneuver, Emmitt says something to you—something innocent, fun, and inconsequential at the time—but something that will linger in your heart for the rest of your life…

"You ready to get your kicks…on Route 66!?" Emmitt shouts with abandoned caution and unrestrained joy.

Your brain places his epiphanous exaltation in long-term storage: The events of today will blot it out for quite some time, but years from now, you'll remember and be deeply grateful that indeed—you, too, visited, traveled upon, and were privileged to be changed forever by the historic and famous Route 66—the "mother" road of America; the road from Chicago to Los Angeles that passes directly through Peach Springs, Arizona…

The road that the downtrodden, yet hopeful, migrants of the Great Depression traveled upon... that John Steinbeck wrote about in *The Grapes of Wrath*...that Jack Kerouac wrote about in *On the Road*...and that Nat King Cole sang about in "Get Your Kicks on Route 66."

Now this great road is *your* road, *your* book, and *your* anthem, in a league with legends. Route 66 is now a part of your spiritual badass journey, as you're on the way to finding out just who in the fuck you truly are.

Take a deep breath, badass—

Why?

You need to get ready—

For what?

Trust me, Breathe...

The second bullet whizzes past your helmet—

Just before this, the events unfold with no time to think or discuss: You and Emmitt exit Route 66 onto Highway 93. You both spot the van with the *Vinnie's Plumbing* logo on the side. Emmitt trails just far enough behind not to raise suspicions. All is well—until the van exits onto an unmarked, dirt and pebble service road which creeps precariously along the edge of a deep and vast canyon: Devil's Gulch.

That's a long way down.

Yes, it is—

While on the service road, Emmitt makes one small but vital mistake: He slip-skids the bike, nearly dumping both of you to the ground. The skid throws a cloud of dirt into the air. The bike's engine, in protest of the steep angle to which it has just been subjected, sputters and stops.

Oh fuck.

Fuck, indeed—

The van sees the cloud and stops. Whoever is driving it is now suspicious. The van makes a slow U-turn in the road. Emmitt rights the motorcycle and begins furiously pumping the kickstart ratchet with his right foot. No go. The van creeps closer—its four tires crunching menacingly on the gravel road beneath them.

Oh, shit. Come on—start!!

Don't worry. He'll get it—

The van gets closer. Kick-start. Sputter. No go.

Closer. The van driver can now see both you and Emmitt—and you and Emmitt can now see *him*.

"How in the fuck!?"Emmitt yells loudly in the helmet microphone.

"*Is that the same…?*"

"Yeah, that's Rick…son-of-a-bitch I left tied to the telephone pole yester-…"

And *that's* when the bullets started flying. The first bullet hits the dirt just below the Honda's front tire—

Kick-start. Sputter. No go.

Okay, fucking start. Fucking start!!

Calm down. I said he would get it—

The second bullet whizzes past your helmet–

Kick-start. Sputter. Boom! Roar. It starts.

I told you so—

"Hang on tight…really tight!" Emmitt yells as he 360s the bike in the road and guns it. The bike takes off along the rim of the canyon. The van pursues. Bullets fly, hitting the dirt all around you.

Holy fucking shit Mother-of-Mary!! Get me the fuck out of here!!!

On the other hand—

There is no other hand!

Sure, there is. Always—

More bullets fly. You hear one nick the bike muffler.

Say yes to the fear! Yes to awareness!

You don't need that. Just Breathe. Let go—

Now!!???

Yes. Even now—

You decide for crazy, desperate reasons, of course…to finally listen.

I am not the voice in my head. I am the one—

You look behind you and see that Emmitt is gaining ground on the van. You speak, but from a new perspective—

—which notices the voice. "Emmitt, skid the bike again." You speak calmly and clearly into the headset microphone.

"What!? Why!? I think we can outrun…"

"Trust me, Emmitt. Skid the bike again."

"Are you sure!!?"

"I'm positive. Do it—now." You urge him with clarity and authority.

Emmitt listens. He throttles back the bike and downshifts just enough for a safe skid exit—if there is such a thing. He does so just as the road takes a sharp bend at a large boulder outcrop perched on the edge of the canyon rim. The bike wobbles, stutters, and then dumps...

"You got this Emmitt!" are your last words before you're thrown from the bike. Somehow, you manage to maneuver your body off the bike in a way that doesn't mangle or kill you. You're calm and focused as the dumping unfolds—seemingly in slow motion. You fall off and, in the process, deftly grab Emmitt by the elbow, pulling him off the bike with you. You both come to a rolling, tumbling halt next to the boulder pile on the rim of the canyon and watch, as his mint condition, black Honda Rebel ...rolls off the edge of the canyon...into oblivion.

You don't have time for shock or mourn, because the *Vinnie's Plumbing* van pulls up shortly afterward. You and Emmitt quickly crawl out of sight behind a single large boulder. The sickening crunch of the van wheels comes to a halt. You hear two doors open and two sets of feet hit the ground.

"They can't see us. Don't worry," you whisper to Emmitt, surprised the headset mics still work.

"I know. All good, man," he whispers back.

You hear Rick exclaiming loudly as he peers over the canyon rim. "Dumb motherfuckers. Serves 'em right. Come on, man. Let's get down there."

"Really!?" his partner asks.

"Yeah, really! We ain't stoppin'. We got product to pick up and deliver. He'll be waitin'. Business as usual. No one's gonna find those dumb motherfuckers for days."

"Whatever you say, boss."

You hear Rick and his minion get back in their van and start it up. They creep off, the sound of wheels on gravel once again worming its way into your brain. You remove your helmet. Emmitt removes his.

"That was one hell of a jump, man. You saved my ass. Thank you. I owe ya," Emmitt says.

"Thanks. Just doing what we had to." You respond with an unusual amount of calm. You're surprised by the new grounded sense of *okayness* in your voice.

Even now?! you amusingly ask yourself.

I told you, even now—

"Sorry about your bike." You peer over the canyon edge and see its mangled remains in a cloud of dust, a good hundred feet down.

"All good, man. It was due for an oil change anyway," Emmitt says, laughing. He stands and then pats you on the back and adds "You, my friend, are no longer a greenie—*at all*."

Chapter 19
Lenny Knows

How to navigate a hot air balloon down the Grand Canyon

A brief aside about love:

Probably like many of you out there in our humble little galaxy, I fell in love for the first time when I was eight years old. It was 1977 and the girl I fell hard for was this grand, beautiful dame named *Star Wars*. She spoke to me like no other girl. And she didn't just speak—she seduced, amused, entertained, and more than anything, *loved*. Huh? How did a movie *love* you…you say?

The answer to that is easy. By the end of the movie Luke, Ben, Leah, Han, Chewbacca, R2-D2, and C-3PO all had one thing in common: They all loved each other. They were best friends. They had traveled to the underworld together. They had gone on the hero's journey together. They had bickered, fought, suffered, journeyed, travailed, overcome, and finally, loved together. They lived it, demonstrated it, and expressed it. Their love for one another became my love for them—and for the movie.

In any work of art, the love, joy, or raw emotion from which that art emanates should be expressed or, better yet, *demonstrated*.

In *Star Wars* that demonstration was largely through the interaction of two nonverbal characters: Chewbacca and R2-D2.

Lenny is the demonstration of that love here.

Lenny knows...

You sit with your legs dangling precariously over the canyon rim. *Devil's Gulch* is one of many "mini" Grand Canyons scattered throughout the Northwest Arizona territory, that presumably, like hundreds of its brethren, had to begrudgingly settle for child status in light of its behemoth geologic mother, formed by the pummeling waters of the Colorado River over the millennia. You're still impressed—even more so every time you gawk at Emmitt's crushed Honda Rebel, eaten alive by the gulch. *You had me at Devil*, you think.

While waiting for J. and Kai to arrive, you peer across the gulch's quarter mile gap at an oddity you've been fascinated by for the last half hour. You pull out your phone to snap a few photos when Kai pulls up in his old, rusty copper-brown Camaro Z28. *Wait till I get my grubby hands on that car*, you think.

"The problem is getting down in the canyon," You overhear Emmitt speaking on the phone with J., who is apparently three minutes out. "They have a thirty-minute head start. By the time we snake our way down in there to find them, they'll be long gone. Not to mention there's no way we can do that and stay hidden."

You listen in and are getting the gist of the problem: speed and stealth. Kai exits his Camaro, walks over to Emmitt, and inserts himself into the conversation. He's 100 percent positive that some sort of illegal transaction is about to take place in the bottom of Devil's Gulch.

Well duh, you think, *Vinnie's Plumbing van and the accompanying shower of bullets from it already cued you in on that shit.*

He's just a kid—

I know. Judgmental asshole I am.

Jedi you are not—

Young padawan I am.

The three-ring circus of Emmitt, Kai, and J. on the phone continues while you sit and watch another circus unfolding across the gulch...

J. arrives in the yellow Jeep with the trailer attached. He parks and jumps out.

"I don't see any other way. Let's detach the trailer and take the Jeep down," J. exhorts.

"Take too long..." Emmitt counters.

"Anybody have rope? Maybe we can rappel down. I see you got a winch on the Jeep." Kai points to the Jeep.

"No rappelling gear," J. responds.

You get up and walk over to the group.

"You doin' okay?" J. asks. "Emmitt filled me in."

"I'm good," you respond calmy. *"and I'll tell you how we're going to get down in there."*

All eyes turn to you. You look across the canyon and point. There, in various stages of setup are four hot air balloons. One is fully inflated and still tethered to the ground. Emblazoned on the balloon's vast multi-colored exterior, in large, ostentatious font, are the words *Vegas Balloon Rides*.

Everyone peers across the canyon. Eyebrows arch. Heads tilt. Smiles form. Everyone's body language shouts a resounding "yes!"

"Hoooly shit!" Kai yelps.

"Might just work..." Emmitt utters.

"Viva Las–*fucking*–Vegas!" J. shouts.

J. has the look of an eight-year-old on Christmas morning when every single present...is *his*.

A rough plan is formed: Kai is to wait here with the trailer and Ollie. He's disappointed, but understands. He'll also be in charge of lookout, communication, and calling the cops when needed. J. provides him with a set of binoculars. You, J., and Emmitt will drive the Jeep over to the balloon launch area and, if possible, bribe a quick ride to the bottom. If all goes well, everyone figures it'll take fifteen minutes to get down in the gulch. The best part: Rick and his minions won't suspect a damn thing. Kai is pretty sure the balloon folks are here all the time.

J. quickly detaches the trailer and places Ollie in a pop-up cage in the back. You and Emmitt hop in the Jeep.

"Good luck, guys!" Kai shouts.

You roll down the Jeep's rear window and give Kai a long-distance fist-bump. *"Thanks, dude. Couldn't do this without you."*

Kai looks pleased, albeit slightly worried, as the Jeep rolls out.

See. He's a great kid—

I know he is. I know...

It takes about seven minutes on side roads to drive around and then over one end of the gulch to get to the balloon people. J. then overlands the Jeep from the road onto a big dusty swath of desert. The Jeep bumps and jostles as J. pushes its limits on the terrain. You arrive. No one seems to notice or care about your unannounced presence. You assume they're used to gawkers...

The first balloon has launched. It serenely makes its way up and across the gulch. You can see about half a dozen people in its basket. Every thirty seconds or so, its burner system erupts with a loud swish of white noise gently propelling it higher. It's quite a sight to behold up close.

The second balloon is nearly filled with air and looks just about ready for launch. You can see another gaggle of people prepared to board it.

The third and fourth balloons are about halfway filled.

"I think we should try our luck with those," J. says, pointing to balloons three and four.

"But if we take that one…" Emmitt points to balloon two. "…we can get down right now. I think I should at least try."

"Of course," J. says in response. "Go for it. I'll ask balloon three." J. looks at you. "You try your luck with balloon four. I have a thousand dollars cash in the Jeep. Do what you have to."

"*Got it*," you respond.

You watch as Emmitt and J. walk off toward their balloons. You stride over to balloon four, now about three-quarters filled. There's a family of four standing nearby, clearly the intended passengers. The children, a boy and a girl, look to be about eight and ten respectively.

Damn. This is going to be tricky.

Just be honest—

Really?

Absolutely.

You walk over to the family.

"*You guys riding in that?*"

"Oh, yes. Pretty neat huh?" the father responds.

"Very. How much does it cost to ride in one of these things?"

"It's costing us about $1,200," the father says gleefully.

Ouch.

No shit—

That's ungodly expensive.

Tell them about Lenny!

"Listen…" you announce, grabbing the attention of all four. "*My friends and I are in a jam. Well, actually—no, my dog is in a jam.*"

Okay that works—

"*He ran away from us yesterday, and now he's down in that gulch.*" You point to the bottom of Devil's Gulch.

Keep going…

"We need to borrow that balloon, just for a short bit, to get down there."

"I don't know, Buddy. We already paid and—"

"*He's a dalmatian. Just a puppy. Six months old.*"

Okay, good thinking. Not exactly a lie…

"Any chance we could…?"

"I told ya, Buddy, we already paid."

Go for the heartstrings…

"*His name is Lenny, and he means the world to me, and he might die.*"

"Oh Daddy, we can't let Lenny die!" the eight-year-old boy sings.

Bingo! We're in!

"*He's probably really hungry about now.*"

"Mom, Dad—let them find their dog!" The little girl is second to sing.

"*Listen, I can pay you if you want. I got a...*" you switch gears mid-sentence.

"*We really don't know how much longer he'll last.*"

"Dan. It's okay. We can wait." The mother is third to sing.

Finish it!

"*It would be a horrible, horrible death...*"

"Goddamnit, Buddy–okay–go find your dog. I'll talk to our balloon guide." The dad finally capitulates.

Slam dunk!

I feel a little bad.

Don't. Go get Lenny—

"Can I compensate you for the inconvenience?" you add.

"Well, um, yeah," the father responds.

"No, not at all. Go get your dog." The mother interjects giving her husband the stink eye.

"Awesome. Thank you so, so much!"

You step slightly away and wave your arms at Emmitt and J. Both of them are mid-negotiation with their balloons. They stop and walk over.

"He wants $1,200," Emmitt says with a frown.

"$1,000," J. adds somberly.

"*Free*," you say with a smile. Both J. and Emmitt perk up. "*Let's get Lenny.*" And then you add "*And for today, Lenny's a dog.*"

"A dog?" J. questions.

"Don't ask. Just follow."

"I don't know what you told them, but I'll take it," J. offers, shakes his head, and laughs.

Two minutes later, J., Emmitt, and you are piled into balloon number four and rising into the air. All of you wave to the nice family who graciously negotiated the arrangements with their balloon guide.

The guide, an older gentleman named Burt, is unfazed by the switch-a-roo. After several burner blasts of hot air, and having floated beyond earshot of those on the ground, he speaks nonchalantly...

"You guys doin' a deal down in the canyon?"

You laugh at his astute observation.

"Hah!" J. chuckles. "No deal. Some criminals stole my iguana."

"Iguana?! What's that? Some sorta new street drug?"

Emmitt smiles at you, rolling his eyes.

"No, no. It's an actual reptile...lizard...iguana," J. tries to clarify.

"I thought I heard it all up here in this balloon, but that one takes the cake." Burt maneuvers a few things on the burner device. "Hang on everybody. We're going down fast—as requested."

You take a moment to absorb the surreal and ridiculous beauty of the situation. The view of *Devil's Gulch* from hot air balloon is breathtakingly gorgeous. The sun shines its late morning rays down into the canyon—a vast painted pool of red, brown, yellow, gold, and amber rock. The immense gulch is peppered with hundreds of dark green shrubbery and cactus islands. From your vantage point, there are empty rainwater rivulets, gullies, arching rock formations, and thousands of single-standing, lost, and lonely boulders. *Devil's Gulch* is another planet—and you're about to literally land on it...

Burt maneuvers the hot air balloon with expert skill down to a flat expanse of red slate and dirt. Numerous large, nearby boulders and small dirt embankments provide cover, so that no one can see you touch down. Anyone in the gulch would just think the balloon was doing some low altitude sightseeing. The balloon touches down. Burt opens the basket, and all three of you jump out onto the desert floor of the gulch.

"Good luck with your iguana," Burt says dryly, while pointing his index finger in a chastising gesture of nonbelief at all three of you. He closes the basket, pulls the lever on the burner, and in thirty seconds he's up and away.

"It's hot as fuck down in here," Emmitt says.

"Yes, it is. Okay. So, what's the game plan?" J. asks.

"The game plan is to get Lenny back," Emmitt says while patting the large buck knife strapped to his hip. "I'll call Kai." Emmitt pulls out his phone. "Lucky. I gotta single bar."

You sigh with relief at the good fortune of decent cell service. The plan would've worked without it, but this certainly makes everything easier. Emmitt puts his phone in speaker mode. The phone rings, and Kai picks up.

"Did you see all that?" Emmitt questions.

"I can't see you now, but I saw the balloon go down," Kai responds.

"You see the van?"

"I do. It's east of your location toward the opposite canyon wall."

"Any other vehicles?"

"Not that I can see."

"Good. We have time then."

"Call me if you see another car."

"Will do."

Emmitt hangs up. "We're headed that way." Emmitt points toward the massive canyon wall east of you. "We'll assess what to do once we get closer. And a suggestion—when we get nearby, take shoes off. We need to be silent."

"*Roger that*," you reply.

You begin the trek toward the east canyon wall. A part of you knows you should be nervous, but you're not. You're still deep in the awake, aware presence facilitated by the medicine sweat lodge. None of this shakes you—everything is just as it is—no drama; no questions; it's just an unfolding—and your part is to *unfold* with it.

This feeling rocks.

Yes, it does.

I asked you this last night and didn't understand your answer. You're my higher self, correct?

Higher self. Great Spirit. Black Shadow. Whatever you wanna call it—me. I am the big YOU beneath the little you—I am the only YOU.

This takes some getting used to.

Yes, it does.

You settle into the silent walk absorbed in the raw, tranquil beauty of the gulch. You understand why Emmitt cautioned everyone to remove shoes once you got closer. Three pairs of shoes crunching against the desert floor makes quite the raucous unnatural sound. *This is why Native Americans hunted barefoot,* you think.

Slowly, you creep closer to the wall. You come upon a small rise in the gulch, just before it. Emmitt looks at you and J. and then points to your shoes. Everyone stops. Shoes and socks removed. You're barefoot now.

Holy shit. This feels great.

That's because you're an animal...

You get closer. Emmitt stoops down to the ground and signals to you and J. to do the same. All three of you are on your stomachs.

"I'm going to survey quickly. You guys stay here. Be right back." Emmitt, then slowly begins crawling toward the top of the rise. You watch, and then—Emmitt's phone rings.

Fuck, fuck, fuck!!!

Don't worry.

Emmitt scrambles to grab his phone and shut it off. He does so, and then slides back to you. He whispers into his phone…

"Yeah…. Okay… Got it… Thanks…You saved our asses." He places his phone in silent mode and then looks at you and J. "Kai says a second car just pulled in, right on the other side of that hill. Fuck, that was close. There's three of them. Two in the van and one in the car."

"So, what should we do?" J. whispers.

"…need a distraction, so I can get around behind them. Let me think… I need to get a look first. I'll try again. Wait here…"

"No, no," J. whispers. "Both cars are just over that hill?"

"Yeah."

"I have a better idea. No time to explain. Follow my lead. You'll know what to do."

Before you or Emmitt can argue, J. takes a handful of desert dirt and rubs it all over his face. He makes a mess of his hair and then—to your utter surprise—strips off all his clothes and gets buck naked. He stands up, his birthday suit dangling in the hot desert air and, without a care in the world, walks up and over the small rise.

"That guy is fucking crazy—and brilliant," Emmitt whispers.

Then you hear everything unfold, amplified by the rock walls of the canyon…

"What in the fuck!?" Car doors slam. Shoes crunch on the ground.

"Who in the fuck is this guy!?" A gun is cocked.

"I need water. Oh, thank God! Lost for days!"

"Shit, Buddy, you need more than water…"

"Just gimme some water. Please, please, please…!"

You and Emmitt slide closer to the top of the hill and see J. walk right into the middle of the den of thieves. He performs brilliantly—slightly drunk, slightly crazy, and very *loud*. All eyes are on J. You and Emmitt take advantage and are able to stand and quickly walk unseen—and unheard—around the vehicles and behind a nearby large boulder. It worked. You're behind them now. You peer around the boulder. Emmitt points to Rick, the only one with a gun, and then to himself. He then points to you and Rick's minion. You understand. It unfolds quickly but feels like slow motion…

Emmitt leaps out from the side of the boulder and in one swift, deft move pummels Rick in the back of his head with the butt-end of his buck knife. Rick buckles and the AR-15 rifle flies to the ground…

The minion goes for the gun, but you leap forward onto his back...

J. spins, and with the force of a karate master, lands a hard clenched fist punch into the third person's chest. You catch a glimpse of him. It's Derek! …from the hotel. Derek collapses to the ground in utter surprise, the wind completely knocked out of him…

You're on minion number two's back, beating him like a madman. He falls to the ground with you on top, locked in a full-on jujitsu wrestling match…

And then—

"Thwack! Thwack! Thwack!" An ear deafening round of gunfire explodes and echoes throughout the canyon…

Everyone stops.

You look up. Emmitt stands with the rifle held high in his right hand. In his left hand is his buck knife. His face is deadly serious.

"Game's over, gentlemen." He says it loudly and, for effect, fires off another burst from the AR-15. Once again, the canyon fills with a thunder burst of rifle fire.

You roll over, minion number two beneath you.

"Stay down, asshole!" you order.

"I'd do as suggested," J. says to Derek.

"You two!" Emmitt barks. "On your stomachs!"

The minion and Derek do as they're told.

"What about Rick?" you ask.

"He's out cold. Check the van. Find something to tie these idiots up with."

You stand, catching your breath, and walk to the van. You open the back, and the stench of animals floods your nostrils. You see bird cages, pens, dog crates, and numerous brown cardboard boxes. A few of the animal captives are whimpering and barking. You see a roll of duct tape on a metal shelf.

"Perfect."

You grab the duct tape and, with J.'s help, wrap the hands and feet of the minion, Derek, and Rick. Rick slowly returns to consciousness...

"Fuck. Are you kidding me. You dumb mother..."

Before Rick can finish his expletive filled rant, J. grabs the duct tape from you and slams a piece of it across Rick's mouth. He does the same to the minion and Derek.

"That takes care of that," J. proclaims. "Now, where's my fucking iguana?" J. throws the duct tape to the desert floor and heads to the back of the van. You've never seen J. this furious. The sight of his anger, raw emotion, utter humanity, and fierce, naked body—smeared from head to toe with red desert dirt—is a glorious sight to behold. He's a wild beast, the restraints of civility completely stripped away…

You see him jump into the back of the van. You hear boxes being torn open, ripped, and tossed. You hear tools moved and clanked. Animal pens are opened. And then—you hear him scream in frustration.

He jumps out—empty-handed.

Your heart sinks. You watch him head over to the tied-up thieves in a strange slow-motion stride. He stands over them and screams with a rage that erupts from the *very center* of the universe.

"I SAID: WHERE IS MY FUCKING IGAUNA???!!!!"

You watch as the minion, Rick, and Derek recoil in absolute terror, certain that the guy standing over them is quite capable of ripping their heads off…with his bare hands.

"I SAID…"

"Mmmmm. Mmmmph—" Derek tries to speak.

J. rips the duct tape off his face.

"In the trunk, man."

Your heart bursts open.

J. walks over to Derek's car, opens the front door, and finds the trunk lever. He pulls it. The trunk snaps. He walks around to the back of the car and opens it. The trunk blocks your view. You hear J. open a box and then walk out from behind the trunk and the rear of the car…

There, perched on his shoulder, is J.'s best friend in the whole wide world. His animal spirit and soul mate—Lenny, looking no worse for the wear.

You have tears in your eyes—you're so relieved. You see that J., too, has tears in his eyes. He collapses to the ground, his right hand petting Lenny—the wildest, craziest, wisest iguana that ever lived...

"Can one of you get my clothes?" J. laughs.

You laugh, too. "*I'll be right back.*"

In five minutes, J. is dressed, Emmitt has called Kai, and the police are on their way.

"Check the back of the van. You'll find another friend in there," J. says to you.

You go to the van and hop in. It takes you a few minutes to put two and two together, but you finally do. You hop out, followed by a six-month old dalmatian on a leash.

"*Emmitt, this is Dottie.*"

"Dottie?" Emmitt asks, then remembers. "Right—Evan's dog!"

"*Yep*," you reply.

Emmitt looks at the three thieves taped up on the ground. "This time, you ain't gettin' away."

A half hour passes, and Kai arrives in the Jeep with Ollie in the back. He takes you, J., Lenny, and Dottie back to the upper rim of Devil's Gulch where the trailer was left. It's decided—thankfully—that you and J. are to ghost the whole affair. Kai returns to the gulch in his Z28. You watch through binoculars as a phalanx of flashing police lights and vehicles arrives at the scene. It's late in the day now. You imagine it'll be even later by the time the mess gets sorted out.

J. puts the Jeep in drive. You peer into the rearview mirror and see Lenny and Ollie both perched in their allotted places on their favorite branch. Dottie has fallen asleep in your lap.

"Everything is okay now?" You make a statement, but leave a question.

J. looks at you, smiles, and responds. "Everything is always okay, silly." He gestures everywhere. "The Great Spirit." You laugh at his disconcerting and all too accurate insight.

You roll out of sight of the gulch and onto the interstate heading north. You look westward and see the sun, once again, taking its daily bow as it exits stage left from the drama of the day.

After a few hours of driving, you're back in the heart of crazy, vibrant, busy, and loud Las Vegas. You meander through a bunch of back streets and arrive once again at a crummy little corner of Vegas called Pebble Street Boulevard. You park in front of the same dilapidated, white, single-story ranch home. You exit the Jeep, lock it, and walk to the front entrance with J. and Dottie. You knock…

This time, from inside you hear someone scramble and fumble around and eventually come to the door. He speaks from behind the door, blind to everything.

"What the fuck you want?" You hear words slightly muffled by the closed door.

"Evan, it's us again. I lost my dog. You helped us out, remember? I have someone here who wants to say hi."

"I don't know, man. I heard you guys stirred up a lotta heat. Just leave me alone, man. I got..."

"Evan. Open the door!" J. gets slightly aggravated. "Someone you know wants to say hi. *Someone* with dots."

"What.!?" You hear Evan quickly unbolt and unlock the door. As he starts to open the door, Dottie goes wild with excitement, whining and jumping. Finally, the door swings open. You let Dottie rush in.

"Oh man!! Oh man!! Dottie, baby. Oh sweetie!" Evan looks at you and J. "How did you…?"

"Long story…" J. says.

Evan falls to the ground and lets Dottie unleash a whirlwind of licks, tail wags, and canine joy. Evan tears up in seconds.

"How did you? I can't thank you enough, man!"

"There is one way you can thank us," J. says.

"Anything man. Anything. Whatevs…"

"Evan, I want you to answer a serious question, okay?"

"Okay, sure man. Like I said…anything."

J. pauses and looks Evan directly in the eyes.

"I've asked you this before, and I'm going to ask you again. Evan—are you sick and tired of being sick and tired?"

Evan becomes flustered and hesitates but, because of Dottie, J. knows he has him by the emotional balls. J. speaks even louder as repeats the question.

"Evan! Are *you* sick and tired of being sick and tired!?"

Evan capitulates. You watch his body collapse with his arms around Dottie. His previous tears of joy transform into sobs of pain, suffering, and loneliness.

"Yeah, ma-." The crying makes his words hard to understand. "I'm so sick a-a-and tired. But, bu- bu- I don't know…"

J. interjects. "You don't need to know. You just need to state your intentions clearly. That's all you need to say."

Evan relaxes. His eye contact becomes steady and soft through the tears. "I am so sick and tired of being sick and tired, man. I can't even begin to tell you, man."

"Good," J. responds. "Remember what I said to you before? You have to *want it*—want peace. Do you want it, Evan?"

Evan slowly stands and looks J. in the eyes.

"Yeah, man. I want it."

With a smile on his face, J. replies, "Excellent. Ask and you shall receive. It's as simple as that. We're leaving Las Vegas tonight. I want you to pack your things. I want you to come with us. We're going to take you to a shelter just outside of the city that a friend of mine recommended and knows. They'll feed you, get you some clean clothes, and if you're willing–*if you still want it*—hook you up with a rehab center. Do you want it?"

"Yeah, man. I do. But..."

"No buts. Yes or no," J. says.

Evan pauses and looks back inside at the disheveled drug den with empty disgust.

"Fuck it. Yes."

"Beautiful. Get your things. We'll make room in the Jeep. Thank you, Evan. You just made *the world*... a tad better."

"Yeah, man. Give me a minute."

Two hours later, you drop Evan and Dottie off at the shelter on the west side of Vegas that Emmitt had recommended. J. leaves him with another $200, gives him a hug and a fist bump, and departs. You watch as Evan enters the shelter and, with any luck, a whole new life.

"Now everything is *more* than okay," J. says. "Everything is Las Vegas, triple seven, delectably, delightfully, and deliciously *perfect*."

"*Yes, it is*," you agree and smile. "Triple sevens!"

And it always has been—

You think so? It's always been perfect?

Of course! Evan is also the Great Spirit...and so are J. and Emmitt and Kuruk, Kai, Rick, Derek, and of course...you.

You drive west, the vast other-worldly glow of Las Vegas slowly swallowed by the glossy-black, star-spangled, desert night sky.

What now?

Now—it's time for you to jump out of your head and fall deep into the vast infinite cavern of your heart...

END PART 3

DON'T JUST READ ABOUT IT.

EXPERIENCE IT.

This is your invitation to a whole new world badass. There's a life-changing *experience* waiting for you online. Something you've been longing and waiting for *your whole life*. You ready? Of course you are…

Go here:
www.spiritualityforbadasses.com

PART 4
Lake County Cave

CHAPTER 20
PLATO'S CAVE

How to escape the cave of shadows

J. drives west late into the night. You know from previous vague conversations that you're headed to somewhere in Northern California, but *exactly* where, of course, has been redacted in black; and *who* hasn't even been mentioned—the shroud of Turin a safer mystery-bet to unravel. No matter. Given all the recent events, you're happy to be lost in the miles that lie between you, wherever, and *whoever*.

You spend the night in a nondescript roadside motel and are on the road again by mid-morning. This time, you're in the driver's seat. It's nice to feel the road through the Jeep's steering wheel vibrating smoothly in your hands. You look in the rearview mirror and all is well: Lenny and Ollie are in their happy spots.

You're now in the middle of California—you guesstimate somewhere between Los Angeles and *Sequoia National Park*. It's hilly, arid, and brownish yellow everywhere you look. You've never been to this neck of the U.S. woods. The hilly to mountainous landscape, robbed bald of all plant and tree life, ain't pretty. You hope that wherever you're headed, there's greenery and trees.

You're also vastly disappointed to discover that the glowing, awakened presence high of the Mescaline medicine sweat lodge has faded to zero.

But something remains, does it not...?

Am I this voice?

Or this voice?

I—I can't tell.

You juggle an inner dialogue that seems to rotate between inspired wisdom and banal chatter—like the classic diminutive angel and devil perched on either shoulder, vying for your time and attention. It's slightly maddening, but you chalk it up to the "washing machine" effect of spiritual growth, as J. called it. You feel completely tumble-dried at this point. Out of sheer boredom, you finally venture out of your inner world and gamble a question...

"So what's next?" you ask while crooking your head and neck toward J. in the fashion of a harried schoolteacher in a classroom filled with little shits.

J. smiles at your vexation and takes a sweet minute to reply. He gives you the same drop of the head back and says, "Plato's Cave...Plato's Cave is what's next."

"...that some sorta California touristy thing?" you respond, knowing the game is afoot.

He smiles. "If only... That's the final *Know Thyself* test. Sorta like the twelve labors of Hercules, except worse."

"Not familiar."

"Hercules, the Greek hero. He had it easy. All he had to do was clean some shit, steal some shit, capture some shit, and kill some shit. Lots of *doing*. Plato's Cave is about *undoing;* undoing the last little bits of your ego-identity. Much harder."

"Um, still lost."

J. pauses, then surmises, "In a nutshell, I think you're close. I think you're close to knowing thyself—which is awesome, right!?"

"Yeah—I guess."

"But I have no clue what final straw will break your spiritual camel's back, so to speak."

"*Go on...*"

"Spiritual awakening, knowing thyself, or becoming a spiritual badass is very much a happy *accident*. There's nothing you can do to cause it, but you *can* become or be *accident-prone*. Escaping Plato's Cave—or at least the attempt—is how you do this; how you become accident prone."

"*Okay. What the fuck is Plato's Cave?*"

"It's a story in Book Seven of *The Republic*."

You shake your head incomprehensively. "*Sorry, not a Greek scholar.*"

"*The Republic* was a sixteen-book masterpiece in which Plato pretty much laid out everything a modern civilized society should know about justice, morality, happiness, governance, democracy, and of course, knowing thyself."

"*Light reading...*"

"The Allegory of Plato's Cave, as I said, is in Book Seven." J. pauses to think. "Well, how 'bout I just share my modern take on it with you?"

"*Sure. No rush here. I'm just killing miles.*"

"Cool."

Once upon a time there were eight people, four women and four men, all trapped—or more like *caught forever*—in a vast underground cave. The cave was their imprisoned reality—dark, cramped, and cold. Beyond being *trapped* in the cave, each person was also *strap-locked* to a chair, all of them pointed at one wall.

Behind them, in one tiny corner of the cave was a small fire which threw shadows upon the wall. Each of the prisoners was entranced by and addicted to the shadows. The eight prisoners had no conception of sun, daylight, or any life outside of the cave. The dancing, swirling, illusory shadow play was their only reality.

From time to time, a master of one sort or another would visit the cave and implore the prisoners to leave.

One day, a Master of Politics arrived. Summoning his best efforts of elocution and argument, he did his best to free them...

"There is light! There is day! Life and freedom are outside the cave!" he exclaimed. The master then proceeded to teach the prisoners about nations, societies, governments, politics, and all that defined a civilized people. Several of the prisoners even unstrapped themselves from their chairs and volunteered to follow the master out of the cave. They all went off enthusiastically to find the light and freedom that the master spoke of. But, of course, several days later all of them, including the master, returned, and strapped themselves to their chairs again; they were soon lost in the shadow play.

A month or so later, another master showed up—the Master of Fame, Fortune, and Personality. "There is light! There is day! Life and freedom are outside the cave!" he exclaimed. He then went on to extoll the virtues of movie stars, famous musicians, celebrity, fame, and fortune. He convinced a few of the prisoners to follow him out of the cave. And, of course, all of them, including the master, soon returned, and strapped themselves to their chairs; they were lost again in the shadow play.

A Master of Science showed up. The same routine played itself out again: Several of the prisoners left with him only to return a little while later and strap themselves back to their chairs staring at shadows.

A Master of Fun, Play, and High Adventure showed up, and, of course, the same thing occurred.

On occasion, masters with more refined sensibilities would grace the cave. Two such masters showed up—one extolling the virtues of bodily beauty, strength, health, and perfection, and the other extolling the virtues of magical thinking through incantations, omens, visualizations, signs, and prophecy. Each master gained quite a few followers, and each group went off to find their destined light and freedom. But, of course, they all returned to their imprisonment.

One day, a Master of Religion showed up. Most of the prisoners were captivated by what he had to say about the world's religions, saviors, and sacred texts. Surely, many of the prisoners were convinced that somewhere in this great body of knowledge and wisdom was the key to finding light and freedom. But, of course…

Finally, one day a master showed up who simply referred to himself as a Guru of the Light. His argument was impeccably refined, convincing, and erudite. Many of the prisoners were once again absolutely convinced that this special man held the answers they were seeking. This man knew *the way*—the way out of the cave and into the light of day and freedom. But, of course, their imprisonment continued.

One day, a little girl no more than ten years of age stumbled into the dark, cold cave. She witnessed all the prisoners strapped to their chairs staring at the shadows on the wall. She had never seen such a thing. Their odd predicament was as foreign to her as her life probably was to them. Being young, naïve, and innocent, she had no agenda…and the little girl did something for the prisoners that no other master had ever even attempted to do: She told them *the truth*.

"It's dark in here, and cramped and cold and all of you seem to be suffering horribly. Can't you see or feel this? Don't you understand?"

She visited them frequently, and over and over she explained to them the same thing: how limited, imprisoned, and dark their lives were. Not once did she mention where she came from or anything about her life outside the cave. Of course, not many of the prisoners wanted to hear this message, and all but one ignored her.

After truly, deeply listening to the young girl, something happened to that prisoner. His eyes changed—his *vision* changed—and the changing of his vision granted him two things: He could now see how truly horrible the conditions were in the cave, and he could now see the eyes of the little girl—filled with a glow, a light he had never witnessed before.

The little girl, noticing how the prisoner's eyes had changed, took him by the hand and slowly led him out of the cave. This journey was excruciating for the prisoner. His eyes weren't used to the small amount of natural light that began filtering into the cave as they got closer to the surface, and the light caused him great pain. Slowly and inevitably, though, he adjusted. Finally, having overcome the transformational pain due to his old, limited vision and limited life, he exited the cave...

Once outside, he fell on his knees and cried and cried. He couldn't believe his eyes! The sky! The sun! The trees! The birds! It was all real! No more shadows! No more damp cold! No more darkness! He was free!

The little girl, still having no agenda, led him to her village. The man lived out a full life of light, freedom, and peace...having escaped forever from Plato's Cave.

J. ends the story. You continue driving in silence for several miles, taking it all in.

"*So you're saying I still believe in something that's trapping me in Plato's Cave?*"

"Yes."

"*And I need to do what, then?*"

"You need to cross every *t* and dot every *i*. You're still identified with something. I'm pretty sure I know what that something is, but I'm not certain. You need to find out for yourself."

"*Okay, but that doesn't explain how.*"

"Oh, we'll get to the how. Trust me. We'll get to the how."

You pause for a good long time and then speak. "*I'm having a total Star Wars moment.*"

J. smiles. "Really!? And what moment might that be?"

"*Definitely a Han Solo moment… I have a really bad feeling about this.*"

"Ha!" J. laughs. "Fucking perfect."

You continue driving and silently acknowledge you are once again charmed, but slightly unsettled by your badass adventure guide. The voices in your head continue their dialogue…

I don't even know what he's talking about.

Well, that makes two of us.

Chapter 21
Political Debate

How to be unenlightened

Interstate 5, which spans the entirety of California north and south, continues to be an exercise in grim Newtonian reductionism and flatland mechanics: If proof was ever needed of a flat, barren, colorless earth, the center spine of California along I 5 could easily provide it. You hadn't realized just how desert-like most of California was.

It's not until you're within an hour or so of your destination (which J. has finally graced you with) that some mountainous, green life returns to your vista. When you finally arrive in Clearlake, California you're rewarded with a vast, beautiful view of lake and mountain, populated with healthy amounts of both conifer and deciduous trees. It's a sight for sore, barren eyes.

J. plugs the final directions into his phone, and after fifteen minutes of windy, uphill, back road driving, you arrive at a small chestnut and burnt-umber cabin nestled on the side of a mountain.

You're greeted by an exuberant border collie with classic black and white markings. It's in full-on wag mode as it rushes out to greet you and J. You hop out of the Jeep, equally exuberant to have both feet on the ground and a place to call home for a little while.

"Maya!" J. excitedly greets the dog. "Come here, girl! I've heard great things about you!" Maya makes her way over to J., suddenly demure from having her name called out by a stranger, but still wagging her tail. J. reaches down and gives her a healthy dose of head and back scratches, which endears Maya to J.—probably forever.

"I see you met my official greeter," a woman calls out. She's in her early forties, sporting a baseball cap and auburn hair in a ponytail; she steps down off the home's small front porch. "She'll never stop pestering you now that you've done that."

"I'm a sucker for a tail wag," J. replies. "Howdy stranger, long time—no see."

"Hey J.!" The woman walks up to J. and gives him a big hug.

J. looks over at you. "This is my good friend, Lynda."

"Just call me Lynn. J.'s the only one who still calls me Lynda." Lynn holds out a hand. You shake it and look into her eyes. She's pretty, but not in an ostentatious way, more in a self-aware and conscious way. Her eyes shine. There's a comforting warmth in her smile that beams a clear message: *I'm down-to-earth, reasonable, and friendly.* You like her immediately.

"How long you guys been driving today?" Lynn asks.

"*Six long hours through the California desert.*"

"Did he share the driving? Or did he do what he did to me and make you drive most of it!?"

A light bulb goes off in your head. *No way. Really!?*

"Lynn was my last student," J. announces emphatically.

"*No shit! Awesome!*" you exclaim.

"Yep. I bet we have a ton in common, especially a high tolerance for spiritually inclined wisecracks."

J. raises both his hands in the air, smiles, and says, "Guilty."

"J. tells me you're from back East."

"*Born and bred in Virginia. This is my first visit to California—actually my first visit to any place west of the Rockies.*"

"J. told me about your adventures in Vegas. Sounded like a big bucket of suck."

"Yes...quite the extravagant experience. No casinos or criminals for me any time soon. The Grand Canyon and the sweat lodge were amazing though."

"Well, there's no black market for iguanas here in Lake County. No canyons, either. So, whatever you guys get into while you're here, it'll be a lot quieter and slower."

"*He didn't take you there?*"

"Where, Vegas? Oh, hell no. My adventure…" Lynn looks at J. "What has it been? Five years now?"

"That sounds about right," J. replies.

"My adventure, from what he's told me, was a lot different from yours. But let's get into that later. You guys are probably tired and want to unpack. Yeah?"

"Abso-fucking-lutely!" J. responds.

"Hey! That's my saying!" Lynn proclaims with a smile.

J. shrugs his shoulders. "Yeah, um—I kinda stole it. …sticks with you."

"*This is gonna be a hoot!*" you exclaim, smiling broadly.

"Literally! From what I understand… What is it? A screech owl, right? Is he in the back?" Lynn asks.

"*Yes, along with his best buddy.*"

"Lenny! I am so excited to finally meet Lenny!"

"*Lenny wasn't…?*"

"Nope," interjects J. "Lynda's road trip adventure was before Lenny was big enough to travel, so he stayed at home with a friend for that one."

"*You missed out*," you add.

"That's what I understand. But now, I have this silly one…" Lynn reaches down and pats Maya on the head. "She's also a teacher in her own crazy canine way."

Lynn does the meet and greet with Lenny and Ollie. Within a short time, you're unpacked and settled in a small room in the back of Lynn's comfy cabin home. The room has a view that any Airbnb would die and charge a mint for: As far as your eyes can see, there's the vast expanse of Clear Lake surrounded by the mountains of the *Mendocino National Forest*. It's breathtaking.

Lynn is a polite, but non-clingy host. J. offers to buy dinner for everyone from a carry-out Thai place in town, so he, Lynn, and Maya all take off in the Jeep. You're happy to give them some private catch-up time, and you're also happy to be left blissfully alone for a spell, in a quiet, empty home overlooking a woodland arboretum paradise.

Lynn said to make yourself at home, so you do: You crack open a Samuel Adams lager you found in her refrigerator, then open the sliding glass door to the back porch, grab one of the Adirondack chairs, plop yourself down, and allow the weary miles of road stress, spiritual awakening, Mescaline medicine, and Lenny kidnapping to all finally—sink—the—fuck—in.

I'm fucking exhausted.

I'm not. I'm just getting started.

I feel like I asked you this before. Who the hell are you?

I told you. I'm your better angel. Your higher self. The YOU before the you.

Is that so?

Yes.

Pardon me if I don't believe a word you say.

...don't care if you believe it or not. It is what it is.

Right. Well—we'll see about that.

The beer softens the voice in your head and returns you, in a sloppy sort of way, back to your body. It's a nice change of pace from all the recent heady conversation.

Sometimes there ain't no substitute for a good liver sloshing...

After the beer, you venture inside and find your bed. You lie down and close your eyes...

It's no surprise that when you open them again, it's the next morning. You're hungover—not from the beer, but from life. As you shower and get dressed, you're apprehensive about taking another spiritual badass step. You still have no idea what's in store for you here in California.

Plato's Cave? What the hell is Plato's Cave?

Don't ask me.

I'm not. Rhetorical question.

Guess we'll find out.

You hobble over to the kitchen. *Thank God—coffee.* You grab a cup and join Lynn on the back porch. She's already caffeinated, and Maya is lying quietly at her feet.

"Good morning, um..."

"Sunshine. Yeah, he said that to me all the time, too. That's 100% his. ...you sleep okay last night? You were out cold when we got in."

"I did. Thanks. Like a rock." You pause to take in the morning view, fresh with newborn sunlight sprinkled over everything. *"This place—is amazing. How long have you lived here?"* Lynn takes a moment to respond, and you notice the pause. You like her even more for her willingness to allow space in a conversation. It's refreshing and immediately puts you at ease.

"Since I woke up three years ago."

This response, however, catches you off guard. It's not what you expected. *But what did you expect? She hung out with J. for an extended period. Very clearly, she's been on the spiritual path for a while. And so, yeah—it would seem she arrived, at least somewhere.*

"And what's that like?"

"Knowing yourself or buying this place?" Lynn asks, smiling at you.

"Um—both, I guess."

"Buying this place was serendipitous. It all came together. I inherited a little money. I got divorced. I found a new job and—*Bingo!*—found this awesome mountain cabin. Knowing yourself? Well, you're in the throes of that. You tell me."

"It's a bitch," you say without hesitation.

"Ah—well, good. You're doing it right, then. Yeah, it's a bitch. But it does eventually conclude."

"And what's that like? This conclusion?"

"Nothing like you expect, of course, but good. Really good. No regrets."

"*I think I'm in this place where I just want it to end. ...can't say I'm suffering from, you know, psychological childhood baggage anymore, but I'm not exactly satisfied or comfy either. Does that make sense?*"

"Yes. Perfect sense. J. shared with me where you are in the process, of course—Plato's Cave."

"*Yeah. The whole cave thing.*"

"*...some advice about it?*"

"*Sure.*"

"As you just said, there's still this subtle itch to complete...all this spiritual stuff. ...a vague notion that something is still missing...a feeling that you're not quite whole. Right?"

"*Yeah. I think that's it. Pretty much exactly.*"

"Well then, the *only* way out is *through* Plato's Cave."

"*I'm apprehensive. J. tried to explain it to me, but honesty I still have no idea what Plato's Cave is.*"

"Oh, don't worry. I had no idea what was in store either when I went through it. It's nothing insidious or tricky if that's what you're thinking. It's just life playing out its last identity cards with you."

"*Explain, please.*"

"I was a political nutcase." Lynn pauses and points to her phone on the nearby table. "As a matter of fact, there's a debate or rally nearby tonight—not sure which. We should go and see if it resonates. You'll see. And then you'll have a better understanding of Plato's Cave. More than I could explain at any rate."

"*Um, sure. What sorta debate or rally?*"

"California has something like fifty—I think—congressional seats in the House of Representatives. So, there's always some Bozo running around stumping or rallying. It'll be fun and crazy and chaotic—all top-notch California shit."

"*Tonight?*"

"Yeah, after work."

"*Right—work. Totally forgot. What do you do exactly?*"

"I'm a manager at a bookstore café in Lucerne. It's called *Sophocles' Books*."

"*Well, that's cool. We'll have to visit.*"

"Certainly. Anytime. And we have good coffee, too. Speaking of which…" Lynn shakes her empty mug. "Want a refill?"

"*I'm good, but thanks.*"

Lynn gets up to go inside for a refill just as J. walks outside with Lenny and joins you.

"Hey. Morning. You wanna feed Ollie? Today's our last day with him."

"*Oh no! Bummer!*" You pause in silence, pondering your feathery friend. "*Really?*"

"I know. I'll miss him, too. But where he's going is awesome, and tomorrow's the only day we can take him."

You stand and leave to go get Ollie and his food. You're a pro at it at this point. Over the last few weeks, you've become his de facto caretaker—smitten with his little warbling, cooing, and wide-eyed presence. You feel heavy of heart knowing that he won't be around after today.

You return with Ollie and his food in tow. In a few short minutes, Ollie ferociously gulps down a handful of chicken livers.

You turn to J., saying, "*Let's take a hike with these guys today. That would be fitting for Ollie's last day.*"

"Sure—once Lynda heads off to work. There's gotta be a trail around here. I'll ask her."

"*Perfect.*"

A few hours later, after breakfast and a shower, you're parked at a nearby trailhead. You probably could have walked to it. You can't believe the sign: *Mendocino National Forest – Emmitt's Cave Loop* – 1.5 miles.

"*A fricking cave? Really!?*"

"Best just to give in to it…" J. says and smiles.

"*…you arrange this?*"

"Swear to God, no."

You head off on the hike with animals on respective shoulders. Ollie has become a true pro at steadying himself on yours. He's a delightful hiking companion. J. walks in front of you. Your heart sings seeing Lenny resting on his shoulders once again. It's a sight that tells you all is right in the world.

…might as well hit him up for those big questions you've been holding out on.

…you think?

Now or never.

You gather the courage and then finally speak. "*J., I have a really stupid question—or questions, maybe. One in particular I've never really asked.*"

"Spit it out. I'm an open book."

"Okay...are you and Lynn...enlightened?"

"Ha! Of course..." J. turns and looks at you half laughing. "...quite a natural question. ...surprised it took you this long. Let me put you at ease: Fuck, no."

"So then, what's enlightenment?"

"*That* is a great question. And the answer is...enlightenment is the booby prize."

"The booby prize? But I thought..."

"You thought. Right. *You thought.* You and fifty billion other people throughout history *all thought.* They *think* they know; they *imagine* they know...what enlightenment is. But until you experience, grok, or touch it—like everything else on the spiritual path—your imagined definition is a far cry from the actual truth."

"So what's the actual truth? You've touched it, I presume?"

"Yes, I have touched it, but I don't live or embody it. No such desire. Like I said—it's the booby prize."

"Go on."

"Enlightenment is the total destruction and self-sabotage of the dream state. It's the final act of the single conscious *one*—the one that paradoxically appears through all of us here—of unplugging from the dream."

"Okay—then what?"

"Exactly: then what? Then what is *Oops! What the fuck have I done?*"

"So, no all-compassionate, eternal, blissful rest among the puppy dogs and rainbows is what you're saying?"

"That's exactly what I'm saying. That's what's hawked in the spiritual marketplace, because that shit sells tickets. But the real truth is…game over. Unplugged. Return to Sender. The Big Sleep."

"*I think…I understand."*

"Like I said, until you touch it, no one ever understands. No one really *wants* enlightenment. What 99% of all spiritual seekers want, if even this honestly, is spiritual awakening or *Knowing Thyself*."

"*I want it. I want to wake up.*"

"Good. Leave it at that. Maybe someday we'll meet and fist-bump in the line for existential suicide—aka enlightenment—but until that time, fuck it! Enjoy the dream state. You'll miss *Disneyland* when it's gone."

"*You don't paint pretty spiritual pictures, do you?*"

"Bob Ross I am not."

You laugh. "*You're frickin' Salvador Dali on LSD."*

"Oh, speaking of which, here…" J. reaches into his pocket and throws you a small sandwich bag filled with brown stuff.

"*What are these? Dried mushrooms?"*

"Yeah, magic mushrooms. Microdose them and they'll help you through Plato's Cave. Mix 'em with some peanut butter—they'll taste better. You'll know when."

"*When what?"*

"When to use them. Small doses will bring back the awakened state of presence."

"*J….*" you pause for effect. "*You are full of surprises and off the charts outside the box."*

"I am Death—the destroyer of boxes." J. laughs and continues walking through the arboreal paradise.

After your conversation, it's only a short distance to *Emmitt's Cave* and the adjacent overlook. The cave is more of a notched indentation; not really the classic cave you imagined, but the overlook is worthy of the hike. You can see all twenty or so miles of Clear Lake and the distant mountains that surround it.

There's no denying the beauty of this part of Disneyland.

True that.

That was a very disconcerting conversation.

Yes, it was, but oh, so real...as usual.

You, J., and Lynn all attend a political debate in the small nearby township of Middletown that evening. Before leaving, you chewed on a very small amount of the Psylocibin mushrooms J. gave you, brave sport that you are.

Internal memo: Mushrooms taste like shit. Mix them next time.

You arrive. There are protesters, supporters, and a gaggle of news trucks outside of the venue, a high school gymnasium. You see a handful of rainbow-colored signs, *Black Lives Matter* signs, white supremacist signs, anti-government signs, and a host of other hot-button topics that people who attend these sorts of things are zealous about.

As you walk into the venue...loosened up from the microdose of mushrooms...you have an *Aha!* moment: *You're* the little girl walking into Plato's Cave, and your job is to help one of the eight prisoners...*escape*.

But the cave you've walked into isn't subterranean; it's the cave of your own mind. And the *you* venturing into these depths isn't the *you* in this book...

It's the *you* reading this book.

You have just entered Plato's Cave and the prisoner you're going to emancipate is the one being held captive by all your ideas and beliefs about race, nation, political party, gender, and sexual orientation.

You take a deep breath...

You notice your body. You notice awareness.

I am Death, destroyer of beliefs...

You place your attention on your skin color, race, and ethnicity, noticing how you subtly identify: as white, black, brown, yellow, Caucasian, African-American, Asian. You know there's nothing wrong with any of these, but *who you truly are* is *not* defined by them.

I am Death, destroyer of beliefs...

You place your attention on your nationality and political affiliation: American, British, Canadian, Filipino, Columbian, Russian, liberal, conservative, Democrat or Republican. You know there's nothing wrong with any of these, but *who you truly are* is *not* defined by them.

I am Death, destroyer of beliefs...

You place your attention on your gender and sexual orientation: Male, female, binary, cross, homosexual, heterosexual, lesbian, gay, bisexual, transgender, queer. You know that there's nothing wrong with any of these, but *who you truly are* is *not* defined by them.

I am Death, destroyer of beliefs...

You enter the rally/debate. It's chaos. There's a shouting throng of people all vying to have their voices heard. The two opponents arrive onstage and fight it out with both impassioned eloquence and rough jocular jabs. It's war, but not just onstage: You realize that it's a war *waged in your own mind*—and there's no end to this war, and there's no solution to this war. The only solution is to transcend it, go beyond it, and escape it…

The little girl journeys into the depths of the cave. She reaches the eight prisoners. She recognizes the one who is lost in national, political, and gender belief. She unshackles the prisoner and takes him by the hand. She leads him out of the cave…into the light of day.

I am Death, destroyer of beliefs…

The debate ends. You exit with J. and Lynn and return home.

Okay. Holy fuck. I get it now: Plato's Cave.

Chapter 22
E=MC^2

How to say goodbye to good friends

It's mid-morning the next day. The *California Raptor Center* is about an hour away. You're en route with J., Lenny, and Ollie, and you're sad to the bone. You've looked at their website, so you're positive it'll be a great home for Ollie, but your heart adamantly disagrees, and is in the throes of a massive *woe-is-me* attack.

"Maybe this is part of your cave. Gotta let the little guy go," J. says while patting you on the back. But all you can do is sigh. You're going to really miss him.

"*Another question…*"

"Sure."

"*What exactly is your relationship to Lenny?*"

"Lenny? Boy, um…"

"*Pet, friend, spirit animal? Kuruk called him that. What's he mean to you?*"

"Boy, that's a good one. So many things. Gimme a sec." J. is driving, and he takes a moment to adjust the rearview mirror, peeking at both Lenny and Ollie.

"Well, he's definitely my spirit animal."

"*Yeah, but what does that mean?*"

"Right. He keeps me tethered here. He reminds me to be present, joyful, and real."

"So, he's family."

"Yeah, he's family, but he's also my responsibility. I have to feed him, care for him, keep him safe—do all the little day-to-day chores that ground me in this reality. He helps because, as you clearly know, I can be pretty *out there*."

"And Lenny helps you to be…down here?"

"Yes. He's my day-to-day expression of being in and loving this world, even when I *really don't want* to be in it or love it."

"Got it. Now I also understand why Lynn has Maya."

"Yeah. We all need someone or something to help us be present—to help us love this world, which is sometimes really tough to love."

"No argument there."

"I think passions also serve this purpose. Lenny is my passion, but so are fly-fishing and hiking."

"I think I need more of both."

"Sure—but one step at a time, Kemosabe. I'd advise finishing this whole *know thyself* thing first before venturing off to own a dog or reptile. Your plate is full enough."

"Right time; right place."

"Yes. Your spirit animal or passion will show up when it's meant to. You just concentrate on the whole cave stuff for now. Speaking of which…"

"Yeah, thanks for the mushrooms. They worked. I think I get it now. Lynn said Plato's Cave was like life's last little identity cards being removed."

"And the debate?"

"Politics definitely removed, amongst other things."

"Good for you. See—nothing to it. Life unfolds."

"Well, it wasn't earth shattering, but I see the point."

"Right. Like I said, you never know which part of Plato's Cave *will shatter* your earth. You just have to go through it."

"*Understood.*"

You arrive at the *California Raptor Center* and are greeted by a young man in his mid-twenties, Tom. He is amiable, gregarious, and a bit nerdy—a likeable science type. For whatever awkward social reason, upon greeting, he hands you the center's brochure. It reads: *Welcome to the California Raptor Center, a hub for research into infectious disease, medical care, biological data collection, and more.*

Well, that was nerdy of him, but clearly this place knows how to care for an owl.

"He's in the back of the Jeep. Want to meet him?" J. asks Tom.

"In a cage?" asks Tom.

"No. He just sits on a branch next to Lenny."

"What's a Lenny?" Tom asks.

J. opens the Jeep's back hatch, and Tom peers in.

"That's an iguana laurenti, not an owl."

"Look a little closer, Tom."

J. looks at you with *Yikes!* crying out all over his face.

"Oh…cool. A screech. *Megascops asio.* We don't see many of their kind around here. They're Eastern."

"*Um, their kind is called Ollie, and he can't fly. It's why he's happy just to perch,*" you interject.

"Is Theresa here?" J. wisely interrupts what soon may be a fist fight between you and Tom. "She's who I've been talking to on the phone; I made these arrangements with her."

Tom stops and gives you and J. a slightly nonplussed look. "Uh, sure man. Let me go get her." Tom walks off.

You fold your arms across your chest in dismay. *"Not a good start, man. Right now, I'd rather take Ollie to PetSmart."*

J. sighs. "It'll be okay. Theresa has been wonderful. I don't know who this Tom character is."

Within a minute, a woman in her early fifties comes out. She's dressed in a white lab coat and sports short blond hair.

"You must be J.!"

"Theresa?" J. holds out his hand. "Nice to finally meet you. We were just showing Ollie to, um, Tom. Ollie's in the back of the Jeep."

Theresa peers in the Jeep. "Oh–my–god! Look at you!! What a total cutie! Awwww…poor little thing. Wings don't work? Well, we've got plenty of other things for you to do here." Theresa looks at J. "May I?"

"Of course."

Theresa reaches in and gently scoots Ollie onto her arm, with zero fear or concern for talons. Your heart sings. You are so completely relieved at the sight and sound of this wonderful woman who just handled Ollie like a pro.

Okay. PetSmart off the table. This lady can take Ollie.

"Oh soooooo cute…" Theresa continues to gush over Ollie. You're smitten and heartbroken at the same time.

"He's been eating okay?" Theresa asks.

"No problem at all," J. answers.

"*He's voracious!*" you add.

"Are you a hungry little monster?" Theresa then addresses you and J. "Well, good. Come on inside; I'll give you guys the tour and show you Ollie's new home."

"Perfect," J. says.

You sigh and grab Ollie's food, then close and lock the back hatch of the Jeep. Lenny sits unfazed in his happy spot. You follow J., Theresa, and Ollie into the facility. It's big—*really big*. There are numerous rooms, laboratories, and a vast housing section for raptors—eagles, owls, hawks, and more—in big, clean cages. You're impressed.

After unloading Ollie into his new home, Theresa gives you the tour. You walk in one of the laboratories and see Tom. He's in full-on science-nerd mode, sporting a white lab coat and goggles…

Catching you entirely off guard, you experience another profound *Aha! moment:* Once again, *you're* the little girl walking into Plato's Cave, and your job is to help one of the eight prisoners *escape*.

You take a deep breath…

You notice your body. You notice awareness.

I am Death, destroyer of beliefs…

You place your attention on your belief in science, technology, mathematics, and all the methods used in this world to understand, control, order, and contain it. …nothing wrong with any of these things, but *who you truly are* is not defined by them. *Who you truly are* is a vast mystery that no science will ever…completely…understand.

The little girl journeys into the depths of the cave. She reaches the seven remaining prisoners. She recognizes the one who is lost in the belief of science, control, and order. She unshackles the prisoner and takes him by the hand. She leads him out of the cave and into the light of day.

I am Death, destroyer of beliefs...

You snap back to conscious awareness. The rest of the tour slips by in a quasi-daydream. You can only think of Ollie. You're a cocktail of happy and sad, and you don't try to push it away.

Before leaving, you're granted some final alone time with your temporary spirit animal. For one final moment, you sink deep into the mysterious, dark, wide, innocent, and *present* eyes ...of Ollie the owl.

Chapter 23
Adrenaline Junkies

How to jump out of a perfectly bad airplane

The next day, you and J. find yourselves lazing around on the back porch with no agenda or plans. Lynn has gone to work. You're happy for a break from all the doing, driving, and Plato's Cave-ing. It's mid-morning. Maya and Lenny are both basking in the morning sun with you. J. is reading a book. You're bored.

"You said something a long while back about jumping out of my head. What's that mean exactly?"

"When you wake up—when you finally *know thyself*—that's what it feels like, sort of."

"Like I've jumped out of my head?"

"Not literally, of course, but something like it."

"Keep going..."

"Just stupid words for the inexplicable bodily feeling of being present, free, and normal."

"Normal? Shouldn't it be fucking extraordinary?"

J. chuckles. "It should be, but it ain't. That's just more hype sold by the spiritual marketplace. I hate to tell you, but spiritual awakening—this whole *Know Thyself* thing—once you've acquired it and settled into it...feels very plain and normal."

"Well, that's disappointing."

"Yes it is, but…" J. takes a big breath and pauses.

"But…what?"

"Stack normal against the way you feel right now. It's a very subtle thing. Like *right now* for instance: how do you feel internally, spiritually, existentially?"

"Incomplete, I guess. Slightly agitated. Lost. Confused. Missing something."

"Right. I feel none of that."

"None of it! Really?"

"Yes—I'm awake. I know who I am. I jumped out of my head, where all the agitation and incompleteness reside…and into my heart, where none of it resides. I went from struggling and surviving in a tin can to living and being in a canyon. Simple as that."

"Methinks it's not that simple."

"Maybe not. You won't completely understand it until you've done it. …best I can offer."

You sigh and bury your head in your phone.

"Hey, speaking of jumping—check this out." J. holds up his phone, which displays a website. "Wanna go!?"

You look at the image and gulp. *"Skydiving!? Really?"*

"Abso-fucking-lutely! It'll give you some practice."

"Practice? At what!?"

"Jumping, of course!"

The next day, much to your utter confoundment, you're at 13,500 feet in a 52' 400 Series DHC-6 Twin Otter aircraft, and you're about to jump—as the old cliché goes—out of a perfectly good airplane…

Yes to awareness! Yes to the fear!

Yes to awareness! Yes to the fear!

You got this.

Two yeses.

You got...

The mushrooms have *really* kicked in. You definitely overstepped the microdose boundary and are tripping balls as you embark upon one of the stupidest things you've ever acquiesced to doing in your life…

What the fuck was I thinking?!

Jumping out of my head?

What does that even mean?

Out of my head...??

Jumper five—go!

Jumper six—go!

But it's too late now. You're committed.

Committed! Ha! To a looney bin!

You slide along the final inches of the bench and somehow remember to crouch and scoot bent-knee into position with your jump guide.

"You ready!?" Josh yells. "Out the door we…"

Jumper nine!

Huh? What?!

Out of my head!?—

Ohhhhhhh, crap!—

Out of my head!?—

Go!

Holy fucking Mother-of-God!

What? Ain't no problem here.

Really? Now you've decided to show up?

Well, sure. I am your higher self and, right now, if you don't mind me saying—you are really fucking high, literally, figuratively, and—um, biochemically—I believe. Mushrooms, right?

You're a complete ass.

Maybe, but I'm also cool as a cucumber.

Fuck! This is violent and loud as shit, but yes, oddly, I'm calm.

Yeah—I'll take the credit for that.

All yours. Don't care. This view is delicious.

Delicious? Really? You are so stoned.

You continue falling for what seems like an hour, but is actually just under sixty seconds. During this time, you descend 8,500 feet and reach terminal velocity of 120 miles per hour. When skydiving, yes—your body hurls through the air at *one-hundred-and-twenty-miles-per-hour*. So it's not calm. It's not

Superman-other-worldly-peaceful. It's loud, violent, and uncomfortable.

Your eyes water behind the goggles. Oddly enough, it's also hard to breathe. And every appendage of your body feels like it's being subjected to some sort of medieval torture rack device. But…

Holy fucking Mother-of-God! This is fun as shit!

And then your guide Josh pulls the ripcord on the parachute release system, and in a single split-second you're yanked and tumbled into an eerie, quiet, and strangely serene parachute glide. The juxtaposition is jarring, but also very welcome. Now dangling at about 5,000 feet, you watch below you as the other jumpers make their final approach to the ground.

So—if jumping out of your head into spiritual awakening is anything like this...

Yep. I'll be a damn pro.

Hey? What's up with your palms?

Oh, man. I know. They sweat when I'm nervous.

Still calm here.

I know. I know. You get all the steel nerve street cred.

You're jolted out of your skydiving mushroom reverie when Josh speaks. "You doin' okay!?"

"*Way cool, man. This is awesome. Thanks!*"

"Yeah man, be careful or you'll get addicted to this shit."

"*I bet. This is quite the experience.*"

"Yeah, me and all my friends are real skydiving junkies."

"Better than crack cocaine, I suppose."

You laugh. Josh laughs also. You continue your slow, peaceful descent to Earth, and then...another *Aha!*: You become the little girl. Your descent from the sky becomes the descent into Plato's Cave...

You take a deep breath...

You notice your body. You notice awareness.

I am Death, destroyer of beliefs...

You place your attention on your belief that life should be a place where your only purpose is to have fun; where you're on a constant merry-go-round of distracting amusement; where you're hedonistically always after the next high or feel-good experience; where you're an adrenaline junkie looking for the next big hit, success, or triumph. ...nothing wrong with any of these things, but *who you truly are* is not defined by them. *Who you truly are* is beyond adventure, fun, amusement, play, and addiction. This life is a learning realm. ...nothing wrong with fun, but you are much bigger than fun.

The little girl journeys into the depths of the cave. She reaches the six remaining prisoners. She recognizes the one who is lost and addicted to fun, accomplishment, achievement, amusement, and distraction in all its multifaceted forms. She unshackles the prisoner and takes him by the hand. She leads him out of the cave and into the light of day.

I am Death, destroyer of beliefs...

The sky and ground swap places in scope and size. Earth gets closer and closer. Josh adjusts the landing pattern and crosswind perfectly as he slows the parachute's descent in the final fifteen seconds. You lift your legs as instructed. Josh gently swoops into the landing run. You make a perfect touchdown.

The whole thing—jumping out of the plane, the mushroomed discussion with your higher self, freefall, canopy glide, and descent into Plato's Cave—took a mere six minutes.

Fuck, that was the longest six minutes of my entire life.

I'm cool.

Of course you are. You're cool...as a cucumber.

Chapter 24
Spiritual Disneyland

How to soak your aura in a hot tub

After a dream-filled night with numerous falling, jumping, and descending themed scenarios, you wake beneath your blankets, surface, and stare at the ceiling. You definitely have a skydiving hangover, but it beats a tequila hangover any day. At this point, you feel like a child's ragdoll, torn to shreds by two large pit bulls in a fighting cage. There's nothing to do but surrender.

Your bedroom door is slightly ajar. For whatever reason, Maya nudges it open, strides in, jumps in bed, and snuggles with you. It's the best thing in the world. She's a sweatheart. You appreciate the attention and so does she.

An hour later, you're in your favorite Adirondack chair in your second home—the back deck of the cabin.

"*This view never gets old.*"

"No, it does not," replies Lynn as she joins you with coffee in hand. "I see you have a new best friend." Lynn points to Maya lying at your feet.

"*Yeah, she paid me a visit this morning.*" You lean down and rub her head. "*What a sweetie!*"

"She does that."

"*You workin' today?*"

"As a matter of fact, no. I took the next two days off so I could hang out with you guys."

"That's cool."

"And I booked us a surprise visit today at a place I think maybe you'll really dig."

"*Please, no more airplanes, adventures, or adrenaline. I've had my fill of all things A and dangerous.*"

"Exact opposite."

"*Oh-kaaaay? Are you seriously gonna pull a J. and not tell me?*"

"I was, but you're right. He did that to me all the time. I'll be nice. It's at a place called *Holly Hot Springs*—massages, saunas, and…well…*hot springs*. Is that your speed?"

"*No shit!? Yes! That is a speed I can agree to.*"

"All arranged. No four-legged creatures, though. Sorry, Maya."

"Did someone say four-legged creatures?" J. joins you on the deck with Lenny in tow.

"*Yeah, Lynn was just sayin'—no lizards allowed.*"

"Not allowed? Where?"

"*Lynn, here, has very generously invited us to soak our weary bones at a place called Holly Springs.*"

"You mean *Holly Hot Springs*!?" J. chuckles. "Really? You booked us a day—*there*!?"

"Yes. Do I sense some cynicism in your voice?" Lynn inquires.

"Hey man, I'll get in line for a soak and a massage any day, but the last time I went to *Holly Hot Springs*, it was a clothing optional, hippy, spiritual Disneyland. Just sayin'."

"Well damn, you really know how to spoil a surprise, don't ya?" Lynn replies.

"Clothing optional?" you ask.

Lynn looks at you. "He's right. It used to be pretty hippy-dippy, but maybe it's changed. I honestly haven't been there in years. Open minds!?" Lynn looks at both you and J.

"Sure—open minds," J. chimes back.

"Open minds—all the way." You look at J. while arching your eyebrows in a comical, skeptical way. *"What the hell."*

An hour or so later, bathing suits definitely packed, you pull into the rural mountainside acreage of *Holly Hot Springs*. While en route, Lynn filled you in on the history of the hot springs, dozens of which litter the craggy, mountainous, earthquake-prone countryside of Northern California. Many of them, including *Holly Hot Springs*, have been in use for well over a century—by settlers, tourists, locals, and um…

"Holy Hollywood Bonkers! You have got to be shitting me." J. is the first to blurt it out when he sees the dozen or so mobile home trailers, trucks, tents, and movie-making apparatus gracing the main parking lot of the resort. Dozens of people are milling around. "I think they are actually making a movie here, right now!"

Lynn sighs and says, "Oh boy, they didn't tell me that."

"Why would they? You're just more cashola for their pockets. Too funny." J. looks at Lynn. "Hey, open mind here. I think this is fucking awesome."

"This ought to be interesting."

"To say the least," adds Lynn. "Okay. We'll just go with the flow and let it be."

"I'm gonna be an extra in a frickin' movie is what I'm gonna be." J. laughs.

J. parks the Jeep; all three of you get out and make your way to the main reception building. The place is deceptively big, with lots of people milling around—none of whom, thankfully, seem to be opting *out* of clothing. There are dozens of buildings, pools, and baths of varying shapes and sizes everywhere. There's also a requisite ton of New Age iconography and statues: Buddhas, Ohm symbols, lotuses, large expensive purple crystals, and various Hindu statues. It's New Agey to the core.

"Well, it doesn't look, you know—nudist anymore," Lynn proffers.

"I wouldn't mind seeing a few naked movie stars," J. laughs again.

"I'll never hear the end of this," Lynn retorts.

You arrive at the main building and check in. It's actually very professional. The woman behind the counter is courteous and apologizes for the movie-making mess. It was some last-minute scheduling by the corporate offices, she tells you. You're each given a day pass and, for lack of a better word, *a menu*. You laugh internally. This is the second time in the last few days that someone awkwardly handed you a brochure instead of just giving you the low-down verbally. You're each told to pick two items.

J. reads the menu out loud. It's a smorgasbord. "Cranial Sacral Balancing, Foot Reflexology, Hot Stone Massage, Thai Massage, Ayurvedic Steam Bath, Chinese Acupressure, Essential Oil Meridian Massage." He looks up from reading and says, "What if I just want to have a beer at the bar?"

The check-in lady overhears him and is quick to interject. "Our facility is alcohol and drug-free."

"Okay—well, that's that," J. says while smiling at you and Lynn. "I'm just gonna stick with a standard massage and a plunge in whatever hot-pool is available."

You and Lynn pick similar items. You go your separate ways to have massages, and the experience unfolds without incident. You're pleasantly surprised to discover that Thai massage is brilliant. Afterward, you're more relaxed than you have ever been. You meet J. and Lynn at a designated hot-pool. They're already neck deep in 100-degree water. There are about a dozen other people in the pool, spread far enough apart to be out of earshot from one another.

"Mine was awesome. How about you guys?"

"Amazing," says J.

"No complaints," Lynn offers.

J. continues in a lower-than-normal voice. "Okay, help us determine something." He subtly points a finger to a small group of people nearby. "Jennifer Lawrence? Jennifer Lopez? It's one of those famous Jennifers, right?"

You take a quick peek, trying your best to be nonchalant about it. You reply in an equally low voice. *"Yeah, it's somebody famous. I recognize her from something, but I don't know her name."*

"Ahhh, Hollywood," J. grumbles. "The perfect mouthpiece for the New Age. All flash and no bang."

You smile at his comment, then sink deep into the warm waters of the natural springs. *Despite its outer Disneyland schlocky cover*, you ruminate internally, *this place ain't half bad.*

Yeah, well—ya gotta start somewhere.

I know.

If crystals and Buddha statues get you in the door, that ain't a bad thing. Right?

Sure—but J.'s correct to be snarky. This shit's a spiritual trap. Most of the time...goes nowhere.

But, in the grand scheme of things, it's all good.

Eh, maybe—you're being awfully generous. It's mostly a bunch of magical thinking and doing.

You're right. Still, I don't see the harm.

The harm is when it gets you stuck...

And then... your next *Aha!* moment: You become the little girl again...

You submerge below the languid hot spring waters and descend deep into Plato's Cave...

You take a deep breath...

You notice your body. You notice awareness.

I am Death, destroyer of beliefs...

You place your attention on your belief in the cult of personality, fame, and fortune... Movie stars, rock stars, sports stars, and talented artists of all walks of life *also suffer.* No amount of fame or silver-spoon good fortune exempts one from the trials and tribulations of this life or this world. We all suffer, grow old, and die. No exceptions...nothing wrong with any of these things, but...

I am Death, destroyer of beliefs...

You place your attention on New Age magical thinking... Ninety-nine percent of what the New Age has to offer is smoke and mirrors. Astrology, Past-Life Regression, Tarot, Dream Interpretation, Channeling, Omens, Synchronicity, The Law of Attraction, and their like: most of it is illusory dream state nonsense, which offers little in the way of actual spiritual growth...little in the way of waking up to *who you truly are*. ...nothing wrong with any of these things, but...

I am Death, destroyer of beliefs...

You place your attention on New Age magical doing... The spiritual marketplace is filled with all sorts of recommendations and admonishments about what to do and what not to do: Extreme yoga, chanting, prayer, meditation, walking on coals, vision boarding, fasting. Doing, doing, doing. The list is endless and so are most of the paths; they promise a grand final result, but almost never deliver. ...nothing wrong with any of these things, but...*who you truly are* is not defined by *any of* them.

The little girl journeys into the depths of the cave. She reaches the five remaining prisoners. She recognizes three of them—one addicted to fame and fortune, another addicted to magical thinking, and the last addicted to magical doing. She unshackles all three of them and motions them to follow. She leads all three out of the cave and into the light of day.

I am Death, destroyer of beliefs...

You reemerge from the silky warm water and gaze around. J. and Lynn have their eyes closed, sublimely lost in the gentle relaxing natural springs. The movie star, with her posse of gilded sycophants, has moved on, burdened by the never-ending trappings of fame and fortune. The New Age thinkers and doers...chant and hope and wish and dream...a never-ending dream of finally...one day...arriving.

All is right in the world.

Yes—yes, it is.

Chapter 25
Namaste', Bitches

How to get kicked out of spiritual clubs

The next morning, once again you find yourself in good company on the back porch of that gem of a little cabin overlooking Clear Lake. As you sit down, you reach into your pocket and throw the bag of remaining magic mushrooms on the table near J.

"*I think I'm done with these. I'm zonked out and exhausted with mind-altering shit—except for this.*" You gesture to the cup of coffee in your hands.

"A most judicious and wise move, Padawan," J. replies. "They're just a tool. Did they help at all?"

"*I think so, yes. They definitely made for an epic skydiving experience.*"

J. chuckles, grabs the bag, and puts it his shirt pocket. Then he turns his attention to Lenny, who is on the table eating his breakfast of strawberries.

"You been sleepin' okay?" asks Lynn. "…noticed your light on late last night."

"*I have been. Thanks. Was slightly restless. Looking shit up on the internet.*"

"Been wrestling with Plato's Cave some more, I take it?"

"*Yeah. No massive life-changing epiphanies. Just letting shit go—mostly shit I already let go a long time ago, to tell you the truth.*"

"But…?"

"*But it helps. Like fine-tuning.*" You pause, reach down, and pat Maya on the head. "*So, I've got a question for you guys.*"

"Sure," says Lynn.

"*I was looking up spiritual awakening on the internet last night and all these nondual and Advaita Ve-something teachers came up.*"

"Advaita *Vedanta,*" says J.

"Kind of like the Zen of Hinduism," Lynn offers.

"*Ah… So, there's a ton—and I mean a ton—of these guys out there. What's their deal? What they teach seems very similar to, you know, J., your whole spiritual badass thing.*"

"In general, I'd say good stuff," J. replies.

"Agreed," responds Lynn.

"*So, are you guys nondualists or Advaita teachers or whatever?*"

"Oh, fuck no!" J. says immediately. "Those guys belong to *The Nondual Spiritual Awakening Teachers Club*—and I am most definitely *not* an invited member."

"*Well…why not?*"

"Because—Namaste', Bitches! —and to quote George Carlin, …*shit, piss, fuck, cunt, cocksucker, motherfucker, and tits.* Ha!" J. laughs out loud. "They don't allow foul-mouthed fools like me in their club."

"And, besides that, you have to be really good at sporting the club-defined affectations and house rules," Lynn adds.

"*Dare I ask what those might be?*"

"Satsang. Lots of satsang. That's the word they use for a meditation gathering. And ya gotta have a picture of Ramana Maharshi next to a vase of flowers on a small table when you do it."

"And you have to take long silent, breathy pauses between teaching words," Lynn says and smiles.

"And you have to sell books, DVDs, workshops, retreats, and action figures at a table in the back of the room." J. chuckles again.

"*Action figures?*"

"Just kidding. Those guys are easy to bash, but I gotta tell you— I learned a hell of a lot from a number of them. Amongst their ranks are some pretty cool and down to earth ones. You just have to be discerning...picky...*careful.*"

"*Why careful?*"

Lynn jumps in: "Because, like in any teaching or organization, you can get lost in all the hoopla and end up going absolutely nowhere."

"They're certainly better than their predecessors."

"*Predecessors?*"

J. smiles, offering, "*The Big Fat Guru Enlightenment Club.*"

"*Oh, those...*" you laugh.

"Yeah, those..." J. picks up his phone and takes a minute to look something up. "You guys wanna go on a little driving tour?"

"Where to?" asks Lynn.

"There's three of them within a stone's throw of the cabin."

"*Three what?*"

J. looks at you with a twinkle in his eye, then says, "Big Fat Guru Enlightenment Clubs."

You shrug your shoulders and smile. *"Sure—why not?"*

"This oughta be fun," Lynn adds, smiling and arching her eyebrows with a bit of uncertainty.

After lunch, the whole gang—including Maya and Lenny—pile into the Jeep. Within a half-hour, you're pulling into a sprawling mountainside campus with a sign out front that reads *The Art of Living Retreat Center.*

"So...we'll do this in descending order of magnitude," J. proclaims as he drives the Jeep onto the campus.

"What does that mean?"

"The good one first and the shitty one last."

"Got it."

You pass a big dining hall, numerous residences, several big buildings resembling hotels, and finally, a plethora of ornately decorated temples scattered across the campus.

"I actually spent some time at this one a while back. ...came here to chill and do some writing," J. proclaims.

"And...?"

"It's cool. Great food, clean rooms, and, as you can see, immaculate landscaping and gorgeous architecture. Totally scandal free."

"Scandal free?"

"Yeah, that's usually the benchmark for places like this. Tax evasion, sexual exploitation, money fraud...lots of stupid cultic shit. But this place has none of that."

"Looks very Hindu to me," Lynn notes.

"It is, but they keep it low-key. They're smart. They know what Westerners want."

"And what's that?"

"Well, it's certainly not enlightenment, knowing thyself, or spiritual awakening...that's for sure."

"So, what is it then?"

"A five-star dining and lodging experience with a healthy dose of Ayurvedic healing and a massage!" J. laughs. "Just like *Holly Hot Springs*—minus the hippies and movie stars."

"Ah..." You shrug your shoulders.

"I had a pleasant stay here, but I never met or saw the guru who started it."

"Why not?"

"He lives in India, and you probably gotta be in the upper echelons of his club to meet him anyway."

"Got it."

"Yeah, not a place anyone's spiritually waking up in, but certainly a place you can get some solid sleep and a good massage." J. laughs again. "So, that's it. Let's move on."

J. drives off the campus; within another half-hour, you've arrived at campus number two. The sign out front reads *The Mountain of Attention Sanctuary.* The front gate is locked, so there's no entering this one.

"I've been to this place once, and the teacher was actually here."

"And you met him?"

"Not really. Just saw him. But it was, I have to say, one of the most sacred occasions—in the traditional sense—that I've ever experienced."

"Really!?"

"Yeah. The teacher was American, but..."

"Was...?"

"He died over ten years ago. But his whole approach was orthodox Hindu enlightenment based. He was pretty cool when he started out, but his whole schtick soured into a big cultic mess."

"Scandals?"

"A few, I think. A real shame. He was a great teacher. Not everyone's cup of tea for sure, but go figure—I learned a hell of a lot from him. He changed my life ...I'll always be grateful." J. pauses and reflects.

"Shall we?" J. puts the Jeep in drive and continues down the winding road for another fifteen minutes. You arrive at a wooded intersection. From your vantage point, there are dozens of old, poorly built ranch homes, burned-out tree stumps, and a massive concrete foundation—all that remained from an old building.

"This is, or *was*, the famous *Hoberg's Resort*," J. says. "It ain't much now, but in the forties and fifties this was the biggest, hoppin' vacation resort in Northern California. Entertainers, tourists, and Hollywood types flocked to this place like pigs to a mudhole."

"Doesn't look spiritual at all."

"Well, not now. The whole place caught on fire in 2015 and burned to the ground. But from 1974 to 2010, it was owned by none other than the *Maharishi International University*."

"*No shit. TM. Transcendental Meditation, right?*"

"Maharishi Mahesh Yogi—the guru of the Beatles and the Beach Boys?" Lynn asks.

"Yepper," J. says. "A few decades ago, before it burned, when I was visiting *The Mountain of Attention*, I stayed here and had a peek around. In that building right there…" J. points to the massive concrete foundation. "…I saw one of the funniest, most cultic things I have ever seen in all my spiritual travels."

"*Yeah…?*"

"It must have been their old gymnasium. It was filled—and I mean wall to wall—with mattresses."

"*Mattresses?*"

"I know. What the fuck, right?" J. smiles. "Well, TM was famous for this thing they did and taught called 'yogic flying' which was Maharishi's ridiculous attempt at teaching his students to levitate."

"*… fucking kidding me?*"

"No. The mattresses were all part of the sham. The students would sit and bounce their skinny little white naïve asses on these mattresses and then call it levitation."

"*And—what did any of that shit have to do with meditation or enlightenment?*"

"My point exactly. To this day I have never seen a more ridiculous display of the utter claptrap bullshit all too frequently peddled by teachers from The Big Fat Guru Enlightenment Club. I only regret I didn't take a picture."

"*Too funny.*"

"Or sad…or pathetic," Lynn adds.

"Yeah, man. It was really desperate and depressing. I couldn't unsee that shit. Afterward, I pretty much vowed to never set foot in another Big Fat Guru Enlightenment Club again." J. sighs. "Okay, let's get out of here."

"Wait a minute. What is that?" You point off into the distance at what looks like an old fountain and statue.

"Don't know. …should I drive closer?"

"Sure."

J. drives toward the statue, rolls the Jeep off-road, and then parks it in front of what is very obviously one of the last well-preserved relics of the Maharishi bygone era. It's a gaudy, faded, concrete statue fountain of the Hindu goddess Kali.

"How perfectly fitting," J. says. "Hey! Let's get out and take a selfie in front of it."

"Why is it fitting?"

"Why? 'Cause that's Kali—the goddess of time, death, and destruction," J. answers.

Everyone hops out of the Jeep, including Maya and Lenny. You pose and J. snaps an arm's length selfie of the whole gang in front of Kali…

…The destroyer of worlds.

Another *Aha! moment* materializes, and you become the little girl again. You sink into the burned-out ground below the statue and descend deep into Plato's Cave…

You take a deep breath…

You notice your body. You notice awareness.

I am Death, destroyer of beliefs…

You place your attention on your belief in nondual satsang teachers, gurus, cults, and saviors. Ultimately, there's nothing wrong with any of these things, but in the end it's always between you and YOU. No teacher, low, high, or mighty—and no teaching, famous, small, or large—can ultimately wake you up...can make you *know thyself*...can transform you into a spiritual badass. *You're* the teacher. *Life* is the teacher. *Existence* is the teacher...

The little girl journeys into the depths of the cave. She reaches the two remaining prisoners. She recognizes the one who believes in and is addicted to spiritual teachers, gurus, and authority figures. She unshackles the prisoner and takes him by the hand. She leads him out of the cave and into the light of day.

I am Death, destroyer of beliefs...

Within forty-five minutes, you're back home sitting in your happy spot on the back deck, with Maya at your feet.

...you think I could ever levitate?

Doubt that shit.

I don't know. Don't you think it's worth a try?

I think, on this hard seat, you'll just bruise your ass.

Damn, you're cynical.

No, I just see shit clearly.

Do you?

Yes, of course.

Call me crazy, but I'm slightly skeptical of that.

Chapter 26
Church

How to rock like a Baptist

A few days pass in which you do a lot of lazing around, YouTube watching, coffee drinking, beer drinking, Maya petting, and hiking on nearby trails.

You're no fool and very clearly see the contrived nature of the Plato's Cave trap that J. has set for you. Northern California is a wicked paradise of alternative beliefs jam-packed with ashrams, retreat centers, sanctuaries, cults, havens, covens, and a club for every whack-job with even the slightest out-of-the box notion about religion or spirituality.

You get it. It's the perfect place to find, expose, and destroy anyone's old, patterned, homegrown internal belief systems caught in Plato's Cave. A part of you is chagrined at just how effective this setup has been. You feel duped, but also relieved to be unloading this shit—because it does feel like it's heading somewhere.

I still have no clue where, however.

Well, you and me both.

I thought you were like my wiser, higher self, and knew where all this shit was headed.

Maybe. I don't know. I have my limits.

Yeah, well—that's obvious.

The dueling voices in your head seem to be worse some days than others. What had started out as something you vehemently feared and ran from—your own Black Shadow, inner dragon, and unknown lower self—has now morphed two times: initially into an all-knowing, all-seeing, time-traveling higher self which seemed to know everything about everyone, and now, more recently, into a fearless, narrating, guardian-angel-like traveling companion with a slight propensity for dufus observation.

You're getting used to it, but it's also dragging on a bit, and you can't wait for whatever is supposed to happen to finally *conclude*. In short, you're probably pretty much *exactly* where you're supposed to be—spiritually exhausted.

J. walks out and joins you on the porch. "Is that smoke I see pouring from your head? Those thoughts were so damn loud, I could hear 'em inside."

You smile. *"Yeah, I'm just wondering how and when all this will end."*

"What...? Life on earth? Game of Thrones? Rock-n-Roll?"

You give J. a nonplussed icicle stare, and then offer: *"My big quest."*

"Ahhh—*your* big quest. Is that what this is?"

"Isn't it? You tell me. I feel like I've asked you this before, haven't I? Where exactly is all this headed?"

"Don't ask me. That's the thing about knowing thyself. It's not an answer; it's a feeling state of body, mind, and awareness. All questions about how, when, where, and why just evaporate. There's no answer. There's just no more *woe-is-me*." J. stops and stands. "Look, honestly—really—I'm not trying to hide any of this shit from you. Let me be as clear as I possibly can, okay?"

"Absolutely."

"*Knowing Thyself* is realizing that there is, in fact, no self; that you, personality, soul, individual, character—whatever you want to call it—does *not* exist. That's it. Like I said: no answers. No grand explanations of the cosmos. No satisfying pat on the back from a supreme god because you've been so good and nice and spiritual and all that. There's nothing. Knowing thyself is a paradoxically satisfying empty shell of a state. J. is just an empty shell."

You sit and stew and take it all in. You know he just said something probably pretty fucking profound, but the arrow doesn't hit its intended target. You sit there like a dullard with a dunce cap who, despite all the teacher's pleading, cajoling, and expert dialectic explaining, *does not and will not get it.*

"*Fuck, this stuff is profoundly frustrating.*"

"Well, that's the first smart thing I've heard you say in days. Yes, it is."

You laugh and throw your hands up in the air. "*I surrender, man. I surrender.*"

"Good. So let's go to church now."

"*Huh?*" You do a double take at J.'s statement.

"Yeah. It's Sunday and Lynda's invited us to attend this really cool small church service just down the road."

"*Ehhh…okay…I guess.*"

"No cults, New Age, gurus, or hijinks I promise. Just good old-fashioned church."

"*What, like Christian?*"

"Yeah, it's a Baptist church. She told me all about it. I'm game. Come on."

"*Well, eh, sure. Why not. Like I said, I fucking surrender.*"

"That's the spirit. That's the holy-fucking-spirit!" J. laughs.

Oh, boy. Here we go again.

Hey! You said it yourself: I surrender!

I'm trying. I'm really trying.

Try harder.

Any harder and I'll explode.

Boom! Stardust!

What does that even mean?

You scramble to find something to wear resembling Sunday church clothing. In the end, the least torn and dirty items win the pious ensemble award. You do your best to tuck things in, button things up, and comb things straight. *At least you're trying*, you think, as you stand in front of the mirror looking more black sheep than dapper.

J. and Lynn clean up well, and have also made an attempt to be presentable. Their efforts actually *do* get close to dapper. You're impressed and amused.

The church is nearby. J. pulls the Jeep into a packed parking lot. The sign out front reads *Shiloh Baptist Church – The Reverend Derek Williams*. The church is small and humble, constructed of typical white board and black trim. It also sports the usual concrete front steps, covered portico, steeple with a cross on top, and red door. It's nice, but nothing special.

As you exit the Jeep, your eye is drawn to a nearby hedge row and a small, leafy, vine-covered arbor. You can see tombstones through the archway and are intrigued. The graveyard looks immense. As you walk toward the church entrance, you have a moment of hesitation and inspiration.

"Guys, I'll meet you inside in a minute."

Lynn looks your way. "…everything okay?"

"All good; I'm just gonna check out the graveyard quickly. Save me a seat. I'll meet you inside."

Lynn shrugs her shoulders. "No worries. Will do."

J. gives you a thumbs up. You meander off toward the arbored entrance of the graveyard.

Okay. Let's just get this over with.

You wait, expecting an immediate response.

Hello! Anybody there? Come on. Let's do this.

You step through the arbor and find yourself in an expansive, rolling, hillside graveyard with tombstones as far as the eye can see.

Come on, damnit. I don't have all day.

What? You talkin' to me?

Finally. Yes, I'm talking to you. Can we just get this whole church-Plato's Cave thing over with?

Um, no clue what you're talking about.

You think I'm an idiot? I know why we're here. Let's just get this over with.

Not in charge of that.

Really? Who is?

Not I.

You stroll down a long, meandering dirt path which weaves in and out of tombstones of all sizes, shapes, and styles. You sigh.

Really? We're not going to do this?

Look, I don't know what you want from me, but even if I was in charge of whatever, I don't do tricks—and definitely not on command.

You're incorrigible.

I'll take that as a compliment.

You continue walking among the graves. Frustrated by your efforts to get one-up on your higher self, you turn around and head back toward the church.

Okay. You win—this time.

Cool. What do I win?

You walk back to the church, climb the concrete stairs, and open the heavy red door beneath the portico. You walk in. It takes a second for your eyes *and ears* to adjust to the spectacle. The place is packed and in full swing. Everyone is standing.

There are three rows of mahogany wooden pews, a vast arched ceiling buttressed with massive wooden beams, and a humble, but elegant altar and front stage. It's not exclusively African-American, which is what you had expected. You see people of all races and colors.

But the spectacle doesn't come from the sight; it's from *the sound. Holy shit! This church rocks!* are your immediate thoughts. Off to the right of the stage and altar you see and hear a five-piece band accompanied by a choir of about twenty individuals. Collectively, they *absolutely* rock. The performance is Broadway quality.

Definitely not your typical churchy experience.

The choir, donning beautifully ornate red, gold, and white robes, belts out a harmony in sync with the band. The music demands the unfettered attention of your soul. With unabashed infection and pleasure, you join everyone in the clapping. You garner a smile on your face as you clap with the music and search out J. and Lynn. You find them and take your saved spot.

You give both J. and Lynn a big look of surprise. J. smiles back at you. Lynn smiles at you, dancing and clapping in place. The whole scene is joyful and raucous.

I'm pleasantly surprised.

Me, too.

The opening volley of percussive, joyful noise eventually winds down, and the church pastor—Mr. Williams, you presume—takes the podium. He's tall, erudite, poised, and African American. Before speaking, he smiles. His smile conveys everything you need to know about him: His stature, presence, and command of the podium captivate everyone in the room. Slowly, powerfully, and eloquently he begins speaking—orating—*preaching*. His words and presence become the perfect complement to the band and choir. You're transfixed, entertained, and humbled.

This church rocks.

You already said that.

I'm saying it again.

You're not, and haven't been for a very long time, a church goer. The last time you attended was with a friend long ago, sometime after high school. Before your parents separated and divorced, however, you actually attended a local Presbyterian church, even with some frequency. You have few, but fond memories of those occasions. Of course, the church of your youth was nothing like what you're experiencing right now.

As the service unfolds, alternating between the reverie of music and the solemnity of the spoken word, you settle into a calm, peaceful, happy presence.

At one point, you lean over and whisper into Lynn's ear, saying, "*This place is just amazing. Thank you for sharing.*"

"I know. Right?" she whispers back.

The service begins to wind down. You're seated when one of the final songs of the service—a song familiar to you from your youth—catches you completely off guard.

> "Oh God, our help from ages past..."

The lyrics and music infiltrate your body-mind, setting off a cascade of emotions and memories...

> "Our hope for years to come..."

Deeply touched, your heart sends signals to your tear ducts. Your eyes become watery and diffuse...

> "Our shelter from the stormy blast..."

Finally, the muscles in your body relent and soften. You melt into a sweet oblivion of emotional resonance...

> "And our eternal home..."

The final words of the stanza shred your heart into a million little golden shards as you're transported to another time and place...

No, no, no. I don't want—

You descend deep into Plato's Cave...

You arrive and there, seated in the last of the eight chairs, strapped and imprisoned, is your eight-year-old self. You walk closer and stand nearby. Your self is crying and in pain. You beckon your younger self to leave the chair and to follow you, but your doppelganger will have none of it. After a while, you give up and simply take an adjacent seat. Your younger self continues to shed tears and emote. You take a small hand and gently cradle it in your own.

You melt into the emotional body-mind of the little you—a long ago version of yourself, trapped in the deeply emotional belief that *church* was the only time you were ever truly happy with *both* your parents. Once upon a time, a complete and *happy* family; then the divorce…and the loss of a parental authority figure…then the *anger* at your parents…and the *anger* at your father…and then, finally, the anger *at church*.

Now you see it. Now you feel it. Hidden away so deeply…so effectively…lost, hidden, and submerged. You had *no idea*. None! All this time, this part of you…trapped, in Plato's Cave.

You meld and fully become your younger self. Except now, you have the conscious, aware capacity of a fully realized adult. You reach down and unstrap yourself from the chair. You get up and turn around. You see the small fire in the back of the cave, which, all these years, has been casting dark, shadowy, scary images on the walls. You walk over to the fire and kick dirt into it, extinguishing it forever.

It's pitch black in the cave now but, oddly enough, you're confident in your ability to make your way out. You begin walking…slowly, sure of foot, heart, body, and mind. At last, for the final time, you exit Plato's Cave into the light of day—forever free from the myriad number of beliefs that had imprisoned you there for countless numbers of years.

You snap back to conscious awareness and find yourself seated in the pew of the small church. The service has come to an end. You look around. Everyone stands. You're invited to shake hands or share hugs with those nearby. You stand and give Lynn a big hug. You do the same with J. You wait patiently until it's your time to exit. You walk out the church's big red door…

So that's it?

You talking to me again?

Yes, I'm talking to you!

Uh, okay—is what it?

You know. Am I done? Awake, realized, or enlightened or something?

Fuck no, you're not enlightened.

Awake then?

Once again, I have no idea what you're talking about.

Are you fucking kidding me?

About what?

This—isn't it?

Um, no. I don't think it is.

Really!?

Really.

Holy fucking shit! Is this crap ever going to end?

Not if I have anything to do with it.

What did you just say?

You heard me.

CHAPTER 27
YOU, YOU, AND YOU

How to find your heart and soul

You wake up with Maya lying on the end of the bed. She's curled up at your feet in a warm fluffy ball of black and white.

If only.

If only what?

Really? Pestering me this early?

Hell—yeah, this early. Again—If only...what!?

If only all this shit were black and white—like Maya.

Actually, Maya is black and white. Ask Lynn.

Not the dog, dufus—reality, spirituality, awakening.

I know, I know. As I said, *it is* black and white. Ask her.

You sigh at being pestered by your higher-screwball-self this early in the morning. You eventually relent and crawl out from underneath the sheets. Maya gets up with you and bounds off, you presume, to hang out with the other humans. It takes a few minutes for you to rouse, get coffee in your hands, and find your favorite chair on the great back deck. Lynn's already up and out there. She's buried in her laptop.

"Morning. Gotta work today?"

"Yepper. Bills to pay and dog food to buy. Good morning. How goes it, Sunshine?"

"Everyone gets infected with that saying eventually, don't they?"

Lynn laughs. "I suppose. Inevitable when you hang out with J. Speakin' of whom—what're you guys up to today?"

"No plans that I know of. I'm assuming we'll be wrapping all this up soon."

"J. told me he has a conference or some teaching event he has to attend next week, so yeah…" Lynn abruptly looks up from her laptop with another thought. "Hey, you guys should visit the store today!"

You take a sip of your coffee. *"I don't see why we couldn't."*

"You can even walk there. It's three miles on foot. You know how to get to *Emmitt's Cave*, right?"

"Sure, I think so."

"Just take the hiking path that splits off from *Emmitt's Cave*. It heads straight down and into town. The store's on Main. You can't miss it."

"Okay. Cool. I'll ask J. if he wants to go."

Maya bounds out onto the deck through her doggy door. You take another swig of coffee and remember something. *"Lynn, I've got another question for you—about Maya."*

"Sure! Oh shit, sorry. Did she wake you up again this morning?"

"*No, no—not that Maya.*" You point to Maya, who is now curled up below Lynn's feet and then gesture to everything around you. "*This Maya.*"

Lynn laughs. "Oh, *that Maya*—the classic illusion thing, right?"

"*Yes.*"

"Of course." Lynn closes her laptop, giving you her full attention. "What's the question? I'm all ears."

You take a deep breath, gathering your thoughts. "*Well, I'm confused—or not clear. I mean, why any of this...illusion? If that's what all this is... I mean...what's the point? I get it. We all come from, or are made of, the same one conscious source or dreamer. So why the dream?*"

Lynn smiles, pauses, nods her head, and then takes a sip of her own coffee. "Yeah, I've bandied that one around with J. for a while—stewed on it, read about it, even researched it—and, um, have come to a somewhat unsatisfying conclusion."

"*Figured as much.*" You linger in silence. "*Lay it on me.*"

You watch as Lynn sinks into her body, present, and at peace, even with this *WTF—Why any of this, God!?* question / conundrum. She looks into your eyes, and you see her fully awakened self...blossom. She rests her hands in her lap with her fingers interlaced. Then she points to Maya, the dog, lying at her feet. "It all has to do with the Tao. Just like Maya here, it's black and white. You know the Tao, right?"

"*Of course. One of the first things J. taught me.*"

"Like I said, this won't be satisfying—because it's only explainable through mythological metaphor. It's too big."

353

"I get that."

"So, your question is just basically...*why?* Why existence? Why this dream? Why the world? Why life at all? Here's my answer. It comes from classic Hindu Vedic scripture."

Lynn pauses and takes a big breath. She gestures to everything. "All of this...is a dream, an illusion, or maya that the one consciousness, Brahman, is having. This dream is said to exist for an incomprehensively long period called a kalpa—something like billions of years—which is like one day in the life of Brahman. At the end of this day, the whole world, *this illusory dream*, is said to be destroyed and reabsorbed into a void of nothingness. Brahman then falls asleep for another crazy long kalpa. When Brahman reawakens, the dream world reconstitutes and the whole thing repeats...and does so forever. This cycle of dreaming and sleeping is called the Tao."

"And the black and white part?"

"When Brahman first wakes up in the dream, everything concerning truth, spirit, and reality—the white part of the Tao—is perceived as being evil, false, or a lie. *The dream* is reality. Ignorance is reality. Brahman wants nothing to do with waking up or knowing thyself."

"But then..."

"But then...Brahman does eventually begin waking up, just like you are now, and the reverse happens. Everything about life, the world, the universe, and existence itself—the black part of the Tao—is now perceived as evil, false, or a lie. Brahman is done with the dream and desires to wake up and *know thyself.*"

"But the truth is none of it's evil—right?"

"Of course not. It's all just a matter of perspective. Wherever Brahman is on the journey through the Tao dictates his perspective. And of course, we're *all* Brahman. Each of our individual journeys, paradoxically, is at a slightly different point on the journey."

"*One man's poison is another man's cure.*"

"Exactly."

"*You're right. That's not exactly satisfying. That just seems, I don't know, to be the mechanics…not the why.*"

Lynn shrugs her shoulders. "…best I got. I don't think we or Brahman can or will ever know *why*. It just is what it is."

"*Well, that at least explains where I am on the journey. I'm fucking done with it.*"

"Right. There's *nothing* you can do except what is true *for you*. I know this whole Brahman-Tao thing sounds bleak—like we're all just puppets caught in some vast never-ending dream conspiracy. But trust me—awakening fixes all that."

"*Really? How?*"

"You stop asking stupid questions like *why*."

You laugh out loud. "*I guess I asked for that.*"

"Yes, you did." Lynn laughs with you.

"*Lynn, you rock. Thanks for listening to all my whining.*"

"Happy to be your knee of listening."

"*Where have I heard that phrase before?*"

"No idea." Lynn smiles and stands. "I'm gonna get a refill. You want one?"

"*Sure. Why not? I'll join.*" Before you stand, you reach down and give Maya—the dog—a big, warm scratch on her black and white head. She wags her tail in canine approval.

Told ya so.

Okay. You were right.

I have my moments.

Before going inside, Lynn turns to you and says, "You know, I have a question for you also. Just curious…"

"*What's that?*"

"Where did you and J. meet?"

You open your mouth to speak, but then hesitate. "*I—ya know—in a bookstore, I think? I…honestly…can't remember. Isn't that weird?*"

"Just curious."

You walk inside; J. is sitting at the kitchen table having breakfast with Lenny.

"Morning, Sunshines. Whatcha guys been up to?"

You look at Lynn and shake your head in humorous dismay. "*Just figuring out the Tao of existence.*"

J. fakes a yawn with his hand to his mouth and lets out "Boooooring."

"*Yeah, I think we both came to that same conclusion.*"

"We were also talking about you guys visiting me at the store today. You can hike there from the *Emmitt's Cave* path."

"I'm game," J. replies. "Actually, drats. I have to make a phone call around noon."

"*Well, bring your phone*," you proffer.

"I hate phones and hikes. You know that."

"*Rules, rules. You know what they say?*"

"I know. Let me think about it."

"Guys—I'm gonna get dressed and head out. I've got the 10 a.m. shift. Just shoot me a text before you come. Aside from my lunch break, I'll be there all day. And if you want, take Maya with you on the hike. She'll adore you forever."

"*Can do.*"

"Cool. Okay. See you in a bit." Lynn rushes outside, grabs her laptop, then scoots past the kitchen again. She fades into the back of the house. You watch as J. cuts up small pieces of pineapple for Lenny. He snarfs it down with gulping, head-jerking abandon.

"*That's Brahman right there.*" You point to Lenny.

J. looks at you; it takes him a second to get it. "Oh, yeah—right. We are *definitely* pawns in the great dream of Lenny."

"*Do you suppose they wrote about Lenny in the Vedas?*" you quip.

"I never read the whole Vedic library, since it's like, you know, 300,000 pages long or something like that, but no doubt Lenny is in there somewhere." J. laughs. "How are you doing today?"

"*I'm mostly fine. How 'bout I fill you in on our hike?*"

"Is that you twisting my arm?"

"*Yes, it is.*"

J. pauses to consider the option. "I tell you what. I'll do half and then come back here so I can make this call. Deal?"

"*Deal. Lynn said it was a straight, easy path from the cave down to her store anyway.*" You look around for Maya, who isn't present. "*Hell, I bet Maya even knows the way.*"

"I bet she does. I'll finish up here, and then we'll leave—okay?"

"*Cool. I'm gonna get my hiking shoes on.*"

Fifteen minutes later, you're in wilderness. It takes you another fifteen to walk to the same location where you parked the Jeep a few days ago. You walk past the *Mendocino National Forest–Emmitt's Cave Loop* sign and begin the trek to the top again.

After your talk with Lynn earlier, you're not feeling particularly chatty. You get lost in the scenery of blue-green conifers, granite-rock outcroppings, ochre dirt trails, and the occasional sparkling, jeweled lake views which occur when gaps in the trees offer a vista. Maya bounds happily at your side, no leash required, and Lenny rides proudly upon J.'s shoulders.

It's not until you've reached the actual cave overlook at the top that you offer the first conversational words. You sit down on a large rock. J. joins you in fawning over the immense Clear Lake overview.

"You know, I don't think we ever hashed out what happened in Vegas. I mean—what happened to you. You went through hell. ...you okay now?"

J. listens to your question and thinks for a few seconds. "I'm fine. Thanks for asking. Yeah, I didn't hold out—as you witnessed. I'm an emotional open book. It sucked, and I experienced the anxiety of that suck like a dagger in my gut."

"You sure as hell did."

"I'm no saint; I've told you. I don't act like a spiritually awakened person should act."

"Oh, I know that."

"Never have. Never will."

"Well sir, I want to thank you for that."

"You are welcome, but I don't do it for thanks. I don't do it as some sort of cheeky teaching thing. I do it because it's real—and it's the truth."

"Well, regardless of whether you do it to teach or not, I find it refreshing—I found it refreshing. It taught me a lot."

"Yeah, hopefully it taught you to greenlight your own sloppy, flawed awakening."

"I think it did."

"So, tell me about Plato's Cave. I have the distinct impression that you've cleaned quite a bit of it out."

"*I—yes, I think I did. I think there is zero vestige of belief left in me.*"

"Oh, I doubt that."

"*Really? Why?*"

"Are you awake?"

"*Um-no...I...*"

"Completely know thyself?"

"*Okay. Good point. I hadn't gotten to that yet. I went through this whole big thing at the church, and when I snapped out of it—out of Plato's Cave, I guess—I had this crazy conversation with my higher self about awakening, enlightenment, et cetera.*"

"A whole conversation with your higher self, huh? And what was the conclusion of that?"

"*Well, as you so keenly observed—no, I do not fucking know myself. No, I do not feel awake. It's aggravating.*"

"Good. Be aggravated."

"*Certainly, I am aggravated. I just—I don't know what else to do. I still feel this fucking itch to be more.*"

"Are you the authority?"

"*What do you mean?*"

"I mean—that's what Plato's Cave is for. It's to remove all external authority and make *you* the authority. Have you actually embraced *being* the authority?"

"*I don't know that I have.*"

"Well, that's part of the problem. You gotta greenlight that shit. If you don't greenlight yourself permission to be the absolute authority, you'll never wake up. …you understand?"

"*I think I do. You mean, you think there's still some other hidden authority in my Plato's Cave?*"

"Absolutely. I can see it right now."

"*Well, what the fuck is it?*"

"Nope. You gotta figure that out on your own. If I tell you what it is, it'll just get twisted and metastasize into some other toxic, bullshit form. It'll hide and go even deeper into the cave. Just think about it. It's really not that hard. It's right in front of you."

"*Really?*"

"Yep."

You sigh and take a big gulp of air. "*Fuck me, this shit is confounding.*"

"You said something like that the other day. It's true. I've never said this was easy. It's actually the hardest thing you'll ever do your whole *entire* life. *Knowing thyself* is a bitch to achieve. But—you are infinitesimally, fucking goddamned close to doing it. Listen to me. I'm going to say it again, loud and clear. Okay?"

"*I'm listening.*"

"Give yourself permission—greenlight yourself—to be the *final and only* authority. This is *your* dream. Only *you* can wake yourself up from it. Do you understand?"

A nerve is struck. You fall into a sobering-truth space of deep, aware, still presence. Strangely, however, your heart is pounding like the heart of a racehorse. You're also on edge, agitated, baffled, conflicted, and frustrated—an unholy, toxic stew of boiling, putrid existential desire and longing. You're close to something, but fuck it all if it *just won't* make itself known.

You shake your head. "*Man—I don't know. Maybe it's just not my time. All this has happened so quickly.*"

"Well, there's no doubt about that. You've traveled a marathon-long way, and not just across the country."

"*I know…and I also don't know. Maybe it's just time for another break.*"

"That may be so."

You continue to sigh and groan sounds of utter exasperation. "*Hey—I've got a question for you. Lynn asked me this morning. Really strange…*"

"Yeah?"

"*Where exactly did you and I meet? For the life of me, I can't remember…*"

J. looks at you with a twinkle in his eyes and smiles from ear to ear. "Hmm? Now that *is* a good question, isn't it?"

"*Yeah, so where?*"

"I'm not going to answer that, either. I want you to think about it—good and long."

"*Well, okay. Isn't it odd that I can't remember?*"

"Yes, isn't that odd? *Very* odd indeed."

J. stands and raises his hands to the view before you. "Oh, man! Utterly magnificent, don't you think? Never gets old. Maya has outdone herself with this one."

You gaze upon the vista of Clear Lake and the *Mendocino National Forest* mountains, which cradle the lake like a babe in arms. You ponder the vast expanse of the world before you. You ponder maya, the dream, the dreamer, and life itself. You ponder your small place in the grand scheme of *all these extraordinary and magnificent things.*

Maybe my place isn't so insignificant after all?

Maybe. Or—maybe—actually, it is?

I feel...so fucking close.

We'll get you there. Just need to hang on.

I don't want to hang on. I want to let go.

We'll get you there. Trust me.

I hope so.

J. gives you a big bear hug and a fist bump and then heads back to the house with Lenny.

Roused from her doggy nap after your conversation with J., Maya bounces around looking for fun. You lean down and pick up the nearest stick. She snaps to immediate attention and jets off when you throw it. You find the path that leads down the lake side of the mountain into town. *It's a straight shot down,* she said, *a straight shot down.* You and Maya hop on it and begin the downward journey…

You walk and ponder …walk and ponder… *It's right in front of me? Some other authority?* But you still can't see it. It feels exactly like that old cliché —"a riddle wrapped in a mystery inside an enigma." You try dropping it from your mind, but it continues to gnaw away at your insides…

What stumps you more, however, than the *Knowing Thyself* riddle is, stupidly enough, *not* remembering *exactly* where in the world you met J. This fragment of amnesia irritates you like an invisible flea crawling across your skin. *It's so damn odd…*

You continue walking. In about forty-five minutes, you reach a small park on the outer edge of town. The shore of Clear Lake is a stone's throw away, and the small township of Lucerne stands before you.

You take a few side streets and then turn onto Main. For safety, you have Maya on a leash now, but she hardly needs it.

Soon, you see the small hanging shop sign for Sophocles' Books. You arrive and stand before the store front, which is comprised of a large glass door and matching side windows. You can see inside. It's not packed, but there are a few patrons. You enter and are greeted by the friendly sound of bells chiming against the door. It's old-school and quaint. That alone endears you to the place.

Lynn is behind the counter; she sees you immediately. "Hey there, stranger. Wondered when you'd make it."

"*Hey. Nice place.*" You point to Maya. "*Can she come in?*"

"Oh, of course. She's a regular."

You reach down and unhook Maya from her leash. She casually tail-wags her way behind the counter, where she immediately slurps water from a large silver bowl on the floor.

You point to Maya. "*Long hike. She was thirsty.*"

"A great hike though, right? I've done it a bunch."

"*Absolutely. Fantastic views.*"

You see Maya take up a spot on a dog bed, obviously hers, also behind the counter. Lynn reaches down and gives her a scratch on her poochy head. "Maya, my spiritually enlightened canine friend, you are the damnedest thing." Lynn says with a smile and turns to you. "Can I get you anything?"

"*Um, sure—yeah. Iced tea works if you have it.*"

"We sure do."

As Lynn prepares your drink, you take a moment to peer around the store. You like what you see. It's soft, inviting, and comfortable on the eyes. There are tables, sofas, and plush chairs strategically positioned. Sturdy golden oak bookshelves sit everywhere; each houses a neat, orderly abundance of new books. You also see a sizable used book section on one large back wall. You take note of one particularly inviting alcove which contains a small table, a matching bookshelf, and a half-sized sofa. It's the perfect place to curl up and, of course, read a book. You internally take dibs on it.

"Here's your drink." Lynn says as she hands you a pint-sized glass filled with tea and ice cubes.

You take a sip. "*Perfect. Thank you.*"

"Where's J. He didn't come with?"

"*No, he hiked up to the cave with me and we hung out for a while, but then he returned home for his phone call.*"

"He's not very good at multi-tasking, is he?"

"*Eh, no, he's not. ...hates it, I think.*"

Another customer steps in the store, and the bells jingle.

"Grab any seat or book and make yourself at home. You cool for a bit?" Lynn asks politely.

"*Yes! All good. Thank you.*" You point to the small alcove. "*I'll be over there.*"

Lynn greets the new customer as you slowly make your way over to your destination, passing by several large bookcases. You arrive at the alcove and sit down on the half-sofa. You hadn't realized just how tired you actually are. You take several sips of the iced tea, then close your eyes and tilt your head back on the plush sofa cushion, taking a few solid moments to decompress.

You feel like your brain, body, heart, and mind have just been rammed through a meat grinder. The sofa beckons you to relax deeper. Your eyes still closed, you drop into your body and take several slow, deep breaths. You open your eyes, your head still tilted back, and stare at the ceiling. You bring your head forward and then turn it slightly, peering diffusely at a small bookshelf to your right. And then you see it!

It all comes rushing back. Your heart skips a beat and begins pounding furiously. Your palms begin to sweat like a pot of boiling water. You're pulled deep into a black hole singularity of horrifying, anxious fear. You reach out and grab the book you see on the shelf: *Spirituality for Badasses*, by *J. Stewart Dixon*.

Holy fucking shit.

Do not touch that book!

What do you mean—don't touch that book!?

I said do not fucking touch that book! Get up and leave right now.

What the fuck?! I thought you were my...

Run, I said!!

And then you get it. All this time—the Black Shadow, the black dragon, the all-knowing higher self, this dufus, authoritarian, higher self-*inner voice*...all this time...fake! Hollow! Not real! Just another belief imprisoned in Plato's Cave!

I see you now!

But I'm—

No, you're not. You're a nothing.

But I am!

You watch, witness, and feel as your fictional higher self, the non-existent, false, higher *you*...

simply *evaporates*...

... into *nothing*.

Your heart continues to pound. *Say yes to fear! Yes to awareness!* You know you're in the throes of a massive existential anxiety attack. With your higher self now evaporated into oblivion, you desperately try to stave off the next wave of fight or flight panic.

I am me! I am real! I am me! I'm the you in the...I'm the you in the...oh, fuck...book.

And then—you remember *exactly where* you met J. It *wasn't* in a bookstore, like you had vaguely, but falsely remembered. It was through a social media post that contained a *link* to his book online. You ordered his book, and within a few days, you were holding it in your hands—and then he introduced himself to you *in his book.* The truth of the matter: you actually...*never* met J. in person—because *that J. doesn't exi-...*

Holy fucking shit. None of this exists! None of it! I'm not real!

I am...I am...I am...not the you... You watch, witness, and feel as *your* character—the *YOU* character in the book—*also* evaporates into nothing. Only the thinnest tendril of primordial awareness is left. You experience this primordial awareness plummet through a rushing vortex wormhole of space and time—*and then* you return to being your true self—you the reader!—with *this* book in your hands. You don't even need to look at the cover. You know *exactly* which book this is: *Spirituality for Badasses Book 2: How to find your heart and soul without losing your cool.* You notice that you are currently reading page 368.

And now, in this moment, you realize what it finally means to jump out of your head and into your heart. *You're awake.* There is no *higher-you* self. There is no *book-you* self. There is no *you* self at all. You, you, and you—all fictional; all a made-up play in the great dream book of Brahman. You are simply the one singular primordial awareness that has *always* existed and will *always* exist, forever and ever, for as long as the great Tao spins.

You snap back to waking consciousness in the alcove of the bookstore. Things are different now: Brighter. Clearer. Pristine. You see reality through the eyes of a newborn babe. How you've reappeared in the bookstore is beyond you. You don't question it. You're simply relieved to be back. Your heart settles down. You take a sip of your tea, and then… J. enters the alcove, with Lenny wrapped around his shoulders…

"But, but, but—none of this is real!"

J. takes a good long stare into your eyes. "Ahh, I see you've finally woken up to the truth of things."

"We, we—don't exist! We're just characters in a book!"

"Congratulations, Kemosabe. Yepper." J. looks around, shrugs, and smiles. "I'm okay with that if you are…"

"But, but, we… *Look!* See the words on the page? My words aren't italicized anymore. What the fuck does that even mean?" And what's my name? I don't even have a fucking name!?"

"Yeah, yeah…slow down. You're hyperventilating. It takes some getting used to. No big deal. We don't exist. It'll all be okay. Just breathe…"

"But how can you take any of this seriously, knowing that none of it exists!?"

Lenny—who is still perched on J.'s shoulders—turns to you, and in one of the most shocking moments of your entire fictional life, *speaks*:

"Dude, calm down. So, we don't exist? No friggin' big deal. Look at me. I'm a damn fictional lizard. ...you see me complaining?"

You almost faint at the sheer audacious absurdity of what you've just seen, heard, and witnessed.

"Lenny speaks!" You point to Lenny. "You speak!?? What the fuck!?"

"Of course Lenny speaks," J. says as he smiles. "He's been speaking to me this whole time. You just couldn't hear him—because *you* were asleep. But not anymore..."

And then, to your utter delight, both J. and Lenny begin laughing. And they laugh and laugh and laugh... It's so infectious, you begin laughing unstoppably yourself, falling blissfully into the whirlwind of their raucous joviality. You pound your hands on your knees and laugh so excruciatingly hard that tears stream from your eyes and your stomach cramps in pain. It's the fullest, most alive laughter you've ever experienced in your whole beautiful, fictional, strange, spiritual, badass life...

"None of this is real! Ha! A talking iguana! Ha!"

Eventually, the laughter subsides. You, J., and Lenny rub your aching sides, hoping for relief. Then, very serenely, you look at both of them, and without a hint of sarcasm or irony, you ask...

"Okay, badasses—what's next!?"

Of course, you—the reader with the book still in your hands—have to take all this with a certain grain of salt, yes? I don't need to tell you this, do I? Okay...you want the nitty-gritty truth? I feel like I've already told you this story. Ah, well...at the risk of repeating myself, here ya go:

When I woke up—when at long last I came to know thyself—I was staring at my computer screen in my small office on a miserable cloudy, cold, and rainy November day...

I had been visiting Plato's Cave for quite some time:

By this point, I had expunged 99% of my old, stale beliefs, theories, concepts, and haughty philosophical ideas. I had whittled everything—*I mean fucking everything*—down to just one small pinprick of a notion: I was existentially unhappy, and I wanted that unhappiness to *go the fuck* away.

I had long ago greenlit the whole process:

I didn't care what it was called—knowing thyself, spiritual awakening, enlightenment, realization, Disco Donald Duck. I just wanted that horrible, relentless, taskmaster of a bitch—*unhappiness*—to die in a hole. I gave myself total permission to do whatever was required. (I *wasn't* suicidal. I was simply existentially done.)

I had become my own final and absolute authority:

I had dropped, killed, and dissolved all philosophical, spiritual, religious, and New Age authority figures, teachings, and advice. I had listened to the sage words of these teachers for a long time, but those days were now over. I had become my own man. I had become, and was now, the single source of authority.

So...

On one very depressing, cold, cloudy autumn day, I meandered down into my office to do some paperwork for my audio-visual business. I had no desire to work, and I began surfing the internet. I happened upon an *amazing* article about spiritual awakening...

For your purposes, the title and author of this article don't matter. Spiritual awakening lightning never strikes twice anyway. All you need to know is this: 1% of me was still stuck in Plato's Cave. The article I discovered and read liberated that 1%.

The article was about *self*—specifically the lack thereof: There is no higher self. There's no lower self. There's no spiritual self. There's no soul self. There is NO self of any sort. There is NO self.

Bang! Mic drop. The End. Boom. Game over. You have reached the end of the spiritual search. *Know Thyself* complete.

As I sat there reading this truth, I finally got it. I had heard this premise before, of course, but like the *you* in our little adventure here—the dullard with the dunce cap on—I just never fully understood it. Not so this time around: This time, the truth sank all the way down into the deepest, darkest recesses of my personal Plato's Cave. This time, the little girl—in the form of this article—reached that final imprisoned 1% of me, took that part by the hand, and lead it out into the shining daylight of freedom.

Up to this point, I had been holding out, hoping, and believing that someday maybe...my higher self would save me...or I would become my higher self...or I would finally realize my higher self. But, of course, there is no higher self, no lower self, no *you* self at all—*not really*. It's all just a ghostly, shadowy sham...

Upon realizing this, I ballooned into a hyper-aware state of blissful presence which, by now, I had experienced 352,432 times. Yes, believe it or not, one can become jaded with the experience of bliss. So I didn't think much of it. Cool article. Nice samadhi experience. But who knows?

After a few weeks, however, a very odd thing dawned on me. *Something was missing. Something was missing*!!!! And what that *missing something* was, was absolutely epic, fire, key, and spiritually badass in its scope and nature: My existential sense of unhappiness was *gone*. I was no longer unhappy, depressed, angst-ridden, or tortured by the feeling of being separate, alone, out-of-tune, incomplete, or lost. I had become the fully rounded package of what it means to be a human being. *Know Thyself?* Yes! Now, I know myself.

So—what do I know?

I am bodily, emotionally, and mentally *present*. I enjoy and suffer all the usual conditions that come with this trifecta: My body is flawed. My mind is a tool. My emotions are the spice of life. Additionally, I am completely and utterly *aware*. This may sound grandiose, but it's not. It's very natural, normal, and dare I say—bland. This awareness is the ongoing, defining feature of my life. Before, during, and after anything else—I am aware. Period.

Finally, I don't have preferences. I'm not trying to exclusively identify with blissful states of spiritual presence, expanded awareness, bodily pleasure, mental acuity, or emotional power. Nor am I running from or avoiding darker states such as sadness, boredom, fright, disgust, anger, or frustration. No state is better, higher, or lower than any other. They're all equal to me. And why do they appear equal? Because they're all happening within the singular dream state of *the one* primordial aware consciousness which, as I so eloquently penned several chapters ago, is pissing this whole ridiculous reality out. Go figure.

So that's my bare-bones, spiritual awakening, *Know Thyself*, spiritual adventure, life-story ending. Thank you for listening, hearing, reading, seeing, and feeling *all of it*...

Now, let's get back to the epic final pages of *your* adventure...

Chapter 28
Epilogue

How to find your life's purpose

You can't believe it's been two years.

You're waiting in your slightly used, mint condition, anodized orange Jeep Wrangler in the parking lot of the *San Jose International Airport* in Costa Rica. You've arrived early. The tropical humidity, exacerbated by the heat of the parking lot, has you sweating. You hear your phone ding and look down to read the incoming text. You smile and your heart begins pounding with excited anticipation.

Your younger cousin, Andrew, sits next to you in the passenger seat.

"Should I get the back door?"

"Sure. Thanks."

"You're positive I did the branch thing correctly?"

You look back and surmise his handy work. The branch is perfect. You know its new owner will approve. And then, you see them...

J. walks out of the airport with a black rolling suitcase in tow and a small carry-on dog crate. He sets the crate down and pulls Lenny out from inside. Lenny assumes his place on J.'s shoulders. You step out of the Jeep and wave...

Two years is a long time. Two years is a short time. But time has a way of catching up to you, and time always seems to deliver the goods...*eventually*. Today, those goods are two of the best friends you've ever had the privilege of knowing in this crazy life, and you're so very happy to see them.

J. walks up to you, smiles, and holds out a fist to bump. You hold yours out, but then break down smiling and envelop him in a big hug. You wink at Lenny as you do so.

"Holy shit! I can't believe you guys are here."

"We can't either!" J. bellows, laughing. "It is frickin' hot as hell here!"

You nod your head in agreement. "…takes some getting used to. Our place in the mountains is cooler, though." You gesture to your cousin Andrew. "J., this is Andrew. He's our test victim."

"You're a brave soul," J. replies.

"Thanks. Happy to hang out. So, you guys are gonna help Cuz here straighten out the whole work, career, life purpose thing, huh?"

"That's the plan. Costa Rica's da bomb. There's a shit-ton of cool things here to experience." J. looks at you. "We'll find out what your purpose is. You didn't wake up for nothing." J. looks around and gestures to everything. "So…you ready to do this?"

You look at J., knowing exactly what answer he expects.

"Abso-fucking-lutely! " You smile and laugh.

And then, you hear it. It's been years. You thought it wasn't—*it couldn't have been*—real. But indeed, it was…

After your exclamation, Lenny, perched on J.'s shoulders, turns his head, looks you straight in the eyes, and *speaks again…*

"Abso-friggin'-lutely dude! Cos-tahh! Ric-ahh! This vacation is gonna be bangin'! …you guys ready to do this? Let the…"

Your jaw drops as you stare at both J. and Lenny. Then you smile and, with zero hesitation, join them loudly, clearly, and triumphantly…

"Let the adventure continue…"

"Let the adventure continue!"

"*Let the adventure…continue*!!!"

Spiritual Badass Suggestion:

Congratulations and a big fist bump to you!

I hope you enjoyed *Spirituality for Badasses Book 2*. And I hope you were *much more* than just entertained. I hope it helped you *and* changed you. I hope it gave you multiple insights and *Aha!* moments about spirituality, awakening, and *knowing thyself*. I hope it gave you...some hope, dawg.

I poured my heart, soul, *and* Lenny muse, joy, and laughter into this book. It was a blast and an absolute privilege to write. So—thank you, thank you, thank you!

Here's my final spiritual badass suggestion: Pay it forward! *If it did*—if the *Spirituality for Badasses* book series (Book 1, The Workbook, or Book 2) helped you, changed you, or gave you an insight of any size, shape, or color—please let me know about it, and please let the world know about it...*because the world needs to know about it!*

Please tell your friends and family. Definitely leave a review on Amazon or elsewhere. And finally, write me an email and share your experience with me. (You can find my email at the SFB website.)

Together, we can make the world a little lighter, a little happier, and of course, a little more...*spiritual badass*.

Fist-bump, friend. Until our next big adventure together...

Peace and laughter,

–J. and Lenny

END PART 4

DON'T JUST READ ABOUT IT.

EXPERIENCE IT.

This is your invitation to a whole new world badass.
There's a life-changing *experience* waiting for you online. Something you've been longing and waiting for *your whole life*. You ready? Of course you are…

**Go here:
www.spiritualityforbadasses.com**

Author

Spirituality for Badasses blossomed out of J. Stewart's life as a spiritual seeker, finder, and teacher. He teaches based on his direct experience, twenty-nine years of interaction with numerous nonduality-advaita-zen-unorthodox teachers, his education in modern mindfulness, and a degree in communications engineering from Syracuse University. He lives in Central Virginia with his wife and son.

References

The A.A. Grapevine, Inc. 1952,1953,1981
Twelve Steps and Twelve Traditions
Alcoholics Anonymous World Services, Inc.

Reviews & Sharing
Hell Yes Please!

Share the adventure!

Things you can do:

Write a review:
Make your world a more spiritual badass place: After reading, please leave a review with your thoughts and opinions. Just search *Amazon, Kobo, BookBub, or Goodreads* for *Spirituality for Badasses* and spread the love, baby.

Share it with influencers, reviewers, or book clubs:
Know anybody well-known who might appreciate an irreverent, potty-mouthed, spiritual self-help adventure? Or know any YouTube reviewers, podcasters, or book clubs? Share away, spread the badass love, and have them give me a shout!

Surprise someone! Buy an extra copy to give away:
Buy an extra copy and keep it in your car. Save it to give to the perfect person—and change the world, one spiritual badass at a time…(I love doing this!)

Fist-Bump & Thank You!
J. Stewart Dixon

Made in United States
North Haven, CT
26 September 2023

42024863R00232